I0692013

Hand and Glove: The Pit

First Edition

Bob E. Genz

Hand and Glove: The Pit

First Edition

Published by The Nazca Plains Corporation
Las Vegas, Nevada
2007

ISBN: 978-1-887895-58-3

Published by

The Nazca Plains Corporation ®
4640 Paradise Rd, Suite 141
Las Vegas NV 89109-8000

PUBLISHER'S NOTE
Hand and Glove: The Pit is a work of fiction created wholly by *Bob E. Genz's* imagination. All characters are fictional and any resemblance to any persons living or deceased is purely by accident. No portion of this book reflects any real person or events.

Cover Photo, Sandra vom Stein
Art Director, Blake Stephens

Dedication

Hand and Glove is an analogy. The Hand represents the dominate, the Glove the submissive each as individuals knows their roles in the realm but when the two combine as equals they becomes something greater than the two individuals. They become the ultimate Ying and Yang, harmony at its best. Being passive does not mean you are weak. Being passive means you have a strength of character that allows you to submit to freely explore variations of sensuality.

Have no friends not equal to yourself.   Confucius

I speak for myself when I say that we each personify the Hand and Glove analogy by how we structure our lives; associate with others and by how intensely we love. I am dedicating this book to my friends. These friends come from every walk of life and social structure. They are creative, brilliant, fun and in their own way extremely Spiritual. We believe in self-empowerment, walking in balance with our inner natures and struggling against the mediocrity of our world today.

To my friends, thank you...Chuck Higgins, Lady Dee, Hal, Lee, Julian & Scott, Kevin Hiza a.k.a. the Pup, Jenna V, Lin F., Lady V., Lawrence F., Timmy Brough, Goddess Lakshimi & Sweet Limey, Peter & Craig, Daddy Brian & boy jeff, dog blu, Papi David, Gene & Master Will, Eric L., Bearman, Richard S., Papabear & Gary, boy jim F., danny T, Grande Mistress Carla, Amy O @ Marvelous Mayhem, the Sabers M.C.C. of Ft. Lauderdale, the Wildcats M.C.C. of Norfolk, SLLAP of Ft. Lauderdale, SPICE of Ft. Lauderdale, and most of all to my Number One...for your friendship, support and love as we walked this road together.

There is only one good, knowledge, and one evil, ignorance.
Socrates

Hand and Glove: The Pit

Bob E. Genz

Contents

Previously

In the beginning, Handler Dan betrayed my trust, love, and devotion. But I fooled them all. I learned the Way of the Slave, learned it well enough to fool my Handler. I learned it well enough to even fool the second in command, Captain Jonathan Hicks. Once a street kid, always a street kid! You learn. You have to if you're gonna find food, shelter and how to earn some bucks. So I turned a few tricks. But I got them to open their doors, feed me, and teach me how to get a better life. I crawled from living in a shit hole as biker trash - up the ranks to be a titleholder in the Drummer contest. Did I use people to get where I was? Of course I did. Everybody does it. At least I thought so until I met retired Major Bruce Hunter. Wealthy, but he didn't show it - and yet he did in the way he carried himself, the way he wore his leathers and the way people sucked up to him.

Being a titleholder, I had to go out to the people I thought were beneath me. I enjoyed the hell out of that time; got my choice of fresh meat, free food, lots of drugs, booze and whatever I wanted. I was the cock of the walk, so to speak. People even listened to what I had to say for once, because I was a goddam spokesman. Everyone listened but one - and he seemed to upstage me by doing nothing, by just being there. God, how I hated Hunter! Even took a swing at him the second time we were formally introduced (as we had met before when he judged the contest). Maybe it was after that party that the idea hatched in my head. Or it could have been another jack-off fantasy of being used like he did those slaves that were always around him. If I could become his slave I would be sitting pretty. Like the other johns from my past, I could top from below.

So I took a year to learn their rules in the slave caverns under his home, Buena Vista. They fucking busted my balls. The hardest work I've ever done in my life was while I was down within those slave caverns, but it transformed me into a docile mountain of muscle whose eyes fixate on anyone who is wearing boots. When I see boots, my mouth starts drooling and, before I can stop myself, I am down on my knees sucking leather. They broke me, got inside my head and flipped switches until I confessed like a blithering idiot. Problem is, my street ego survived, it's deep down inside of me where damn few dare go.

Months into my training, I was taken to a processing center where I was installed in a cage. No explanations were given, but why should they? In their minds I was only a slave. One of those baldheaded processing geeks entered to give me and the rest of us in the cages a shot in the rump. Most of the slaves in the cages around me had never been sold before, so they hadn't a clue what the fuck was about to happen. The shots were given so we would be calmer for packaging. I had been sold, Master Dan knew and that's why we partied the night before.

Calm and woozy from the shot, I was packaged in the rubber gear that most of us leave in. Believe me; you are snug as a bug in a rug when they seal the top of the crate. The music begins, and you're away. I awoke a couple of days later at what I first thought was the home of my Master, but found out later was a huge corporate building in some unknown city. I was suited in a leather straightjacket, bondage pants, heavy boots, and a thick hood. Onwards and upwards – literally – as I was loaded into a helicopter and off on the second leg of my journey to meet who they called the Master of Masters, he who would soon be the Deus of Castle Enterprises. As I gathered it, I was to be his gift from Buena Vista.

Carried from the helicopter, I was dropped onto my knees and made to wait. Someone was in the room with me because I could feel the floor vibrating with his movements. He stood with his legs on either side of me, lifted my hooded head, removed the gag with a jerk, and filled my mouth with his fingers. His arms encircled me and drew up upwards; he was much taller than I and stronger by the feeling of his arms. The panels over my tits were opened; his fingers found my nipples and began rolling them expertly, taking them slowly from low pain to screeching. With his hand on my hood, I was moved across the room until I could go no further. Then my legs were kicked out, my head pushed over and the zipper over my ass opened. The rubber cock was withdrawn and his slipped in to fill the void. Who was this man that takes time to make this slave feel as good as he?

He moved me back to kneeling, placed a boot toe under my lips, and tapped my head to start me licking. When he did remove the hood I could've shit. I was kneeling before the man of my dreams, my Lord and Master, Hunter. I had come full circle. Destiny had brought me before the man who I had worshiped even while in the slave caverns; however, one problem appeared to ruin my idyllic reunion with my Master Hunter. Dan had arrived under false pretenses. The straightjacket I had been wearing was transferred to another body and I was told in no uncertain terms, "What happens on the yacht says on the yacht."

Returning home, I was trained in my duties within the household and my ego found reasons to begin to surface. At first while Sir wasn't around (which was often), I would shirk my duties, fail to mop the floors, or forget to take out the ashes in the main fireplace. Then mikey got caught doing the unthinkable and I found I could bully him for more grub, extra snacks. Hunter refused to listen to the house gossip until he caught me red-handed with my hand in the cookie jar. One thing led to another which led to another and, before I knew what was happening, I had done the unthinkable and the panic button was hit. All hell broke out, literally! All doors to flee were locked and I had to stare into a red-faced Hunter in one of his rages. I knew if he caught me, all or part of me would pay dearly. I was right; all of me died that day. Many months later, I needed to ask myself: Could I be reborn as his glove?

Chapter 1

There is nothing permanent except change.
Rogers: Student's History of Philosophy

It seemed decades ago when it signed the contract that took this slave away from the man it loved. In fact it would be three full years come next June, now being December, that it had been away undergoing positive reaffirmation. This slave could have been serving its one and only Owner if it had come to realize earlier in the program that only its mindset held it from happiness and true destiny. Foolishly, it thought of only itself and not being one as it is now with its Sir. Those first days with Sir were very memorable. Everything had changed and yet nothing had changed. It was as if this slave still served Master Dan, so was the routine of Master Hunter with little variation. Sir seemed to awaken with a enormous appetite in the morning, be it for sex or a large breakfast. (Which he believed to be the most important meal of the day.) Those first few days were definitely days of learning and reacquainting this slave with the body and appetites of its new Owner.

Sir awakened early, as is his normal nature. He rolled over to see who was in bed with him, pulled its hands up to the headboard cuffed them in place crawled around the mattress, spit on his hand and slid his cock into home plate. This slave thought this was far more fun that having to serve the coffee and a blow job that Master Dan required as his eye-opener. Hell of a way to get the heart pumping and the blood flowing. Sir took his pleasures with his slave, shot his load, rolled off and took a shower. Returning, it was released and sent down to the galley where it retrieved Sir's tray before returning to the stateroom.

Entering, it found Sir in a heated debate via the phone. While it listened to a one sided conversation about Buena Vista renovations, it set out Sir's breakfast on a table, leaving the metal chargers in place until he could actually ring off to dine. It was about to kneel as was its training, but Sir set it to work while he wolfed his food in huge gulps as if he were starving.

It was ordered to pull out shorts, tank top, a billowing Hawaiian print shirt and sandals for this morning's meeting. That done, it was given a note to deliver to the galley and return with a bowl - which this slave knew would contain nothing but slave slop. Sir ordered the bowl placed on his table and it to kneel between his legs. Sir kindly filled this slave's bowl with nice chunks of food from his own plate, added his bowl of fresh fruit and ordered it to eat as he watched over another cup of coffee.

This slave was amazed how much better the food was topside. The slave bill-of-fare slop tasted better or enriched as it had larger chunks of meat and dried fruit that would keep this slave in a healthier condition and serving its Lord to the best of its abilities.

Having dressed Sir, it was permitted to do its hygiene rituals under his watchful eye. On board the yacht, the slave was permitted to squat over Sir's commode with seat elevated to shit; afterwards, it flushed out any residue and oiled its hole for Sir's enjoyment. It was permitted to shave itself unattended. Upon exiting the bathroom it found Sir speaking to another slave kneeling at his feet.

He pointed in this one's direction and ordered, "Take my slave, 9-745. Show it the quickest routes around the boat so it may better serve me, introduce it to the others of your breed so all may be aware of its presence."

Sir took the slave's chin within his hand and lifted it. "This does not mean I will not use it any more or less than I have. My slave will lighten its load. Send it to the conference room in about three hours with refreshments, but only then; after much heated arguments we will all need cooler heads. Dismissed." He turned to this slave. "9-745, go with slave 5-221 and it will show you around. Learn what it has to teach you. You'll be tested daily. 5-221 has orders for both of you. Dismissed. Now get your ass moving!"

It hadn't been gone long until it heard Master bellowing its number over some public address system, "9-745 report to its Owner, stat!" It was in the engine room when it heard the announcement and ran up too many flights of steps, totally bypassing the stateroom and finally had to get directions from someone else's slave to find Sir's quarters. Upon arriving I found Sir standing quietly in the middle of the room one fist on his hip. He turned as this slave entered. "Where in the fuck have you been, slave. I have been buzzing you for over an hour!"

This slave had to have had a puzzled look on its face as it tried its damnedest to ask, "Buzz?"

Sir walked to the nearest table picked up a remote control box and pushed. Looked up at this slave and depressed the button again studying this slave's face. "Fuck," he bellowed, "9-745 is not fucking wired! Go to the galley, ask Cookie for my apples. Bring me two, three if they're small." This one ran off on his errand. Found the chef who directed this one to take what he needed from the refrigerator. The apples were medium sized. It considered Sir's needs and brought four.

Entering, this slave, found his Sir naked. Sir took the apples, tossed one to someone at his rear and ordered this one to the floor, head down. This one hadn't heard the other speak until it was nestled down on the floor. It thought to itself that voice is awfully familiar but it was out of place here. It knew that voice from the its…oh, God, not here, it thought. Why now, why here?

It must have jerked, or done something to call attention to itself where it was kneeling as Sir barked a command. "Crawl over here to me, 9-745."

Rising on to its hands and knees it crawled the short distance and saw my Owner's bare feet and boots. Was that Master Dan? Why was he here? Sir lifted his feet, indicating to this one that it was to serve as his footrest. It crawled into place, settling down as Sir's big feet took possession of its body. It listened intently to their discussion.

"After tonight, I will have this group of elders out of my hair and we will have the boat to ourselves. Then you and I can get reacquainted and you can brief me on the renovations. Is that apple going to hold you until dinner? If not, the slave can get you a sandwich or something. OK?"

"Sir, I had a light lunch in the airport and the apple will be fine until diner, thank you, Sir," said Master Dan. "Sir, using the electric jacks, the slaves in mining opened a corridor and found yet another huge domed room, it is absolutely massive and the engineers believe it could easily be transformed - with a little shoring - into the great hall you have always dreamed for. All the engineers are asking is that you look at the blueprints I have brought to you and give them a go-ahead. They have included a proposal for costs, man-hours and materials."

"Hold up there, Dan. Just how big is this room? Have you seen it?" Hunter began directing questions to Dan as his mind went to work on the new proposal. Papers were rustling overhead as he studied what Dan had brought.

"Sir, we believe this room could, with some minor modifications, easily hold all our shields and their mates. And Sir, if we do not have any unforeseen accidents it could be done in time for the October Run. Which, Sir, would be a major feather in BV's cap, don't you agree?"

"By God, Dan! Did you see their figures for this venture? Money does not grow on trees, nor do slaves!"

"Sir, couldn't you approach the elders for a loan or levy a tithe on them? BV has been carrying more than its load for years - and didn't you say that the England house has their loan coming due at the first of this year?"

"Ok, Dan, show me the blueprints. It might be time that BV sells one of its assets to Castle Enterprises. Only this Lord knows how much Captain Hicks has been after me to sell to that end of the business firm." Master Hunter began to scrutinize the diagrams and blueprints, growing excited. "Damn, that is one huge room and look how close it is to yet another water way, nice." Sir kept pouring over the blue prints had risen to see their farthest extent when a knock came to the door. "9-745, go slowly to the door when I gave you the cue, open it. Dan, roll that thing up and hide the proposals. I do not want this greedy bunch of whores seeing them until I am damn ready for them to see it. If anyone asks why you are here, you earned this vacation." He turned to me and motioned. "Ok, slave, open."

As it opened the door, it was pushed open by a manimal on a leash - by its looks a puppy dog - followed by another leading an elderly Grande Dame. She was elegantly dressed in a tight fitting leather dress with a split up one side, a lacey bodice and the mark of an elder; boots with golden spurs. She did not even falter when she saw Master Hunter standing near the desk where he had been talking with Master Dan in his birthday suit.

She purred, "Bruce, are you wearing that old thing to the formal cocktail party tonight? I should have known you would have to steal the show by being unconventional." She laughed, walked to where he stood and took his seat. Her dogs sniffed as far as they could on their leashes and finally settled at her feet. Absentmindedly, she put out one hand and began scratching behind one pup's ear while the other pup licked her hand. Her dogs looked to be identical twins, mirror images of the other. "Ah, Daniel how good it is to see you off the farm. Has the world come to an end that you, Hunter and Cappy are off the farm at the same time? How do they survive?"

While getting some clothes on, Dan began to speak with her while Sir stepped into the bathroom to shower and this slave went about pulling out his evening attire. His water shut off and it was standing there with a warm towel to pat him down. This one became a touch bolder and suggested that it give his Sir a shave as he had failed to do that routine this morning. He looked at this one in the most peculiar way before sending it out to prepare for his dressing.

I heard Master Dan calling this elderly lady Mistress Beatrice. Alarms went off in this slave's head: she is the retiring Deus of Castle Enterprises! That helped explain why all the elders were on a yacht in the Bahamas, which opened the doors for more questions. Why are they all here and who is running their Houses while they're away?

Hunter spoke from the bathroom, "Mistress Beatrice, why don't you take Master Daniel up to the cocktail party and get a head start with the mind games. I will be along in a moment. One must keep up one's pretenses in this snobbish group and I must be fashionably late, shouldn't I?" Hunter's deep laughter told them that tonight should be interesting. "Besides Beatrice, you can protect Dannyboy from the vultures. They're scared of you!"

Cutting in to their conversation Master Dan stammered, "Sir, I did not bring formal leathers!"

"Fuck that nonsense, boy! You are going to the ball," Master Hunter laughed, "and I am going to be your Fairy Godfucking Father! So you don't have any excuses! Besides those whores upstairs will eat you alive if they are drunk enough," he laughed again. "They will think you are me!" Master Hunter filled the room with deep gut-busting laughter. Master Dan made a face until Master Hunter corrected his negative thinking. "You came here to serve me. Now is your chance, boy!" Not to be halted at this game, Master Hunter turned to me. "Slave, Hand and Glove: The Pit of his clothes, now!"

While this slave was about his task of removing from a hesitant Master Dan his clothes, Master Hunter was rummaging in his wardrobe. Dark brown leather pants were tossed to the floor behind Sir while he continued to rummage through the hanging clothes. A handsome black and brown leather shirt followed the pants. Handsome it was, black leather trimmed in brown leather. It dressed Master Dan as fast as things arrived for. Odd how he seemed to struggle with the wardrobe change.

Lady Beatrice liked the idea of mind-fucking the elders and eventually, once Master Dan realized Master Hunter intended to have his way, he submitted and accepted the idea. Master Dan stood and offered his hand to Mistress Beatrice who accepted. Together they departed Master Hunter's stateroom and, with the two manimals in tow, headed off in the search of the cocktail party.

Hunter sat as soon as the door closed, "I will be really fucking happy when I get rid of these bitches tomorrow. Then I can honestly try to enjoy a few days before we return to Buena Vista. Slave, dress me!"

Returning to where he sat with his pants this slave found him with his head buried into Master Dan's shirt. This one coughed to get his attention. He laughed, wadded up the shirt and tossed it aside. His way of explaining his action was to say something about how he loved the scent of a hot boy. He smiled as this one dressed him in white breeches, knee high boots, spurs, a light blue uniform shirt, Sam Browne belt, badge and gloves. Into his breast pocket it inserted two Churchill 50 ring cigars and Sir placed the cutter and lighter in a pouch that was hung from this slave's neck.

Sir was the picture of perfection, standing there in full police uniform. He turned to me, looked down and realized why it had been late this afternoon. He turned and opened a cabinet, then took from the closet one silver tipped riding crop that he inserted into the outer edge of his left boot. Reaching deeper into the closet, Sir pulled out a cock and ball strap with a small black box attached to it and added a small button box to his belt.

"Slave, quickly go shower, clean out its hole and return. We must not keep the guests much longer." While this slave did as ordered, Sir must have gotten bored cause when it returned it found Sir smoking one of his cigars and playing with something he had prepared for his slave. It was ordered to come to him and stand holding its cock and balls out towards him. A cock and ball strap this one was familiar with, but not one that had this attached black box like Sir held in his hand. Sir made certain the strap and box had full contact and locked the strap in place with a tiny padlock. Then Sir took the box from off his belt, touched it to the box under this slave's nuts and activated the system.

This slave looked up to his Sir with puzzlement written all over its face. This one just could not figure out how, unless the box beeped, that it would know Sir wanted it.

Master's sadistic chuckle forewarned this slave. "Slave, be attentive, listen. It will hear a beep that tells it that it is to report to me, ASAP. Once it hears the beep it has five minutes to call in via phone or I hit the button again. Phones are all over this tug, pick one up and call my number; 555." Sir let this slave hear the beep that was obnoxious enough to get through even this slave's hard head. This slave thought the demonstration was over until Master hit the button the second time.

This slave jumped from its kneeling position up to the ceiling and began dancing around, wailing as it nuts not just caught fire but were stomped to death by the electric jolt that passed through them. It was not at all pleased by this evil contraption that Sir had locked on to this slave. It knew then that it would find a frigging phone quickly so as not to have that lesson repeated any time soon!

Once Master stopped his fit of laughing and caught his breath he turned serious again. "If it's not here or it has failed to report in by phone, I will depress the button a third time and hold it down. That kicks up the punch to another notch and its ankles will sprout wings! Bend over and open its ass cheeks!"

He inserted a condom wrapped cigar into his slave's ass, pushing it past the muscle and leaving a leather lace dangling out of its hole. "Stand up, and turn around." Sir bound the balance of the leather strap around his slave's nuts. "Tonight it will serve me as my humanidor. When I next order it to get me a cigar, it will shit it out of its hole, remove the condom and it had better pray that its ass is clean, because it is your job to cut the cigar, prep and light it. It will place the lighted end into its mouth, holding it between its teeth and offer it to my hand. When it sees the ash to be about an inch its mouth will open and I recommend that it have collected some spit in the back of its mouth or it will get burned. It will not make a sound if it does get burned."

Before we parted his stateroom Sir laced its cock, making it hurt so good and had this slave slip into a leather jock. It felt more naked with the jock strap on than when it was naked. It opened the door, Sir stepped out into the hallway and this slave followed in his wake.

We arrived in time to watch the moon rise from the ocean. Sir had this slave standing as it had been taught, within arm's distance so that this slave could always be alert to the needs of its Master. Interestingly, with Master Dan present this slave knew that it was to be attentive to only one Sir - its Owner. So why was this one kicked out of a daydream when it heard the beeper going off within its jock and found that this slave had been separated from its Sir? Its heart skipped a beat when looking around on the deck. It could not find its Master and would have died had Master Dan not stepped up and pointed the way to its Sir.

It entered the sitting room off from the deck just in time to see and be seen by its Owner - who had the box out and was about to blow this slave's nuts into another world. His cigar had reached a critical point. Sir needed his ashtray. Sir was in a heated debate when it dropped to its knees beside its Owner. Oddly this one could see Master Dan watching it from the corner of its eyes with its mouth open, waiting for the ash that Sir had promised this slave.

Master's hand descended, the cigar cupped between thumb and forefinger. This slave's mouth was open, waiting, spit slick and hungry for Master's hot ash. Sir did not seem to notice, did not look down, just knew it would be there waiting with mouth open. Sir gave a quick glimpse before he placed the cigar between his slave's teeth, then used its teeth to cut the ash which fell into the depths of this one's mouth. Without command the trap shut and it swallowed. Sir's hand patted this one's head as if to say, *good boy*. It was pleased and when it looked, Master Dan was no longer nearby.

A slave stepped from below, rang a small gong and announced to all that dinner was ready. We were ushered into a small but beautifully appointed dining room. The walls were covered with mirrors, giving the impression of a much larger space. Slaves held the chairs of their Owners until they sat. One of Mistress Beatrice's pups held her chair and stood at her back while the other one was ushered under the table at her feet. There were eight place settings at the table, seven were occupied and the one missing was Master Dan. Sir signaled that this one should come to him, and he whispered into its ear. "Go find Master Dan, inform him dinner is being served and I will not tolerate his drama tonight. He will report to me here and dine with us. No excuses. Run and return!"

Eight place settings indicated Buena Vista, England had sent a mousy looking man and one female slave; France had sent a perky female Domatrix with her breeder male slave; Germany sent a dark man and a sickly looking slave who looked as if it was all skin and bones; Mistress Beatrice represented Castle Enterprises; Laos sent a handsome Master with his equally handsome male; Cambodia sent a white Master with a berry brown male slave and Master Dan would make eight.

Fortuna smiled upon this slave as it found Master Dan in the opposite direction of the dinner party. Dan was on the front of the boat looking off in the distance when he heard its bare feet running towards him. He turned and put out his hand as if to stop this slave from running into him. Or to say *don't say a thing*. But this slave chose to ignore his silent command; one time, not long, ago it would have remained silent.

"Sir, my Master has sent this slave to find you, Sir. Sir said, inform Master Dan that dinner is being served and I will not tolerate his drama tonight. He will report to me here and dine with us. No excuses. Sir!"

This slave was confused as to how this situation must be handled. One part of it wanted to grab his hand and drag him back to his Master's dinner party, another side wanted to throw myself at him. My balls beeped this slave ignored the sound, preferring to be close to Master Dan and trying to silently beg him to come to dinner. The blast hit my nuts. It screamed and dropped to its knees holding its balls. It rose and ran back to my Master. As I looked back, Master Dan had turned back to the ocean and this one returned to the man to whom it belonged.

Seeing this slave return empty-handed, Master was not pleased. He excused himself, walked over to the phone and called (if this slave heard correctly) security. Sir spoke with his back towards this one and returned to the dinner party in a somewhat lighter mood. By the way he spoke, he was enjoying the conversations and the company. I did notice when Master Dan did not return, Sir had one of the kitchen slaves remove the table setting. He gave an excuse for Master Dan mentioning he was tired from his flight in this morning. But this slave could feel an undertow. As must have Lady Beatrice, she seemed to be studying my Master and her eyes held questions.

The dinner seemed to go on forever. Seven courses in all, each with their own wine. While the Owners dined at the table, each slave that could be spared from serving their owners was fed in an out-of-the-way place. Once that was completed, we returned and others departed to their meal. The table scraps given to us did not become our whole meal, they only added bulk to our diet. Having had dinner when they chose to take coffee, brandy and cigars on the deck, their slaves could be present to serve their needs.

My Owner took Lady Beatrice's arm as if to escort her to the deck; instead, she halted him and they had a quick exchange of words that related to Master Dan's absence. This slave was sent to warm Sir's brandy as they talked and walked slowly to the deck. Mistress Beatrice was pretending to be tipsy by the wine. He sat her down near him and put a pillow at her back, but her final comment gave this slave an item to ponder.

She said, "Hunter, you know he still cares. Be careful with his heart."

Master Hunter rose and got everyone's attention. "Ladies and Gentlemen, raise your glasses to a toast, 'To the Dream and those Departed.'"

Sir and Lady alike tipped their glasses of whatever they were drinking so it spilled to the deck then they lifted it to their lips and tossed it back in one swift gulp. Sir cleared his voice, getting everyone's attention again. "We are lucky tonight as we have live entertainment. Laos will show us their native dance and Cambodia has agreed to share with us some of his beautiful music while we relax this final evening of Union. When you return home tomorrow, think of the things we have discussed, implement the programs that we have all agreed upon and, please folks, send in the necessary medical papers or Castle will be forced to send a team to collect what is rightfully their's. Now I will shut up, so sit back and enjoy the show."

This slave was holding Master's brandy snifter between its legs, warming the brandy as most Sirs preferred and it was shocked to hear Sir call for his cigar. For some reason this slave thought he would ask for that in private, not here. It balked for just a second, but enough time passed for Sir to repeat the question until it responded, stood, grabbed its ankles and produced Sir's cigar. Mistress Beatrice was giggling while this slave humiliated itself for the pleasure of its Owner.

It licked off the condom before it broke the cigar out of its packaging, clipped the end, took the cigar to its lips and lighted it, placed the cigar between its teeth and offered the smoke to Sir. Sir chose to punish it for him having had to order his cigar twice. He was watching the dancer as it bent in upon itself until it resembled a human pretzel.

This slave was coughing when Sir noticed the slave's predicament and removed the cigar from its burnt mouth. The slave learned to pay closer attention to its Sir; the blisters in the roof of its mouth would help it remember its act of stupidity.

The moon was high overhead when the Sir left the party in route to our stateroom. Walking down the corridor, it noticed a security officer standing before a suite door, Sir stopped spoke quietly to the guard. "How is he?"

"Quiet now, Sir. We had to take action to secure his safety, Sir."

He turned to this one. "Kneel and wait. I will not be long." Sir turned to the guard, "Open the door."

The guard keyed the door and opened the door inwards. As Sir passed beyond, this one saw a man bound upright in a chair, his back was to me, then the door closed and it knelt to await Sir's return.

This one heard Sir's voice rise in anger. "How dare you think? It was one thing to come here, totally another to come under false pretenses! Do you think I'm stupid?!" The door was jerked open, Sir stepped into the hallway and the door slammed. It could feel the anger like electricity bristling off a generator. Master turned to the guard and snorted, "Tighten its bonds, you were too nice to it! Let it think before I take its rank!"

Sir stopped and looked down at me. "Get up slave! Get to the room; I will be along in a moment." He paused in thought. "Return here with its straightjacket, now!" This one ran, found the jacket where it had been hung and returned. Hunter was no longer in the hallway. The guard took it and told me to go back to the stateroom and await its Master.

When this one was exiting, the guard opened the door and it heard flesh hitting flesh. It knew Master would be in a mood tonight. Returning to the stateroom, it prepared the bed, tidied up and, when it found nothing else to do, dropped to its knees, placed its head to the floor and prayed that Sir would not take his anger out on this slave.

The door opened and slammed shut; his walk said he was angry. He paced a few minutes and walked to the bar. Poured himself a shot, tossed it back, poured another and threw himself into the chair. He snapped his fingers, signaling that it should crawl to where he sat. Sir put his boot out, this one leaned forward and kissed the sole of his boot. It felt his eyes boring into its hide as Sir bellowed, "Get me a cigar!"

While he watched this one ran to his humidor and returned, dropped, cut and lighted it as he had directed. He took the cigar instantly from its offered lips. It watched as Sir took the cigar, placed it in between his lips, took a long draw, savored the smoke and exhaled. He opened his legs and pulled this slave into the comfort of his crotch. While there, Sir played with his property lightly touching its face, cupping its chin, raising its head and fingering the collar around its neck. He came to a conclusion, sighed deeply and muttered, "I will give him one more chance."

He dropped his cigar into a glass ashtray and began unbuttoning his shirt. The hand that had been toying with this one's collar pulled it up onto its feet. As the shirt was pulled from his pants its head was inserted all he said was, "Make me feel good."

While he smoked, this slave licked his armpit, sucked and chewed lightly on his nipples. As it was chewing, Sir ordered it to chew harder. As it did Sir seemed to relish the pain as much as this slave loves the pain on its nipples. His cock formed an outline within his pants as this one's head worked across Sir's chest and downwards towards its goal. The fly unzipped and my tongue snaked inside to lick the rising cock. Using its mouth and hand, Sir's cock and balls were withdrawn from captivity. Sir allowed it to mouth his cock, suckle his balls and work its tongue below Sir's bull balls.

Sir took that time to stand, grabbing this slave's collar to drag it into the bedroom where this slave was leaned over the footboard. Sir pulled this slave's arms outstretched, found straps and bound them in place. He removed his belt and went to work on this slave's ass, making it twist and yell as he blistered away. When Sir got it to the shade he seemed to prefer, he lifted this slave onto its toes and impaled this slave's ass. Sir gave it no time to adjust to his invasion but took his pleasure fucking this slave's hole hard. Slamming his full body weight against this slave's upturned ass, grinding his cock. When Sir paused for a breather, his cigar down trailed this slave's back burning it, making this one cry out with a Master's need for someone to suffer. Resuming, he leaned into this one, it could feel the heat of his cigar at the nape of its neck, smell the tobacco as it and he drove this slave forward like a locomotive. His hand found its collar and he used that to gain more purchase as he slammed his cock deep, choking this slave as he blew his load. Another withdraw and slam, he shot again. He withdrew, released this slave and pulled it off the bed to drop on the floor. Master stood above it like a massive tower of boots, breeches and cock. Sir looked down, snapped his finger and commanded, "Clean it, faggot!"

This one's lips encased Sirs cock and tongued it clean of any of this slave's ass juices, but it must have done something wrong. No sooner than it had its lips around Sirs cock did he push it off, place his boot on its cock and leaned down, starring at this one who was terrified of what might happen next.

"I own you slave. Others may have broken and trained your sorry ass; but I own you until I see fit to sell your worthless hide!" He stood back up and made a new demand. "Undress me, slave!" Once this one completed removing my Master's garments, Sir bound its legs and arms, tossed it in bed climbing in beside it. Sir pulled it into the 'V' of his body and wrapped his big arm over his property. One hand rolled and tweaked its left nipple as he dozed off.

It lay there beside him, wondering what could have happened to Master Dan that would have brought about his outburst. Was Master Dan's arrival here for more than just to bring the blueprints, or was it to see this slave? That had to be banished from its mind, elsewise it would find more trouble than it needed. Master Hunter owns this slave, Master Hunter owns this slave, and this slave is owned by Master Hunter. It chanted its new mantra until it too drifted off to sleep.

When he awoke the sky was still dark. It felt him move, crawl over this one's body and heard him exit the room without so much as putting on any clothes. This one snuggled under the blankets and returned to sleep. It awoke when it felt him climb back in bed. He must have gone for a jog around the boat while the others slept as his body was sweaty when he returned. This one gave it no extra thought, pressing into his chest and licked him as he pretended to catnap. His arm opened, pulled me into him and held me in place as my tongue wrote love notes through his chest hairs. Again he sighed, exhaled and was asleep.

The ships bell wakened him with a start. He looked around, saw his slave, released its hands and ankles from bondage and pushed it over the edge of the bed; there while it knelt Sir fed it his tiger piss, then sent it afterwards to the kitchen for coffee and a sweet. It returned with his huge cup of coffee and hot sticky buns fresh from the oven. Those he wolfed, turned to me and ordered leather for the send off of the elders.

He showered; this one tidied the room, greeted him with his towel and had laid out his shaving gear. While he lay back in a chair, it had the honor of shaving his Sir (without a nick, mind you). Sir was pleased and ordered the slave to complete its cleaning rituals while Sir's breakfast was brought by one of the kitchen slaves.

Exiting the bathroom, Sir ordered it to eat its own breakfast of champions while he began his morning calls. When finished with gulping down this one's breakfast, it went to prepare Sir's boots, leathers and ready him to meet the day. Damn, he was in a good playful mood, as he would tweak this one's nipples while it tried to dress its Sir.

Sir chose to wear side-laced pants, his ever-present tall boots, spurs, a Sam Brown and no shirt. The way those pants molded to his body as it laced them snuggly made him look even more delicious than when he stands before this one naked. The glove leather silhouetted every pore on his body.

Dressed and booted, Sir directed this one to open a cabinet and remove two large paper shopping bags that contained beautifully decorated boxes. He went upstairs, this one following with the bags. He found them eating their breakfast as an airboat banked and swung around to land. The pilot came aboard and was brought up to meet his passengers.

By the way he reacted to seeing this one naked and Master Hunter in leather and boots we knew he was family. Besides, who in their right mind today wears brown knee high boots and breeches to fly an airboat? Sir seemed to like what he saw in this young man and extended to him an open invitation to return a couple of days early before we were to fly out.

With packages in their clutches, the elders gingerly climbed aboard the airboat. Being the generous host, Sir waved at them as they taxied across the open waters, gained speed and rose into the air in route to Miami International Airport and home to their countries. Once they were gone Sir seemed to relax. It was ordered to remove his spurs, return them to the room and return with its hood.

Upon returning, it found Sir stretched out over a huge divan that had served as seating for all those he had hosted. One leg up, the other stretched out, and his hands laced behind his head as he studied the clouds. He knew it was present as his hand detached from behind his head and a finger crooked in this one's direction. He pulled it into his lap, drew its face up to his chin and allowed it to worm itself into a position that Sir's chin could easily touch this one's head. Sir took my right arm, pulled it behind this slave and used it as leverage to get this slave where he wanted it. His leathered leg pinned it in position while a hand found a nipple that Sir began absent-mindedly rolling as it turned and kissed its Sir's chest. We laid like that for most of the morning until the sun got too hot, then his head turned to look down at me.

"What happens here, stays here. Does it understand, slave?"

This one acknowledged Sir's comment and he ordered it repeated.

We rose up from the divan, crossed the deck and descended into the darkened silent corridors to the corridor below deck. Sir stopped before the guarded doorway, dismissed the guard, took the key and opened the door. He pulled this one in behind him, directed this one to kneel, then he stepped beyond and allowed it to see who was under lock and key. It was as this one assumed, Master Dan, except he was bound within this one's straightjacket.

This one wanted to ask why, but knew better and lowered its head, sat back on its haunches, placed its hands at its back and waited for enlightenment.

Sir, on the other hand, walked over to Dan, pulled him to his feet and snarled at him. "You like this better, don't you boy?"

Hunter turned and was not expecting an answer when Dan spoke quietly, "Sir, this suits this one better, Sir."

Master's hand rose as he turned the power of that blow across Dan's lips and knocked him across the room. Hunter looked down on him then glared at this slave who had risen up on one leg as if to help Master Dan.

"Get back where you belong, slave! Don't fucking move a muscle! Press its worthless head to the floor and pray." It dropped its head as Sir commanded. Sir made it very aware that it was to stay put as his boot ground its face into the floor. "Stay down, slave!"

Dan was trying to struggle to his feet; Sir wanted otherwise. There seemed to be a brief struggle and Dan's body hit the floor. This one could not keep its head down; it looked up just as Master's boot slammed into the midsection of my Handler,

Dan. This one wanted to help but its confusion as to who it should help kept it in place, thankfully so. Master Hunter was not taking any lip from Dan and this confrontation spoke of times before. Why was Master Hunter so angry with Master Dan? Besides the obvious fact that he had come to the yacht on false pretenses, that he came to see this slave, or was it something this slave was not privy to at this moment?

Master Hunter, having taken the wind out of Dan's sail for the time, took that opportunity to pull the man to him, pull the hood over his head and lace it tightly in place. Dan's attempt to protest was silenced as Sir shoved one of Dan's own socks in his mouth before locking the mouth closed with the snap plate. Sir lifted the encased slave to its feet, jerked and pushed it forward as he ordered me to open the door. Dan sailed past me as if Sir was tossing a bag of garbage into the corridor. Sir directed me with his head; it ran ahead and opened the door to the stateroom. Master Hunter goose-stepped Dan down the corridor and pushed him into his private suite. Dan got his feet in a twist and fell hard; Master seemed to think it was another of his ploys. His boot descended, catching Dan as he was attempting to push himself off the floor using his head as leverage. Master's boot caught Dan's butt broadside; the impact slammed Dan about three feet into the room. There he lay, struggling to suck in air through the hood. Master Dan looked up at this one, his eyes displaying pain and fear as he - like this slave - had never seen Hunter this angry before. This slave crept into a corner, found its knees and placed its head to the floor.

Master did not even look in this one's direction but turned, walked slowly towards the door and left. It knew that he would be back once he got his anger under control; unlike Master Dan who hits when he is angry, Master Hunter knows his own strength. One of his blows, when truly angry, could easily kill a man. He went upstairs to walk off his anger and to calm down before he really did damage to Master Dan.

While Master was away, this one took it upon itself to check to see if Master Dan was alive and breathing. This one knew better than to loosen the binding or remove Sir's gag from Dan's lips. It was limited to what it could do but this one felt better having checked Dan before returning to its corner and waiting. It had a long wait. We both did.

Master entered the stateroom and snapped his fingers, calling me to him. I crawled the short distance as he walked towards me, put my head to his boots and held position. His tap on my head told this one to rise. He looked deeply troubled by what had happened to piss him off with Master Dan's actions and his reactions; this one guided him to a comfortable chair and put him down into it. This one quietly made him a stiff drink, fetched him a cigar, prepared it for him and offered it to him. He took it and the drink, pulled this one in between his legs and pulled them around it.

Sir looked down on this slave, cleared his throat and began speaking in low tones, "9-745, you have been mine since I first saw you long time ago. I knew you were part of my destiny. I also knew that I would not have the time to train you as you so richly deserved, that's why Dan was found."

He took a sip on his drink and a long draw on his cigar. He leaned forward and blew the smoke into this one's face. This one drank his smoke, wanting more, needing more to feel useful. "Like you, 9-745, Dan has made it known in the wrong places that he wants to serve me like you, as my slave. He wants to serve and be with the men he loves. That's all wonderful and fine except he is a trusted Handler with rank at the BV compound. If I collar him like I would any other slave, his companions would feel betrayed if I let him continue as he has been doing. Sucking cock while on duty he will eventually betray himself. Slave, you may not know the rules that apply to Handlers. They may use any slave sexually as they wish but two Handlers may not be sexual with each other on base. That one has almost broken all the rules, his commanders have informed me."

Master put the cigar in his mouth, held it while he stroked this one's head, feeling the hair on its head tease Sir's open palm like a bristled brush. The ash had grown long while he smoked and talked to me. This one opened its mouth, Sir looked, understood and flipped the ash into his private ashtray, the ash was swallowed and Sir continued, "According to Commander Schmidt, Handler Dan has already been caught servicing another Handler on the base. That was before you came into his clutches. Your presence was an experiment in training and to see if it being there would help Dan overcome his masochistic side.

"It would seem that Handler Dan must to be taught to fear me. Then maybe I can drill into his slave mind that he will serve me best as my slave while serving as a Handler. Besides, there are more ways to mark a piece of property than just a collar; yeah, that's what I'll do." Mind made up, Sir's course of action established at least within his mind, Sir ordered me up, "Open that second door and bring me the black doctor's bag. Then open the fourth door and pull out the stocks that are inside. It's time that this slave Dan thinks about its actions."

This one returned with the doctor's bag and, while Sir rummaged though it to find a syringe and two small bottles, this one opened the indicated cabinet and removed wooden stocks from where the feet and neck could be mounted. Sir left out the bottles and syringe, making a comment they would be used later, then gathered up a handful of cord that he pitched in my direction.

"Bring me that big dildo, slave!"

He took it out of my hand, pulled Dan to his feet and carried him by the straightjacket to the foot of the bed. Master had this one remove Master Dan's pants and boots while he held Dan over the footboard. Once that task was completed, he pushed Dan's upper torso over the board, grabbed this one's head and forced it between Master Dan's butt cheeks with an order.
"Eat ass, slave!"

This one set about doing its job for God and country by digging into to those handsomely bruised butt cheeks and burying its face. This one's tongue did the best version of a true lap dance any Master could ever have the pleasure of enjoying. Not only did this slave lick around the ass muscle but parted those cheeks, and my tongue dived into those pink lips. Master Hunter let this slave have its fun and even shouted encouragement to his worthless slave. "Come on faggot get deeper, bury that face, slave!" His hand always followed his words of support as he tried to push this one's head beyond the muscle and bury it deep into Dan's butt.

Slave Dan was not an inactive participant; his ass unfurled and sucked this slave's tongue within his hole. By the way he responded. this slave knew that Dan liked to have more than just a tongue buried into that musky smelling hole from hell.

Master Hunter, however, had other plans for that dank smelling hole of Dan's. His hand grabbed a hold of this one's collar, pulling this slave away and forcing Sir's dildo into Dan's butt. Sir met no resistance. Dan's hole sucked that rubber cock right into that boy butt and sat there chewing on it as if it was saying, what's next? Hunter locked the plug within Dan's bowels using the same harness this one arrived wearing. Interesting how the same gear that fits this slave also fit Dan, a little tighter in places but they fit as if made just for him.

Dan was pulled upright, the plug was set as Dan groaned and walked as if he had a log buried up his ass. (Which is just about how Master's plug feels the first hour or so.) Master Hunter guided Dan towards the open closet, flipped him around and backed him into place. This one handed Sir the neck stock. The wooden stocks were set into grooves before being slipped into place, pinned and locked around Dan's leathered head and neck. A second stock placed at Dan's feet locked those in place.

Sir took the leather lace he had tossed this one and used it to bind Dan's balls - to which were added what looked like about three pounds of diver's weights. Interestingly enough, Dan's cock had remained erect and got harder when Sir applied the lace and weights to its nuts. Sir opened the panels within the straightjacket, produced two forceps that were locked on to Dan's nipples. Extra leather lace was bound to each clamp, those laces pushed through holes on the door and the door was shut and locked. Sir took the extra lacings pulled them tight and tied them together. Completed as Sir saw fit, he directed this slave out the door down a flight of steps into his private dungeon that was located near enough to the screw room that any screams would go unheard.

The balance of the afternoon was spent with this slave worshiping my owner, Master Hunter. He worked this slave over until it was a quivering mass of meat on the floor then snapped his finger and it crawled to him only to beg for more. God, what he could do to this slave! He taught this slave the very meaning of trust. That day, like so many that would follow, this slave screamed its love and fear of this man it called Master. As many ways that he fucked this slave throughout the afternoon, he did not permit himself to cum. Only to build what this slave knew would be a huge release.

We both napped after the workout. This one taking comfort in my Master's arms, feeling the welts he placed upon this one's body for his pleasure, to satisfy his needs and to let his dark side feed. In his arms this slave drew comfort knowing that it had fed Sir's inner demon well.

The ship's bell called us from our nap. Sir stretched liked like a big cat, stood, walked over to the cabinet and jerked the door open. Dan's scream could be heard beyond his stocks and this one witnessed Master's cock swell with anticipation of this evening's entertainment. Dan was released, this one led him on its own leash to the upper deck where dinner was set for one. Both of us were ordered to the floor and this slave was positioned to the left of Sir's left boot, the other creature on his right. Sir removed the other's gag, gave it water, and even leaned down to give it a kiss. Sir knew when to give support and when to withdraw it, that kiss made the slave melt. He turned to this one, signaled it should rise on its knees. His hands cupped this one's chin and pulled its face forward. His reward was one of his heavy kisses that sucks the breath right out of a slave's lungs and promises the slave that there will be more.

Sir had opted for dinner under the awning. The galley slaves had mistakenly set the table in the adjoining room. Sir remained steadfast until they brought the table to him. Dinner was placed all around him as he sat looking into the distance, one hand on each of his slaves. Fresh conch salad, lobster, some type of yellow fish, kelp steamed rice rolls, fresh baked plantains, steamed carrots and other things filled his table to overflowing. Sir took a lobster, broke off its tail and peeled the shell off before tossing it over his shoulder and into the ocean. The first bite went into his mouth, the second into this slave's and if there was a third into the other creature's. This way Sir fed us all and we did one hell of a lot of damage to the food that had been put before us. What was left was returned to the galley and fresh wedges of pineapple were placed before us. Together the three of us ate about half the pineapple. Plates removed and table relocated, we were left on our own.

He pulled the creature's body between his legs, unzipped his fly, pulled out his cock, placed the cock head on the creature's lips and began to piss. This one was amazed to watch - knowing who was under that hood drink and not miss a drop. Sir rose to his feet, walked a few feet and resettled onto a huge divan that would easily have held six. He looked in our direction and called us to him. "Get over here, slaves!"

Both of us crawled the short distance and resumed our positions. This slave on his left tucked neatly up and under his beautifully veined arm and the other one with its head resting on Sir's right thigh and Sir's booted foot resting on its crotch. We lay that way for however long a time he felt it necessary. One Master and his two slaves, the perfect triad for those that live the BDSM lifestyle.

He had asked me long time ago when we were dating if this slave would be jealous if it had a brother slave to care for him. At the time, due to this one's own insecurity it said yes. Yes, it would be too jealous to allow my Sir to be shared with another. Now if he asked this one, it would reply no. This threesome could work. Sir needs one to beat and another to care for his needs while the other one heals. Besides, any more than two slaves and the Sir is no longer in control. He is working for his slaves, not the other way around. Still, Sir will sell to anyone more slaves if the owners can prove that they can care, train and maintain more. He is, after all, still a businessman. He makes the new owners very aware of the fact there is a restocking and retraining fee should one need to be returned.

One man and two slaves lay snuggling together until a galley slave coughed and Sir had to take a phone call. He withdrew into the sitting room to take it. He returned, mumbling something about Cappy having to have emergency surgery. This one was sent for a cigar and a brandy. When this slave returned, it found the creature licking on Sir's right boot and this one was put on his left. Together we matched each other as we synched our pacing. First cleaning the soles of his boots, working upwards to tongue his boots and together we crossed the bootshaft, working our tongues into his leather-covered legs. Master loved it; two slaves really loved it. Worship of one's God should be often and plentiful; Master Hunter made our worship sessions both of those and more. When we got within chomping distance of his cock, he rose laughing and told this one to take its brother downstairs to the dungeon, it was time that one learned its place.

As this one did his bidding, Master followed, stopped by his stateroom and retrieved his doctor's bag. When he joined us, this one knew Sir had a serious need for two slaves to carry his pain for him. Dan was released from the straightjacket, stripped, and its arms were secured in heavy leather restraints. The creature was bound to an 'A' frame fuck bench, its legs spread, after which Master pulled its arms downwards and locked them to its own ankles. Then Sir came for this one. Sir placed this slave on an elevated kneeling fuck bench, its arms and legs bound in place. Just by the way Sir smoked his cigar, you could see his excitement of having his two slaves under his care.

Sir walked to a cabinet on the opposite wall, pulled out a set of keys and unlocked the doors. As this one watched, Sir pulled out a tray of little vials, lifted out a disposable needle box, and placed what looked like strings of needles on a tray and a handful of syringes. That tray was placed at our rear. He made one more journey to that cabinet before he closed and locked it. Sir stepped before a small refrigerator took out a few ice-cold vials and returned.

He was being evil - his face certainly looked it - as he stepped within this one's view. It watched as Sir loaded four syringes. One vial went into all four, two of the cold vials went into two syringes and he laughed a very dark laugh as he passed this one's head in route towards its rear. Master announced to the room, "This is going to hurt a lot. Scream when you boys feel its necessary, your screams will only make me happier!" Again, that sadistic laugh.

He rubbed this one's ass with an alcohol swipe, flipped the syringe into this one's butt cheek and left the syringe in place. He stepped over to the creature and repeated the process, but with that one he depressed the syringe, letting the fluid enter the slave's meaty butt. No sooner than he withdrew the needle did that creature begin screaming. Sir depressed this one's syringe withdrew the needle. Whatever he had injected into our butt cheeks felt like liquid fire that did not just stay isolated in one spot but radiated as it moved down the leg. This one's scream joined the creature's in a duet to sadistic delights. We must have not been singing clear or loud enough as Sir took his belt to our upraised asses, and that only increased the spread of the fluid within our burning ass cheeks. Another needle entered our butts, a different type pain awoke and we raised our voices again. He must have dropped about twenty needles into each of our hips before he tired of that game.

Once the needle had dropped its agonizing liquid within our butts, time halted as we gave lung to the pain. Even when he no longer swatted our asses, the pain continued to flow across the buttocks, down into the thighs and it actually felt as if the fluid drained into our cocks and balls. Our whole backside was one massive hurt; he had done nothing more than a few whacks with his belt and we were a sobbing mass of pain.

During the height of the pain, he removed the plug from the creature's ass and shoved his cock into this animal's ass. His cock resting quietly within my hole was the only comfort it had since Sir began feeding his dark side on our pain. His cock felt like a lifeline cast out on the water for a drowning man to pull for safety. Sir took his pleasure, grinding his loins into my pain filled ones. Each time he slammed his cock home and his weight hit this slave's butt, the pain reawakened. One moment his cock was buried in my ass, the next moment he had his cock in the creature's ass. Its volume changed as Sir's cock worked its magic. Sir worked up a mighty steam, plunging his cock into one aching hole then into the other, back and forth. Twice this slave neared a climax of massive proportions, yet somehow Sir seemed to know. He would swing over to the other creature even as this one begged him to stay. God, was this one a blubbering idiot. But this one was not alone as the other slave was begging just as loudly. Master Hunter had two bitches about to take the place apart if he did not soon blow his load in someone's hole.

Damn if he did not take a breather and use a rubber cock on both of us. That bastard laughed as he churned our guts into mush. When he climbed back into the saddle he used the rubber cock on the other slave, making us match his need for a full-course climax. The closer Sir got, the more frantic he seemed to become. First in this one's hole then out into its, back and forth, neither of us knew if it was his cock or his rubber cock pumping and grinding these slaves sick with cum lust. Luckily he chose this slave to blow his load within and when he finally shot, he dropped over its back and blew two loads into its guts. All of us screamed in unison. Sir shot first, this one joined him and the creature blew its load as well.

One very happy Master returned to the stateroom with two very sore but happy slaves. All slept in his king-sized bed per his orders. This one on his left, the other on his right. This one cuffed, the other in leg irons and Sir in the middle. Sometime in the night, this one heard him fucking the other creature and, by the sounds of the other creature's moans, this one was very happy it was Dan that got his third load.

Awakening in the morning, two slaves finally realized the depth of his sadistic pleasures as we rolled on to our butts and jumped from his bed as if shot. Sir had gone to call the hospital for information on Cappy and found us checking out our extremely sore, bruised, butts in his floor-length mirror when he returned. "I take you two like my handiwork and are dying for another round?"

Sir chuckled deeply as this slave paled and responded with a very polite, "Sir, yes, Sir." He knew - like we slaves knew - the term 'No' was no longer a part of our vocabulary and our punishment for using it would have been really severe. In no way could we deny our Sir anything by word, thought or deed. Even daring to be slow in responding to his question could, if he was in a bad mood, get these two hurting slaves in deep shit.

Over breakfast Sir told us that Cappy was improving and would be recovering at the BV hospital at home on our mountain. It was nice to know that Sir's best friend was improving. Just that made his mood lighten and he went diving while Dan and this slave were left to complete a number of chores. If all was done before he returned we would be permitted to enjoy the comfort of the sun. This one spit-polished Sir's boots to his preferred mirror shine while slave Dan cleaned up the dungeon from last night's play. When Dan had completed his chores, he joined this slave in the stateroom to help finish Sir's boots in record time so we could enjoy the sun together. Our Master was kind enough to place upon this slave at the beginning of this slave's journey his collar. Since Dan was still a Handler back at the base, it would be hard to explain the presence of a collar when he returned; instead, Sir locked a logger's chain around that slave's neck. The weight was extreme but not so bad that it would cause circulation problems. The weight in itself was its own lesson and punishment.

Two slaves ran gleefully upstairs to enjoy a moment's respite from our Master. We were so bold that we even had the kitchen help provide us with large pitchers of mixed tropical fruit juices that Sir had left orders we could enjoy. Dan was asleep and this one's mind was tracking down some information within its own head. That is, this one was trying to put two and two together to create four. It was attempting to balance rumor with fact on people that my Sir had around him.

For instance, Cappy, his best friend, was known to be an evil bastard when he was infuriated. When he was angry, not only did you see him red-faced, shouting and mad but you heard him approaching. Plus, he loved to verbally debase a slave or anyone that enraged him. Whereas when Master Hunter was fuming mad even Cappy ran for the hills. No one liked to face our Sir when his anger was aimed at you. Still, Sir had a saving grace that Cappy did not. Sir would, when boiling mad, order whoever had pushed him over the edge to be silent until he regained his composure. Else wise he would strike out in anger. His fists without the fire of anger held enough of a punch, add the fire and someone was going to be hurt, badly beaten or left in a puddle of their own blood. Sir turns brutally cold when his buttons are pushed. That aspect of my Master this one had heard about and seen recently when he blew up at Dan. This one learned a lesson at his slave brother's expense.

Sir found two slaves lounging on the wooden deck taking in the sun, asses held high in the air. Failing to acknowledge his presence got a wet towel to each upturned butt and brought us to our feet dancing. Master seemed excited by something he found while diving and wanted this slave to take notes.

He found some old coins as he and his diving companions were capturing dinner. They had shot a fish with a spear gun and the fish had sunk into a crevice. At the bottom of the crevice Sir found earthen jars filled with clumps of blacked metal. Using the spearhead he scraped the metal and found both silver and some gold in the clumps. Laughingly, Sir dropped the heavy fish sack. One lump weighed about 30 pounds and could have been gold or brass; the smaller did have a silvery cut in its surface.

He was excited with his find and more excited about what he had considered giving his team of Handlers. He was rambling about trying to do a huge vacation for all the Handlers within BV as a way to say thanks to them for all their hard work. A week or two of high seas adventure and buried treasures to be found by the BV team would do the whole team a world of good. He and Dan exchanged ideas most of the night as this one took notes of the exchange. Two days were spent in his company enjoying the tropical paradise and our Master.

Thursday arrived, as did our airboat, and a fourth joined in on the fun. As luck would have it the pilot was a shield mate in good standing. One Master, one Top and two slaves who got buggered in more ways than this one could think. Friday, Dan and this slave packed his luggage and made preparations for our departure on Saturday morning. We three would be back on the home court by Sunday evening.

This one was shocked by the way people treated my Master and his two slaves. It was one thing for the airboat pilot to join us on the yacht a day early for play-time. It was something totally different to see the preferred treatment shown Sir and his entourage as we landed at the Port. No one blinked an eye as Master Hunter and his two slaves went through customs without so much as a search for contraband. Seeing our Master for the first time would have made this one want to question him - much less his two handsome slaves walking at his side, carrying his briefcase and personal luggage. Hell, a customs guard (complete with slave collar) escorted us through the lines of waiting tourists disembarking from huge cruise ships to an awaiting limousine. Once in the limo, Sir directed the driver to go first to the downtown gold district and there we were met by another slave who took us into a skyscraper. This one loved how the common people reacted on seeing one of us open Sir's door, holding it until he passed through. Sir loves the little things that we did for him. Always giving him reverence; holding doors, holding his chair at dinner, standing until ordered to sit, waiting until ordered to eat, carrying his bags, serving as his ashtray, table, boot rest - anything he desired, we slaves fulfilled.

He had come by the gold district to bring to an old friend from his Vietnam days his findings. Sir was talking adamantly to a lady about the find and her life while he sat in her office. Her slave took the lumps of metal into an adjoining lab and returned, announcing to his Mistress that the findings would net more profit for historical reference than for the metal that they contained. Sir elevated his booted foot, snapped a finger and Dan crawled under to act as Sir's bootrest as he was the closest. This one had been studying their conversation and was amazed that she was nonplussed by Sir's command over his slaves. Sir thought nothing of using us anywhere as long as we slaves suited his purpose. We seriously did not break too many taboos so we would be left alone. The meeting broke up after Sir reached a conclusion. The metal and the coordinates to the find would be sold. This way, if the lady was correct, Sir could tackle one of his pet projects earlier than next year.

Before we departed, this one was made to undress and it was measured for a custom piece of jewelry that would be inserted into its cock and work in conjunction with the holes already present. This slave would soon be placed into strict chastity and cum control. Sir had Dan measured for a small ring - his mark of being Sir's slave - that would be fitted behind that slave's cockhead. Dan was taken into a private sterile room, his shorts opened and Sir had three piercings placed in the groove behind his cockhead, curved barbells were inserted and when they healed Sir's mark of ownership would be installed. The three barbells would be removed and the solid ring installed, woven actually, in and out of the skin until a ring of metal encircled the cockhead. He could get an erection but it would hurt like a mother as the ring would not expand, as it was smaller than Dan's circumference. As much as Dan loved the idea, he hated the thought of no longer having control of his own cock; he was now more than ever Sir's slave.

Master wanted Dan to go home with a changed attitude one way or another. Sir set about reaffirming Dan's commitment to Him with the help of a cane laid heavily across the boy's butt and thighs the night before departure. Saturday before departure, Sir had this one dress Dan in knee length leather bondage shorts that were padlocked in place over which was placed a standard baggy slave's jumpsuit. This one got away fairly easily, having to wear only the shockerball collar and another baggy jump suit.

Dan seemed reluctant to return to Buena Vista for two reasons. The first was that he had gotten a suntan and now had a collar of white skin where there should have been darker flesh. That actually did not bother him as much as the second reason. He loved serving Master more as his slave than as a Handler. He really begged Sir to allow him to remain where he belonged. Sir did not want to listen to Dan's interpretation as Sir had his own plans. Dan was to serve him as his Handler and that was that. Master even made him sign a contract stating that he would be Sir's Handler until Sir said otherwise. This would be a very short-termed contract if Dan returned home and resumed his old ways of blowing Handlers in the back corridors.

Returning to the limousine, we took our places as this one returned to the comforts of sitting between Sir's legs and Dan sat on the floor under his hand. We rode to the airport in relative silence until Sir announced to us that he felt like we both needed to join the mile high club and that would be a very pleasant way to wile the hours before we returned home. Our car was passed beyond the security gate, onto the tarmac and it was driven up to a private black jet with a silver crest on its tail. Men in Castle livery loaded our trunks while we climbed the steps and entered the cabin. Sir ordered water for the two of us and a shot of Jack for himself. A stewardess, wearing a collar, served drinks as Sir was showing his slaves the plane proper.

The back tail section had been transformed into a private suite, complete with its own bathroom, bed and closet. There we were ordered to strip out of the jump suits and be comfortable. Here, on the plane, Sir was home. The next area was plush seating for eight passengers; each chair transformed into a twin bed and the forward third of the plane was given over to the pilot, small restroom and kitchenette. Once aware of our new surroundings Sir took Dan into the back bedroom to change its cock dressing. Sir returned leaving Dan to rest.

This one was kneeling between Sir's legs while Master was having a phone conversation, he tapped this one, ordered a cigar and it went to fetch his desire. Sir waved his hand in the general direction of the back. Entering, this one found Dan resting on the bed, bound spread eagle, his ass impaled with a large plug and his mouth equally plugged. By its eyes, Dan was loving all of it, both were glazed and pinpointed from having had an endorphin rush. This one found Sir's humidor and returned rapidly to cut and prep his cigar, kneeling within his presence.

Sir kept this slave kneeling, straddling his boot, hands to the floor, focused on serving as his ashtray. Its mouth remained closed until Sir's cigar approached then it would open to receive the ashes or serve in other means. Sir liked placing his cigar between this slave's teeth, there resting until he reclaimed the smoldering stogie. Being used this way reminded this one of times when an old man taught it the pleasures of serving a man who smoked cigars. Master Hunter had helped this one to transform a negative experience into a very positive pleasure. Serving Sir in this manner was most pleasing to this slave, as no other slave could provide this service. Hadn't Sir helped it realize through his deep programming that this slave was happiest when Sir used it as his ashtray, butt and boot boy? Besides, when Sir rewarded this one with the butt, didn't Sir always give this one his piss to assist with washing the cigar down?

The phone call ended, Sir leaned back into his chair, took a long draw on his cigar, looked down at this hungry face, smiled and exhaled his smoke into its lungs. Sir was happy by the phone call and the results of the trip. He ordered another drink for himself, placed this one's face in his crotch and closed his eyes thinking, while this one toyed with pleasing his Sir's rising need. He chuckled and looked down. "Look what you have done to me, slave," he said in mock anger. "Looks like I am going to have to take this in hand and make two slaves club members. Up, get your sorry ass into the bedroom."

There are many aspects of control when one owns human property. Master Hunter has shown to this slave that he prefers to have total control over his possessions. He enjoys the pleasure of having a slave or two in bondage while he is working elsewhere. Just the knowledge of having a person locked in his bondage feeds his dark side. He loves to walk into a room and see his slave just where he left it, writhing from the pleasure-pain of his toys working. It is a lesson in trust for the slave as well as the Master. The slave has to learn to accept this treatment, this level of control over its own freedom. The Master has to learn that his property will be safe while he is out of the room. Most men that this slave had played with prior to my Master Hunter would never consider leaving this slave or another alone in any form of bondage, but that is what makes our Master different than the others. He has a way of establishing a link, a connection with his slaves that goes beyond the spoken word. It simply is a knowing or a trust based on the security of two humans forming a unique bond. Plus he has the uncanny way of being able to see through another's eyes.

Instead of immediately jumping this slave's bones, Sir wanted this one to suffer, to anticipate his need. And by the rise in his pants his need was getting very excited by the prospect of having slave butt. Sir had an evil thought; if you watched his eyes like we were trained to do, you could see those evil thoughts pass from the left side of his brain to the right. Sir released this slave's cock, got it hard and had this slave kneel between Dan's legs. There it was ordered to insert its cock into Dan's butt. Once in place, Sir bound this slave to Dan's already outstretched body.

Sir's sadistic laughter filled the air as he pulled out one of his suitcases and produced his electrical toys. This one assumed that Dan got the same treatment as this slave. Its ass was filled with one of his toys and something was wound around this one's nuts. Then the electricity began to work on this one's cock, which was buried in Dan's ass. His jump told this one that he, too, was feeling the electricity. Sir set us in motion as one jolt of juice went into this one's nuts, paused while another jolt traveled down its cock and into Dan's hole, which jumped to his own music. Sir actually left this one pumping its cock into Dan's ass while Dan was getting bumped by his own electrical jolts. Neither of us would cum this way - that was not Sir's intention. His intention was to make us more sensitive to his needs and his needs were that we suffer while he worked. Before he closed the door on two humping slaves he promised that he would return.

One thing this slave learned early with Master Hunter is that one should not piss him off. He believes in protecting his property. When out in public with his slaves he can be very protective and does not cotton to others touching or slapping what holds his brand or collar. Normally, Sir is one that rarely gets upset. When everyone else is running around like chickens with their heads cut off, Sir is the calm in the storm. Then there are those rare times when someone foolishly pushes him once too much, and when that occurs, almost everyone with some sense will run for the hills and take cover. Dan mistakenly pushed him once too often when he appeared on the yacht and suffered greatly for his mistake. Sir is not one to scream or yell when he becomes irritated. The more irritated he becomes the quieter, calmer and colder he becomes, until he turns into a black cold fire of brutal energy. If he reaches that stage and it's you that he is pissed with, grab your ankles and kiss your ass goodbye. Because no manner of apology will warm his heart until he has concluded his judgment and sentenced the fool that started his anger. Those within the caverns know that Master Hunter does not reward bad behavior and his idea of punishment can make strong men weak-kneed.

God, how badly this one wanted to cum. Sir knew how to place his devices so that when this slave was just on the brink of pushing over the edge, a jolt of electricity would stop that thought. This way, Dan and this slave were almost constantly on the brink of slipping over the edge and cumming without permission only to be driven back from the edge of pleasure by Sir's pain. This one was on a mini-power trip, its cock lodged within the very Handler that had broken its will and fashioned it to suit our Master. This slave wanted so badly to hurt the man below it and yet, it was his brother, the very man it loved. Together we rode Master's jolts of electricity, squirming, writhing and riding each wave until Sir finally called a halt.

There he stood, handsome as hell itself, pleased with how we had suffered for him. This one was disconnected from Dan's backside, it was ordered to release Dan. Together we undressed our Master, replaced his boots and followed his orders. He had us both strung up and facing each other when he was disturbed by a phone call. Tossing on shorts, he departed, leaving us swinging with toes barely touching the ground. Dan opened his legs, encircled this one's body and pulled it to him, where he kissed it, longingly, lovingly. Neither of us heard his return, both felt his presence as a bullwhip encircled our bodies and burned in its message. Dan's legs dropped as he mouthed the scream and mine joined in the duet. Another stroke kept us singing, the flicker caught and tagged Dan's right nipple, painting it brilliant red.

Master's anger was fanned to a black heat as that kiss must have brought all his worries forward and brought them to bear on Dan. Master beat him six ways to Sunday with that whip before he stopped, tossed the whip away from him as if it was a snake and sat down abruptly. He sat there holding his head in his hands, not moving, just sat there. He got up mechanically, walked over to where this slave hung and cut its bonds; pointed at Dan, silently ordered this slave to cut him down. Dan dropped like a sack of potatoes and lay there breathing heavily. His body was cut with angry red welts all over.

Master stood, looked down at Dan and screamed, "Damn you! Damn you to hell!" He snapped his fingers, this one crawled to him, and he pulled me hard into the 'V' of his legs, closing them around it and sat there staring at Dan. Sir's right boot slipped forward, Dan's eyes took on life. His head and body was pushed up slowly to a crawling position and he began to crawl forward towards Master's boot. Master cursed again in a whisper. "Damn you to hell, slave!" Dan inched himself forward, crawling as each movement caused him great pain. Master continued to whisper, "damn you, damn you, damn you."

Dan put his lips to the underside of Master's boots. He kissed them and Masters boot jerked back, then forward to slam into Dan's face. Dan's lip split, blood began to trickle down his chin, still he held his position. He lowered his head; kissed his Master's boot sole again and this time it held its place. Locked in silence, Master watched as Dan tongued his boot sole clean and moved up to the upper side of the boot, weaving his busted lip, blood and tongue across and up to Master Hunter's shafted leg. There at the top of the boot he paused, head bowed, waiting.

Masters chest rose as he inhaled and exhaled a long, drawn out and deep sigh. His hand went out to touch Dan's bowed head slightly. Dan turned to look at his Master; his eyes were filled with love.

"Why must you two always make things harder than they need to be?" Sir seemed to speak to the room. No one answered.

Master leaned forward, his right hand stroked Dan's head then he grabbed a hold a handful of his hair, twisted his head and drew him closer to him. Sir began knocking on Dan's head when he spoke, "Get this through that thick head of yours, slave. YOU remain a slave to me and a Handler as well. Double duty. You are strictly forbidden to suck or be fucked, nor are you permitted to cum while in the caverns below! YOU have sex when I say you do. You'll report to me weekly for discipline until I see fit to change things. Commander Schmidt will be advised that you are on special assignment, thus your need to oversee the building of the great hall. Fuck this up in any way and I – personally - will castrate you. Understand me, slave Dan?"

Dan made him aware of his acceptance with a prompt smile followed by, "Sir! Yes, Sir!"

Master rose, dumping us both to the floor. He climbed onto the bed, lying on his stomach, pulled a pillow under his head and looked over his shoulder. "Slaves, come here, please me!"

We feasted well during that flight; this slave pried open Sir's ass cheeks and buried his face while Dan found comfort licking out his armpits. He made us bath him with our tongues then he fucked us both. Once exhausted, Sir laid back with a slave under each arm, all of us purring in satisfaction. Both Dan and this slave joined the ranks of the Mile High club.

A limo met us at Washington National. Both slaves kept to the floor while Master occupied the seat. Phone calls were patched through to our car while we returned home to blessed Buena Vista. We slaves remained quiet, each lost in our own thoughts. Dan was worried about how he would be received back into the caverns after his departure and this slave was worried how it would fit into the main house routine.

Master Hunter seemed to know what was going on in our heads. He pushed a button on a console, the window rose between the driver and us. The glass frosted and we were left alone to ponder our fates. Sir picked up the phone and told an operator on the other end to hold all phone calls, hung up and turned his attention on us slaves kneeling at his feet.

With his boot he got this one's attention, "9-745, it will do fine once at home. They will teach it my routine, which will be done daily unless I break it out of the routine. Slave Dan, it has the harder of two jobs. First, it owes its worthless life to me, its Owner. Second, it owes its allegiance to Buena Vista. It has my orders, break them and I will castrate it and hang its dried nuts from my keys as a reminder of what it once was. Do not fuck with me on this. You of all people know what I am very capable of doing should you fail me." Master Hunter seemed to watch Dan digest his words before he ordered it to speak.

Dan cleared his throat, "Sir, this slave will do you proud. It does not deserve its nuts if it fucks up Sir's orders, Sir."

"You have the harder job of you two slaves, you must be diligent to prove to those who know you that you have not changed, and if I hear that you have sucked off any other Handlers, boy!" Sir's threat hung in the air; enough had been said between them. Master looked down. "Hands behind its back. Now suck my cock, slave Dan, make me feel good to have its sorry ass back where it belongs."

Master lay back in his seat, spread his legs and allowed Dan to crawl between them before they closed to encircle his working torso. Master winked at this slave. Master and this slave both knew it just might be a long dry spell before Dan was going to getting any more cock like his owner's.

Dan transformed a simple blowjob into a worship service as it made love to his owner's cock and balls. This one admired his brother's talents and felt deep compassion for the man that was once his Handler, now turned brother slave.

By the time we passed the security gate, Dan was dressed and sitting beside his Master and this slave rested quietly between both men's boots. We had said our goodbyes earlier when, after Dan had given our Sir the best blowjob this slave had ever witnessed, slave Dan was ordered to blow this slave. He who this slave had serviced many times in that capacity did now serve. The subtlety of the act told to both slaves who was to be the leader in Master Hunter's personal slaves, this slave 9-745. Slave Dan would always be the lower of the two unless this slave fucked it up somehow.

A honk from the limo brought all slaves to the front door, at least those that were not attending to Master Cappy's recovery. We carried in Master's trunks and followed Sir up the stairs. Mike, Cappy's slave, showed this slave where to take Sir's trunk and poor Dan was left downstairs holding Master's briefcase. Sir went into a private room to check on Cappy and his recovery from the emergency surgery while this slave was directed where to place the trunk before returning to fetch the other. No one helped this slave. Even as much as Handler Dan wanted to be of assistance, he had to hold his place and watch this one drag the second, heavier, trunk upstairs. Luckily J.D. ran to this one's rescue. Either he was sent or was afraid this one would destroy the trunk with the drag-and-drop method it was using to pull the suitcase to the upper level. Luggage finally located within my Master's suite, this slave returned to the main floor of the house to take the briefcase from Handler Dan. Dan winked his eye and refused to give up the briefcase. He waited until Master Hunter returned to the entrance hall and together, with this one in tow, we adjourned to his office.

No sooner had Master Hunter seated himself behind his desk did a knock come upon the door. Slave mike stepped within to thank Hunter for returning and to inquire if we had eaten. Sir ordered food to be brought here for all three of us before he dismissed mike. Sir sat behind his desk, ordered Dan to check the mail for anything that he thought Sir needed to see and put this slave to working on lighting a small fire within an old barrel-shaped cast iron heater. All junk mail went the way of the stove; all that Dan thought Sir needed to read was opened, proofed by either Dan or this slave before being given to Master Hunter. This way the three of us found the surface of his desk in less time than it took mike to return with dinner.

There was a light rap on the door, Master Hunter sent Dan to open the door just in case mike needed assistance. The door opened up to reveal a huge red-faced man wearing white and carrying a hot bowl. He entered, begging Sir's pardon, and began stammering in his nervousness. This one knew him as the Master Chef of the kitchens below ground and whispered this information to my Owner.

Master Hunter rose from his desk, ordered Dan to give the man his seat and when the elder chef was seated, put his fears to rest by calling him by name. "Ah, Clyde, what brings you out of the depths tonight? What's this you have brought me to taste?"

Clyde was a beefy man with strawberry red hair, beard and warm dancing eyes. He was stronger than one might expect, but the years of working in the kitchen beating eggs (and slaves when they failed to submit to his needs) seemed to pay off for him. He had bought his freedom years ago, lived underground where he was closer to his work and the extended family of the caverns. This one found Sir Clyde happiest while in the kitchens, driving his staff to fulfill their tasks and quotas quickly. From past interaction with Master Chef Clyde, this slave found him to be a just man with a vicious swing if you got caught nibbling on duty.

Clyde had cleared his throat in preparation to speak with Hunter when mike entered with a tray. This one was sent to help mike make the necessary arrangements so Sir could be fed. Master offered food to Clyde, who quickly refused it saying he had eaten in the kitchens. Clyde was on a roll, so once he had Sir's ear he pushed on to explain what he had brought to Master Hunter.

"Master Hunter, I think I have perfected the recipe for slave fare. I have been working on it since you asked me to see if we could make it healthier for those who were doing more work. Well, Sir, I think I have it. Would Sir like a taste?"

Hunter leaned forward, a smile crossing his face and stuck three fingers into the goop that looked like poi. That which clung to his fingers was deposited within his mouth; this one wanted to giggle so badly but knew better than do something that disrespectful even when Sir made a face at the taste of the goo in his mouth. Sir seemed to swish the goo around in his mouth before he swallowed it.

The Master Chef had transformed into a vulture watching his next meal, he was so intent on Master Hunter's reaction. All of us got a surprise when Sir picked up the bowl passed it to Dan and ordered him to take a taste before passing it down to this slave with an order. "Eat it slave!"

How quickly things got back to normal once we were home at Buena Vista. Dan was once again a Handler and this one was still only a slave. This one dug in after the initial finger full and was shocked at how good it tasted. The Master Chef smiled as he watched this one licking its lips, as did Master Hunter when he asked this one if it was good.

This one mumbled with a mouthful of gruel, "Sir, yes, Sir," and happily returned to my bowl, finding it odd how deeply this one missed its slave gruel while out on the yacht. Human food was too rich for this slave; too much human food and it got a sick belly (as Sir found out while on the sea).

Sir ordered this slave to stop eating and answer some questions. He was told that the new recipe suited this slave's taste, that the goo was palatable. Strangely, this slave had only eaten half of the bowl and felt full. It would have taken approximately twice that amount to reach this state with the old stuff. It tasted sweet while in the mouth but had a pleasant salty taste when it left the tongue, and it seemed to give this one a buzz.

Taking his cue, the Master Chef told Sir that an additive had been discovered that would make the slave population more compliant and more willing to please. Sir asked to see the recipe and nearly shit when he realized that this slave had ingested THC. Master Hunter suggested that this new gruel be tested more completely before it became the main bill-o-fare for the whole slave population. Handler Dan would subject a dozen slaves to this test and he would report the results to our Master weekly. That said, the Master Chef rose and took his leave, happy with how the meeting had ended.

No sooner had the door shut did mike ask to speak. "Sir, please don't use that stuff. This one can find a better alternative to having to use narcotics to get the slaves to conform to the Chosen Way. Please, Sir, let this one try!"

Master rose, crossed the room and sat down at the small table. Another chair was placed nearby for Dan and they were served while Hunter mulled over the conversation in his mind. He spoke to both slaves, "Dan, you'll conduct the test on the most unruly slaves in our pens and you, mike, will get to work on finding an alternative. If this stuff works as well as it seems to be doing on 9-745, it will be an easy way to convert some of our troubled ones to the Way. Mike, you'll find me an alternative to the slave fare, one that has more nutrients for the mules, horses and the heavy work animals. Accomplish that and you'll be allowed to continue your chef training."

This one had resumed nibbling on the contents of the bowl until Master ordered mike to take it. This one was not willing to give up the bowl; that is, until its Owner took the bowl from it and got this one's attention by grabbing its neck. Sir stopped this one from making more of an ass of itself by grabbing a hold of this slave's neck and forcing its face into the wooden floor. Sir's boot held it in place as he drove the point home; obey or hurt. When it was released, it scuttled to its owner's side and there it knelt as he and Dan finished their dinner. Mike was dismissed for the evening, as the plates could wait until morning. We had our final dinner together. As soon as mike departed and the door closed, Sir had Dan dropped to his rightful position on the floor at his Master's boots. Like before on the yacht, we dined well on roast beef, veggies and stuffing. The food did not matter as much as did the company we kept.

With our dinner finished, Master rose to his feet, pulled Dan upright, wrapped his arms around the man and Dan did the same. Master pulled Dan's right arm to his back, pinning it with his hand, then reached up with his other hand and grabbed Dan's chin. Sir's head lowered and Master forced his kiss onto trembling lips that parted to accept Sir's darting tongue. They held onto that moment until Master broke the contact. Master pushed Dan back a step and addressed him as a Handler. "Report to me here, next Friday. I expect you to have records of your first week's test with the new recipe and details from the builders about the cavern hall. They have my permission to start the project. Dismissed, Handler!"

Crisply, Handler Dan saluted, turned and exited Master Hunter's office. He returned to the caverns below with a new lease on life, this one would have to assume. Hadn't he come from being a Handler of men to being an owned slave in less time than it took some people to change their oil? Handler Dan was no longer alone in this world. Now he belonged to a family of three: one Master and two slaves.

A Boner Book

Chapter 2

I care not what subject is taught if only it be taught well.
Thomas Huxley

The return to routine was nothing new to this slave. At least it was almost the same routine that had been trained into it by Handler Dan. Save for here within the main house, this slave had extra duties befitting its rank as third slave to the household but number one to our Lord and Master Hunter. Master Cappy healed from his emergency surgery. This slave never really found out what happened to him, but from the way Master berated him once Cappy had healed the accident was not to Master's liking.

Between the two men, Cappy was the elder and a graduate from the USMC, a Vietnam veteran (as was Master Hunter) and, unlike Hunter who held the rank of Lieutenant, Master Cappy was a Captain. He was a handsome man, German stock, and dark hair with salt gathering in and around the temples of his flat top haircut. Hazel eyes, 6 feet 1 inch tall and built like a brick shithouse that weighed in about 197. He was the typical lean, mean, fighting machine. Brute strength with a slight tummy that stuck out over his belt no matter how he tried to hide it. Cappy had proven time and time again just how well disciplined he was by the way he took orders from Master Hunter. It was as if Hunter's orders had originated from God's own mouth when Hunter spoke to Cappy.

As the foreman and close friend to Master Hunter you could see that their love affair had gone on for years. It was a friendship that was like a blood bond with deep trust and something else. The something else was a closely kept secret held between the two of them. Too much went unsaid between these two men - especially when they had a disagreement. Those occasions were rare, as Cappy preferred to defer to Master Hunter. Still. there were times when Cappy just up and disappeared off the face of the planet. Usually his twin slaves kept their mouths shut about these occasions. Almost all men who could leave our tiny island of sanity would on occasion take a much needed break and returned refreshed, renewed, and ready for another month of slave breaking and training. One such occasion happened to Master Cappy; he disappeared and reappeared in a 24-hour period. The reason the twins voiced their concern is their Owner returned welted and bruised. Hunter told them to mind their own fucking business, it was none of their concern.

Then there was the bet between Master Hunter and Cappy. It had started as a friendly bet placed between each of them over dinner. Neither the twins, Handler Dan nor this slave could find out what the bet was about, but we all knew who lost it. For a week, Cappy had to wear heavy leg shackles that were locked over his boots and this only made him more evil. Everyone except Hunter was subject to his crop for any minor screw up.

Cappy owned the twins. He actually found them when he was a pipeline pimp on the oil rigs in Texas. He broke and trained j.d. first and, with help, they seduced the younger brother mike into the triad. Cappy would not tell anyone how long they had been with him, but both boys were in their mid 20's and they were devoted to their Sir like this one was to its Master Hunter.

Where the twins were concerned, Cappy normally meted out punishments when one screwed up. Except for one day, when slave mike was caught using a computer for something other than bookkeeping. Slave mike had been caught chatting with men online when it was suppose to have been working on the books. Supposedly, or so the story goes, slave mike had been using the computer this way for over three months. This one was sent to fetch Cappy from out of the logging zone. Cappy was still in recovery from his recent surgery and this one did not think while passing the stable to pick up a mule for Cappy's return to the house. This one found itself being used as a bareback mule as Master Cappy drove it with his crop back to the main house. Nearing the house with Cappy on this slave's back, we could hear Hunter's bellowing voice chastising slave mike. He was pissed!

Cappy entered, pulled Hunter back from the cowering slave and asked it to explain itself. Slave mike admitted it had been wasting valuable time and had basically blown off about three months of work time intended for the books. Cappy turned beet red began screaming and kicking at the slave until Hunter pulled him off and took Cappy into the kitchen to calm down. When Cappy returned, he was cold like a dead fish. He picked up slave mike by his collar, drug him into where Master Hunter was standing, and tossed the slave before his friend. Cappy screamed to mike and anyone in the room, "Take this piece of shit to your shed, Sir, and teach it a valuable lesson! Teach that slave why even I fear you, Sir!" Cappy kicked at mike, who had paled from its sentencing, and then Cappy turned and stalked out the front door.

There, in Master Hunter's private domain, slave mike would relearn fear of his Lord and Master Hunter. Few slaves that had been returned to Hunter's shed ever spoke of their experience while under his care; but, we could read the signs that told us enough about what went on. The shed equated to hell's gate in these slaves' book.

The second day home, this slave was refitted with a slave harness that earmarked its status among the slaves on Buena Vista. Like the other harness, it was riveted in place; however, it was an abbreviated slave harness. Two shoulder straps, a chest and back strap, one strap around its rib cage, and it held its cock and balls encircled by steel along with a strap that kept this one's hole filled until Master chose to use it. Slave mike had a harness that indicated it was well trusted above and beyond all other slaves on the base. Slave mike's harness was attached to his collar; one single strap ran down his spine between his ass crack and attached to a ring around his cock and balls.

For slave mike to overstep his boundaries and lie to both Masters, we slaves knew he had made a major breach of trust. Hunter bound slave mike's hands behind his back, Sir's boot placed on the slave's ass helped it to its feet and, with Sir's hand on its collar, mike was taken to the shed. Screams were heard from the shed, long drawn out screams that ended abruptly when we saw Master Cappy enter.

The day wore on while j.d. and this slave went about our preset tasks, priming the house for weekend occupation. We slaves were in the kitchen prepping vegetables while we waited our house chef to be returned to us, slave mike. Our backs were to the shed as we worked, hoping and praying that neither of us would be required to cook for guests. We heard the back door spring open, and then something was tossed in and splattered against a cabinet. We slaves turned to see what the noise was. There on the floor was a very pale and shaking slave mike. Mike was wearing a mule harness, thick cutting heavy leather that ran over his shoulders, down the slave's torso, two straps around its ribcage and it even had thigh cuffs. Our look in its direction caught us in a verbal tongue lashing from Master Hunter.

Master grabbed the closet phone, called the main kitchen and ordered the Master Chef to send up a cook to replace slave mike. We heard a sob from mike. A slave in soiled whites ran into the room; Hunter pointed to the menu hanging on the wall and ordered him to put those slaves to work. This slave was in route to dry storage when it noticed that slave mike's hands were sealed within heavy metal balls.

Hunter was on the phone, summoning a mule trainer who ran the short distance and entered the back door. Slave mike was taken from us that day and mike did not return to us until he had worked off its debt to Master Hunter. When slave mike returned, he'd changed. Its dedication to its Lord and Master was extremely altered as slave mike had learned to fear our Lord.

No matter how hard Cappy or Hunter tried to hide their true natures from us slaves, it would periodically slip out to torment us. For instance, this slave was walking down the hallway with a huge bundle of soiled linens in route to the laundry room when its Sir caught it, flipped this one around and pushed its shoulders to the wall. This one feared it had done something wrong, lowered its head and waited. His hand grabbed this one's chin, quivering under his touch. His face loomed close and he tilted its head upwards as if he was preparing to reprimand it for some failure. Instead Master forced a kiss to its lips, sucking the air from its lungs. The kiss made this slave weak-kneed, it dropped the soiled linens, which broke the magic spell. He laughed at this slave's dismay and continued down the hallway whistling while this slave had to pick up the dirty laundry and try to regain enough composure to could finish its routine.

Another day after slave mike had returned to the kitchen, this slave heard pots and pans hitting the floor. This one thought mike might be needing assistance or was having another asthma attack. Thankfully this slave did not rush into the kitchen but gingerly pushed open the door. Peeking in, it saw slave mike's hands grasping the pot and pan rack overhead while Master Cappy was busy eating his slave's ass. Cappy (so this slave was told by the twins) was a mean ass-eater; god how he loved it. And from what this one witnessed before it departed, slave mike did, too!

Before the deception, slave mike had always been a go-getter; he seemed filled with nervous energy, as did his brother j.d. Neither of them ever really sat down unless ordered, as they were constantly flitting around the house, doing chores or at Cappy's bungalow. What this one learned of them was from observation while they were present in the main house. Hunter kept slave mike in the heavy slave harness as a reminder that mike no longer had preferred treatment. Another slave was given the bookkeeping detail and Master Hunter made certain he was occupying his office when that slave was present.

Everything within the house was not all shits and giggles. We all had our chores, including Masters Hunter and Cappy, to keep this House up and running. We slaves had our routines and by far the lighter duty between our Masters. They had the hard job of keeping everything moving and working in unison. Imagine running a household. Next, add a slave compound that not only broke the beasts but also trained and educated them for duty. Add farm production, crop rotation, logging, opening new fields, slaughtering animals for our freezers, energy production and having to deal with guests. Standard household personnel for the main house were only five to seven slaves and two Masters. Downside - depending on the time of the year -there could be from 45 to 400 slaves in various stages of re-education. We housed 30 full-time Handlers, 6 foremen, three doctors, 5 trained RN's, and security personnel could reach as high as a couple of hundred during auctions. During auctions there would be up to 300 slaves underground awaiting the block and half that many buyers. Place all that around, under or above ground, on at least a 1000-acre farm. Add a small herd of dairy and beef cattle, a few hundred chickens, pigs and real horses. Plus the planting or harvesting schedules. Not to mention all the other bullshit that goes on with daily living and we could understand why our men, our Masters, would come home grumpy and loved being fussed over by their personal slaves.

It was our jobs to make them feel appreciated. We slaves of the main house did our parts to keep the house spit-shined like their boots, meals on the table at appointed times and the home life worry free. Many nights after Hunter and Cappy were fed, we would retire to the living room, there the men would sit and talk about the day's events, make plans and arrangements while one or more slaves were on call should they have need of anything. When we were not on call, our jobs continued; scrubbing dishes, serving coffee, breakfast prep, boot polishing, serving as boot stools, ashtrays, whatever was the need of our Masters. Once the evening's chores were complete, the named slaves, mike and j.d., along with Cappy, would usually withdraw to their own private cabin in the woods and this slave would be left with our Sir. These were the times that this slave loved the most, our quiet time.

Master Hunter had his own routine. This one awoke its Sir at 6 A.M., got him dressed as he wished and down to the breakfast table by 8. By 9, he was in his office or out on the farm directing things. He would catch lunch - if he were so inclined - either above or below ground. This slave, once breakfast was served to the Lord, sucked down its meal and went to work; that is, unless Sir had plans for this creature, which was rare. This one tidied up Master's suite, put away any rope or toys left out and cleaned up the bathroom before reporting to slave mike for more duties. Normally this one, if guests were present, tidied their rooms, changed linens, got those in the washer, set about polishing Master's boots, guests' gear and being on call for guests' needs. It was in charge of dusting all surfaces at least three times a week, running the vacuum cleaner daily, mopping all other floors, sweeping the ceilings of any spiders, cleaning ceiling fans and making certain the fire boxes were full of dry wood at all times during the winter months, plus, it (or mike) would haul out the burned embers and clean all fireplaces during the winter months. When this one had slack time, it was to report to mike where this slave would.

Master and this slave had a few things in common. My Master had a boot fetish and this slave did, too. This slave loved serving my Man's boots; this one loved the satiny taste of his boots, loved working them to a high mirror shine. Sir had a wardrobe the size of a small bathroom dedicated to his love of boots. Opening the twin doors gave this one such a rush of Boot Power that it could not stand upright in the presence of all those boots facing this boot-humper. Hunter owned just about one of every variety of knee-high boots known to exist out there and some he had customized to suit some of his more exotic tastes. Thigh-high Wesco's engineers with five straps, thigh-high lace ups, knee-high loggers, Hiatt's, Vogel's, Dehner's, Matterhorn's, jump boots, Justin Polo, and all of them were Sir's to wear and this slave's to serve lovingly. Ah, how this boot-fuck loved serving his boots.

The first night this slave was bound up nice and tight and locked into the boot closet, this slave thought it had died and gone to heaven. In the underground, this slave had been trained how to care for a Master's boots - yet nothing prepared this boot-fuck how Sir wanted them cared for by this slave. This slave looked forward to a repeat of the time that Sir sat one sunny day on the back porch and taught this slave how to give his boots a proper boot shine. Applying paste wax with its hands would not do for this Sir, it was forced to use its bound balls with its cock locked up high and out of the way. Damn few want that care to detail to sit there the whole afternoon while a slave lovingly works the paste wax deep into the leather of a warm boot being worn by its own Master with its own nuts. Once complete to Sir's likes, Sir tossed it a tight jock strap and bound a soft split apron around its waist. Using only this slave's legs and crotch, was it permitted to buff Sir's boots to a high shine. Afterwards, this one was ordered on its back. Master stood, placed his beautiful boot over this one's cock, positioning his heel until it rested on its nuts. Master brought this slave to climax using the pain in its nuts and the stroking of his boot on its worthless cock until it blew a load.

Sir loved being in his boots and loved having this one locked in boots of his choice. Most slaves within the house during winter months wore boots just because the floors within the cabin were cold and our Masters liked them locked in place. Bondage can come in many forms; boot bondage is one of the sweetest and the hardest to get used to when one must sleep in one's own foot gear. Still, boot bondage did keep us slaves safe from harm when our Sir's chose to place us all in heavy steel leg shackles. All of us got leg shackles after slave mike betrayed our Master's trust, it was their way of saying, *do not fuck with us!*

Gladly this slave ate his ass, drank his piss, snot, farts, ate his ash, boots, cigars and got beaten when Sir thought it needed a head adjustment, fucked as Sir desired and still this slave craved more. This slave loved serving Hunter; nothing was too extreme for this slave to do to honor his orders.

My Dad had been a bastard, he had treated his son brutally and Master Hunter helped this slave overcome some of the fears and traumas dear old dad had placed into this slave. Dad had been a biker, an outlaw one to boot. He had caught this slave giving one of his brothers a blowjob out in the back shed when he realized that he had something better than another old lady. At first, this slave wanted no part of dad's idea. It was one thing to blow a hot biker, it was another thing to be used by dear old dad. He gave me no choice in the matter. This slave was bound to the bed and he raped me when he returned from a night out drinking. He was remorseful for about a day but he kept me at home, chained by one leg.

Hunter helped this slave overcome the trauma of dad. Helped this slave accept and move beyond the hardship and abuse dad heaped on his own son. Hunter found out more than he wanted to know about his slave when, one night bound over his bed, he came home a little drunk, smelling of stale beer, cigars in full leather. This slave was bound spread-eagle, blindfolded, gagged and left for his return by orders as he departed in route to a Shield event. J.d. did the honors with Cappy supervising this one's bondage. Together they made the ropes tight and this slave's extension wider than normal, it suffered with cramps while it awaited its Sir to return and it began to remember things that had been done to it by its dad, horrible things. This slave struggled to be free, nothing gave, it knew when dad returned, what this slave imagined he would do.

This slave heard his Harley roar up the mountain and thought dad's home. Fear and foreknowledge of what dad would do when he came home made me struggle within my ropes. Lying there, this slave heard his boots on the wooden stairs as Sir - or was it dad? - returned home from a night drinking with his buddies. He sat on the edge of the bed, his cold leather glove stroked this slave's back and it began fighting the ropes again. Dad laughed, his hand cupped this slave's butt cheeks, his breath drew close, his cheap cigar blew in this one's direction and he climbed in bed, took position. This one felt dad kneeling between its spread legs, felt dad as he pulled out his cock, pulled open this slave's butt cheeks and spit into the hole. Dad leaned forward driving his cock between this slave's ass cheeks, its butt hole opened as his weight drove it deep into its hole.

Master's larger than dad's body covered this slave's backside as he lay down upon it. He leaned into this slave; his cigar was near to its ear by the heat it felt. Then the whisper came that filled this slave with reawakened fear, "Daddy's home!" Like daddy's, his breath stank of whiskey and cigars, all of it triggering the old memories flooding back.

This slave began screaming through its gag and bucking at the same time. All Sir did was hold on and wait until it settled down then he fucked it slowly, tenderly, as he knew this was not normal behavior. Sir plowed his slave's ass, its eyes uncovered so it could know Sir's presence in the reflection from a nearby mirror. Afterwards, Sir, held his slave captive within his arms. That was the first of many demons Master Hunter had to drive from this poor slave and why this slave believes its Master is more of a God. Master Hunter may own this slave but he shows it genuine care. Something few in the outside world did, ever.

Slave mike had been caught doing forbidden computer time in the later part of February, it returned to the household strangely modified, fearful, and this slave found it had clout with slave mike where it once did not. 9-745 had endured over a year in the mule-training program, whereas slave mike had only to endure the three months it had failed Master. The mule trainers made mike pull and work doubly hard if for no other reason than it had been a trusted house slave who had failed in its duties.

Slave mike returning to the fold was the next best thing this side of Christmas for this slave. I found out early in its return that this slave could bully mike into feeding it more of the table scraps and other foods. In this way, this slave began to dig its own grave, literally. Master Cappy did not believe slave mike nor did its own brother when they were told that this slave, 9-745, was bullying mike for more food. This slave made certain neither Masters were present when it played its stupid slave games. This slave was blessed that Master Hunter would not listen to gossip or slave rumors - with exception to Cappy - when it came to how 9-745 behaved while he was away. Still, this slave was reprimanded more than once for this one's failure to complete its assigned tasks promptly. Cappy called it lazy-good-for-nothing more than once and used his whip to help this slave move faster in its duties around the house.

This slave had been in the main house for about eight to ten months after returning with Master Hunter and Handler Dan from the Elders of Castle Enterprises meeting they called Union. It had been giving j.d. and mike attitude, bullying mike in the kitchen and being a generally lazy snot of a slave when this one was out of earshot of its Masters. Its bullying had gone on for over a month when Master Hunter caught it tapping on mike's shoulder for more food. This one, like a fucking fool, denied its actions! It tried to lie its way out of any wrongdoing, hell this slave tried to pin the blame on poor mike. When that did not work, it tried to run out of the room and into the laundry room. Anywhere to be away for Sir's anger. Still today, this slave has no idea why it tried to run, true, it had seen Master's anger and how he punished slave mike. This one just did not want any more punishment for its own wrongdoings. This one feared Master Hunter and even mike showed signs of distress as Sir vented his anger at 9-745.

This stupid slave had been testing the boy's and everyone's patience just to see how far its leash extended before Master would jerk it back to reality. Master Hunter stepped quietly into the kitchen, he may be a big man but he can move like a cat at times, to tell mike we would be having guests for dinner when he caught this stupid slave with its own hands in the cookie jar. This foolish slave's back was turned to Sir when he entered as he was supposed to be down in the caverns for the balance of the day. When he coughed this slave froze, cookies mid-mouth.

Master crossed the distance rapidly with his huge giant steps, his hands reaching out for me. He was like an avenging angel sweeping down on this slave as it turned to face him, and this one choked on its cookie as it darted under Sir's extended arm. He made a grab as it passed clutching its arm and flipping this one around, back and down to fall onto the lower cabinets. Sir grabbed ahold of this slave's shoulder, dragging it to its feet. This one was scared out of its wits, Master's eyes were filled with hatred and disappointment, it knew if it got caught Sir would flay it - or worse, castrate it - for failure. When this slave fell into the cabinets, something clicked inside of my head and its years living on the streets kicked into high gear. Foolishly, this slave kicked its Owner in the stomach as he reached for it. Sir was stunned by the vicious kick, his face became blood red and his eyes, oh God, his eyes were just evil looking. The kick to his stomach made him step back to catch his wind. This slave scuttled to the opposite side of the kitchen, the farthest point away from my Owner. This slave was shaking in fear of what it had done to its Hunter. Still, deep inside it knew that its Master had never struck in anger; but it had never seen its Master this way before. He seemed cold, perplexed and hurt as he stood clutching his stomach in the middle of the room.

Master turned to where slave mike stood in shock of what he was witness to. Master pointed to mike then to the door and told him to go to the office to make the call. This one shit! It knew that the call would be on the intercom, Code Red-Main House! All free Handlers would beat their way to the main house to see what the problem was, double time!

As mike moved to exit, this slave rose to its feet and began screaming at Hunter, who stood at a distance and blocked any exits for this slave to flee. God, how this slave was angry for his fucking patience with this slave! How this one hated him and dad and how much they were alike! The only sound in the room was this one screaming, cursing him and his ways until there was dead silence as this one ran out of things to say. That's when this one thought he heard boots out in the hallway. Master had turned to see who was coming when this slave grabbed an appliance cord and swung it, hitting my Owner.

In slow motion, this one watched him turn to face me. The appliance cord that this slave had swung ran a whiplash path across his shoulder, up his face with the plug cutting a gash just above his left eye. Blood spewed from the cut on his forehead and began streaming down his face. Master stood there in shocked silence as the blood quickly covered his left eye, cheek and began dripping off his chin to the floor. Master went dead calm in shock. Slave mike had just poked his head into the kitchen from the hallway in time to witness the swing and its damage; he too stopped dead in his tracks.

The instant it saw the cut, this slave was sorry. But it was too late. The blood cascaded down his face and dripped casually to the floor. This one watched the blood flowing with its own eyes. This slave watched in horror as a change came over him, a visible shudder ran over his huge frame. His hand rose to his eye and pulled away, covered in bright red blood. Slowly, he turned to the island cabinet, opened a drawer and pulled out a terry cloth towel. Slave mike had run into the room in hopes of helping Sir with the cut, Master flicked him off like a fly and told him to keep everyone out of the room. Slowly, almost mechanically, Hunter tied the towel in place, held his hand over the cut, and waited until the blood slowed and stopped seeping from the cut on his forehead. His once handsome face held a blood seeping welt up the right side of his face, running over the bridge of his nose and stopping at the gash above his eyebrow.

Slowly, Sir turned his bloodied face in this one's direction. It was horrible! This slave had hurt him badly, had struck out in anger where my Master hadn't. He glared down at this one as it tried to crawl in upon itself. He did not move, just stood them staring at it in shock and disbelief of what it had done. Master was wearing the red mask of death; the only other colors were the brilliant blue eyes glaring at the slave who had struck the blow. For the first time in this slave's miserable life it knew it would die soon and no one would care of its passing. Here, Master was the judge and jury. This slave grew more terrified as Sir stood there in silence, glaring down at it with all the hatred of the world staring out of his once warm and loving eyes.

Like a mouse cornered, this slave began to look for an exit - any exit! Looking out the back window, it saw what it knew would be there, Handlers watching, waiting for permission to enter, all seeming to hold their breath while waiting to see what Sir would do, how he would correct this situation. Handler Dan stood at the door, ready to jump in the foray and drag this screaming foolish slave back into a hell from which it would never return.

Master held his hand upright, basically telling them to stay put. This one tried to scurry towards the laundry room door in hopes of getting past Master before he could react. That simple act began the dance of death as Sir went ballistic. He tripped this one with a well-thrown stepstool, halting any attempts of this slave making it to the doorway. Sir stormed in this one's direction and it scuttled back into its corner. It watched as Sir's boot elevated and stomped down rapidly, transforming a once useful stepping stool into wooden splinters littering the floor; that should have been this slave, it reasoned. When this one ran toward the back door and hopefully into Handler Dan's arms, a well-aimed pot hit this one's shoulder and that exit was cut off. Together we danced a pathway of destruction as we danced from one side of the room to the other, any attempt to leave his domain was cut off for this slave. It rationalized the Handlers would be better than facing the wrath of the Master, and it was right. If Sir could get his hands on this slave, it would be lifeless matter between his hands!

Sir did not vent or curse his anger - he did a systematic destruction of everything that got into his path. The ceiling pot rack was ripped from its moorings, pots, skillets and tools crashed to the floor. A heavy two-inch butcher's block was transformed into splinters, all this one could think of was that it should have been me. A cabinet door was ripped off its hinges in passing. The only exit this one had open to it was closed completely when Sir tipped the refrigerator over onto its side and blocked me off. A heavy oak chair was shattered into more splinters and what was left was picked up and hurled across the room. This slave ducked, what was left was stomped to death by Master's avenging boots. It should have been this slave under those boots, except it was on the opposite side of the room and shaking in fear and terror of what it had done to its Owner.

When someone had the misfortune to stick their head in from the hallway door, a frying pan filled with hot oil and eggs slammed it closed! Another pan was beaten into a lump of worthless metal and tossed aside. All the while the destruction of the kitchen was going on, Hunter never even approached this slave. True, he did heave things at it but they were easy to dodge. He should have grabbed this slave and beaten it to death; instead, he held his distance.

Then this slave watched him as he inhaled deeply and let out a long, drawn-out sigh as he fought to control his anger. The blood on his face mixed with sweat, the towel was solid red with his blood and even the towel no longer stopped the blood flowing down his face to mark his shirt. Finding an intact stool, he righted it, sat heavily and leaned his aching head onto his upright palms. The kitchen looked like a cyclone had struck it. The floor swam with a reddening slime as liquids from the tilted refrigerator mixed with his blood splatters on the floor to create a disgusting river creeping across the floor.

Hesitantly, this slave made motions as if to crawl to his side and beg forgiveness. His head rose up in a flash of pain, his eyes impaled this slave and quietly he whispered, "Don't move one fucking inch, don't say one fucking word. Sit there and shut up! If I get my hands on you right now, I will kill you!"

This slave drew back into a corner, pulled its ankles up to its butt, hung its head over its knees and began slowly rocking back and forth. Silence reigned in this once too noisy room; the only real sound was the drip, drip, drip of his blood striking the surface of the island where he sat in stony silence. This slave began to cry once the realization of what it had done to its Owner, lover, Master settled in to his brain. It started shaking out of fear and the dread of what Master would do to punish this one for this action against the only man who ever truly loved this slave. Stupidly, this slave had done something that his Master would never do while angry - strike out! This slave had brutally hurt the one man that mattered in this world to it and now would pay greatly for this error.

Cappy took that lull to enter the mess of a kitchen. He opened an orange first aid kit and began to clean Hunter's cut. Master seemed oblivious to his presence and when he did notice that Cappy was fussing over him, Sir tired to push him aside. Ignoring Hunter's blustery comments, Cappy directed the twins to lift the refrigerator back upright, allowing Handler Dan and two other Handlers to enter the room. They blocked this one's exit completely and by the looks on their faces - including Handler Dan's - they were totally disgusted by its behavior today.

Cappy spoke quietly to Master, "You need stitches, Hunter."

Master growled a response, "Then fucking stitch me up, goddamnit!"

Cappy told him, "This isn't Nam, you need a doctor, fast! I can halt the bleeding with pressure but you need stitches. Lots of them!"

Master seemed to turn and see Cappy for the first time. "Cappy, patch me up so I can take care of that animal. Then I will get stitches!" Master pointed with his bloody hand in this one's directions and all eyes seemed to see this one for the as something less than human.

This one must have spoken audibly as it was thinking, Oh God, what had it done to its Owner? Hunter looked down at me when this one thought that statement out loud, his voice cold and harsh. "God has nothing to do with you now, slave. This devil will get his due from you in spades!"

Cappy was screaming at Hunter, "Damn it, Hunter, hold still! These bandages will not hold! You need stitches, now! A little lower and that bastard would have taken your eye."

Hunter looked up to see Handler Dan. "Go get some rope and burlap bind that piece of shit real tight. I do not want it to think it can escape. Drag it somewhere it can be kept until I am able to skin it alive. Do not break it, it's mine. All mine!" Hunter rose shakily to his feet and spoke directly to Dan. "Keep it up here, topside. I do not want its kind contaminating the others with its stupidity!" Hunter put out his hand to Dan. "Better yet, hang it in the slaughtering house. Let it hang with the other animals to be butchered. Let it think and know I will be back! Ok Cappy, get me to the doctor. My head feels like it's split in half!" Cappy and slave mike helped Hunter out between them as j.d. ran to find the items Sir had ordered for this slave's containment.

This slave was sorry for what it had done to him. It wanted to beg him for his forgiveness, but he was no longer within this one's range. Instead, this one kept silent, praying that its death would be quick and painless and yet, it knew better. All those who witnessed its transgression would help to make it suffer until its Owner could skin off its hide as promised.

Handler Dan took charge when j.d. returned with the rope and burlap. "Wet the burlap, j.d. On the count of three, jump the animal, 1...2..." They jumped on two; many bodies pulled this one down to the floor, flipped it on its stomach and began lacing it into tightly bound ropes. This one did not struggle, it knew it was wrong for what it had done in anger, and it surrendered. They bound its hands at its back, pulled rope around to the front and doubly bound its arms; its legs were cinched at its ankles and again at its thighs. The burlap was pulled over its head, ropes wrapped around its throat held the bag in place. When it opened its mouth to scream in protest, they laid rope in the open cavity and wrapped its head with the rope. It found a new agony, the fear of the unknown.

While it lay there on the floor, the Handlers helped right the area. Dan began issuing instructions. "Take it as Sir ordered to the slaughtering pen, boys! Make the trip eventful so it will have something to worry about when we come for it again. Post a guard, this one does not escape!"

Two pairs of hands grabbed this slave's legs, rolled it onto its stomach and drug it across the wooden floor. For the first time in its life it was thankful for all the long hours it has spent on its knees waxing that floor, the wax allowed it a slow but gentle passage. The waxed floor was too short lived. They pulled it across the threshold and onto uneven rough planking that made up the back porch. At first, it was jerked along the planking by its feet until it remembered the steps at the back door. The planking was minor pain compared to this slave's journey down the steps and its halt on the gravel at the step's base.

This slave was rotated until it faced the steps. They drew it slowly forward, it became a ship in the sea, the steps its own private ocean of hellish waves! The boys let gravity do its job as it drew me forward. My chest cut the wave, the fiery Pacific Ocean scraped down this one's chest from its neck to its navel, raw burning blistering scrapes across the rough hewn wood. Thirteen steps from top to ground; its chest felt like raw hamburger sizzling in the heat as it took one step at a time and yet it knew, once it hit bottom, there was the gravel path yet to traverse. The pain in this one's chest kicked a flashback to the time the sheriff had forced it to lay across its red corvette and the fire in the hood baked its chest raw.

The path that it took daily to the chicken coop to gather eggs for mike became threatening and ominous. Again it was rotated, my legs grabbed by over zealous hands that dragged this slave forward over the sun-hot pick-axe sharpened gravel drawn up from the pits of hell. In the past, this slave had to swing that axe in silence, now this one gave voice as each swing of the hammer cut into me. The mountain reclaimed its toll from my flesh as each sharp edge claimed its blood debt. Again it was rotated and pulled forward over the gravel, its voice giving song to its passage. Those that held it within their hands only laughed as they pulled it closer to its new residence, the slaughtering shed. Crawling the Apian way would have been a gentle stroll compared to the rendering of this slave's chest into ground meat. My chest and my legs, shoulders, hands were caught between numb and self awareness, making the snail-paced drag and pause journey a pathway painted heavily red. Deep inside of this slave, this one knew no matter how bad this journey lasted, it was not over until my Lord and Master began it again.

They halted, it missed their conversation. I'd given over to the pain that was washing this body from the rope and dragging to its new location. It began to rise and spin out of control while, at the same time, its legs were drawn up and its ropes drawn tight, cutting into its body. It was floating free of the earth, spinning slowly as they pulled it over a fence. Suspended, the air around it was filled with a putrid noxious odor that burned into its lungs and made it want to vomit. My arms and legs jerked, the pain in them was horrendous! Jerk, stop, swing back and forth; jerk, swing, jerk, swing; blood was rushing to this simple one's head. What were they doing with me? What were they doing to me?

It wondered and realized the same moment the rope was cut. It dropped a short distance; hitting with a plop before the runny putridness began to flow back over. My head went under the muck and my open mouth was filled with the rotting foulness! Stupidly, it swallowed the wet shitty liquid of the pigpen when it opened its mouth to scream, the ooze soaked through the burlap bag and filled what little breathing space was available to this slave. The oozing liquid was sucking my body down, vomit spewed from my mouth, nose and was trapped within the burlap bag around my head. This one had been whimpering until it hit the pig pen, the acid within the animal piss found every cut on this loathsome slave and it gave long constant screams of anguish. It writhed and attempted to lift its enflamed chest from the muck that lay all around it. This slave was silenced by a boot at the back of its neck, forcing its head into the muck!

Dazed and totally at the mercy of uncaring Handlers, this slave was lifted from the muck, thrown over a concrete flush pen, washed off with a hose, and allowed to drain before it completed its journey by the ramp into the butcher's room. Voices of the men who had drug me to the location filtered down to where it lay heaving, "Bet you 9-745 won't forget that trip for the rest of its worthless life. No matter how short it is after what it did today!"

They repositioned its legs, locked them with a new binding to something at its rear. Its arms were elevated, adjusted, bound into location so its chest was lifted from the floor at an arc, head slumping forward onto its chest. Its head was lifted; one removed the rope that bound the burlap bag in place while the other removed the bag. It felt a jerk on its head, the bag refused to relinquish this one's head. A wet vacuum had formed within the bag, drawing the vomit and pig shit into my nostrils even as the bag was being drawn off its head.

A boot toe lifted its head as this one lifted its face to see who had carried out Sir's orders. They took turns washing its face with their private hoses. j.d was there. He dropped to his knees, leaned down to it and helped it see who was speaking to this slave.

"Now, its true colors have been seen. Master Hunter will have no other choice than to take me back to where this one belongs - between his legs and on his cock! When you are being fucked by Pappy, that mean old fuck, think how good it was being beneath Hunter and remember, this slave will be there, serving as I did before you entered our world." j.d. pulled the burlap bag over this one's head and roped it tightly around its neck. The door slammed as he and the Handler's departed and it entered hell of its own creation.

Damn me, damn this slave, it did thousands of times. It waited painfully as its arms and legs went thankfully numb from lack of circulation. It tried wriggling, moving itself and realized that was a mistake after the circulation within its limbs screamed from the awakening pain. Like a fool, this slave played over and over the event in hopes of clearing its head from that ill-fated blow to Master's head and the cut that draped his face in blood. All of it was its own fault. The shed in which this slave lay bound was silent as a tomb; mine, what had Hunter said long time ago? Yes, pain would be its educator. The only sound it heard was its own cracking voice as it labored to breathe, sucking air through the disgusting burlap bag that clung to its face.

This slave cried in shame and fear of what was going to happen to it by its own Owner's hands. Hadn't Sir once said if it had disappointed it, that it would be castrated or worse, sold? Closed within this slave's self torment, its own world of terror it heard nothing but the crackle of the walkie-talkie of the guard watching over this slave, blocking any escape. As if it could fly out of these vicious bonds that held its body in a forced arc.

What if this slave's blow cost Master Hunter an eye, or what it he had to be hospitalized until he recovered, how long would this pitiful slave be here? Did it matter how long? Now, whatever it got from Master Hunter or any of his minions, this slave deserved it all. Why had this slave struck the only man it had ever really loved? Why would this stupid, lazy, no-good slave want Master Hunter to castrate it? If only castration would allow this slave to crawl back into the graces of its owner. If only...

It jumped when someone spok. "Looks like the boys did the job well in getting this sack of shit out of the Master's house. Glad to see they made certain it will not escape!" Who's voice was that, speaking to this slave? The voice spoke again, "You are not going anywhere especially after we drove all this distance to be with you."

Oh, God! No! That voice sounded like Daddy; but he was or should be still in jail. What the fuck was he doing here? Another voice spoke up, this one chilled this one to its core, "You deserve every damn thing Master has planned for you, 9-745, everything! Today, you'll pay dearly for your actions against my only friend. How dare you attack my rescuer? I have prayed for this day, that my Lord would permit me the honor of showing just how devoted I am to him. Hopefully, he will permit me the honor of cutting you down to size. I owe him that much, yes, making you suffer would be great fun. Did it in Nam to that black bullyboy, can do the same to you, yes, to you. How you'll suffer for me, slave! Uncle Sam taught me the trade well, making men suffer. I can make you beg in ways you have not even realized yet." The sick fuck who was talking began laughing to himself. "Yes, you'll suffer for days for me, days and weeks.

Then I will help you heal and do it over again until you cannot live without pain in your worthless life!"

Before this slave had time to truly digest the full extend of those words, this one's chest hit the ground hard. The wind was driven out of its lungs. While it struggled to regain some oxygen, it was flipped with a heavy boot thudding into its ribcage. Someone grabbed the burlap, removed the rope around this slave's neck and pulled it off. There kneeling beside it was Officer Jack, wearing a slave harness, Doc stood peering over his shoulder as the big greasy biker from the sheriff's hellhole stood looking down at this slave.

The big biker ordered slave jack to grab its ankles and drag it out to the blooding tree. Doc danced for joy - or attempted to do so as he looked more like a marionette that was shy a few strings. Screams were no longer muffled as it sang out as jack viciously added his welts and bruises to those already layered into this stupid slave's hide. Slave jack hauled this worthless creature over hard packed ground and stopped under a huge oak tree that all here on base knew as the blooding tree. This is where all the deer and cattle were hung as they drained of blood. The soil here was enriched by many a butchered animal, here the grass grew greener than any other location save a few springs on the farm. Here it was halted, thankful for the thick grass upon which it lay. This one begged slave jack and the men who escorted this slave out of the slaughtering shed and down to the blooding tree for mercy, all were cold and indifferent to this slave. Turning its head, it noticed lawn chairs had been placed under the shade of the tree. It almost looked like the makings of a picnic. Yes, this one noted in its head, a picnic fit for sadists.

The crowd seemed to be fluttering around a central figure, and then the crowd parted there stood my Master. He starred down at his slave, his eyes were cold, distant, and totally without love for the slave he had once held within his arms. He saw this one looking at him and barked an order to those men milling around him. "Doc, grab slave jack and mike, put that thing on the cross and wash that shit off his body!"

Doc almost jumped with glee when he heard his name called and the order given. He seemed to have anticipated this move on Hunter's part and produced a gallon jug of liquid he shook vigorously as he watched and directed the slaves. They lifted, released this one's ropes, and bound it back upright to the St. Andrews Cross.

Doc reappeared, wearing for the occasion his bright red rubber body suit. He poured the contents of his jug into two buckets, passed out heavy rubber gloves to the attending slaves and gave all toilet brushes. Slave mike started the washing process as he used only cold water pumped from the nearby well to wash off the crud that was buried into this slave's skin. He worked quietly and completely as Doc directed washing this slave's chest almost tenderly, making certain to get all the major dirt out the open cuts before tossing a bucket for rinse. Doc danced gleefully forward once slave mike had stepped away. He dipped his brush into the bucket and tossed the cold fluid over this slave's cut, gnashed and battered chest. No sooner than the fluids hit the cuts did this one begin to give voice to a new agony that flamed white hot across its chest. Doc was laughing and scrubbing this slave's chest with that damn stiff bristled brush, making certain each and every cut was scrubbed clean of any dirt. This slave could not stop screaming and its voice raised an octave when slave jack began to assist Doc in his efforts to get the cuts clean. The bastards scrubbed my front, then flipped me and scrubbed my back. Once done, mike rinsed it and left it to drip-dry in the sun. It was a sobbing mess and no one seemed to care, not even my Master.

Master's voice cut the air. "mike, cut off his harness, it will no longer need it where it's going!" Slave mike sawed through the harness that Sir had placed on it the second day home from the boat trip. This meant this slave it was nothing, not even a slave, worse than an untrained animal! So it had become for it to have struck its owner.

The biker approached where this one hung on the cross, slapped its face and told it to shut the fuck up. He grabbed this slave's waist belt, cut the straps and pulled the ever present butt plug from this slave's hole, sniffed it and tossed it to the ground. His knife cut the balance of the chastity harness to shreds making certain that it knew just what he was doing. Then he teased this poor slave with the comment, "Hunter has agreed if there is anything left after he is finished with you today, that I can have your sorry self." His laughter told this slave more than it wanted to know, there would be nothing left of this slave after its own Master finished laying on his own form of punishment. This slave emptied its bladder and the men laughed.

Handler Dan was working with a rope, casting it over the large oak tree limb from which the animals were hung to be gutted and bleed. Once he got the rope in proper location, a chain was hoisted up and over the old tree limb. He worked quietly, watching this slave, shaking his head as if to say, how dare it do this. Still this slave could not stop watching as a metal bar with a central o-ring was attached to the chain and slowly hoisted up. This one knew in a few minutes it would be hanging in that place, helpless to stop its own death by its Master's hands. This slave deserved to die.

Master Hunter sat in the midst of the throng of men. He was sporting a thick bandage around his forehead that covered his left eye. He looked as if he, too, was suffering along with this slave. Good, it thought, he made this one strike him! Let the bastard suffer!

Handler Dan approached this slave followed by slave mike, jack and j.d. Dan showed me a big bottle of water, he opened the lid and put the mouth to this slave's lips and began feeding it the water. The slaves worked as a team, one would release one hand, one held it while the others worked a suspension cuff around its wrists; those got locked behind its back before they released its legs. Together, jack and mike pulled this one forward, caught it in their arms and drug it the short distance towards that metal bar. They released its hands and each was locked into place, spread wide on the damn bar. Slowly, its arms were lifted until it rose up onto its toes and swung midair.

Hunter bellowed to them, "Lower it! It will last longer with solid footing!" That was all he had said in its favor since his last statement in the kitchen. This one knew it was doomed. Still…someone cared enough to place its hands into suspension cuffs, meaning that it just might survive this ordeal after all. That is, if it did not die at Doc's hands when or if it was permitted to heal.

Slave mike ran off on an errand. While they waited, Cappy fussed over Hunter's bandages. The biker was being given a blowjob by j.d. and Officer Carl was seated next to Hunter; jack was under his boots, serving as a boot stool. Returning too quickly for this one, mike dumped an armload of heavy twigs stripped from a weeping willow near Hunter's outstretched boots.

Hunter directed each slave to choose his or her weapon. They went at the pile with gusto, each had a grudge against this slave for some reason that they needed to release. Finding their chosen weapon, they sat back and stripped it of the green, revealing brilliant white under bark. Master rose to his feet, bent down and picked up something coiled at his feet. This he slung over one shoulder before he started walking in my direction.

Step by step, he drew closer to this foolish slave. He was chewing on a lighted cigar as he drew closer. The bandage, which covered where this slave had struck him, seeped blood through the stark white material. The man that stood before me was not my lover; this man could kill me joyfully and be done with the job at hand. He had other plans; plans that would make this one suffer for what it had done to him. There was no joy in his eyes…this slave had taken that away! His eyes had transformed into an icy cold metallic blue, devoid of emotion. This one tried looking away, but found that it could not and continued to watch him stepping closer to it. This one's stomach tightened, its heartbeat increased as this one's fear increased to terror. This one could not even speculate what would happen to it when he did reach it.

This one flashed back for the thousandth time the encounter we had had in the kitchen and the damage this fool slave had done to him. This one had no clue why it had struck him. It pleaded forgiveness with its own eyes; Hunter did not warm in the least. It begged in silent anguish that he give it another chance, no response. As a last resort, it tried a simple smile; his hand flashed up and ripped that smile from its face as he slammed its head with his open palm. His distant stare told this slave all it need know. There wasn't a snowball's chance in hell that it would get out of this one!

What he had draped over his arm before he started walking in this one's direction caught its attention. He let the hemp rope drop to the ground and stepped closer to this slave. We locked stares; nothing melted his, this one looked away. His hand jacked its jaw, forcing it to look back into his eyes. He dared this slave to move again. He took a long draw on this cigar, held it in his mouth before exhaling it into this slave's face. Still locking his eyes to this slave's, he took the cigar out of his mouth, held the cigar between our two faces. This one prayed that he would not grind out that cigar on its face or mark its face in any way. Hunter moved the cigar closer to this one's face and it tried to back away. Moving this one's head to avoid the glowing ember, Hunter latched on to this one's chin and drew it closer. The cigar touched this slave's neck and coasted down it slowly burning it here and there as it descended. The cigar came to rest upon this slave's right tit. He held it there, daring this slave to flinch, to move, to do something; it did as it screamed as he burnt the flesh.

Master whispered, "Equal time." The cigar strolled over to this slave's left tit, it too was burned and this slave screamed again. The fucking onlookers applauded!

While they clapped their hands, this slave, whispered, "Please Sir!"

He withdrew the cigar from that toasted tit. Took a long inhale from the cigar until it glowed bright orange and placed it back on this slave's flesh. Slowly it descended this slave's torso until it found what it sought, the underside of this slave's balls. There he butted it out, grinding into the underside of this helpless slave and stood back to watch it scream. The cigar was tossed aside and ground into the soil with his boot.

Although terrorized, this slave knew that it deserved this punishment - even wanted it. This was the only way that it could purge itself of the guilt for hurting the one man it had ever truly loved. This one took a chance, it whispered to its Master those fated words, "Sir, I love you, Sir!"

He looked up, "I love you too!" Hunter turned and called to Dan, who ran down to his Master and where this slave hung, "Say your farewells to 9-745, Dan, it's the last time you'll see him."

Master stepped back allowing Dan to approach. Handler Dan placed a thick padded posture collar around this slave's neck as the whispered so only the three of us could hear. "Why did you have to ruin things, boy? We were a happy family! "

This slave started crying as he worked a buckle under its chin and slipped the leather between the stays, pulled the leather and made certain a padded flap extended down to cover a small patch of flesh over the spinal cord. "Sir, thank you, Sir," this one sobbed.

His face drew closer, "I don't think he is mad enough to kill you. But you'll have to prove yourself like never before if you survive this punishment session. No Handler's can help you now. You're on your own to improve your fate and to win him back. Do it, David, come home!"

Master told Dan to kneel where it was, without care of those who witnessed what we had tried to hide from the others. Dan sunk to both knees while our Master stepped closer to this sobbing mess of a slave. From his breast pockets he withdrew two heavy cotton eye patches. Those were placed over my eyes and taped into place. As he taped them and wrapped an ace bandage over to maintain their position, he spoke to this slave his parting words. "I never raised a finger to you, any other slave or a boy in anger. I am calm right now. Stupid, stupid slave, your attack on me was unprovoked. True enough, you would have been punished for being caught mooching food from the kitchen but you were not the first to do that. And you won't be the last. That punishment would have been a breeze compared to what you now face! An animal attacked its Master and an animal is going to be corrected in the only fashion it can understand. You'll be beaten like an animal that has gone out of control. If you survive, you'll live among your own kind in the pit until you show signs of change.

"Before, when I flogged this slave," using his finger he jabbed this slave's chest, "it was love making. We both enjoyed the scenes that unfolded. Before any heavy whip work, I'd give it a warm up; today is different. Today is punishment; it does not deserve that kindness! I gave you my love, strength, the warmth of my heart. I fed your mind and body, even gave you routine and discipline. Perhaps I was too good to you, slave?"

"Sir, no, Sir! You have been just what this slave needed," my head dropped. "Sir, I am sorry for what I have done to you. Please forgive me."

Master stepped back as if stunned. "You have reason to fear me now, slave. I am beyond normal anger now; your Master is more of an avenging angel or the angel of death! Before, when you first came to me, a part of you died in the shed, you learned there was no going back to your old self. Today, I will see to it that your wildness is harnessed if not outright destroyed. Right now, slave, you are no good as you are. You are like a worn, cast-off, single leather glove. Useless to yourself in this present condition and useless to your hand until we purge your deep-seated self-hatred. Today you enter rebirth. If you survive this ordeal it is only because of the strength given to you by the Way of the Slave."

He continued to ramble, this slave wanted to shout to him to just shut the fuck up and go on with the whipping; instead, this slave heard out his preaching. "Too many bottoms, wannabe slaves have come to me for help after someone like you had finished with them. It wasn't a mistake or a fluke of the draw that I was at your first title-holder gathering, I was on a hunt. You were the prey that I was seeking. I wanted to see the animal in its wild - and brother, did I see more than I needed to know. You were pathetic! You still are! How dare you think the world owes you anything? How dare you abuse those men that submitted to you in that fashion? Yes, I know how many you damaged beyond repair, some of them are here today! Some I am going to allow the pleasure of watching your punishment. How dare you abuse them like you thought you could handle? Today, we will test that theory, put it in actual practice. Today is retribution day! We shall see if you can get a hard-on after today. A child who cannot play with his toys without breaking them does not deserve toys!"

Master must have backed away. "Rise Dan, give me your shoulder." Foot falls withdrew, then this slave heard him bellow, "Carl, front and center! Your turn with the fuck up!"

Carl approached, whistling. He stood before this slave, grabbed its cock, balls and pulled them away from its body, almost lifting it from the ground. Something was fitted at the base of its cock and balls, then he began wrapping them tightly, drawing them out and away from its body. Dull pain awoke in its nuts and spread down into its cock as the blood was trapped and forced forward down the hardening shaft of its own cock. He cleared his throat, hocked up a big goober and spit, it hit this slave in the face. Then he began to speak, "slave 9-745, you should know by now that only Master Hunter wants your sorry ass. You belong to him like that tractor over there, he can do with it as he wishes, even sell it to the very willing Pappy, who would take you back in a second. They have already begun bidding on what is left of you. If you want to survive this test, fight with every ounce of strength you have to return to your owner, elsewise you are lost and will be sold. Believe me, there are worse things then Pappy or Biker Ben, far worse things!"

Officer Carl, having finished wrapping this slave's cock and balls, withdrew. Leaving this slave to wait for the next part of the event. Someone was kind enough to lower the bar from which it hung until it could drop to the ground and wait.

Hunter mentioned to the world that he was hungry; Cappy sent mike, jack and j.d to the kitchen to fill a hamper with picnic items. Officer Carl and Hunter began talking while they waited for lunch. "Carl, was Pappy excited when he heard that shit head had hit me?"

"Lord God almighty, yes! He is so fucking excited that he went home to change his bed sheets and make arrangements for when the boy was given over to his care. He told me to tell you it doesn't matter how badly busted up that boy is. Just bring him home to Pappy and he will nurse him back to health his own special way!"

"God, can you imagine that? Pappy nursing anything," laughed Hunter. "How are things working out with you and jack, Carl? Problems? Bring him over in a couple of weeks and leave him here, after today, witnessing this punishment, I believe he and a lot of other slaves will realize just how unwise it is to strike out towards any one. Hey Ben," Hunter greeted the big biker. "Yes, it's ok. Cut was deep. Doc had to give me over 30 stitches. Yes, yes, it will be a week or more before I can see out of my eye, thankfully the fuck up missed it or he would be dead and buried."

Feet hitting the sod ran quickly past where this slave sat waiting its punishment. Someone announced, "Sandwiches all around." Hunter was offered first pick from the tray.

Master said to j.d. with a mouthful of food, "Go upstairs into the closet. There on the wall you'll find a huge black snake whip; bring it to me."

j.d. hesitated. "Sir, begging your pardon, Sir. This slave knows it needs this punishment; but, please Sir, don't use that one on it. Please reconsider your choice in whips, Lord!"

This slave heard a dull wet thump and then Hunter bellowing at Cappy. "Punish your slave for talking back to me or I will rip off his nuts where it lays!"

Cappy bellowed, "j.d, here!" It sounded like j.d got slammed in the face again for having spoken out of turn by the sounds of the gasp of air and moan of pain that followed the outburst in this slave's favor.

Another pair of feet ran past this slave, laughing as it passed. A few minutes later, Doc's voice could be heard from the balcony outside Hunter's suite, "I found my baby!" Doc returned laughing and cracking the whip mid air. Each crack of the whip sounded like a loud gunshot. "Damn this whip has a life of its own," cackled the twisted fuck for a doctor, "but then it should. It took a life to make it! Had it made for you, dear Hunter, while we were stationed in Thailand. Remember? Excellent choice. This whip will rip the hide off an elephant!"

"Dan, help me remove this shirt," Hunter was quietly preparing for what this slave knew was coming its way too soon, the breaking of its spirit.

"Sir, your right shoulder is cut too!" Dan was speaking, "Doc, come here, bring your black bag, look at this. You missed one!"

Doc giggled, "Oh, you'll live Hunter. I will check it after you have completed your exercise session today. You should be hurting from all those stitches; but you aren't showing any signs of distress. I would love and hate to be on the end of that single tail once you start. Whew, it is gonna be a blood bath!"

"Dan, take those slaves down to the animal," Hunter ordered. "Pull him back on his feet. I want every inch of his worthless body covered. Your team is his only warm up session; make it good, long and lasting."

This one's arms were pulled upright and it was lifted off the ground. Feet ran to stand around it. Everyone waited for the command, it came and from Dan, "Light the fire. Burn him!"

They struck as one, then became random blows up and down this slave's body; it was a fiery rain from hell that descended as each slave that this slave had hurt in its short life took up a switch to vent their anger at its abuse and deception. Flames crawled across this one's stomach, over its shoulders, front, back…they hit everywhere, and all was engulfed in flames that rose higher, hotter. This slave jumped about, twisting and turning in hopes of avoiding the abuse. Nothing saved it as they followed the struggling, beating a red-tailed path across its worthless hide. This one did not withhold its voice but sang out with the first blow and continued until the command was given for them to halt. Even then it did not stop. It felt like it had run a hundred yard dash through a thicket of nettles, its lungs ached from screams and it hung there panting, trying its damnedest to suck air into its burning lungs.

Sir bellowed, "Lower it to the ground, it will last longer that way!"

Someone stood nearby, its nose got pinched off and when its mouth opened a bottleneck was shoved between its teeth. Hand and bottle helped lift its face towards the sky as the liquid was forced down its raw throat. Was it beer, piss, or beer piss? Did it matter? It was liquid, it helped appease this ones raw burning throat.

They lowered it to its feet, but this one's arms kept dropping lower and it willingly followed them to the ground. Its legs were drawn out behind it; two sets of hands spread and held them in place while two hands spread this one's asscheeks wide. Cappy stepped up to the plate. "Remember, dick-wad, what you said about my collection of crops, canes and quirts? Does it, slave? Let me refresh its foolish mind, it said, 'who would own those tiny thin whips or canes? Only Dykes on Trykes use them, and never on real men.' Well, slave, it is no longer a real man in my book. It's nothing but an animal!"

He must have turned to face the men under the tree when he next spoke. "Today, Gentlemen, I will be demonstrating what I learned as a Master Drill Sergeant in the Marines; how to apply a crop, cane or quirt to an area that no Marine ever wants abused. A place that no doctor will check for abuse should you have to prep a prisoner to go before a judge. Officer Carl, please take notes on this for future application at your next jailhouse party!" Cappy stepped over this slave's grounded body, straddling this slave's back. "Hold it tighter, and jack, Dan, spread its ass cheeks wider. Use duct tape, it will hold better on its flesh to keep the ass cheeks spread. Yeah, that's the way, boys. Spread'em wide!"

The first blow to this slave's pretty rosette jump-started its heart and made it arch off the ground. He used something to lay in welt upon welt from one side of the left inside ass cheek to the right side. Then he began pounding this slave's rosette until this slave knew it had to be chopped, raw, bloody sirloin. From initial contact of his first blow, this slave did its damnedest to kick off the men holding its legs open and crawl away from Cappy's assault. Any time this slave moved, Cappy laid his idea of the law deeper into this worthless slave's bunghole. Screams had to be heard down in the caverns, all of which came from this one tortured soul. When Cappy stopped, this slave continued to scream, when they released its legs, it did its damnedest to draw its legs into a fetal position. Even that was not permitted. The duct tape was removed rapidly and its butt cheeks once again covered its badly blistered hole.

The cleft of its ass was then repeatedly packed with white hot miner's fuse that ignited, drawing its brilliant fiery hot embers deep into this one's core and triggering a massive explosion of pain that radiated outwards. My screams rose a pitch, cracked and halted all together. My mouth was open, but no sound exited.

Again it was lifted. This time into a kneeling position by a chain, clanking link by link. Again someone fed it another bottle of fluids, followed by yet another. They wanted it to endure its punishments; they wanted it well enough for it to take Master Hunter's beating. Rebellion in any form would soon be beaten out of it, no more would it dare to lift its voice, eyes or hand to its Master and Owner. Today it would learn fear from the only man who loved it enough to care. Today, all rebellion died or I died.

"One of you bastards remove its eye patches, I want it to see its Master's anger and lift it to its own feet," Hunter bellowed yet another command to the crowd. Someone ripped the patches from its head. It was turned to watch Master rise to his feet and gloweringly, step by step, cross the short distance to where this slave hung. This one began to moan and tried backing away. There was no escaping what was going to happen next, this slave knew it would soon be just another animal cut and bleeding under this damn tree. Master stood before his slave.

"Shut up, slave!" His open gloved hand shot across this slave's jaw, splitting its lip and almost knocked it out. When this one's eyes cleared, Hunter was lifting back up from having stooped over to pick up the rope. His hand reached out and caressed my chest almost tenderly, moving gradually downwards until he found what he sought, the base of this slave's rib cage. There the rope was looped. He wound it around and around in a slow spiral down its torso, covering the kidneys and lower back from any ill-fated blows. A knot was tied at the back and then the rope was pulled between its raw ass cheeks, around its cock and balls before being pulled back through the ass cheeks where it was cinched tightly in place.

It was obvious what Hunter had in mind for this slave. He was going to whip the living shit out of it! Even though he was protecting its kidneys and lower back, this slave knew that if it struggled excessively during the whipping there would be no skin left when the rope was removed; on either, nuts or back!

Master turned to the slaves. "mike, jack, and j.d front and center. Mike, bring me that flogger, the thudder, that's the one. Good boy. Take your positions. I had better warm up this arm before I do any serious work."

Even this slave knew what the slaves were doing without turning its head. They were forming a circle; each boy's hands were placed on the other's lower back. This way everyone braced the other one. A shudder ran down this slave's spine as the whip cut the air and landed solidly across one of the slave's backs, a slave who moaned in pleasure. Another blow sailed past its ear; another moan escaped the second slave's lips. God, how this slave wished that it was he who was receiving this loving warm-up session. He swung a few more blows to each slave's back, then he stopped abruptly. "Back to the men folk, slaves. Thanks!"

Master stood looking down on his pitiful slave. "Open your cock sucking mouth, slave!" He inserted a bite guard. "It will not stop the screams but will stop it from biting off its own tongue!" He backed away, "Doc, bring me that damned whip! The lesson begins!"

Chapter 3

None are more hopelessly enslaved than those who falsely believe they are free.
Goethe

Oh God, please no! this one thought to itself as it watched Doc almost glee-fully skipping down the hill and place his big single tail into Hunter's outstretched hands. "Shall I bind his legs so it can't run, my Lord?"

"Yes, but be quick about it," replied Hunter. Hunter took a few practice swings, popping the cracker against tree limbs, cutting them from the tree as clean as if he was using a machete. Dear God, please help this lowly slave! Even as it watched in horror it knew, no one - not even the devil himself - would stop what Hunter was about to do. It was his right, after all, to correct this slave's errant ways.

That man was still handsome as hell, even in his fury. The whip arched over his head, muscles rolled over his back and cut downward each time he stripped larger pieces of wood off the tree. This slave would be lucky to survive this whipping, would be lucky if it had any flesh left on its bones. Hunter stopped, walked behind me, and took some practice swings to get his position so that just the cracker would connect with this one's skin. How fast would that bastard of a whip travel and how much dam-age would each blow do to this slave's already tender skin?

A half a dozen times he popped that damn snake, each time this one jumped to the glee of the audience. And then he stopped popping the damn thing! Everything grew silent, quiet, waiting for what was to come next. The black snake trailed out over the ground at this one's feet. It flicked with mock life, moving like a cat's tail, waiting patiently to pounce on its prey. Then the snake began to crawl backwards, this one saw it through the eye in the back of its head as it arced up and backwards, sailing over Master's head, back and then forward. This one could hear the whip screaming through the air - then it connected mid-shoulder, pushing this one shudderingly forward as the whip drew back to its Master. This one screamed like its heart had burst as the pain washed back to front, like a rock thrown into a pool. The second blow cut into its right shoulder blade. It felt blood, real or imagined, oozing down its own back! The third struck the left shoulder. Another deep cut was impressed into this slave's psyche. Hunter paused to allow this slave to suck in air, then he began again. He allowed the snake to coil around my heaving chest, the tail biting deep into its right nipple. Blood drew from the cut, then he pulled and the whip ripped off skin as it broke away from this slave and took to the air! Its screams were being heard into town as Master's black snake worked one cut after another into this slave's hide.

It begged, mindlessly, for him to stop. It screamed, giving voice to the pain he was inflicting. It cried out in shame, hurt and anguish as he forced that snake to take possession of this slave like nothing had before. Its mind quivered like a bird trapped between hands and wilted as the next blow ripped into its tender flesh dragging from this one's lips, "Oh, God!"

Hunter stopped and shouted back at this slave, "God has no place here! Call on someone you know!"

Master set up a pattern, one, two, three blows in rapid fire then a pause for reflection. This slave tried its damnedest to skip, turn, move, dash, run away from that possessed whip as it carved this slave like a rare roast on the dinner table. It lost the count when a vicious cut nailed its padded balls and forced this slave to vomit. Master halted long enough that Doc could flush out its mouth and give him the thumbs up to continue.

Master took his own sweet time working his marks deep into this slave's hide. It was being laced by a red-hot flame, stitching all over its body. No longer did Master just work the back or chest - he worked lower, burning its legs, making it dance, jerk and spasm. Still the black snake would rise and fall, crawling mid-air to this slave and grabbing it, forcing its lungs to empty as it screamed before it wrapped itself tightly around the slave's torso and bit deep.

Sir halted his delivery, someone was speaking to him as this slave hung limp like meat in a slaughtering house awaiting the butcher. Hunter seemed angry, shouting, "Go ahead, just fucking do it!"

Doc approached this rung out dishrag of a slave. The sick bastard was loving how his handmade whip was biting into this slave's flesh. Damn if the bastard didn't make as to lick the cuts; instead, he leaned in towards this slave and began taunting, "How do you like my special whip, slave? If my Lord only knew what it was made from, he would be disgusted. Bury it or burn it if he could. My whip's a cut above the rest," the sick bastard started laughing at his private joke. He released the knot and began unwinding the rope that tore at my waist. He unwound it slowly, whistling at what he found beneath the rope, the raw scraped flesh. "Look how handsomely you bleed slave! Oh, poor little slave, does it hurt? It will hurt worse when I get a hold of it, that I can guarantee, slave!"

He held before this slave's eyes a bloody rope; the groans it had been hearing were its own. The rope was slowly ripped from its moorings, revealing to all that were bearing witness the job Hunter's torments had done to me. The flesh was blood red, angry and painfully animated with a life of its own. The skin beneath the ropes had to have looked like the time this one had to lay its motorcycle down on pavement. Thank God it had worn leather chaps, however that time its arms took the worst of the road rash. Its stomach and back felt like it had been laid down and dragged a mile or two over gravel.

My mind flashed back to another time when it had removed the ropes from around a boy's wrists, they too were just as raw and bloody. Then, I told the boy as I fucked him, that his wrists would be good as new in a day or two. If the circulation didn't the return, I didn't care in the least! What goes around comes around. This slave must endure the pain and suffering it had given to others. Would anyone care what happened to this slave? The question today, would this slave survive this test of wills?

Hunter laughter echoed hollowly within this one's ears. What had made Doc so goddamned twisted? Slave rumors speak of his time in Vietnam, only God-Hunter would know for certain. Hunter stomped into view, cigar to his lips, drinking a beer. He seemed refreshed from his warm up. He studied this hanging slave, guzzled the beer, crushed the can and ordered another brought to him. That damned whip hung like a boa around his neck. Damn, this slave was it swore that the thing moved, coiling itself around its Master like a snake.

A slave ran forward, dropped to its knee and presented its Master the beer. Hunter shooed it away with a kick in its direction. He took the beer, popped on the top, walked towards his woefully hanging slave and poured the contents over this slave's head. He even gave this one a drink. Another beer was produced and was fed to this slave. "Drink slowly boy," Master coached. "That's it, slow swallows; this will help you hold out longer." Nothing more, he wanted this slave's screams to be recorded dutifully by all that witnessed this event. Someone swam into view; it did not register at first what was being pointed at this slave. It was a camera; the bastard was filming this event. Whatever for, why?

Master lifted this slave's chin, held it in his gloved hand and this slave moved its head to rub its head on those gloved fingers. He held me so it was forced to look into his burning eyes, "Time to go back to work. Phase two of its reconstruction."

As Master backed away, this slave's eyes followed his slow withdrawal. His hand reached up and the snake moved to become an extension of his arm and will. He swung it overhead, the light catching it as it dropped to pop loudly, startling this slave to open its mouth in a fearful scream, "No!"

"What did you say, slave?"

"Please Sir, no more!"

"You should have thought of that earlier!" Master bellowed at this slave, "I am going to take that word from your mind, Slave, now and forever more!"

The next blast forced this slave backward with the power of its strike. This one fought back, forcing itself to stand before the next charge. It held until the snake rose into the air, gathering power as it arched out and returned flying straight as an arrow to thud deeply into its right tit. This one screamed a god-awful scream that ended in deep, chest-exploding sobs! Its head fell forward and it fought to remain awake. This one hated the darkness even more now as an adult than when it was a child. It struggled to stand itself erect to keep its legs from dragging it down into hell. It fought and stood its ground.

Hunter laughed, "That's it slave, stand tall and proud!" His arm rose, the snake took to the air, it rose high up before it descended. This one watched in rapt horror as the snake swung mid-air, cutting through the vapors and screaming its need for slave blood. Like an arrow shot from a bow, it came and placed its shaft into this slave's heart. It faltered and this one passed out.

Something putrid rushed into this slave's nostril, forcing it to return to its pain-filled body. Who was crying? Everything was foggy as if this slave was looking through sleep sealed eyes. Doc was at this one's side, rubbing its face with a damp rag, forcing something that smelled like rotten eggs under its nose until its eyes opened. This one sagged, its legs no longer supporting its own weight. Doc fussed, clucking his tongue like a chicken as it worked to revive this one. He'd get it ready for more whipping by its sadistic owner.

"Go ahead you motherfucker. Get me up and ready for more cutting from that son of a bitch! Go ahead, you evil fucking little prick!" What this one hoped it had spoken aloud, in truth it only mumbled incoherently. Like a marionette with a broken string, this one fought to drag its feet under its sagging body. As if it would break if it moved too fast, it pushed itself upright until it stood before its Master as if to say, damn you fucker! Do your worst!

Hunter chuckled, pointing at this one, "Damn, you make me proud, slave!" The whip swept backwards and its bravado fled as the whip came for it.

What was it Pappy use to say to me? "Boy, you are just to damn stupid or dumb to get out of harms way. Why are you so damn stubborn?"

Like a robot, Master would knock its feet out from under it and this fool of a slave would slowly rally, pushing itself back up, standing there taunting and damning Sir. Each blow cut a bloody path across this one's body, but it was no longer feeling the pain. It had stepped beyond that threshold. Nor did it find pleasure in it what it was doing to its owner.

Voices could be dimly heard, someone was shouting, "Cut him down, he's had enough!" Was that Cappy bellowing at our Master? No, but if not Cappy, whose voice was that? The mind recognized the speaker. It was Dan imploring Hunter, "Its on automatic drive, it will keep coming up as long as you stand before it, Sir!"

"Fuck you, Dan! Get out of the way or you'll taste the whip, too!" Hunter shouted. Hunter would continue until he was ready to stop, just for now he was driving his point home. Making this slave well aware that this was no longer just passion play. This was punishment. Complete and total control of this one's being. The whip sailed through the air one more time, struck its body and this one faded from existence at last.

This one had started screaming at the onset of his punishment, somewhere along the journey its voice had given out. When Master stopped, tossing the whip to the ground, it no longer had a voice and was lifeless. It dreamt that it crawled the short distance once it had been released to where its owner stood. It drug itself the short distance using its last reserves, it knew beyond all things it had to get to its Master. There it stopped, put out its lips and kissed his boots. There it died.

It awoke with a start! This one's world was dark an oppressive, its head was filled with cold molasses; slow, dimwitted. Breathing was agony; every inch of its body hurt! Turning its head, it found what it hoped would be there - a tube near to its mouth that was sucked. Its thirst quenched, it returned to the darkness from which it came.

The second time it awoke, men in white were moving it; it woke mewling like a wounded animal. They worked on it, silently cleaning and working ointments into its hide, it was ordered to suck on the tube more. The liquid took it back into the darkness, dulling the pain that every inch of its body felt.

Movement was forbidden by straps on its ankles, wrists held it in check. Men came and departed, all worked on it silently, they moved as if their feet were padded. Making no sounds, they spoke in hushed tones, all working quietly and efficiently. One arm was sealed to a plank, tubing ran liquids into this slave's body, and someone had plans for it after all. A male slave nurse smiled at it while it placed in injection into the tube that entered its arm. Again it slept.

This one dreamt that Master stood at the foot of the bed looking down at it. His shoulder was freshly bandaged; as was his head. j.d. was helping him into a shirt. Hunter turned when the slave doctor entered, "You can have him until I heal. Then he is mine and I have plans for that animal. It will no longer think before it acts after I finish its new training schedule, it will be nothing but a robot built of human flesh and bones."

Time had no more meaning to it as it slept, awoke, crawled from one day to the next. Suffering, always suffering, as men in white worked to help it mend faster. Master had plans for it. He wanted it to continue to suffer; he wanted it to remember its place, lowest on the totem pole, last rung in the ladder.

It awoke to find the room filled with Handlers, two were enough to fill any room. They scowled at it; every moment this slave made was watched and noted in a book. They watched it all day then departed. It had solid food that day and felt better than it had in a long time. The agony had passed.

But the following day it nearly died! The Handlers were back with Hunter, who was pushing the slave doctor to the wall and demanding this one's release. This one was shocked to hear the slave doctor tell this ones owner, no! Hunter was not pleased. He left in a huff, shouting over his shoulder that it better be packed and ready tomorrow.

The following day, it was taken from the hospital. The Handlers took it down into the caverns and placed it in a very small cage, the door closed, locked and they departed. The cage was made of small gauge heavy wire, something like a shipping crate for large animals. There wasn't any room to move once inside, no comfort was permitted this one. It stayed within the cage for what felt like an eternity, by the cramps in my body.

Two Handlers came for me. They drug this slave out of the cage, cuffed its hands and set off in a brisk pace down the corridor, turned right where another Handler opened a wooden door, allowing us to pass beyond. This one was stopped, one Handler ran up the steps, this one began climbing behind when the Handler at its rear pushed a metal rod to its butt and depressed a button. This one could have sworn it had wings when the electricity of that evil baton hit it. It ran up the spiraling steps following the hollow sound of the Handler before it until it was halted. Another oak door was opened; they escorted this one through and into the main house. We were in the recreational room, the dungeon within the main house. All the standard furniture had been pushed back to focus on one piece of equipment. To that this one was lead.

Cuffs removed, they rebound this one's arms in upon themselves, wrists to upper arms. While they were binding it, this one studied the device before it. It looked painful! It was a very rough 4X4 locked between two high sawhorses with its apex aimed towards the ceiling. Once bound, this one was lifted and its legs were forced apart. Thus it was mounted onto what they called the horse. Its ankles were lifted and bound to its upper thighs; one Handler grabbed hold of its nuts, pulling them away from its body then produced a hammer and U shaped nail. Holding this one's balls, the U shaped nail was forced over the flesh between balls and body before it was nailed to the Horse.

Hunter entered the room and they saluted. This one chose to ignore him until he made it very aware of his presence by adding alligator clamps to this one's badly bruised and barely healing nipples. The 'V' of the 4X4 was working its way into my ass crack and rubbing against this one's backbone by the way it felt. The Handler's took position on either side of this slave. Hunter walked over to the television set and slipped in a tape. There this slave was in all its blood and glory as Sir slashed the hide off its worthless body.

Master pointed to the screen; spoke over his shoulder to the men, "What do you think about this, men? Think it will sell on the open market, or is it just too gory? It has got to pay for its room and board somehow. Your input is important to me, gentlemen. Give me an idea if you think the market is ready for this tape."

This one paid them no heed. It had other things to think about - like its ass on fire! The apex of the wooden V was burying itself deep within the crevice of this one's sore ass and driving Sir's message home. It was there to please him, however, whenever! The pain grew excruciating. When this one dared to voice a complaint, it got gagged and slapped by the Handler. How dare it try to stop them from watching their movie of this slave's whipping session! Hunter left the room, but before he left he told the Handlers there were more tapes if they found the time too boring.

This one sat upon its Horse watching in rapt horror at the scene that was unfolding on the television. God, how Hunter must hate this slave, look at how viciously the other slaves beat it, it needed to understand that it had been a spoiled brat and worse to its brothers within the household.

One Handler kept his eye on this slave, who was crying unashamedly. It knew the whipping session was needed to keep this slave in line; it had wronged its owner in the worst way possible by striking out in anger and confusion. They watched the movie; this one watched the sun setting on its life and the world beyond the windows. It was filled with yet more pain and uncertainty with each passing moment.

It tried to adjust itself, hoping to ease the pain that was like a nail being driven between its butt cheeks into its brain, it almost fell from its perch, caught and slowly righted itself. The Handler at this one's side just stood by, watching with this huge shit-eating grin plastered all over his face. Bastard!

The movie ended. One Handler pulled from a stack of tapes one that caught his attention, labeled *Jail House Cock*. It was installed, ran through its credits and opened with this one bound on that fucking metal cot! The reality of what was being shown to this slave made every fiber of its being raging mad! Everything that happened to it while in the jail was a fucking set up by Hunter! Rage raced through my head - *Evil fucking Bastard! I am glad I hurt you!* That thought almost cost this one its nuts. If the Handler hadn't caught this one and righted this slave would have been castrated.

I seethed as they watched the bastards, Officer Carl and jack working me over! God damn him for this! Hunter knew I was there! Probably set the whole thing up just to teach this one a lesson. I hated him!

Still the pain in this ones body was working against it. Every wiggle this one made while on that damn Horse only made the pain slice deeper into this one's mind and body. It felt like it was like sitting on the edge of a knife as it was slowly drawn back and forth between bone and flesh on this slave! This one screamed through its gag, screamed in anger and pain at what was being done to it by someone it thought was beyond this shit!

Hunter entered the room; pointed at this one and ordered, "Remove it from the rail!" He looked at the television, walked across the room and turned it off, "So you know. Good."

One Handler pried the nail off its nuts, together they lifted it and set it on the floor and began removing this one's bindings. This one was crippled yet again from his brutality; this one could do nothing to him, yet.

Doc and Cappy entered from the other door while Dan, Carl and his slave jack entered by the same passage this one had climbed. Hunter was sporting a series of band-aids on his forehead; his neck and shoulder were bruised from my handiwork. If only this one could have done more to him than just that blow. With the new evidence that this one had seen, Hunter deserved more! Lots more!

Hunter stepped away from the cluster of men, stepping in this one's direction. He stopped about three feet away and looked down at it.

It did not cower, it snarled at him.

"Crawl to me, slave. if you want to be forgiven," Hunter ordered.

Where the Handlers had placed me, there I was rooted to the floor.

One of the Handlers at its back kicked its ass lightly, as if to suggest that this one should crawl to its owner and kiss his boots and beg for to be forgiven.

This one studied the crowd, jack was motioning me forward and he got backhanded for his attempts to urge me into motion.

Doc looked at me and smiled. That chilled this one to its core. Something wasn't right when he smiled, someone was going to be hurt.

Hunter snapped his fingers, getting this one's attention. As if to say, here I am, find me by the sound. Fuck, I knew where he was, damn it! Tentatively, this one put out one hand as if to test the floor for hardness or booby trap's, the other one followed. But my backside just would not budge. It was as if it had sent tentacles into the ground and there it would stay. This one looked up to Cappy, down at this one's hands, up at Carl, down to the hardwood floor, up at jack, and began to think. Did it really want forgiveness from Hunter? Shouldn't he be begging me?

This one looked up to Hunter. He had done this to me, stripped away everything to get me to this spot. He had destroyed my life, had me raped and brutalized in his god-forsaken jail, forced me to become a slave. Made me fall in love with a Handler, and then destroyed that. If I could have gotten my legs to work, I would have strangled him on the spot. Instead, I yelled, "No!"

Hunter's head shot around in an instant and he took one step towards this one. "What did you say, slave?"

Tears were streaming down this one's face, when it looked up again and said, in a quieter voice, "No."

A smile crept across his face and damn if that bastard didn't laugh. "Damn boy! I had hoped you would say that."

He turned to Dan, "you own me fifty dollars, Dan! I know him better than you think you do."

My blood froze, turned to ice within my veins and my heart stopped.

He turned to his friends, "I am the Lord and Master, Hand and Fist of Buena Vista, the upcoming Deus of Castle Enterprises. I have searched for a slave that would suit my needs, today, I have found the one." He pointed down at this one. "Today, gentlemen," Hunter said, "I have found the one I have sought. Out of that animal on the floor I will fashion the Glove!"

Everyone in the room seemed to understand his reference to the Glove except this one. They applauded, clapped him on his back and all departed the room, except the Handlers, Hunter and this slave.

"Come here, slave!" He said it quietly.

This one was losing its defiance; now, it was uncertain that it had done the correct thing by refusing to crawl to him. It looked up and repeated its first answer, "No."

It didn't matter that every bone and muscle in its body ached badly. This one just did not want to move an inch to save this one's life. It just no longer seemed to care. Too stubborn for its own good, my Pappy use to say about this one. Stubbornness runs in the family. Stubbornness had always proven to be this one's downfall. Shit, hadn't this one been warned by other friends not to sell prescriptions to those fisters? Did it listen then…or now.

Hunter stood there, patient as always with this one. Stood there shaking his head in wonderment, "Slave you have made me very happy. I am glad your Pappy told me what he did about you." He motioned with one finger to his men. A boot pressed this one into the floor; hands grabbed this one's hands, pulling them sharply back and binding them tight before dropping this slave to the floor.

Hunter's Vibram soles squeaked across the floor to where this one lay, he knelt, grabbed this one's chin and lifted. "When I am finished with your training this time, that ego of yours will be dead. Slave you'll remain, one way or the other. You may hate me now; in the end you'll be devoted to me. You'll never think of lifting your voice or hand to me again. This I guarantee, slave, this I guarantee!" He rose, "Put him back in his cage. I will be along in a few. It is time he learns about the Pit!"

Two strong hands lifted this slave from the floor and it found its voice. "Please, Sir?"

We took a circuitous route to the cage where this one had hoped it could finally get some rest from today's activities. Instead of a quiet trip in its cage, they took it down an all too familiar corridor, turned left, entering a very sterile white room. The room was lined in pure white cabinets; the floors and walls were white tile and in the center of the room stood a huge steel picture frame.

One Handler held this one in place while the other Handler pulled a stool close to the picture frame. Shackles hung from the upper and lower corners of the device. It was helped up, turned and positioned. One Handler locked its wrists in leather lined steel shackles, after which this slave's ankles were also bound. The larger of the two Handlers withdrew a round ball from a cabinet and tossed it to the smaller Handler. The ball gag was forced within this slave's mouth before being buckled in place. This one was not uncomfortable in its position, its arms hung loosely until the smaller of the Handlers found the controls.

The rather small Handler made adjustments to a console, watching this slave as it was slowly drawn taut within the picture frame. Another set of controls drew its legs taut. Once complete, the machine was locked and they withdrew to a corner to wait whoever was coming to work on this slave. Overhead hung a light this one had once seen in an operating room, a hose reel hung on one wall and below this slave was a drain. The room smelled of antiseptic, which foretold that this one would be suffering under someone's hands sooner than it wanted.

The door opposite the one we entered squeaked open. In walked a thing in black rubber. It could have been either sex - no one would have known by the way it was covered literally from head down to its feet in black shiny rubber. Even when it turned to look up at this slave, it showed no visible eyes, just silver mirrored eyes that looked alien and its mouth had to have been filled or gagged by the way it looked. Skintight rubber covered its hands, feet and head. This one walked into the room, looked up at it then went to work, pulling items from the cabinets and laying them on a tray. The tray was brought around to where this one hung.

The door opened again. In stepped a man in red and black rubber suit. It looked up at me and spoke, "Glad you could join us, 9-745."

This one nearly shit, it was that twisted fucker we slaves hated, Doc. Doc chuckled under his breath when he turned to face me. A little man with an angelic face with the soul of the devil himself, sadism personified. Hitler would have loved Doc's attitude. If slave rumors were true, Doc and Hunter had been stationed together in Nam as Uncle Sam's official unofficial interrogators.

He surveyed this slave like a hanging slab of meat, approached while speaking quietly under his breath. "Poor baby. Doc will make you feel all better."

A stream of piss trickled down this slave's leg and a mewling sound could be heard echoing around the chamber.

Doc only laughed, "Glad you got that done before I really started to work." As I continued to whimper, Doc stepped up on the stool. He slammed his open palm into this slave's jaw, snarling, "Shut the fuck up! Soon you can scream all you want. But after I have hurt you. Not before."

Doc turned and pointed to the tray. The boy in the rubber body suit brought it to him. Doc was rambling again while he removed the ball gag in this one's mouth, "Some men like to gag their victims when they work on them," he giggled while rubbing his crotch obscenely, "I don't. I love to hear a slave scream."

He turned to survey the healing cuts from Master Hunter's whip. "Sorry I could not start this process of your healing sooner, but they have barred me from the hospital for cruel and unusual treatment. Still, it's nice you came for your check up. Real nice. When I saw you upstairs, I helped convince Hunter that you needed a check up before he dropped your ass into one of his pits. Can't have you dying from some horrible infection. Just won't seem right!" Doc began washing this slave's body, gently working the suds deep into the cuts and checking some for infection.

"My, my, my, how my whip cut you badly here and here and there. Yes, you need some extra attention to those cuts. Lovely whip, isn't it?" Doc began applying salve to the smaller cuts before ordering a tool from the tray and began digging in one. This one screamed at his sudden attack!

Doc stopped the attack on that cut moved down to work on this one's rope burns, clicking his tongue and whistling in appreciation at what he found. He spoke to me as he worked, "Hunter tried to protect your kidneys and back but he did not realize how much wiggling you would be doing. The rope has burned about two to three layers of skin away. You really shouldn't have struggled so much, this is your fault, you know! 9-745, you know Hunter probably better than any of us. You should know by now that once he is mad or has his mind set, there ain't a damn thing you can do to stop him. It was the same when he was in Nam."

The Doc pointed at a spray bottle, the rubber slave passed it to him. He sprayed this slave's waist liberally until its cuts began to fizz and bubble, then he sprayed more until the fizzing foam turned red. Using another tool off his tray he dug around, opening cuts so the foam could dig in deeper; he so loved his work, the bastard! His gentleness betrayed his real desire to make this slave suffer beyond even his imagination. Doc was well known to those of us slaves who had the misfortune to come under his hands. He found the pleasure of his pain to be wildly erotic and loved sharing it with all that came to him. His hands were so gentle as he worked the salve into this slave's tender skin.

He stepped off the stool, the slave moved it to this one's back and Doc began to work its back. "Can you keep a secret?" Doc whispered to this slave while he worked on cleaning this slave's cut up back and ribs.

This one nodded its head and murmured, "Sir, yes, Sir!"

Doc began, "Did you know that Hunter saved me from myself while we were in Nam? No? To make a long story short, I came to Nam by way of a flagship as most Marines did in those days. Men hit on me left and right to service them, I refused. Anyway, three MP's had me tossed in the Brig on trumped up charges. While in the Brig one night I was raped by these brutes, gang raped, repeatedly all damn night. They thought I had a pretty fuckable face and ass. One in particular admitted that he had talked the other two into helping him get me for snubbing his advances. He was a big muscled fucking loud-mouthed blue-black southern spade! He thought it was cute how I begged and pleaded with him while he plowed my white ass. I swore when I was released that I would get a taste of him later. When Hunter and his men found me, the

Marine and I had been in our little love nest for over a week. I had stripped him," Doc giggled like a schoolgirl telling a story about her first kiss, "of everything. Including his skin. It is amazing how much pain a body can take, isn't it slave?" As if to prove the point he dug into my skin with something until I screamed for his pleasure.

"I even fucked him with his own cock before that spade lost consciousness. Bet you won't believe this, but that damn nigger begged me to fuck him harder with his own cock," Doc sniggered so hard he just about fell off this stool.

Fingers pried open this slave's ass, Doc was clucking at this slave's back. "Look at the way the rope and that damn horse as cut his butt cheeks. Get me the other spray bottle and get the hose." A cool spray began to hit my back and I felt it running between the ass cheeks. It could feel a minor trickle of pain, like a small ember being blown into a high flame until this one could no longer remain silent and it screamed its displeasure. Cold water eased the pain in this slave's ass, rinsing bloody foam down the drain below me. An ointment was rubbed into the abrasions and Doc's fingers probed this slave's ass, as if to work the salve deep into this slave's hole. One moment this one felt his fingers working into its hole, the next it felt nothing.

"Get me a large flanged butt plug, chrome. We must keep this hole stretched and open or it will heal incorrectly."

The thing ran for what Doc needed and returned momentarily with a huge chromed plug that was forced within this slave's butt hole. It held once Doc removed his fingers. The weight was unbelievable and very erotic feeling. Bandages were passed to Doc by his slave and its hole was taped over the plug, locking it firmly in place. Doc circled this slave, checking cuts, abrasions and bruises before he climbed back up on the step stool and began speaking quietly, as if he was confiding a secret to a dear friend.

"I am glad he used my whip on you. Somehow it was a fitting choice for your punishment. Yes, fitting. The one man that beat and raped me should be used to beat another into submission." Again his sick laugh echoed around the room. He leaned in real close as he whispered into this slave's ear, "Hunter and his men searched all over the place once they found our love shack in Nam. They never could find that MP's cock or his skin. Can you guess where it is? Hunter thinks the whip is made of water buffalo, but I know the difference. Now you do too." With his confession completed Doc seemed to change. He got down to the business at hand, me.

He looked down at the rubbered slave, "Pass me that crock of dry acid, get me a bag of saline and bring me a bowl and a spatula." Whistling some show tune while he measured the acid, he added the saline solution and began applying the thick paste to different deep cuts on this slave's broken and torn skin. No sooner than he had scraped the spatula of goo onto the first cut did this slave begin moaning. This one's cuts were on fire. That shit hurt as it worked its way down into the cuts, burning out any possible infection until it hit fresh meat. Mewling changed to low screams as more cuts were doctored with the slimy shit! Doc seemed oblivious to this one's screams until he grabbed his rubbered slave and began humping him, pretending to fuck his ass.

Doc moved to my back and worked more of that shit into my cuts. Low screams became desperate pleas for him to stop. It was ignored as usual. The twisted fuck of a doctor was jumping around, wildly excited by this slave's outburst as if in celebration of this one's pain. Fucking sadistic bastard!

He turned to the slave, "Hose him down." The slave played the water all over this one's body, it felt refreshing in a way to have the cool water stop the burning heat where Doc had applied the solution. Its skin was extremely tender from the whipping and now this added insult. It felt raw, like all its nerves were being slowly torched. When will this nightmare end, it thought? When will it wake up and be beside its owner?

"Turn that damn hose off shit head. Give me those probes, fetch me a box of swabs, and move your lazy good-for-nothing ass or I will make you suffer more than this stupid slave." The slave ran to do his owner's bidding.

Doc leaned the weight of his body on to mine. He held up one probe so this slave could see it. Curved like a sickle with a sharpened edge and point. "Scream out if this hurts, I will enjoy it all the more." Damn him and Hunter too, both are on my shit list for making me continuously suffer their pain.

Doc began touching here and there with the probe. All the while he was doing that, his tongue stuck out of his mouth and rested on his lip while moving back and forth in rapid jabs at each corner. His concentration was extreme as he worked to open and remove minute particles of dirt - real or imagined. This one could not stop itself from giving Doc the pleasure he sought, its voice screaming.

The bastard went to work, scraping and cleaning cuts up and down this body. By the way he kept up a running dialogue you would have thought he was a dentist doing a routine cleaning on my teeth instead of digging around inside cuts on my chest, back, and thighs.

"Poor slave, look what Hunter did, your poor nipples they are blistered. That's where he must have used his cigar, yes! Oh, and under your nuts, oh, my, that's gonna be fun to heal. Blistered from his damn cigar, poor little slave. You deserved every bit of it and more, you cheap whore!" Doc made his point by digging the chisel deep into a cut and ripping it around until this one screamed and broke into begging! "How dare you strike my Savior?"

Doc's voice changed, "I wonder if my Savior would permit me the pleasure of making you really suffer like only I know how to do. You know you deserve it, you really do. One should not strike the hand that feeds and cares for you, even if he bites like Master Hunter does. It's all good; now, isn't it slave?" Doc stepped down from the stool walked to the intercom and depressed the button. "Rinse it with the diluted alcohol bath, slave." He began speaking as this slave's body drew up taut before it let out one massive gut-wrenching scream after another.

Returning to this sobbing slave, Doc climbed back upon his stool, plucked a huge jar of crème from his slave's hands and began rubbing the ointment into this slave's aching body. This cleaning was almost as bad as the whipping had been as Doc had no care for this slave except as a means to inflict pain.

Hunter entered the room through the corridor door, a slave on a leash moved before him. To my surprise, it was officer jack who was now sporting a full leather mule harness, fingerless mitts and a pair of Master's vicious alligator tit clamps. Slave jack wasn't happy. His back showed Master's handiwork, a recent whipping. By the way jack was moving, something was hidden under the folds of his bondage shorts. Jack had looked hot in his officer uniform, but how he looked now was even hotter, every muscle showed down to his toes. Master and jack could have been poured from the same mold by the looks of their physical attributes.

Master was in one of his moods by the way he was not giving any slack to the leashed slave at his feet. Slave jack did not move fast enough until Master leaned over and grabbed a hold of the chain between his nipples, then the slave jumped out of his skin trying to please. Master Hunter nodded to the Handlers, raked the room seeing Doc and this slave held within the steel frame, "You called, Doc?"

Doc stepped down from the stool approaching Hunter, "What are your plans, Sir for 9-745?"

Hunter was watching this slave, eyeing his craftsmanship with that fucking evil whip when he turned to Doc, "How much longer, Doc, before it's healed?"

The Doc looked up at this slave, walked around to its back and returned to stand before Hunter - who just dropped jack to the floor with a vicious kick to his nuts. "Sir, by my reckoning it will take the better part of a month to get it totally healed, Master."

Master Hunter seemed to digest the information, smiled and put his arm over Doc's shoulder, pulling the smaller man towards him. "I will give you one more week to have him ready for me. Do not torture him, I have plans; it is all mine. Bake it, give it super antibiotics, hell do voodoo if it will get him up to speed. Where that animal is going it will need all its wits about it to survive."

Doc started wiggling in closer to Hunter, "Sir let me break him for you. I did it in Nam, hell we both did it. Let me do this to repay you all your help, please? We did it in 'Nam, Hunter, we can do it again, like old times, eh? No one will catch me this time. That animal deserves my special treatment. No one, I swore when I was over there Hunter, that no one would ever hurt you, my Savior, ever again and I mean to keep that oath. Please, Hunter?"

"Calm down, Doc. Just you calm down," Hunter was speaking to Doc in quieting tones as it his voice could soothe the savage beast who was his friend. "Not this time, my friend. That one," Master nodded his head at me, "has to be handled like the Senator's kid, with kid gloves. I want that animal to remember it made its own death bed. I plan to write its story on its sorry good-for-nothing hide! I want it to remember who broke its will and destroyed its ego - and brother, I know just how to destroy it." Hunter hugged Doc to him. "Don't look so glum Doc. I brought you a new toy." Hunter kicked at jack, who moved like a crab on his hands and knees sideways to dodge the boot.

Master handed over jack's leash. "Here Doc, encase this cocky son of a bitch in one of your rubber goon suits. When you bring it to me I want all holes plugged and no way it can be recognized. Consider this a test of your talents, Doc. I want it so no one knows who is inside your suit. Once the suit is in place it will not be removed for at least a month, so plan accordingly Doc. Also, I want it to have one zipper from its belly button to the small of its back, that's the only zipper I care about. Fuck with it Doc, as only you can."

Ex-officer jack was putting up a struggle, screaming and begging Master, saying he did not deserve to be Doc's plaything. Damn if he did not cling to Hunter's legs as if he were a child refusing to go to his grandparents' for the first time. Hunter didn't seem to care. His face got redder the more jack screamed, moaned and begged; until Hunter's hand shot out, closed around jack's throat and choked off any protest midstream. Hunter pulled jack up slowly to his knees before he backhanded him and tossed his ass on the floor below where this one was bound. Hunter slammed his boot into jack's crotch as the slave tried to skid away.

Doc was dancing in excitement of having something to do for his Savior. Hunter opened the door into the corridor, stood there for a moment, turned back and opened his arms wide. Doc ran into them and they closed protectively around him. The two men shared a hug. "Thanks, Doc. You take care of my slaves while I am gone. Have dinner with me, will you Doc? We can catch up on old times. Besides, the house feels empty nowadays and I could use your company."

The door closed behind him and Doc moved to my side. "It is going to be so nice to have you here for a week. We get to repeat this exercise at least one more time before you have to leave for reassignment."

Slave jack was cowering in the corner while Doc studied the tile flooring. His head snapped up, he turned and went to a cabinet. A heavy key chain was pulled from a lab coat; the cabinet door was keyed open before Doc pulled out sterile hypodermic syringes. Two were filled and placed with cotton swabs on a tray. Doc called his slave to him; the thing extended his hands to take the tray.

Doc locked the cabinet and spoke to the largest Handler in the corner. "Grab that runaway slave and drag it here, will you?" It took both Handlers to finally grab the skittish slave who was crying and begging both men to stop. He was caught and dragged over to Doc. Doc had them hold him long enough to give slave jack a shot. The drug - whatever it was - would have its affect by the way Doc watched him. Slave jack crawled to the extent of his leash and melted onto the floor.

He turned to the Handler's, "Gentlemen will you be so kind as to help my slave take these two to the recovery ward? Slave, go get a back board, a gurney and three sets of linens. Two sets are to be taped to the board and one will be used to cover it. Once the shot has knocked it out, give 9-745 a Code 3 immobilization and take it to the burn recovery unit. The other one goes to my workroom, make certain it does not escape."

My hip stung where he placed the shot. My head became light and fuzzy as the drugs hit my system. All the dull throbbing pain lessened and faded, as did this slave.

When it awoke, it found itself bound. Strapped to a heavy wooden board, arms at its side, head locked by tape over its forehead, it was incapable of any movement. Something moved just out of range of this slave's blurry eyesight. A blue rubbered thing slipped up to where this one lay. This thing placed a tube between this slave's lips and it was locked within its mouth with tape. It sucked on the plastic straw and drew into its mouth the familiar fruit drink that it had had long ago in Handler Dan's. The same stuff that took it then from its pain-filled suffering.

Another doctor walked by and checked its vitals; this one wore a lab coat and actually looked like he knew what he was doing. Lab techs entered while he was there, cleaning this slave, reapplying salves, rolled it on to its side and removed the packing between its ass checks. It was moved to a waterbed and rebound on its stomach, its ass taped open, exposed so the air could circulate and heal that area faster.

It slept again and was awoken to find Sadist-a-Doc peering down at me. Doc worked quickly, applying ointments and ordering an IV for forced antibiotics. He was making an all out effort to get this one well before it was taken from him. Another shot was administered and it slept.

When this slave woke face up on the third day, it found its Master standing next to its bed. He did not speak nor touch, just stared down at his handiwork. His face was cold like a wintered concrete wall, cold and impersonal. His eyes were filled with sadness. This one took that time to turn in its captivity to show him the brunt of his craftsmanship, how his whip had cut this slave to pieces. This one wanted him to see it all and his eyes registered and reflected his pain. We both were suffering in our own way.

Thank God this slave's face was gagged, because this one really wanted to hurt him. I wanted him to suffer like he had made me suffer. I wanted to tell him, *look at me you bastard! This is what you did to me; you did this, not I.* However untrue the statement may have been, this one knew in the pit of its stomach it was I who created this retribution upon itself. This stupid slave pushed its Master too far. Dad had tossed me to the streets, I had hoped and prayed that Hunter would too.

Hunter stood there for the longest time. When he moved, he did something that this slave was not expecting. He lowered the bed guards down on one side before he climbed into this slave's bed. He released this slave's legs from their locked down position, slipped beneath one leg, opened his fly and pulled out his cock. Two strong hands closed around two legs. Hunter lifted, pushed its legs towards its head and impaled his cock into his slave's ass. Hunter ravaged this slave's ass, pounding it hard, driving his point home…no matter where it was, how it suffered, it was owned forever by its Master and he would use it as he saw fit. Quickly, he blew his load, withdrew his cock, wiping it with one hand and cleaning his hand by placing its own ass juices over this slave's face and nose. He rose, rebound its legs and departed.

The next day, this one was taken by wheelchair into a shower room. There it was bound and made to wait. Doc entered with two black rubber encapsulated slaves. Head to toe coverage, both slaves had their eyes covered with mirrored shades. The thin one was the same one that had worked with him in this one's recovery. But my eyes were drawn to the other one. Its rubber looked to have been painted over his body, each movement, no matter how pained, expressed strength. It was like looking at an encased lion, all its muscle rippled under the layer of black rubber. Even that slave's cock and balls were encapsulated by the rubber and hung out of the suit as a vulgar display of prowess. That slave had head tubes extending from its nostrils and mouth with inflating bladders that either recycled its air or kept it working to suck air within its rubber cage. If it was jack, there was no way to tell from outside appearances. Doc had even added a corset of rubber that forced that slave to stand erect and a posture collar that kept its head locked forward at all times. To move it had to move its whole body - not just parts.

Doc had his two rubberized slaves gave this slave a shower, cleaning out its hole and all other aspects. They made certain to shave it of all hair and chemically remove any residue before it was pronounced clean, dried, placed on a wheel cot and bound in place.

We moved as a team into the hallway, down a short corridor, and into a private room. The slaves lifted this one off the cot, placed it on a fuck bench, pulling its arms under a wooden dowel before being bound and locking its kneeling legs by straps to the device. Once done, the three of them departed and it waited, knowing Master would be along in a few minutes.

It actually felt good to be waiting for him to arrive. The body had almost healed from all but the most serious cuts. The whipping had been about two weeks ago from this one's reckoning. The door opened and closed, this one heard his boots on the floor and his footfalls as he stepped closer to it. A gloved hand stroked down this slave's back. Forcing goose bumps to crawl this way and that on my skin. His hand strolled down its spine, down to cup its butt cheeks to grab a handful before giving it a pat. Sir stoked this slave's body all over, using his gloved hands. He found a buckle and strap near its head, pushed this one's head down between a 'V' of wood and leather before setting the strap, locking its head downwards, facing his knee high mud caked logger boots.

He played his way down my body, coughed, and then spoke quietly, "I heard his plans for you, 9-745, and had to come see for myself what he had done to my slave and brother. You have looked better that is for certain."

This one could have shit! It was not Master but Handler Dan, "Please Sir, get out of here! Master is on his way, please don't get caught here by him. God only knows what he will do to you! Please, Sir, go!"

Dan started speaking, "There is no place we can hide from Him. Still, I can give you courage for your darkest hour; this is the only way I know how to give it."

His cock entered my ass. He leaned his weight over my back to kiss the nape of my neck as he began slowly fucking me, tenderly driving his cock deep into my soul and heart. The risk he was taking to give me courage, to give us both pleasure was too supreme. If caught, he would be stripped of rank, something this slave knew he wanted; but as Master had said, there is a right place and time for that. This was not the proper time. But this slave melted into him, worked its ass muscles around his cock, milking it as he worked to increase his tempo and our joined pleasure. Our union was a short sweet fuck that made me melt into him. If anything could give me courage, this simple act of making love to a bound slave was hopefully enough. He came, withdrew his cock, walked around to where this one's head was bound towards the ground, unbuckled the strap, lifted my head and kissed me long and deep. We both heard a commotion in the outside corridor. He rose, whispered to me to be brave, and was gone.

This slave was crying when Master entered the room from the corridor, somehow missing Dan in the passage. Hunter looked down at this one's sweaty backside and punched the intercom screaming for Doc. The door opened and Doc ran in to face Master's wrath. "What is it doing sweaty and why does the room smell like someone just had sex in here?"

"Who would dare play with that slave, Master?" Doc asked before he pulled apart my ass cheeks and inserted his finger. "Whoever it was fucked him, too!"

"Get me the surveillance tapes on this room, Doc, and I will speak to you later about this matter. This is a secret between you and I understand me?"

Doc fled the room on his errand for a very pissed Master. By the time Doc returned with the tape, Doc would have found out everything his Master Hunter wanted to know.

Master stomped around fuming, "This smells like something Dan would have done. It was him wasn't it slave?" He would know soon enough, this one rationalized, once he saw the videotape of the security camera. But this one held his tongue and remained silent.

Hunter's boots walked over to a wall, stopped and returned. Slowly his hand glided down my spine following the same trail that my lover Dan had just traced with his glove. Master's hand grabbed butt cheek and patted it lightly like Dan. He seemed to be thinking of something.

The air came to life, it seemed to my ears, as I heard something descending to slam heavily against my bound butt cheek. The strength behind his blow and the impact of the swung paddle pushed this slave and its fuck bench up on its front legs and forward, the bench and I dropped with a dull thud. My scream was loud, sharp and abrupt, as this one did not expect the paddle.

"Slave, you are going to confirm to me one way or another who fucked your ass. Either by your continued silence or by your screams you'll tell me what I want to know." Master spoke in clipped tight words as he yelled down to me.

One of his hands rested on this slave's back, the other lifted the paddle and, like a dart, it quickly descended to hit both buttocks in a white hot flash of fire. The paddle only lighted on this one a moment before it was lifted and slammed back onto my bound wiggling butt. He may have succeeded in forcing this slave to scream but this one remained silent to who had lovingly fucked its ass.

Master kept at his exercise, working this slave's ass into a flaming fire pit of pounded hot flesh. Master was angry at Dan's betrayal and use of this slave without his permission. This one could almost hear his Master's mind churning as he beat his slave's butt black, blue and white-hot! Master was in fine form today. He beat slave ass until his arm gave out, then switched arms and went at it backhanded. He was furious at both his slaves. This one gave him the screams of anguish he so richly worked for, but not the information he had sought to damn Dan.

The paddle was flung hard against the opposite wall. Hunter forced his cock into his slave's burning ass and leaned down, forcing his cock to impale this slave. There he held his position, leaning his weight into me and lifting the back legs of the fuck bench off the floor. Elevated and tilted, its ass was lifted with his cock still imbedded, this way Master worked on dumping yet another load into this slave's butt.

This slave gave him none of the normal bill-o-fare, meaning its ass did not assist its Master by milking him while he slammed his balls and cock into my ass. It was nothing but a thing under his heaving hips. Master realized the change in it, dammit! In a fit of rage he withdrew his cock and slammed out of the room.

My minor victory was short-lived. Doc sent his goon patrol to retrieve me. They washed out its ass and took it back to its bed. The following day, Master returned with two Handlers and four heavy labor mules. This one was bodily lifted from the bed by two mules that carried it into the corridor and forced it into a heavy steel cage. Hunter took this one's head between his hands, pinched off its nose and held its lips shut until it knew it would black out from lack of oxygen, then he released. It opened and fell for the oldest trick in the book, again. When it opened its mouth a tube gag was inserted as a Handler forced a gag plate across its lips and the device was buckled in front to keep it silent in the passageways. Two poles had been attached by chains to the upper portion of the steel cage upon command the four mules lifted as one. This one was now captive to its Master, held in cage, hands bound at its back and gagged as the mule team began the swaying walk towards what ever would be this slave's end.

Hunter drew Doc aside and directed the Handlers to take this one to the pits, as he would be along in a moment. That was the last time this slave saw Doc and this one was never so thankful. Hunter was talking to Doc about something he wanted done to slave jack and asking him to do a quick, quiet check up on Handler Dan. Doc handed him a cassette, saying he had it all on tape. It was walked out of earshot as they talked and this one grew concerned about Dan's fate.

Like an animal in a cage in a Tarzan flick, this slave was walked down huge hand hewn corridors cut through solid limestone by slaves. The Handlers called a halt to the little procession and waited at a junction for Master Hunter to direct them to the proper set of pits. Some pits were more wretched than others. Those nearest the lake were for those like this slave, the incorrigibles who had foolishly overstepped the lines drawn between Master and slave.

My owner approached at a quick pace, "Well, men what the fuck are you waiting for? Take it to the pit."

"Begging your pardon, Lord. Which section of the pits did you want this one taken?" a boyishly handsome redheaded female Handler asked Hunter.

"Right! Follow me. We will be going for a long walk. You were wise to bring extra mules. We go to the private sector." Hunter led off and my little caravan followed.

Finally, this one thought to itself. I will get some much-needed sleep away from the administrations of the fucking evil doctor. Now I will heal myself. It was interesting to watch as we walked the corridors to see the reaction of Hunter's Handlers and slave foremen as we passed them on their way to work details. The slaves seeing this caravan, the Handlers, the mules carrying cargo - all seeing Hunter in his glory made the slaves drop to their knees and place their heads to the floor or suffer a whip strike from a foreman. The Handlers saluted, he knew most of them by name and spoke to them as he passed. He stopped the caravan to watch a slave being whipped by one of the Handlers, then stepped over and assisted the Handler with the whipping. Another Handler was congratulated for her upcoming promotion.

This one grew bored, as it seemed this one was being carried the full length of the cavern system from the hospital at one side of the mountain to the opposite opening. The caravan halted before a familiar door, Hunter entered without knocking and drew Commander Schmidt to the corridor. She looked down at this one in the cage, and then turned to Hunter. "Shall I mark it for dead, Sir?"

"As you wish Katherine. Until it shows improvement, it is as if it's dead to me. It is nothing but an animal," Hunter replied. "These men and mules will be with me for the next hour. Place them outside on private duty on your roster and give me the keys to the mining shack?"

Commander Schmidt looked up with surprise registering on her face. "If you are taking it there, I will mark it as deceased," she handed him a set of keys she had hanging from her belt. "Sir, when you are finished there. Bring those keys back personally. We have a problem we must discuss, a major problem," she seemed distraught by what ever she had to speak with him about.

Hunter handed her the tape. "For your eyes only. This I think is the problem."

I wondered could the problem be Dan. He had been reporting to Hunter weekly after his return to duty and there were many nights that he stayed overnight at the main house, serving our Master in whatever capacity Hunter sought. Hadn't Hunter made it a private celebration when Master received the custom cock ring by inserting the ring in and out of the piercings behind Dan's cockhead? Was it possible that this slave's action had somehow affected his brother slave Dan in such a way that Hunter had two slaves behaving badly?

Commander Schmidt and an extra set of guards escorted the caravan through the huge steel portico and through the gate beyond. As the door closed with a heavy dull thud it felt like this slave was saying its last farewell.

How long had it been since this slave had been carried in through those doors on a wooden pole? Then they called it a runaway slave. Now it departed those same doors feeling more like an animal than before. Would it die over the next few hours, it had no clue.

They marched slowly down the road that this one had run up naked in route to be Master Hunter's slave. I could still see me in my mind's eye as I ran barefooted and naked to the door of the main house, knowing that once I was within Hunter's arms all would be fine. Then I joyously signed the slave contract, never even reading the damn thing and signed my freedom away. Why? Because I foolishly thought Hunter was like all the other tricks and johns in the world. Like all the others I could manipulate to fulfill my desires. They proved how incorrectly this slave thought. How they shattered this one's dreams on the very first night! Hunter knew this one was a gold digger, but knew he could make something useful from the pig's ear and almost accomplished it. But he had failed to destroy one aspect of this slave. Its ego!

The mules walked down the gravel roadway and stepped onto an old path leading into the forest. Two mules carried this one in its cage while the other two moved forward to make its passage easier by holding sapling trees back from the path. The journey drew it deep into the forest and the forest seemed to close in upon it. This one had always been a city dweller; it was used to the constant rushing wind of moving cars in the distance. This one loved the sounds of others being nearby, the sound of doors up above closing in an apartment complex, the feeling of never being alone even when this one was alone. Living in the city to this one was something like how a bee must feel living in its hive, alone but never alone. The lack of sound in the forest was deafening. The only sound was the footfalls of boots and bare feet on twigs and molding leaves on the floor of the forest.

The caravan moved until Hunter called a halt. This one's cage was lowered to the ground while he and a mule forced open a rusty-hinged door. We had stopped before a building made from what looked to be hand-hewn lumber as the bark was still on walls. The shack looked old, nearly rotten by the way it sagged towards the center. There was only one door and a single padlock, this Hunter keyed open. It took the combined effort of Hunter and one mule to get the door to move on its rusty screaming hinges.

Hunter entered the building, returned with a kerosene lantern asking the Handlers if anyone had a match. A lighter was produced and the lantern lighted. We waited while Hunter entered the shed then he called for us to enter. The inside of the room betrayed the outside of the shed. It was Spartan. but clean. On one side of the room were huge cogwheels and gears protruding from the floor. As the Handlers walked across the wooden floor, it sounded hollow, their boots echoed within the room and below. The other side of the room was littered with rotting wooden crates, old rusty cages and barrels of stuff. In the center of the room was a platform that had what looked like a line slicing it down the middle. The mules placed this one's cage on the platform, centered on that damn line. The wooden poles were removed from this one's cage and chains were added. Four chains in all, each holding a hook at one end and a ring at the other, were attached to the corners of my cage. A Handler stood on my cage to reach a chain hanging over the platform that was lowered, but the chains on the cage would not reach. It took all four mules to lift this one's cage high enough so that a Handler could hook the rings of each corner chain. When complete, it swung lightly back and forth, suspended over the platform. Once completed, Hunter inspected their work and dismissed the Handlers and their charges.

This one was kind of puzzled by all the extra activity, but I just didn't give a fuck. Nothing I could have done at that point would have changed anything in Hunter's mind or mine. We had both set our courses and we would follow them to the end; but to what end? My mindset was that I would not back down until Hunter apologized for brutally beating me, for having me raped in his jail cell and for fucking getting all that brutality on tape.

Hunter pulled a rickety chair out of some corner. He walked over to where this one's cage was swinging, reached into the cage and removed this one's gag and arm bindings. He withdrew and sat heavily, pulled out a cigar and began removing the cellophane wrapper. He rolled the cigar between his fingers, listening to the tobacco, sniffed it, cut the end and lighted it from a wooden splinter he held into the lantern. He took a long slow draw on the cigar, rolled the smoke in his mouth, inhaled and slowly exhaled the bluish smoke perfuming the air with the flavor of a rich cigar.

My cage was tight. My legs were forced to remain tight to the iron bar walls. My arms, even released, could not move around to my front. The cage was damnably small, almost too small for this slave. Perhaps that is why he chose it, to force it to remain in a fetal position, who knows better than Hunter and his misplaced symbolisms. What a wacko pair they make. Sir and Cappy, and now Sir and Doc. What was the real story between those men? What gives them the right to make this one a captive?

Hunter sat there enjoying his smoke. He willed my eyes to meet his as he looked down the cigar between his teeth. He did not say a thing. Enough had been said already, but this slave knew beyond any doubt that it had pushed its owner one step too far. It had crossed the line of no return and if it survived this next ordeal it would be a miracle.

God only knows why this slave did not apologize to him. Why we both held our silence as we both stared at each other. Hell, how many owners would have given their slave a chance to be forgiven? Damn few. Why, then, did this one constantly refuse to give him his due and beg for his forgiveness? Was I really as hard headed as Pappy had said? This slave knew that answer all too well. Too many backlashes had proven that it was incapable of thinking for itself, especially when it felt cornered or asked to apologize for some wrongful act.

Hunter was sitting close enough to lean back in his chair and place his boots on this one's cage. His eyes darted down at his boots, imploring me to kiss them and be done with the charade. Instead this one withheld his lips and missed its last chance to be forgiven.

Hunter's response was to clear his throat, coughing up a huge hocker of snot and tobacco juice, and then spit the damn thing at me. The goober hit my torn and bruised chest before it flowed down and dropped to the floor.

The Lord only knows why this slave held its tongue; perhaps it thought that if it said anything it would go worse on it. Who honestly knows? But this slave remained silent, screaming inside its own head, blasting Hunter with every curse word it could create and damning him to every hell it could imagine. The fury that this slave felt had to be like a projectile as darts were flung viciously from my eyes to nail his hide with my rage as this one seethed silently. Not opening its mouth was only from fear of worse retribution.

Having cleared his throat he began speaking to the room. "Everything that has happened to you, 9-745, both here at the base and outside at the jail was because you are the most stubborn asshole alive! You have to be one of the most stubborn ego-centered boys of all time!

"All you had to do was get on the bus and everything would have been as we had planned. None of this would have happened to you. None of it! That's why I had to teach you a lesson and put fear into you. I used our shield mates to drive that point home. After they finished with you, you knew there was no place outside of Buena Vista that wanted your kind. Hell boy, you have no friends, no one that cares for you as much as I once did.

"My pap used to say, 'if you can't catch fish with one type of bait use dynamite. Once they are stunned you can scoop them up with a net.' The sheriff and his goons were my dynamite and nothing that happened to you there was anything that you hadn't jerked off thinking about. Hell, boy, you told me that was one of your fantasies; well it got played out in full." Hunter laughed a cold distant laugh. "You could say those inbred morons were my best teaching tool. They were my visual aides," his chuckle filled the room and me with hatred.

If I could have reached him then he would have been strangled by my own hands. Instead I opened my mouth screaming at him, "You fucking bastard, you used me! Do you know what they did to me, fucker! I was raped repeatedly!!!"

His laughter was dark and sinister when he replied, "Yes, I know all of it. I was behind the curtain filming it. That tape has made me a lot of money and you have a fan club. You are more popular now than when you had sash rash and were a title holder!"

"LIAR!!! You are nothing but a Goddam lying sonofabitch!" I screamed and jumped at him, which only set the cage to rocking back and forth over the platform. I tried to shut out his voice. My heart turned into a lump of slag fresh from the iron furnace, hot and brittle. "I'll find a way to pay you back, Hunter! Some day, some way, you'll pay for this, you bastard." I was furious and tasted blood, mine. He seemmed to want to provoke my hatred, he said things to make me scream at him. He was infuriating me, making me rage at him. All the while he sat back, patiently waiting, smoking his cigar, listening but not listening to the shouting of a slave.

"Good to see you still have anger and hatred. Hold onto that thought, savor it, maybe it will keep you warm where you are going," he whispered to me after this slave had calmed down.

I tried to reason with that sick bastard, "Why did you choose to destroy my world?"

He replied, "Boy, you did the damage to your own world. I did nothing; I was your only disaster relief." He leaned in towards me as if to speak quietly between ourselves. "Did you know I have been pursuing your butt like a dog on a fox hunt ever since I was a judge at your *Drummer* contest? I knew after your talent competition that I wanted to own you. No, I let nature take its own course once you had the title. Well, I did set some things in motion, knowing that sooner or later you would be drawn to me like a moth to a flame," Hunter confessed as he was looking up towards the ceiling. "Hell, boy. I could have kidnapped you if I wanted you so desperately. But I wanted you to come to me by your own free will, you did; only when you knew the outside world had turned cold, brutal and unforgiving."

He coughed and spat on the floor, "I was happy enough waiting for you to come to me; but your dear old dad changed my mind about you and a lot of things." He laughed, crushed the cigar butt out of the floor, rose from the chair and started pacing the room.

I shouted at him, "How did you find that bastard! You both have a lot in common, I hate you both!"

Hunter farted loudly then scratched his ass. "Your dad thinks you liked him fucking that hole of yours because you kept telling him to go out with his brother bikers. He even thinks - like I do - that you love provoking a scene because you love pushing it to the limits, don't you slave? He even said you were just like your mother; cock hungry and biker crazy."

"Don't shake your head at me, slave. Your dad and I had a long talk. We both know you love sex to be hard and rough. Some people cry when they get a busted lip or a few bruises from sex, you thrive on it, that's what you think is love. Yeah, your dad said the same thing." Hunter walked to where this slave hung, unbuttoned the fly on his jeans, hauled out his cock took aim and pissed on this slave. "Drink it, it may be your last, fuck up!" He shook his cock and put it away then began talking again. I hated everything he was saying but could not block out his words it was as if he was writing them on my soul and I was forced to listen.

"Stop It, Stop talking this bullshit, you fucking bastard! You know nothing, nothing!" I screamed at him.

"Hell, slave, your dad was really talkative those few days I visited him. Hell of a man, shame he had to go to the gas chamber for killing those men."

"What? Oh God, I didn't know! I'm glad he's dead! Like you'll be if I can get out of this cage, fucker!" I wanted Hunter's blood on my hands for forcing me to hear this old shit again. Wasn't it enough that I was locked in his cage, at his mercy? No, I had to listen to my life at the hands of my dad replayed for Hunter's twisted pleasure.

"What was it your dad said? That's right, your mom had abandoned you and him, run off with another biker. She had been gone for a few months when he found you on their bed with one of her old nighties, it was the way the fabric was draped over you that got your old man excited and he raped your ass that night. He said you looked just like her, yes he did." Hunter moved over to the machinery, clicked a button and an engine purred to life. Then he returned to torment me some more with my past history.

I was crying for some fucking reason, frustration or shame or a combination of both. "Please, no more," I begged.

"It seems your dad was possessive of his new found toy. He found ways of keeping you home from school, hog-tied in a closet where he stored his leathers and boots or bound to a chair. He said you would beg him to come home and when he was home you would beg him to go out to the bars. What age were you, 17 or 18?"

Sobbing, I said to Hunter, "I could not fight him off. He was much bigger than I was and after all he was my pap. It was the first time he had ever showed interest in me, ever, and I loved his attention."

"You have blotted out what really happened just before he tossed your ass out on the streets, haven't you, slave. Just as I thought."

"Sir, no, no, please, don't..." I begged Hunter to stop the story. I was being flooded by too many old memories, too many feelings, and too much heartache.

"Seems your dad came home late from work one night to find three Harleys parked in the alley behind the old house you and he shared. Entering by the back door he found one of his club brothers eating a sandwich and guzzling a beer. This brother told your dad that you had a mighty fine piece of ass. Dad shot him where he sat eating. Running towards a commotion upstairs, he shot the second man as he walked down the steps zipping up his fly. He stepped into the bedroom and found you with your hands tied to the headboard and his best friend fucking your ass. Your dad's best friend was so focused on riding your sweet ass that he was totally unaware that two people were dead in the house and he was next.

"I do agree with your dad, you do have a very talented ass and I do love the way it milks my cock when its buried in that hole of yours; but it's not something to kill over," Hunter laughed before he continued, "Listening to your dad as he recounted his story, he had no guilt about keeping you tied in the closet or to the chair or bed. He believed he did it to protect you and that it would make you a stronger man today. Like his dad did him. He had no guilt about raping your ass or mouth or about 'teaching you to take it like a man.' But he does have guilt about killing his best friend and hearing you begging him to fuck you harder. I bet you didn't know that your dad got a hard on watching the two of you fuck! That's what toasted his cookies, that he enjoyed watching his club brother use you and that is why he put the gun to his bro's head and shot him."

"Hunter!" I screamed at the top of my lungs. "You fucking bastard, Why? Why did you tell me this, you son of a bitch, why?"

"Because I want every ounce of hatred you've got to be aimed at me, slave! Because you are going to need it where you are going. Let your hatred fuel the fire that keeps you alive. Your dad told me that if I was set on making you my slave, that I should give you no options for escape. That I should keep your ass and cock chained! Make it impossible for you to flee in any direction. And to keep a belt nearby for when you screw up. Boy, you are an easy mark. The Federal Government taught me well. Nothing you can do will stop this pendulum's swing."

Damn him, everything thing that evil bastard had said about my life was true! Everything up to now was his way of forcing me to conform to the slave's path and this cage was just icing on the cake. Every truthful word was like a nail he drove into my coffin. His words hurt me more than his whip. My head rose slowly as I twisted my body, pulling my arms under and around me, using the new pain to fuel my growing bonfire of hatred. I willed the son of a bitch to look at his slave locked within his cage. The hatred that my eyes projected had to have burned holes in his armor because he looked away. I won a momentary confrontation and it gave me false bravado.

He was the animal; I was in the cage safe from him. He was cruel, brutish, and sadistic and I was safe from his touch within my cage. I screamed at him, "I am glad that I struck you. I wish I could have made the cut deeper! Bastard!"

He shook his head as if in a dream. He looked tired, old, battered and I rejoiced at seeing him this way. He deserved that and more. I let him have it with both barrels, screaming and calling him every foulmouthed name in the book. I lunged at him with my hands clawing the air like a wild animal, even as I verbally vomited my hatred at Hunter. I wanted him to remember me after I was gone! I wanted him to hear my anger aimed at him! My words hurt him, only his property knew the buttons to push, so I rode his elevator to the top floor then slammed it back down to the lobby before I finished reaming him a new asshole!

He walked slowly towards a tall lump of nondescript rags and pulled them off, tossing dust into the air before dropped the rags to the floor. Beneath the rags were two long heavy-looking handles extending out of the wooden floor. Putting his hand on one he pulled back on the pressure plate, the other was moved forward and the platform below me gave off a loud grinding sound as metal kissed metal. My screaming outrage hushed abruptly as Hunter looked at me, winked.

He pulled back on both levers and the floor beneath my cage fell away, leaving in its place a black open hole in the floor. Cold dank earthy frigid air swept up and wrapped its chilly fingers around my hatred heated body, attempting to snuff the flames of my hatred. My body shivered from the deep dark coldness of that open tomb. The pits by the lake where the incorrigibles were normally placed were a sunny day on the beach compared to this nightmarish hellhole that Hunter had opened beneath me. From a slave in a cage I had been instantly transformed into a worm on a baited hook, dangling over a black fishing hole awaiting an invisible toothy smile to close around me and draw me down deep below the surface of light into His intended hell! The reality of the moment silenced my insane mutterings. Up to the time the floor fell out from beneath my cage, I thought this had all been a game played out my benefit. Hunter would never submit me to the rigors of the pit - or would he? Sheer absolute blindingly silence filled my void as I hung over that huge black hole. Even the sound of the engine was silenced as the reality struck home. Sound returned, first with the sound of rushing water, blood rushing into my temples and followed by a low pitiful outcry of "Nooooo!"

My hatred beat a hasty retreat, slipping deep inside my body and turning my heart into stone even as my mind wheeled and my mouth spit out false sentiments of love in hopes of stopping my descent past these hell's gate. I dared Hunter to move. Slowly he turned, walking a short distance to a huge wooden support bean and pulled another lever. This one's cage clicked its descent into the open orifice. I felt my rage rising to boiling point and I screamed again.

Link by link, the cage clicked downwards. Slowly the floor rose and this caged animal passed beyond. Click…click…click was the only sound as it dropped downwards. I felt like a cat trapped in a burlap bag that had been tossed into a river.

Hunter turned from the lever and was walking toward the door. My scream of anguish stopped him dead in his tracks. I wanted out, pleaded with him, begged him to forgive me. I even told him I would do anything, anything to please him. He halted mid-step to turn and looked at me, saying "You should have thought of that earlier."

Still the cage descended. I tried using my arms to hold the cage up and out of the darkness into which I was sinking. They held it for a moment then gave out from the weight being too much for me to handle alone. My cage slipped past the halfway point, I was suspended between light and darkness and all I could do was watch his retreating back.

He shouted back at me, "Remember, slave, I am the light. Only through the light shall you rise from the darkness."

My eyes were level with the floor. Hunter stood with his back towards me. a dark shape silhouetted by the brilliant light of sunset. This slave's cage dropped beyond the rim of the floor. It heard the door slam and the lock replaced. Hunter had departed.

A Boner Book

Chapter 4

"Madness need not be all breakdown. It may also be break through.
It is potential liberation and renewal as well as enslavement and existential death."
Robert D. Laing

Link by link, the heavy cogwheel that hung high overhead lowered this cap-tive slave in his heavy steel cage into a velvety black open. The cogwheel overhead dropped one link at a time, making the cage bounce itself down into this sucking dark world below.

Nothing could describe the despair this slave felt when the floor slipped out from beneath his cage and it finally realized that Master was not playing games. This was not a mind fuck, this was really happening and nothing would stop this runaway train until one of us broke from the stress of what would be unfolding below in his pit.

This slave would last longer than most as it was in good physical condition. Now it was a battle between Master and slave to see who was the strongest and whose will could control the other. All the cards were stacked in Hunter's favor. He had the sun, food, water and freedom to use as he saw fit, and he had taken all those away from his misbehaving slave to teach it a lesson. Hunter would win eventually. Still, this slave had its hatred and that could, if I used it correctly, work to destroy that bastard Hunter like he destroyed my world. I *will* fucking win this skirmish! Hunter will be on his knees begging me for forgiveness after I finish ripping his head off!

This slave screamed as the chain slipped through the cogwheel, making the cage drop unchecked until the descent caught on something, jerking this slave up short of hitting the ground. How far had this one's cage fallen before it was jerked up into the air and hung dancing around in a wild arc until that settled down to a wildly swinging pendulum. It felt as it was swinging in a huge circle the room had to be huge since the cage did not bump into anything.

Click by click, the chain dropped. Link by link, inching the cage deeper into the ever widening yawn of a darkening hell. I hated darkness ever since dad used to chain me to drain pipes in the basement before he left for a work or on a run. One night in a huge dark basement made all my fears rise to the surface, which would not be dispelled until dad returned home and drug me up the steps. Hunter's darkness was less comforting; at least Dad's I knew I would come back up basically unchanged. Here in Hunter's this one knew deep within that pit below its descending cage, a major portion of it would die before it was dragged back into the light.

Finally the swinging cage veered, caught at something that sounded like gravel and stopped its descent. The machines sounded a long way up as they coughed and died. My tomb became silent, too silent for my tastes. Not even the sound of pass-ing vehicles on the highway could be heard at this depth of Hunter's Hell. The only sound other than my panting breath was water dripping from somewhere and hitting a small pool with a tiny splash.

This slave grew worried that it would be left in this overly tight cage. I wiggled and turned myself until this slave could find some comfort. Even with hands before its own face the pit was so dark it could not see them. Cramps from the forced position were rippling all over its body, minuscule movements were all that it could force its body to accomplish within its iron cage.

I began sounding out the size of the room by making hooting noises. The sound that returned said this one was in a mid-sized room with hugely tall ceilings. Working with its hands, it could find only pea-sized gravel. There was nothing of any use to help it escape from the cage. The gravel did, however, fill its mouth and give it some moisture. At least it was something to consider as it fucked with its own head about food. Its stomach was growling and it was a damn fool for not drinking Sir's piss.

If I closed my eyes I could pretend that I was asleep, but I wasn't tired. If I opened them, it was the same darkness that lay behind my eyelids. A song wandered into my head and I sung it loudly to keep the rats away. Basements always had rats, especially in New Jersey where this one grew up.

Wait, what was that sound? I screamed until my voice broke, then lay there sobbing and listening to the echoes of my strained voice. The darkness drew closer to me. I could feel it like a tangible thing, like a heavy blanket being pulled over and around my body. "No, no, no," I screamed, wanting this nightmare to end. I prayed that I would awaken and be in bed with Hunter and Dan. No one came to my rescue; no one cared for this slave as it was. This one knew it had been a bad slave. I had been a bad human.

Each scream was sucked into an awaiting vacuum that ate it up and gave this one back nothing. Horribly alone, I ranted, raved, screamed, cursed, cried and even begged for someone to come take me home where I belonged. For the first time in a long time this slave, this man, was alone. Really seriously alone, and it did not like this at all. I grew afraid. My body began to chill - not so much from the cold air of the mountain as much as it was from my fears.

One moment I wanted to tear Hunter's body parts off, the next I could not think enough good things about him. Hadn't he, when he got angry, sent us out of the room so he could get control over his demons? Hadn't he said he would never strike while he was angry? That if he hit while he was angry the blow was kill-force? Because when he was angry, he could not control the demon within.

Death had to be better than this living hell! The common sounds that one takes for granted within a household were strangely absent here. No one lived within this room, save for this slave. This was hell, my personal hell, total darkness and total silence! Trapped in this goddamned cage of Hunter's!

My body tired and it slept, only to wake with a start as something crawled over me. What had it been, a rat or a dream? This one knew nothing of cave systems except how to dig holes in them. Those nights with the chain gang we had no bugs crawling over us. Then again, if we did we would have probably caught them and added them to our diet.

Suddenly a sound...foot falls on gravel. I would have jumped for joy if I could have. Instead I let out a loud yell, "I'm over here." No response was given, only the sound of booted feet making their way across uneven ground, the crunch of gravel under someone's boots. How could they see in this gloom, or did they know the path to this one's cage from being down here? This one had no knowledge to answer the questions that ran through its mind. Its only thought was release, food, and freedom. My laughter filled the cavern and echoed back to me; Hunter had given in too easily, I had won this battle.

I screamed when I saw the green glowing orbs hanging mid-air, twined ghostly apparitions, night viewing goggles that not just one but four people were wearing as they approached my cage. The orbs of glowing light stopped, a tube of red light was shaken into life and tossed like a comet over my cage until it landed, rolled and remained on the floor, illuminating the area. Three other red trails of fire arched over my cage and landed, giving the cavernous rock formations an eerie ghostly presence.

Three moved forward while one stood his distance, barking orders. They moved towards a spot not far from where this one lay in its cage, fiddled with something on the floor, found purchase and lifted the squeaking metal while the other placed a metal pole under the hinged door to keep it open. One climbed in, then out again. They turned, moving in the direction of my cage. The lock was keyed open and it was taken out.

Struggling, screaming and biting did this one no good, three mules grabbed a handhold and bodily carried it to the upraised gate, tossed it into the depths of its new hell and they lowered the gate while I tried to raise myself. Two mules stood on the gate while another found the gate latch, pulled it over the hasp and locked the gate door. The sound of that lock closing was the coldest sound in the world. It spoke of the finality of death.

Three withdrew and the fourth walked forward. Looking up through the gate this one realized it was not Hunter or Dan, but a mule that had been barking orders. It was this particular slave that tossed a paper-wrapped fist-sized lump through the gate. He turned and withdrew; leaving me to explore the confines of my new home while light was still available from the glowing red cylinders that were left on the floor.

The paper wrapped lump held food, a cold lump of sweet tasteless matter that went chokingly down my throat. My exploring hands found a groove chiseled into the above ground stone floor. Following the groove with my fingers down the solid stonewall, I found a cup cut into the surface of the stone where there was water, a blessing. I had to drop to my knees to lick at the moisture collected within the small basin, still it was a welcomed gift that helped wash down the thickening lump of food in my throat. Food within my stomach, I set to exploring my new residence. High above me were stalactites, some dripping mineral fluids that splashed to the floor, some of which ran into the water groove feeding my small catch basin.

The air in the pit had a deep earthy taste, cool yet not overly cold; however, the rock from which my tomb had been carved was cold and seemed to suck the warmth right out of my pores, numbing me and my aching body. At first the cold was welcome - then I realized that I had to constantly keep moving to keep warmth in my body. But there wasn't any place to go.

The tomb was a roughly rectangular shape. The two longer sides were rough-cut and still held the lines of a pneumatic drill cutting down into the stone face. One short end held a catch basin for water and the other had a square cut 'V' in one corner. Feeling with my hands, I found a tilted stone floor about a foot down from the main floor of my tomb and, to one side, an opening that seemed to open into nothing. Laying down on my back, placing my feet up and through the grating overhead I wormed my arm down into the opening to see if there was any way I could use this to my benefit. The opening was no more than six inches at its widest and the tilted stone ran out a short distance from the opening before dropping off. Extending my arm further told me there was rock directly across the gap. My hand touched stone on three sides and it took some twisting that almost got my arm stuck to find out the reason for this depression. Withdrawing my arm I found my hand and arm was covered in a heavy rotten stench of decaying shit. This area was to be my toilet, the tilt of the stone floor allowed my feces to drop and hopefully roll down the cut chute, this way I would not be living in my own feces. Someone had gone to considerable lengths to make certain this pit was a lot healthier than those old pits I had cleaned down near the underground lake. Those poor wretches had no water or a means to get rid of their own shit; they lived in it. Most died in it.

Interestingly enough, I had the pleasure of watching the cage ascend back up to its lofty height with the help of the waning glow tubes. I was transfixed, as if it was some awe inspiring movie on television. It could have been a movie by the way it affected me with its going. I had become cold from the hurt of my body and the mental pain was somewhat detached or unmoved as the cage rose into the air, pulled by four ghostly arms beyond the door. The clanking of the chain halted. Mouth open like a turkey about to drown in its first rainstorm, I watched as the trap door was drawn closed and then I broke my self-imposed silence by screaming, "Hunter!" My word was flung back at me as the walls picked up my pitiful cry and bounced it around the room, then snuffed the outburst.

The red tube lights slowly diminished, giving me less and less illumination to the cavern walls. They glowed like hot embers in a long forgotten campfire as my eyes adjusted to the creeping gloom. I attempted to fight my waxing depression. Alone, horribly alone, I sat there rocking back and forth while trying to comfort myself. Hoping this was all a joke and knowing it wasn't, this was my hell. No sounds from above filtered down, no light from the sun above. What time was it, anyway? What day of the week had it been when I was lowered into Hunter's pit? God, I was so alone! Then I cried deep soul tears, making my heart hurt with the depth of my own anguish.

The fight was on - me against myself, the winner would serve Master Hunter or not. That all depended upon if I survived the entombment for all my crimes against the BV state. Like a spiral out of control my mind wandered through my memory seeking out the good times that we'd had above ground, but they always were overshadowed by my darkening mood. It seemed that each time I brought a picture of something wonderful that was going on with me and Hunter into the light of my mind, a dark shadow would appear to show my faults. It became a dark dance with the devil, one step forward, two back, turn, swirl and one step forward, two back. Eventually, I bored of that action and took up singing any song I could drag out of my memory bank at the top of my lungs.

Up there, I used to make fun of show tune singing, hip-moving faggots. Down here in the dark recesses of my mind, not only could I recall a lot of the words to the show tunes but also my hands and feet worked out patterns to keep me busy and warm. Laughingly, I danced and sang songs from my childhood idols. Cher, Barbara, and even some Kitt songs found their way over my lips and out to a most appreciative silent cavern. Hell, I even made up verses they would have never considered. The singing kept my spirits up and my body warm. I sang the second day away and lapsed into a quiet restful sleep.

I awoke to darkness, no idea what the time was, and no way of telling. When I did reach above the grating, exploring with darkened fingers, I found another parcel of food. I finished the one from the day before and ate only a small portion of the second one, thinking that they could just as easily starve me to death down here and that I had to hold on to something that would get me through the hard times yet to come. My water basin had filled during the night and it gave me welcome drink.

I continued my recasting of show tunes, reviewing movies within my private movie theater and even imagined that I was eating popcorn, only to find out that my recall was a mistake. Like a fool I sucked my water basin dry and panicked when it took the better part of the next day to fill up. The basin held about a cup of fluid before it would begin to run over the edges and after the first time I sucked it dry I found that the basin filled to almost full twice a day - giving me about two cups of water per day. Not the required amount one needs daily, but with luck hopefully enough to keep my body working without a kidney shutdown.

I became very inventive while in the pit and recycled the paper that my slave bill-o-fare was placed on. That became either my ass wipe paper or I soaked small bits of the paper in water until it became pulpy. That was eaten to add something else to my stomach. The fist-sized lump of food was basically tasteless but had a very sweet aftertaste. It seemed to give me false energy, but nothing to cover any distance as my stomach seemed to be almost constantly growling for more food. So I sucked on rocks, recycled my piss when I could get it aimed the right direction and even ate the paper that each parcel of food arrived in.

To keep busy the first few days, I sang songs, replayed movies in my mind, did multiplication tables, sit ups, exercises until even that grew boring and the weight of this darkened hell pulled its heavy cloak tighter around my shoulders. I sank into the gloom of my own night. Lost within the confines of my mind, I watched over and over all the things I enjoyed while I had lived topside and replayed all the wrongs that put me in this damn dark hell. Me stealing food from the main house kitchen, me shirking my duties, me lying about things I had failed to do. All the time I thought I had gotten away with something, only to see within my mind how it was nothing but another stone tossed into the pond creating yet another ripple effect in my life of lies.

I jerked off reviewing times Hunter had made love to me. Jerked off again thinking about how men had held me in high honor as I walked down that runway with my sash over my shoulder. Fingered my asshole thinking of Hunter's cock buried deep inside me and how good it felt the first time when I was bound, helpless and begged him to fuck me harder. Why had I been so bad to get here, why?

I cursed Hunter for all his good intentions and the ways he used me. Cursed out the boys, Cappy and Doc for how they misused me. Found great satisfaction in seeing them each tortured and torn; but then, my mind would show me something wonderful and I would get a hard on. I jerked off just thinking about things. Like a monkey I once saw in a zoo; jerking off made me feel alive! Giving myself pain also made me feel alive. God, how I use to love grinding my nipples using two stones while jerking off or gagging myself with my hand like Hunter loved doing with his cock. I tried fisting my holes, playing with myself, jerking off, eating my own cum, drinking my own piss until one day it no longer held an attraction for me. That day I realized I needed someone else to make it work, that day I cried and begged forgiveness.

My depression made me mostly unable to sleep. When I did, it was a fitful night or no sleep for days as I studied a problem that I was trying to see my way around. Only to find myself up against a wall and Hunter with his ever-patient ways holding me, making me see my errors. Alone, hideously alone.

One day succeeded another followed by yet another until there was an endless line of dark days. At first food came daily, then there were days with no food followed by days with more than one parcel of food. The first time I found more than two parcels of food I was horribly worried that I'd missed one day of food, not eaten anything the day before. Or had I been given more food because they were not going to feed me for the next few days? I tried hording the food and found that it grew hard as a rock if not eaten soon after it arrived. Even softening the hard lumps in the limited water only made more of mess than for anything eatable.

Odd how things stick out in one's mind when it's occupied by abstracts of a world gone beyond grasp. I had jerked off time and time again thinking of how great it felt having a cock rammed into my holes, or how it felt to be touched by a flogger until my cock lost interest. That's when I realized how long I had been locked away in this pit. My hand glided over the top of my head, it was just that simple. That's when I noticed that I had hair! I had entered the pit freshly shaved to the scalp and now I was sporting a growth of about an inch and a half. I tried to figure out how many days had passed for this to have happened a month, two? Oh, God! He plans for me to rot in this pit!

Something came over me and I began picking at my scalp, pulling out the hairs in hope that it would stop the feeling of loneliness. It didn't but it did start blood trickling down my forehead. Then I started rocking back and forth, just rocking and hitting the back of my head against the stone; those little jolts of pain felt good! I continued and began crying, *I am sorry, I'm sorry, I'm sorry!* Then it happened and I screamed. I screamed as a brilliant blue light arched overhead and slammed noisily to the ground. I jumped and buried myself in the darkest corner of my pit, quivering from fear and excitement with my head tucked in the corner. Even with my eyes covered by my cupped hands, the light was blindingly bright. I could see just by its reflection off the rocks around the cavern into the depths of my rock prison.

I became hysterical and screamed, "Off, the light, off, off!" My voice seemed weak and mewling in my own ears. When I quieted I heard what I feared; the sound of footsteps approaching. Like an animal, I crawled around in my pit trying to hide, tossing my spare food packages down into the shit chute in hopes that they would not steal them away.

Pressing my face up into the grate, I tried to see who was coming. I saw nothing, but heard what sounded like an army of booted feet walking in my direction. The noise of their passage, their grunts, groans and boot soles crunching into the little gravel on the solid rock floor was too loud for sound sensitive ears. My ears bled sound. They had become increasingly cognizant of even a cricket's fart across the cavern. It was as if I had been deaf for months only to finally hear a thunderstorm, too loud and drawing closer. I was being assaulted by brutally rich common sound; the same noise no one would normally notice became, to me, deafeningly thunderous!

Arriving at my gated tomb they found a half-crazed thing in the bottom of the pit mewling from the excitement and fear.

"9-745, close your eyes tight, put your hands over them and face the floor or go blind!" said a stern voice at the rim of my tomb.

Without hesitation this slave complied, the sounds had hurt bad enough, the light would be beyond brutal. Cowering on the floor eyes clutched tight, palms pressed hard over the sockets with thumbs pressed hard into my ears praying silently. I felt the grate open through the rocks and into my bones. Two grunting mules worked it open as its hinges squealed. The grate slammed harshly into the rock surface, making me jump with fright from the sound.

Someone jumped down into the pit, grabbed a hold my neck and pulled me upright. My hands were pulled from my ears long enough to hear the command, "Stop fighting slave, we are here to help. Remove your hands, 9-745, but keep your eyes closed. We will cover them with bandages."

Shaking in fear that my eyes would be damaged beyond repair and excitement of being rescued, it took all my limited self-control to hold position on my knees. Eventually, I placed my hands on two strong rubberized legs at my back and drew both warmth and strength. Eyes bandaged, my hands were locked in steel cuffs and he helped me rise slowly to my feet. How long had it been that I had had this pleasure of standing straight and tall? When I entered the pit I had been freshly shaven. Now I had a short beard and about an inch of hair on the top of my head. How long had I been down here, living in my hell?

Strong hands lifted me from out of the pit and almost gently set me down again. Warmth radiated from the people around me, they smelled good. One or more wore leather and rubber; a hint of cologne perfumed the air, as did ripe man sweat smells that had long been taken from me when I entered the pit.

"Damn it stinks like rotten flesh and look at the fresh blood on his forehead."

The same stern voice ordered the others, "Hose out that pit, he smells of an infection. We will be skinned alive if it dies. Two of you lift and carry him to the interrogation room."

"No more, please," I cried and struggled within their arms.

Heavily muscled rubber encased arms slipped under my legs, lifting me and supporting my back in a fireman's carry. Air from the rubberized mules hissed and wheezed out of tubes, either in their nostrils or mouth or both. More swiftly than this slave could have walked the distance, they strode to the place where this one's interrogation would take place. Gravel below me turned into silence as we entered a warm space, there it was lowered to the floor and pushed down onto its knees. Two hands one from each mule held it lightly in place as they too waited for whoever was to come.

A familiar voice hissed at the mules, issuing orders. "Wash off some of that grime, put proper blinders over its eyes. It will go blind if it's not kept in total darkness. And see to its cuts. We can not permit it to get and infection down here."

The mules drug me back a short distance and began washing me with tepid water. It felt like this one was being rewarded instead of just being made presentable for whoever would be doing the interrogation. They soaped it good, then rinsed me as I stood quivering against a rough wall. Instead of letting it drip dry, it was rubbed vigorously with coarse cloth after which my cuts were anointed with ointments. Gently, a hand worked on applying a spongy bandage over its recently cleaned eyes so that no light might filtered in to cause this one any distress or damage. Once complete, it felt as if its head had been wrapped in numerous layers of bandages and upon opening its eyes found no light but a friendly cloak of darkness.

It was glided by the rubberized hands where directed, hands pushed it downwards until it found itself seated. The mules went about securing this one to a low wooden rail, a belt around its waist, its hands bound by rough rope and its legs lifted, stretched out, and bound straight out in front of me.

I jumped when a vise-like hand grabbed my chin then began to apply pressure, forcing my mouth to open and another hand helped pry my jaw open. One held it while someone fed a thick metal tube just down to the edge of my throat. Pills were blown down my gullet followed by fluids and someone massaging my throat to make certain the pills reached my stomach. Once done to someone's whispered commands the tube was withdrawn. Soft music could be heard playing just in front of me. I listened intently trying to figure out what had they just forced down my throat. It didn't matter, nothing mattered right then, I was out of the pit, clean, sitting comfortably in bondage. Someone wanted me! Someone cared about me!

I nearly jumped out of my skin when he spoke!

"Why did you bring me here, slave?" A quiet voice asked in a low whispered tone.

I giggled and got a belt slap across my stomach, "Sir," I said meekly, "this one does not remember asking for anyone, Sir."

"Wrong response, slave." The belt hit ran across my chest, hitting a nipple. He repeated his question. "Why did you bring me here?"

"Sir, this one does not remember asking for anyone, Sir, please believe this one, Sir!"

The voice spoke quietly, issuing an order to someone at my back. "Begin."

My arms were pulled back and lifted, tilting my torso and head forward. Someone held them in place while another wound rope from my wrists up to my elbows, making certain that they drew them tight then halted. Burning pain climbed up my arms and into my shoulders. They would break or dislocate a shoulder if I could not find an answer soon.

"9-745, think! Why did you bring me here, slave?" His voice raised a pitch as he screamed. I could not rationalize why or what I had done to bring him here to me. I honestly did not know the answer he wanted me to give him.

"Why did you bring me here, slave?"

I was terrified and began blubbering like a baby, shaking my head back and forth while screaming, "Sir, I really don't remember asking for anyone. Please Sir, believe me, Sir!" The rope rose up to my armpits. It felt like my shoulder sockets were being ripped from their joints when they stopped. I heard the slaves moving around to either side of me as I began moaning in dismay. I could not rationalize an answer. My mind seemed to no longer work, it was mush inside my head!

"Think, 9-745, think! Why have you brought me here?"

They did not wait for an answer but began wrapping the rope around my ankles, drawing it tight before wrapping it up another level. Over, draw tight, over, tighter yet, over and up until the blood felt as if it was being pushed up my legs. I panicked and screamed. "I am sorry! Sorry!!"

The rope stopped. They let me calm down. Then he spoke again. "Who is sorry?"

Babbling I replied, "I am!"

The rope renewed its winding attack around my legs - tightly from the ankles, skipping the knees then continuing up my thighs. I was lifted from the stool while they covered my crotch and ass with the rope. A knee at my back kept me sitting upright on their damn stool. My legs, just like my arms, throbbed horribly with each pain filled heartbeat. I knew if I failed to find the correct answers soon my brain would succumb to a sea of pain.

Gently a gloved hand glided over my sobbing face, collecting the beads of sweat that were running off my face. "Who are you?"

Gaspingly this one muttered, "Nothing. Nothing!"

The man laughed, patted my cheek, and said "That's right!"

Again I was lifted, the stool kicked out from underneath my butt and I was set to the ground. That allowed me to lay flat on my throbbing arms while my feet remained elevated and bound in position. Someone started crying, begging forgiveness asking the room for help, begging, crying screaming but no one came to help. I was besieged by doubts wondering why he was here. Again I was alone in hell. It took time immeasurable to stop hurting and the numbness to settle over my body. The numbness gave me an ounce of relief and a dull full-body throb with each heartbeat. It was self-awareness like nothing this slave had ever experienced and it quieted as the numbness crept throughout my limbs.

My senses had long been playing tricks with me while in the pit. I smelled bread like it was being freshly baked in the ovens, not the rot and filth of my own putrid existence. Here lying on this floor, bound up like a Christmas goose, I smelled the fresh scent that denoted Hunter's presence, his cigar. Was the scent real or imagined? This slave did not care. It smelled good, wholesome and gave me such good memories that my sobbing halted and I turned my nose towards the scent as if to fill my lungs with it in hopes of pleasing him again.

Like a sigh the next question was given to me. "Why?"

Then silence, long drawn out silence only shattered by my sobs. I could not rationalize what or why he was here. Was it time for me to confess to all my crimes, was that what he wanted? Did he wonder why I had hit Hunter? Why I had stolen food, bullied mike and otherwise blown off my duties? Why I had tried to manipulate Hunter and everyone else important in my life? Or was it why I was a total fuck up?

I replied with a question. "What do you want from me?"

His response was not expected. A cane was laid across the soles of my bound feet, not just once but twice, hard! My screams turned into sobs of anguish. My mind went into tilt even as my whiney voice changed into a long drawn out babbling chant of disbelief that ended in a pitiful scream. Would this nightmare ever really end?

He screamed down at me, "Answer me, you lazy good-for-nothing slave! What did you do on June 27th at 3PM?"

"Sir, I don't know!"

He might as well have been hitting the soles of my feet with a 2x4 as badly as his cane hurt with each repetitive blow. His boots stomped the short distance to where I lay. He stood over me looking down, lifted his boot and pressed down on my rope-bound stomach and arms while screaming down at me. "Think! What are you here for? Think!"

His bullish bellow for me to *think* halted my pained outcry. His outburst jerked me back, forcing me to ignore my fear and the rising terror of my present situation. Instead of thinking, I began rocking back and forth, giving myself comfort like a mother would her baby. When my gears did finally engage and thinking resumed, this one found its head was swinging in the negative.

His response was designed to help me break out of that negative headspace. Each time my head gave a negative signal his cane would strike the bare soles of my feet. It was a game he loved to play, one I would loose. He struck the soles again and again, pausing between blows as if to give me time to find the necessary answers that he was demanding of me.

"Please, stop, Sir!"

He halted, waited. Hunter was ever so patient when he wanted something from someone. "Are you ready to be forgiven, slave?"

I did not hear him or he didn't wait for the answer. Perhaps none was needed; I do know mules were summoned. My arms were locked to my heaving torso and I was returned to my pit. Maybe he called out to the mules before I could answer him. "Finish what you have started, lock his arms to his chest and take him back to his pit! Maybe in a couple of days it will remember why it's here!"

They secured my arms to my chest by wrapping a few straps of rope around my torso, giving me room to breathe only barely before hoisting me like a roll of carpet onto their shoulders. My anguished scream, an outpouring cry voicing pain, echoed off the walls of my hellish home. I screamed as they lifted me out of his terror then screamed in fear of what was to come and the reality of going back to the pit. Bound helplessly in this cocoon of rope, I was unable to get even the slightest relief from this situation. They lowered me to the ground and, with their boots, kicked me over the edge. I dropped the short distance, landed and screamed no more.

When I awoke, I tried my damnedest to will myself back into sleep. Anything to escape the hell my body was suffering. The drop did not kill me. It did, however, awaken all the aches and soreness within my once numb body to a full-blown massive vivid beat. It felt like every heartbeat was reflected off of each rope that encircled my body. My pain filled arms glowed brilliant, like an electric blue diamond with fire while my legs pulsated with the brilliant radiance of an opal. All the ropes ground one point home; damned, damned, doubly damned! Lying there, I could feel my blood fighting to get under each rope, could see the dammed flow washing back upon itself building up a tidal wave of blood trailing back towards my heart. Even my heart seemed to slow and skip beats as I felt my body dying. All of this was due to my own stupidity. Like a flash from an explosion, a thought blossomed in my mind, could it be just that simple? All I need to do is beg him for forgiveness? As quickly as it came it was dispelled scattered like a fart on a breeze and another more pressing detail filled my mind with need. Thirst!

When I hit the floor I had fallen and rolled onto my bound arms, which is probably why I passed out. Using my feet and bent knees I flipped over onto my stomach, the sobbing scream that tore from my lips echoed around the chamber. By the feel of the floor and the smell of shit nearby I knew they had dropped me in the wrong direction, the water basin was opposite where I lay and up the wall by about 2/3's of the way. To get there would be absolute horror! I could bend my knees without too much pain, but still the journey would be paved with my blood.

Lying there, I did my damnedest to draw on any reserves and plan out my course of action. I had to somehow flip my position, change directions if I was to find any liquid to quench my drying lips and thickening tongue. If I could bend my knees and get my feet up on the pit wall, I just might be able to pull my torso around. But that would mean that I would have to be lying back onto my arms, which could quite possibly make me pass out. Perhaps I could flip onto my stomach and use the same process, it would be slower and I just might take off a few layers of skin on my chest but it would lessen the pain in my arms.

Knees bent, exposed chest to the floor of the pit, it took considerable effort to get my feet up to the wall. Using just my toes, I had to rock back and forth to work up enough momentum to turn my body in the opposite direction. It was incredibly slow, painful steps that seemed to suck out life with each motion. The rope around my torso helped initially until a boulder sized piece of gravel found its way under my chest and threatened to slow my progress. I bit my lip and forced myself to move. What agony those few small steps became. Sweat was pouring off my face as I pushed and toed each tiny step until I was forced to bend my torso in upon itself. There I had to fight fainting from the pain. I had to collapse in on my legs, forcing my shoulder joints to pop loudly in protest to the tight position. Struggling to make the turn on the floor of my pit, I nearly passed out again from the pain and was shocked when stones fell from the ledge above.

I was panting like I had run miles and must have gasped in surprise or fear from being caught because a voice spoke down to me. "Are you thirsty, 9-745?"

"Yes," I panted to him and then added with a pain filled voice, "Sir."

"Roll your face upwards and open your mouth, 9-745."

A zipper was pulled down, mentally I could see him standing tall and proud above me pulling his watering hose out of his pants and taking aim. I had no choice in the matter. I was horribly thirsty and this was the best water at hand, recycled water that, if I was in luck, was once beer.

The first splatter of piss hit my bandages and was guided down to fill my mouth. I could not swallow fast enough, not wishing to lose more than a drop of that precious fluid. I drank it quickly and prayed whatever I missed would be easy to lick up from the floor. His fluid was graciously accepted as if it was the best beer in the house, but it petered out and was gone too fast for my needs. He must have sensed my desperate need cause he stood there looking at me. It was as if I could see through those bandages as he stood there. Who was it, could it possibly be Hunter? The echo within the cavern seemed to play with the tones of voices; I found that out when I was first in the pit. Speaking to the void always gave me back an echo of another voice.

Lying there in the pit I realized the worst of my fears had been conquered; death by thirst. My skin burned where his piss touched, but I no longer cared and tried my best to will myself to sleep. My body refused to obey; instead, my cock hardened. What about this situation was so fucking sexual that would make my cock hard? My cock has always been my worst traitor. If he could, he would have sold the meat of its body to Hunter years back and it would have lived happily within some chamber at his beck and call. Like I was now. I waited, damn him, for him to forgive me! Fucking bastard, I missed him and wanted to feel his arms around me again. My panting broke and I cried deep gut wrenching sobs of despair as I realized more than anything in the world, I needed him, Hunter, at any cost.

I could have shit when I heard the bastard that had given me his piss shout out to the room. "Drag him out of the pit. Round two is about to begin!"

Mules clothed in heavy rubber body suits and gas masks (by the sound of their breathing) hopped into the pit where I lay. Rubberized hands rolled me over before picking me up and passing me hand over hand to others gathered around the edge of the pit. Three arms carried me back into the warmth of the interrogation room before lying me down. They waited while air in their hoses cycled into black rubber bags and hissed back into their helmets. I could see them clearly in my mind. Heavily muscled men with shiny liquid bodies cloaked from head to toe in rubber. Black satiny rubber that clings to every muscle - a bondage suit like no other, trapped behind rubber masks that alienate them from the other slaves. How many of these rubber slaves had that twisted doctor made while I have been down here? Who were they and why did they feel so familiar?

The voice began again, this time it was deeper, more bass than baritone and I knew that voice, it was Hunter! My mind reeled with hatred but my body betrayed me. Upon hearing his voice, I began to cry and beg him in little whispered gasps, "Forgive me, forgive me, forgive me."

His all too familiar boot steps drew closer until he stood above me, toweringly looking down from a distance damn few can appreciate. "What did you say, 9-745?"

It was his voice, his presence, his smell, him everything about him and everything that he had done to me over the past years and more lately past few months that made me realize. Without him, I am no thing, nothing, nonexistent, a thing without purpose or pleasure.

I broke like a handsomely built sand castle that succumbs to a wave as it washes over it. I broke and howled in misery, realizing he had done everything out of love and a need to control me. Something we both needed more than life itself. Through deep chest throbbing sobs I cried out to him, "Please Sir, forgive this fool?"

He did not respond to my pleas, but spoke in my direction to the slaves around my bound body. "Remove the rope from that thing."

I passed out from the agony into the whirling darkness of oblivion. When I awoke no longer was I bound by ropes or bandages; however, to my shock I had been returned to the pit and the grate had been sealed back in place. What had I failed to say to Hunter? Why was I back in the pit? No sooner than I thought that statement did it occur to me that as much as I wanted to hate him, I wanted to love him more; instead, I chose to fear him.

Locked within a cavern deep within a mountain. Locked into the depths of my own hell, the lowest thing in the universe from these depths. There were only two options left to me. One was death and the other was life under Master's control. So I came to learn to fear the man I learned to call Master.

I could barely use my arms from the damage that the rope bondage had done to them. But it was still enough for my needs within the pit. Feeding my face, drinking water and watching memories play out in my mind were my only entertainment. Things had changed since Hunter had heard me begging for him to forgive me. In the distance within my cavern there shone a dim light. He had plans, or so I hoped. What he'd said; that he was the Light, only through him could this slave rise from its pit. The darkness sucked at me, draining away all resistance and fight. I wanted to be with him. I needed him to exist. One day I stopped eating my chunks of prepackaged slop. Laid down and gave up. He came to me and I damn near missed him because I thought he was a dream. I'd failed to hear his approaching footsteps or even notice the increased blue light until a shadow moved down the side of the pit and illuminated coldly the bottom where I lay. From my position lying flat on the floor he seemed to be a black giant standing on the grate over me.

He coughed and hocked up a wad of spit that was dribbled from his lip to hit me in the face. That was when I realized he was not a dream, but real. As if in slow motion, I pushed myself up to my knees and timidly extended my hands through the grating in hopes that he would allow me to touch his boots. He was swifter than I. As my hand approached his boot moved and pinned my fingers of one hand under its sole. Slowly he rocked forward allowing his superior body weight and his boots to do the work and drive the lesson home.

No scream escaped my lips as the Vibram sole ground into my tender fingers that were pinned to the metal grate, nor did I damn him for his use of me; instead, I whispered a thank you. His boot rose, releasing my pinned fingers and, with the side of his boot, were pushed off the grating. He waited, watching as my other hand glided up through the grating and touched gingerly the welting of his boot. His boot did not pounce on my hand as the other one had but held its place. Was this his way of luring my hand closer? Picking up courage, drawing strength from him I pushed my hand higher. Affectionately my fingers glided over the oily black surface. I shattered the moment with a lustful moan. His boots turned and he withdrew.

I wanted to cry out to him but I had stuffed the freshly ground fingers into my mouth in hopes of tasting what I so richly craved. When he departed, my mind played tricks on me, forcing me to go to greater lengths to please him if or when he returned. This lesson this slave must not fail or it would die in this pit due to my own stupidity.

The light on the far distant wall drew closer. It was still a great distance from my pit but it was closer. That, for some reason, gave me hope. The simple gift of light to a thing that was locked in a pit of darkness was a reward better than extra food rations. Master Hunter came and departed as he chose, this one stayed with its pit and rotted. Each time he came, a glimmer of hope flared into existence only to be snuffed out as he departed. Once I looked forward to food. Now I sought Master's presence, he was far better for my mind and body than any food.

Master had a way about him when he came to me in that pit. Always commanding, yet tender. He knew that I would do anything for him to get out of that pit, still he kept me there waiting for some invisible sign. He would stand on my grating looming high above allowing me to grind my face and tongue into the soles of his boots. Or beg for his piss, the ashes from his cigar anything that would give him pleasure. Yet he held himself back.

When next he came to see his thing in the pit I was ready for him. He made me very aware of his presence as he walked down the cavern to where I lay in wait. He stood over me as he had done before. Instead of my hands passing beyond the grate I pressed my face and tongue to the under soles of his boots. He stood there saying nothing, just letting me lick, suck and lap at the soles until he became bored. He backed away, I called after him and he halted, turned and ordered me to open my mouth. He unbuttoned his pants, pulled out his hog leg of a cock, took aim and fired.

I was ecstatically happy, laughing in joy of what had just happened. Not only did he allow this thing to suck clean the soles of his boots, I was permitted to drink his piss. My pleasure came from being of service to him. My enjoyment was not important, that lesson I learned well in that pit.

When I realized that I had been jerking off while he was pissing in my mouth I damn near shit! Afterwards, once he had gone, I knew I had to punish myself for this infraction. A thing, I rationalized, does not own its own cock, nor its air, nor its water or food. As punishment to myself I pushed small pebbles into my cock slit, withheld from myself any water from the basin until all the fluids I had carelessly spilt on the floor of my pit were sucked up. When completed to my sense of self-satisfaction I knelt in the corner, bowed my head, took up two rocks and used them to grind my nipples raw and came without touching myself - blowing pebbles and cum all over the floor. That too was licked up and savored as if it had come from my Master. That was the first climax this slave had had since its cock lost any satisfaction.

Nothing gave me a sense of time. Food came at irregular intervals; water dripped constantly in the cavern and filled my little suck basin. Master could have been coming day after or day or hour upon hour and this slave would not have known. The only thing it did know is that it craved Hunter, his boots, his touch, even his spit. A touch from him, no matter how brutal or tender, would be like being touched by a God, my God.

That's when an idea hit me. A slave needed a prayer that would help it during its darkest hours. Maybe I had heard it somewhere or made it up, but the words came to me easily and when I said it out loud it gave me strength to deal with the loneliness and fear. "Holy art thou oh Lord my God, Holy art thou whom nature hath not formed, Holy art thou who the vast and mighty one, Lord of Light and the Darkness!"

Hunter was the Lord of both Light and Darkness. Had he not placed me here within his pit to learn to fear his wraith and to earn his compassion? This slave in the past was not an acceptable vehicle to properly serve its Owner, Lord and Master. How could I convey to my Lord and Master that it was ready to be lifted, how?

Master came to me after I had been reciting the prayer until it had become a mindless chant. His boots crossed the distance to where this slave languished, waiting a time to show to my Lord and Master the newly awakened bud of patience that was growing within it. This slave waited, kneeling, head bowed, praying silently the prayer of entombment.

He stood above me, listening to my whispered breath as I recanted the prayer. He snapped his fingers like a gunshot in the cavern, causing me to halt and look up to the glowing form haloed in light above me. This one waited, its new patience holding it in place on its knees.

The first words that I had heard form his lips came at that instant as if to confirm that the prayer and my new attitude was proper for this slave.

"Good, slave," was all he said. But it was enough to kindle a flame within my void soul and to toss me a lifeline this slave so richly needed at its darkest hour. His words and my prayer gave me validation to this new existence. The dim light showed him to me. Chiseled features leather chaps, boots and above that darkness. "Service my soul, 9-745."

I assumed he wanted his boot soles cleaned and buried my face into them, but the boot I had chosen was raised and slammed back into the grate to hit my face. I was dazed by his action and tried again to lick his boot soles. Again the boot stomped my face below the grating.

I screamed out of fear and revulsion and realizing that I had once again failed him. I was not ready to be his slave. Would I ever be? I cried out in total despair until the cavern walls echoed back to me my wailing voice. I cried there, hoping for a footfall on the gravel in the corridor of my cavern. Food did arrive by its usual means as a wet plop on the stone floor above my pit. By sound alone did I find the small parcel. I took up my prayer, singing it with the cavern's voices echoing it back to me. Together the cavern's voices and I took heart. Master would be back and this time this slave would be ready. I meditated until I fell inside of my own soul, my own mind. Parts of me began to battle for the control of my destiny.

What was that? What did you say? Stop whispering, he has gone. Yes, I failed him again just like you said but I wasn't ready. Remember you said something and I looked over to where you sat and I missed my chance to catch his snot. Damn you animal you made me miss my chance to serve him! But did you see how I tricked those guards into binding me. Ah God it was delicious it hurt so good. What? Your eyes were blindfolded? Ok, ok, nevertheless you would have loved the bondage like this slave did; it was good, real good. He saves the very best for me cause he loves me. Yes, he does give great pain. Yeah, it's like this pit, I hate it and I love it still I need it. You know how the old song goes? "He made me love him, I didn't want to do it, I didn't want to do it."

What, what's that you say? I should punish myself for failing him. I can you know, punish myself but it's not the same as when he does it, not the same. Would punishing the animal help the slave? No, not really, both of us would hurt that we know from past experiments. It's just not fun without Him.

Stop saying that I am not an animal, you are! I am a slave put here to better learn how to serve my Lord and Master. No, no, no, I am not the creature in the bottomless pit you and when he comes to rescue me you are staying behind, so there! I am his slave; He will come and take me back if I can only prove to him that I really ready and that I know my place.

Speak up damn it, what's that? Yeah that just might work this place is the pits. Maybe with your help we can clean this dump up get is all spit and polished before he returns next. But what am I going to do with my hair, he hates hair why else would he keep me shaved. Plucking it out only makes us bleed. Really, I didn't know shit could be used that way. Sounds like a plan, let's get to work.

Wait, did you hear that! Yes! Master comes; foot falls on the gravel. "Aggghhhhrrrr!" This one screamed as a stream of water hit its chest and played over its head, washing off the crust that marked it different from the other bad slave. The bastard was washing away all details that this one had worked so hard to create! Even as this slave fought the water if found itself very aware and alive. It was as if the water was there to make certain that bad slave was washed away, down the drain and beyond to some unknown cavern below. The water stopped, the grating was lifted, tossed away and this slave was pulled out of the pit.

Two hands attached to very strong bodies dragged this sobbing scared slave down the cavern corridor until they dropped it in a quiet room and departed. One single candle burned in a niche on the opposite wall to where this one lay dripping and shivering, not so much due to cold as to fear of what was to happen next.

The candle gave me adequate light for one who had been locked in darkness for how long only Master knew. That one candle illuminated the room to my light sensitive eyes as if I was standing in the middle of a stadium with floodlights on. In other words, the room was almost too bright, light enough for me to see barren walls broken only by two doorways and one small platform opposite where this slave lay on the floor.

A black rubbered hand parted a curtain over the doorway opposite this slave's position. In walked a huge well-muscled rubbered man who walked like a lion in full control of all he surveyed. He walked quietly towards the platform, his eyes pierced me where this one lay, eyes that (if this slave did not know better) belonged to Master. I became confused by his presence, began coughing up water but his eyes never left me as he willed me to be silent.

The giant of a man was covered in satiny black rubber from the top of his head to the very boots on his feet. Huge gauntlet gloves covered his hands, rose up his corded arms, thick strong legs were supporting his well-defined torso and big black thigh-high boots with yellow striping seemed to coat his legs and feet. He took a position before the platform directly in front of the candle. There he stopped, crossed his strong arms and spread his legs wide in a power stance daring me to so much as breathe without permission. My mind kept playing tricks with me because it kept saying it knew this person and yet my eyes said otherwise.

Then he spoke and this slave knew that it was none other than Hunter. How he had changed while this one faced its darkest hours in the pit! Somehow he had bulked up, laid on new layers of muscle. None of that was important; what he said was. "Last chance for forgiveness, 9-745. Will it obey without question?"

Hesitantly this slave mumbled the prayer under my breath and replied, "Sir, yes, Sir."

"Crawl!" His fingers pointed to a spot on the floor before him.

This slave dropped down until its torso was laid on the floor, it bowed its head before crawling the short distance to where he indicated. When it arrived he stepped aside, kicked it onto its back and ordered it under the clear acrylic platform. Once in place, he dropped and locked panels around this slave's legs to make certain this slave would not refuse him again.

It was interesting to watch him as he walked around the platform and made ready to help this slave make the final transformation. Pins were pulled on either side of the platform so that he could lower the oval to within inches of this slave's head. Standing at my feet, he ran his gloved hands over his black rubber torso, squeezing one of his nipples while the other hand coasted down the oily surface to cup his crotch and hold it out to me. With a quick grasp and pull, the cod-piece was pulled from the rubber suit. His handsome full meaty cock sprang into view, looked down at its slave and began to swell with anticipation. His hand grabbed up his own nuts, circled them, clamped them tightly until his head rolled back in appreciation of the pain-pleasure he was giving himself.

The hand that had been playing with his nipples dropped back behind him where the other hand joined the first. He bowed forward, reached between his legs and pulled a zipper open that sliced his blackened body in half and opened his crotch and ass to full view. How handsome my God had become while this slave had been away.

How wretched this slave had become rotting away in its pit, no longer did it have the fine muscles, as did its Master who stood high above it. No longer was it presentable to anyone but him. The weeks, months or years of solitude without exercise had done its job. What this slave once held as a proud overture and had lorded over others it no longer had, it was weak and flabby. No one but its Owner wanted it now. My eyes could not see enough of him this man of contrasts. Rich black oily skin of rubber and his pearly white blood-engorged cock and balls were seared into this slave's mind and soul. This slave, 9-745, was owned by this Master. It was there for one purpose: to serve to submit totally to Master's will or be damned.

Master Hunter sat down upon his throne; his ass was close enough that this slave could kiss it and did without permission. This slave needed him to know how much it had changed for the better; it needed him to know that its old self had died in the pit. The only way this slave could do that was to accept his gift without question and to accept and appreciate all his pain or pleasure for what they were, his love.

Master's body began jerking and it realized he was fisting his cock. Not to destroy his pleasure but to add to it, my tongue snaked out and began worming its way around his ass ring. One of his raunchy farts tickled my tongue as it exited, filling the head box full of trippy-rich ass gas. This slave was once again where it belonged, below its Master and locked in heaven.

Two months it took to break and crush this thing. Finally my ego died and this slave was reborn. There are no positives or negatives in a life of service only a life focused on ones Master. Life is neither good or bad - it is focused.

Master once said, "Anybody can break or destroy a human will; but only a God can mold that shattered thing into a thing of splendor." Master Hunter gave me a reason for living, service and he became my one and only God! It had taken Master three months to totally and irrevocably destroy my will and seven more months to re-create this slave. All the values it had learned in the outside world were stripped from its mind and replaced by Master's rules of order, his dictates, and his will. When this slave crawled out from the darkness it returned to topside as a new being it had been reborn, remade into a shadow slave. One who feared being outside of his Master's shadow because it knew that if it did something horrible would befall it.

No matter where Master went, this one was not far behind him, always within an arm's reach, under his boots, because it feared being far from him. Little did this one know that it was the first subject of a brutal experiment to create slaves that were so dedicated, so devoted to its Owner that it was termed a shadow slave. So it came to be his number one.

Chapter 5

*Every prison, and fetter, and scaffold, and bolt, and bar, and chain is evidence
that man believes in the depravity of man.*
Tyron Edwards

My Master is a shrewd businessman. Sir has a knack for seeing below the surface bullshit of his friends or us slaves. Not only does he see our potential, but also he has a way of drawing it out of us; so that when we are around him we try to imitate him and live up to our highest potential. He has a personal following like no other Master in the region and a dedication among the Shieldmates that equals fanaticism.

When everyone had given up on me. It was Master Hunter that cared enough to destroy my old self and rebuild upon this body a new being - a slave that feared him totally but was wholly devoted to him. All other men in my life I had topped from below, manipulated them until I got what I wanted. Not so with Master Hunter. He was the only man in my wretched life that gave me just what this slave needed, discovered in a pit deep within the bowels of the earth and hard love. He broke my will, utterly destroying it and reformed a new being from the tattered flesh, breathed life into its lungs, gave it purpose, taught it fear and a devotion that turned into love. This slave was no longer the being that it had been on the outside. Now it knew its purpose and that objective was to serve however, whenever he chose, completely giving unselfishly of myself to his gratification without thought of my own pleasure or pain. So this slave came full circle and returned to the Master's house reborn in his image of a slave, his number one. If need be, I would graciously lay down my life for him without even a second thought. He - as that twisted fucker we know as Doc says – is my savior.

My Master is a retired Vietnam vet, a class act, and an honest man who just happens to be a strict disciplinarian who is fair and actually very kind hearted. He runs a large farm in Virginia that houses one of the largest slave training faculties in the United States that is hidden in the bowels of the earth in the Luray caverns subsystem. He runs the world from his position as the Deus of Castle Enterprises, Inc. My lord and Master Hunter rules our known world from his estate in Virginia. He works hard, plays harder and should he have any spare time, he retreats to his private studio where he creates. He says that this slave is his best creation, still there are times he needs to splash paint on canvas, rip and mold metal or spin clay on a wheel. In his studio he finds his peace and time for much needed reflection. Thankfully he is one of the first to poke fun at himself and his artwork, as he loves a good joke and enjoys life to its fullest.

If I have learned anything since I have been his slave it is this; you do not want him for your enemy. He once told me "Leave me and mine alone and everything will be right with the world; fuck with either and you're dead!" Master is a lighthearted man who loves to share his good fortune and hard work with others; however, if you are foolish enough to cross him, be prepared! He can be the typical personification of a sadistically brutal bastard! He would just as soon rip out your heart and eat it like an apple than take a swing at you. It takes a long time for his pot to boil but once its boiling, run for the hills and start praying his sights are not aimed at you.

After being with him for over four years - I have honestly lost count - you would think that I should know him pretty well. That is not the case. Master Hunter is damn secretive and fucking scary at times. The way he knows things tends to give me the hebe-gebes. Plus he is an odd duck - as odd as they come. He refuses to wear a lot of black, the color that most of us love to wear. Due to his religious beliefs! That's why he has a wardrobe of all sorts of colors, even in leather.

Once, a long time ago, I dared ask him why he chose to wear a rainbow of colored leather instead of the basic black that most other leather men chose to wear. He laughed and told me it was because he could. Then he turned serious and laid some heavy shit on me. Supposedly when he was born into his Native American tribe, the shamans said the heavenly stars had some weird alignment that pointed out that he would be a man of power, a holy man. Well, he's that for certain. Soon he will be the Deus and he is the Lord of the Buena Vista manor but that does not explain all his weirdness. He went on to tell me that he is of the Shaawaanee tribe out of Kentucky, the land of misty shadows, where the ghosts roam free. In his world as a child he was taught the old magic by many elders within his tribe and that to him magic was as commonplace as was a sneeze. Magic to him has neither time nor space, it was to him as simple as stepping off the face of earth and out of time. His power animal is a huge Kodiak bear and I nearly flipped when he took me into the forest and showed me that circle made out of rocks. Strange place that area is, it's just really weird feeling out there. All slaves that serve him have been out there once, to kneel in the center of those stones while he chanted in some strange language. We know when we see him heading that way to leave him alone, he is doing important business out there and its not for us to disturb him.

He says he walks in balance with his nature. Claims to be a warrior priest from some decades gone by still if you put all that aside I know him best. He is kind and cruel, lovingly tender and brutal a contradiction in terms but I cannot help it I do love him and fear him.

This slave learned while in the pit that I will live out my life serving Master Hunter and when I die he will assign my ashes to be used in a fashion that suits him. Even in death there are ways in his world of magic that I can serve him. This is my fate and I go to it joyfully. Master Hunter is a man like no other men and one this slave willingly serves with all its abilities.

****

The phone rang and I overheard a conversation, my Master was saying, "Hot damn, my man! Glad to hear that you've gotten the project finished so soon!... Sure! We will be expecting both of you and the boys this weekend; but can you do me a big favor? ...Yeah, swing by and pick up Prissy will you? That way I don't have to send a car for her. She will be waiting for you at her office, 67 M Street...yeah you got it. ...Yes, she is still one hell of a Dom. You'll hit it off with her but don't let her bully you, she loves doing that to men, it's her thing!" He laughed loudly at his own joke and resumed, "Hey, let me send down a big flatbed, we have a couple of deliveries coming your way today and they can swing by after their drop-offs. ...Sure. Not a problem. Two mules and one Handler, the mules can lift some pretty heavy shit. ...Oh? Ok? ...Hell yeah, take the second exit and stop by a bar on the way in. It's called Hog Heaven, ask for Charlie and tell him I sent you. Call us from there, I will send down a 4x4, your town car will not make it up the hillside, winter and spring did one hell of a washout! …Good, we will see you about dinner time."

Master Hunter was talking on the phone while I remained where he had placed me, between his legs at his boots. The best place to be in my way of thinking. My back was nested into the 'V' of his crotch. We had been playing with a wonderful new hood when the telephone rang and slave mike brought it to him.

Something was amiss. Slave senses know these things. Call it our second sight if you'll, we just know things about our Masters and Mistresses that they don't want others to know about. It gives us an edge, as if that would do us any good, but still it keeps us up on our toes. The Manor Motorcycle run wasn't until October; that gave us plenty of time for all the things he has on his agenda.

Phone call completed, he laid it aside and returned to me. I don't know which of us wanted that new hood in place more, him or me. Both of us were enjoying ourselves. While he was speaking on the phone he'd completed lacing up the back of my neck and head. With a tap on my head and a push from his hand he told me that he wanted me to turn around so he could view the hood, I did as ordered. I drew my kneeling body as close as I could to his crotch, draped my arms over his thighs and locked them there, turning my face up towards his.

The phone rang again. He bellowed and tossed it away, ordering the other house slaves that he was taking only emergency phone calls and that emergency had better be a call from God himself. He turned his eyes back on me kneeling patiently between his legs. "Are you trying to get on my shit list today, slave?"

"Sir, no, Sir!" I mumbled through the hood. The hood he had on me was, by the looks, a standard humdrum issue. Which was a let down, as he had promised that this hood would keep me locked into silence. He pulled my head closer. Put a blood pressure bulb into an inflating nipple and began depressing the bulb, forcing air into a pocket over my lips. Interesting how it felt as the leather inflated over and around my mouth, cheeks, and chin, locking them tightly by nothing but air pressure.

He smiled and asked me if I wanted to suck his cock. I could only nod my head in response as my jaw would not move. "Cat got your tongue, slave?" he laughed.

I nodded and let my eyes answer the question. He removed the bulb and relocated it to another side of my head. The space over my ears became tight and when his mouth moved I couldn't hear him. Again he laughed and pulled me to him. He seemed happy by my forced silence. If he was happy I was overjoyed.

Too quickly for my tastes he released the pressures and removed me from the hood. I must have looked displeased by the early release because he looked down at me and said, "Ain't finished with you yet, meat." Together we played with three or four different hoods before he made selections for his personal use on me. This way, we shared a wonderful union, a lazy day which was unknown with his typical busy schedule.

Master had put aside the hoods and taken up a handful of straps that he wound around my head before buckling in place. He was talking while he put me into the Bishop's hood. "Master Jude and I put our heads together to come up with this just for you. I think you'll like it. Hold still, damn it!"

Two of the straps ran on either side of my nostrils was attached a chin cup. Once in place he tightened it locking my mouth closed. A big shit-eating grin slipped across his face and with a flourish of his hands he produced one of my favorite toys in his leather gear, his old leather codpiece. It was rich with dried cum, smegma, piss and had been worn so often by him that the leather was incredibly supple. It was that codpiece that he snapped in place and to the straps that ran down over my nostrils and mouth. He chuckled as my eyes rolled heavenward. He knew that his scents, tastes and touch drove me wild, this codpiece over my nose would send me to greater places than any poppers. This was filled with my drug of choice my Master.

"Like that, don't you little pig?" His laughter told me he did not need an answer as my eyes had glazed over and I had entered ecstasy. "Looks great; however, there is one more addition I have been meaning to try."

He pulled out something that looked like a leather bag or a pillow without any stuffing. Over my head the leather bag was pulled, taking away the light and locking me back into that comfortable darkness that this slave had learned to love. With the tug of a zipper the bag closed in around my face. He added a thick, two inch collar around my neck to add to the burden of sucking air through tiny pinprick holes hidden somewhere on the bag before pronouncing it complete and to his liking.

My body told him how much I liked the extra confinement to my head with hard nipples and a more than happy cock trying to get his attention from its own cage, enforced chastity. He knew before he put it on me, he knows me better than I do myself.

His hand pushed gently but insistently down on the back of my neck telling me he wanted me on the floor. Using his boot toes, he moved me into place on my hands and knees before the man I feared and loved. I knew what was to come next and braced myself as his boots rose from the floor and dropped onto my back. The way he had me positioned, his legs ran down my spine and his boots rested just off each shoulder near my head.

He settled down and got comfortable in his chair. I heard him barking orders to the twins and making a few phone calls. One boot lifted from my back and settled down on my upraised ass check. When he finished his phone calls, that booted leg was repositioned down on my back and over my shoulder. Again he settled down and his movements seemed to cease all together. I prayed he was napping. He needed it as last night he had been more than just a little hungry for meat…he wanted it raw and bloody. He worked me over double time.

My back was welted and bruised, but this one paid it no mind. They were, after all, badges of honor and pride. I loved wearing his coat of many colors. Not only did it show to others how much he cared for me, but how well I served him. Among us slaves there was very little that we could display except the colors of our Master's pride and those we showed off without so much as bitching or moaning about the pain. It was how we showed others our satisfaction.

True, he had dozed off. He was too still and my legs were cramping, my shoulders hurt; but I dare not raise myself or think of myself at this time. He finally jumped as if startled. His boots hit the floor suddenly and I felt his boots on the wooden planking as he walked across the den and was gone. I held my place, relaxed my aching back and shoulders by stretching while he was away, even dropped down onto my stomach to rest my knees. This was permitted as long as I did not try to move from the area; blind as I was I just might damage myself or break something. I could have reached up and removed the head bindings, but this slave dared nothing that stupid. No, there are things far worse than being locked into darkness and waiting his return. I endured enough of that hell to earn my place here at his feet and here I'd stay until he tires of me or sells me to another.

A cold gust of wind from outside as well as the feeling of the wooden floor told me others had entered our home. I could not tell anything except someone was moving towards me, so I rose back into position, the same before he left. His hand touched my back and patted me twice; our code for this slave to rise to its feet and wait at his side for other orders. No one but those who had close ties with our family knew how much he cared for this slave or I for him. Simple little gestures like his coded pats told me just how much he cared for my wellbeing and show his level of control over this slave. He has trained me so that when I am without eyes, I am to place my hand on his elbow. This way, he can lead me wherever he wants. Slipping my hand out, I found his boot and rose to his side. He put my hand on his elbow and led me into the den before pushing me back down in place at his feet.

By the movement of the floor I knew exactly what was going on. Unshod feet were running about the den, getting the guests settled and taking luggage to their private rooms. Another time I would be doing that, but for now I was at his boots where I belonged. Even blind, I was constantly diligent to his needs. Having survived the darkness of the pit, no simple device like a hood would ever keep my mind's eye from seeing beyond those simple folds of leather.

The group from Washington D.C. had arrived, if my senses proved true. Miss Priss' perfume cloaked the air with the fragrance of more flowers than one person should ever wear. Hunter was walking before me. I had my hand resting lightly on his elbow as he'd trained me. He was leading me up the steps to check on his guests. We stopped at Miss Priss' suite first to see if she was comfortable and moved down to the dormitory that the other men seemed to prefer, where we stayed a few minutes while he chatted animatedly.

Normally those of the household slaves ran around naked. That is, naked as one can be when wearing a slave harness that all of us were fitted with after my and mike's indiscretions. After I had returned from the pit he had my harness fitted with snaps instead of rivets. A simple difference, but one that did not go unnoticed by the other household slaves.

Master dates our anniversary according to the day that I crawled from his pit. By his standards, on that day I was reborn and in truth I was. Only now I understood the quote I once used on stage, "S&M love play binds like no other." As a cardboard top I never really understood the depths of that statement; nowadays I live by the statement and agree with Larry Townsend's comment whole-heartedly.

Master Hunter is the type man that if he sets his sights on something or someone he is going to have it - one way or another. Aggressive in bed and in business and cutthroat if required. But there is a side to him that only I and a few others see; the big teddy bear. It's that side of him I love the best. The one that comes in tired from a long day and puts his head into my lap or who cuddles with me lovingly. Yes, my Master Hunter is a paradox but I love every inch of him.

Our lovemaking is as spontaneous as a will-of-the-wisp. As carefree as the wind. I may be working alongside of slave mike in the kitchen peeling spuds when he walks in, grabs a handful of my butt, presses me into the counter and whispers into my ear, "I need that ass, now!" Without so much as a howdy-do, his cock enters me. I love giving him pleasure. However, despite the times that I would prefer not to be used, I do it anyway because I love him. After all he has the choice of others. He comes home to me. He does not belittle me like other Masters do their slaves, but elevates my self-esteem. Few can handle the amount of pain Master Hunter likes to dish out when he is hungry and damn few could handle the depths of the commitment we have between us.

He had completed meeting with everyone and we were in route to our quarters. Up three steps, the door swings in to our right and we are home. He is in a festive mood as he rips my harness off my body, turns me and whispers how excited he is seeing me in that hood. He pushes me backwards towards what I know is waiting for me - a butt plug and the bondage chair. My ass gets plugged and I am lowered into position, straps lock my butt in place with more straps to spread my thighs wide. Each arm is lifted, swung up and over to the back where they are bound over a T-bar on back of the chair. He so hates it when I slouch, so this is one of his ways to correct that matter and it works for both of us. A strap over my forehead locks it to the cushioned headrest and, with the addition of a few more straps down my legs, I am complete.

He withdraws, but returns a moment later. He cups my balls and binds then deep into a ball stretcher that makes me wince, as it's the long one. Slowly, he drops a sound down into my piss slit. Just the feeling of it entering that hole makes my cock harden with incredible sensations as it gets fucked. An electrode is secured to the end of the sound and the ball stretcher has its own connections. He sets the charge on the Tens unit, whispers a good-bye. The charge of juice runs down my cock and begins pumping my prostrate as he departs. Both my cock and my balls are on fire and I'm loving it.

Once before the pit, he had placed me on a bondage board, had me wrapped nice and securely then was called out of the room. While he had been there I was grooving on the situation, but when he departed I became worrisome, fretful and lost my headspace. He must have sensed my fright and returned. As he calmed my fears he told me the way of his world. "Boy," he said, "you think I need to be at your side every moment while you are in bondage? Wrong! It gives me a hard on just to think of your suffering in my ropes while I have to be away doing boring shit like book keeping or entertaining. I get a high like no other thinking about you here in my room, bound, helplessly struggling. Bondage isn't bondage until it goes beyond your limits, then it become real bondage."

Returning to his guests, he left me all alone to endure the test before me. I settled back to enjoy what he had set for me and got into the situation. I knew he could sense me and if I were in any manner of danger, he would be at my side in a flash. He'd proved that more times than not.

He was watching me now, I can sense his presence. All of us within this household can sense him when he is nearby, and it's our slave sixth sense kicking into high gear. Goose bumps crawl across my bound body, my way of saying Master is nearby. We have a link; psychic perhaps, I just don't know or care to explore it for more than what it is. A Hunter barometer. It isn't a localized phenomenon, it happens to all of us and I bet if Cappy would own up to it, he is also affected by his presence. The sensation is not unpleasant as it begins with a tingling, goose bumps follow, our tits get hard and followed not soon after by our cocks. It's not just isolated to us slaves, but others that have served him as a bottom or have some other affiliation with him.

His fingers closed around my nipples as be began rolling them, slowly increasing my pleasure-pain. Once up and fully erect, clamps were added, weighted and tugged on gently to set the teeth of the alligators that he preferred using on me. The pain was delicious, as it coaxed my desires to have him instead of that butt plug in me. He knew how to work this slave into a fucking frenzy and loved making it crave him. As quietly as he had entered, he departed again. But not before turning up the Tens unit to another level of impact. Leaving me alone to ride out his pain for his pleasure and I loved how he treated his thing.

My cock was on fire when he returned and he stomped out the flames with his boot. The suddenness of his boot on my cock made me nearly jump out of my skin and made him laugh in delight of catching me off guard. He lifted his boot, walked closer, straddled my bound legs and sat down on them. His hands fondled my bagged head teasingly, kissing, nibbling my neck. One hand stroked my cock, rolled a nipple, giving me the pain pleasure we both craved and blending them like an expert chef. His hands teased me as his mouth slid down my struggling body. I was on fire with desire. I felt him lift, move away and walk around the room.

He returned to his captive, coaxing my body to squirm and wiggled on that butt plug, making me grind my ass on that plug lodged between my ass cheeks and fight the ropes that bound me to the chair. The bastard knew just exactly what he was doing to me. Goddam, I wanted his cock shoved in me or down my throat and he knew it!

He straddled my legs and sat back down. His weight shifted as my collar and leather bag were removed. There, before my eyes, was my Master grinning like a Cheshire cat, studying my face. Tenderly he kissed my forehead, "Like this, don't cha pig?"

No answer was necessary. He knew what I needed. One hand fingered the chain between my tits. He studied my reaction, drawing the pain out of my body and drinking it like no other man could. He leaned back, holding the chain and watching me wince, struggling to accept his gift of pain. The chain dropped, his hand lowered to my hard and oozing cock. The Tens unit was removed as he slowly fucked my cock with the sound. He allowed it to flow out before pushing it gently back in. This was only a prelude to what would soon happen if I could have my way; his cock would replace the plug in my ass. All the time he was fucking my cock with the sound, he was watching my eyes and I his. God, how he loved to fuck with me!

He removed the balance of my headgear so he could have his way with my lips; he loved sucking face almost as I did. He whispered into my ear, "The guests are resting from their long trip. I think I need to rest, too. Don't you agree, slave?"

I wanted to scream *no, you want to fuck my ass*, but agreed with him that he needed to rest. He laughed, stood up and backed away from his bound slave. Damn him, he had no intentions on resting. There he stood in his favorite (or was it my favorite?) outfit, thigh-high big boss Wesco boots, his leather jock, gloves and one of his big Churchill cigars. The game was afoot; I got to service his boots as long as he smoked that cigar. After which, if I pleased him and his boots well enough he would fuck my butt off.

I growled at him, "Grrrrrr!"

He laughed and released me from the chair, backed off and took one of his power stances; legs spread wide, crotch humped forward, cigar to his lips and just daring me to move. I dropped to my hands and knees. He looked down to me while he was lighting his cigar, "Crawl to them, boy."

I crawled to them, willingly, head bowed and growling as I came towards him.

He put out one boot, caught my head and stopped my progression. "Let's see if you can earn them." He cocked back his head, summoned up a huge wad of snot from his innermost depths, reared his head and spat it into the air. I watched it sail in a high shimmering arc over head before it began its descent. I shuffled forward and caught it with my mouth, stuck out my tongue to show him and swallowed. He had backed away after he spat his load into the air, taken a seat in his huge leather wingback chair and sat with one leg tossed over the arm, laughing at my antics. "Get over here, slave, you have work to do."

I scrambled to that left boot; sole turned up and aimed at me. Paused, looking up at him waiting for his permission. Once given, like a man starved for water, I dived onto that boot. Some bootblacks only clean the uppers of the leather. I have been trained to service all of my Master's boots from soles up, and it's only proper. After running my tongue around the Vibram soles, it coasted over and into the welting of the boot, gathering all the dust and grime my tongue could find. Once both boot soles were clean I returned to my love, cleaning and worshiping his leather covered legs and those incredibly huge, wonderful, oiled leather boots. Completing the upper, I straddled his left boot and, like a monkey clinging onto a tree branch, ran my tongue higher and higher around his limb. I was in heaven. Especially when he flipped his cigar ash onto his boot where I could have two taste treats in one, leather and 'gar ash! One boot done, I moved to the other as he shifted his body and boot in my direction. He loved my worship sessions as much as I loved giving them to him and his boots.

I had reached as high as I could on his boots with my tongue when he ordered me to stand. He wrapped a doeskin strip of leather around my nuts, drawing them deep into their sack and ordered me to straddle one leg. "The best oil in the world for my boots, slave, comes from slave nuts. Take them in your hand and put back the oils you just sucked off!"

I had to straddle-squat like a crab to work my balls over those boots, but it was worth every moment and sensation he ground into those nuts. If he felt that I was not doing the job well enough, his boot would suddenly leap from the floor and slam into my bound nuts, damn but it hurt good. Each time he did that made me go crazier. The bastard knew it because he had me licking and rubbing my balls on his boots; fucking boot lust!

His cigar was getting down to finger length when he abruptly rose to his feet, tossing me onto the floor. One boot rose quickly and grabbed my attention by slamming down onto my nuts, trapping me from going anywhere. With a snap, his jock was ripped off. "Look what all that tongue action has done to me, boot slave. Get that face up here, now! Lick my balls, cocksucker!" He held them out to me in his fist and grabbed the back of my head, pulling my open mouth towards his nuts. All of them got forced into my open mouth; there he held my head as my tongue did a waltz over his ripe nuts. "Chew them, slave!" Teeth were applied as ordered and, in response, he began moaning and grinding his hips into my face while his cock tried to poke out my eyes.

He was sweating when he leaned back, disengaging my mouth from his balls as if to sit back down in the chair. But he'd failed to remember that he had moved. Somehow he didn't gauge the distance properly and sideswiped the chair on his way down. For a moment I was stunned, not knowing what to do as his face registered as much surprise as mine. For that moment, the world stopped. I didn't even dare to breathe, then his eyes twinkled and he burst out laughing. "There goes my dignity," was all he said and he continued to laugh riotously.

He looked down at me, wiping tears from his eyes. "You moved the chair didn't you, slave? Go ahead you can tell me. No?" Easy laughter rolled out of his lips. "Shit, slave, now you know my secret. I don't have hindsight! Well, since I am down here already, why don't you straddle those boots and work your way up here," he was holding out his cock as he leaned back on one arm.

Gladly I straddled his big legs and worked my tongue up his boots to his cock. He let me tongue his cock before he pulled my face higher and onto his nipples then into his armpits and on up his neck. I hoped Heaven smelled like him, rich warm cinnamon spicy musk, Hunter.

"Get your cute mug up here, slave, I need a smooch." Hunter purred into my ear as he pulled my lips to his. Our tongues did the slash and parry of seasoned warriors and before I knew it, he was on top of me and had me pinned to the floor. He laughed lightly. "Got'cha just where I want you, piggy boy!"

Using his boot toes, he pried open my legs and nested his boots, crushing my cock and balls. Damn. he knew me too well, I thought. He crawled forward until his leather knees were wedged into my armpits, then he leaned forward, pushing my arms overhead and pinning them to the floor with one hand. He looked like a conquerer ready to rape another captive. He leaned back, took a long draw on what was left of his cigar and leaned down. Blowing the smoke in my face, he pressed his cock between my lips.

My tongue connected with the underside of his cock as my lips opened to take in the cock head and shaft. He started thrusting his cock into my mouth and lifting his boots to grind into my cock, with his rocking action I was being driven nuts. It felt like I was sucking on my cock and hurting my cock at the same time, it was perfectly delicious.

My teeth traced his cock. One grating plunge past my teeth made him shudder. The second time it happened made him collapse as he rammed his cock down my throat and shot his load. That's when we both heard the knocking at the door. Neither of us paid any attention to it, hoping it would just go away. Except it didn't. It just kept knocking until he bellowed, "Come in!"

He was still sitting atop my chest when the door opened and in stepped mike carrying a tray of food. "Begging your pardon, Sir. You asked that I bring this tray to your at exactly 5:30 PM. Is there anything else you might need, Sir?"

Master rolled off of me, stood and placed one of his big boots on my chest and held me down. Then he turned to mike, who was about to depart the room. "Yes, mike, lay out my dinner clothes. Nothing too formal, your choice!"

While mike was preoccupied with pulling out leather pants, a shirt and the standard knee-high boots and gloves, Hunter was busy rubbing his boot soles over my cock, making me hump the soles of his boots in hopes I would have the chance to cum. Once he realized what I was about to do, his boot shot off my lap as if I had scorched his foot. He looked down at me and leered, "Later if you've earned it. Get your ass up off that floor and start me a bath, then return to remove these boots."

He was near the bed, having changed the shirt mike had chosen for the evening. I knelt on the floor, my back to him as is the custom of his bootjack. One boot slammed not so lightly into my balls and my legs closed around his boot. Using my hands, I helped him pull his boot off and his leg out. Once out, he took the boot and placed my head into the shaft so that I could drink the moisture from his feet. That is my job as his bootblack, bootjack and boot slave; to properly care for his boots and all foot gear. The second boot followed the first. Once completed, I chewed his socks from his feet, then helped him into the bath, and then I returned to put away his boots.

After a moment I was there to scrub his back and body. A water fight broke out and I was pulled into the tub to lovingly tend to his bathing ritual. Meaning: I did all the work while he laid back and allowed me the pleasure of caring for him. He cleared his throat; looked down to me as I was chewing on his toes, "Slave, will you do something for me knowing that it will hurt?"

I paused as if I was thinking, removed his toe from my mouth and replied, "Sir, I am yours to command, Sir!" Then I went back to chewing on another toe as he squirmed lustily. We finished his bath and I dried him tenderly with a nice thick warm towel, gave him a quick touch up shave and tidied the bathroom as he padded out into the bedroom.

When I joined him he was almost dressed. This was odd, as I had been dressing him now for almost a year and he had never done that before. Even when he was in a hurry. I finished his dressing, adding socks and boots to his wardrobe, stood back, eyed him carefully and made a few adjustments. He grabbed me then, pulled me into his arms and raped my mouth.

"Under the bed is a box, pull it out and go get the talc you are going to need it tonight." His big smile told me either I was in for a wild time or he was going to have some fun at my expense. Either way, I was his to command. He helped me powder my whole body lightly with the talc before he permitted me to open the box. As I pulled out the contents of the box, I could do nothing but babble incoherently in surprise. Inside the box was a catsuit, head to toe encasement made from rubber. The first rubber that I had ever owned, and it was being given to me by my Owner.

Amazingly enough he helped me get into the suit and watched as I pulled on the booties before he walked into the closet and brought me a pair of rubber Dehners styled boots. I thought I had died and gone to heaven. The suit was fashioned so my cock and balls hung out of the suit but I was covered from my head down to my toes in rich satiny black rubber that felt like a second skin. Each step made me feel like I was in a liquid bondage suit, as each step tugged against an invisible bond. What a sweet suit and, in the excitement of the gift, I tossed myself at my Master covering his lips with kisses.

"I take it you like my rubber suit, huh, slave?" Master asked me with his smile plastered all across his face.

"Oh Sir, thank you, Sir! It's the first rubber I have ever owned."

"Go get a moist bath towel; you need to clean me up. I'm covered with your damn powder."

While I ran to do his bidding, he must have stepped into his closet. Because when I returned, he had two extra packages laid on the bed. I busied myself wiping off his boots and leathers from any and all stray talc before I ran to toss the towel into the hamper. I felt like a child at Christmas

My mind must have been wandering until he slapped my cock and asked a question, "What's that thing you keep waving at me, slave? Did I give you permission to have a hard on? Well, did I?" I was so excited by the gifts that I was blinded by his earlier question. The gifts had just whisked that question out of my mind so I was a touch stunned when he pulled out a codpiece.

I looked up at him quickly to see what his eyes were registering and noticed he'd gone cold and deadly, "Sir, your cock, Sir! Forgive me Sir; it got excited with the rubber and all, Sir! I will never get a hard on again, Sir!"

"Don't lie to me slave! You are a fucking liar!" Then he laughed and grabbed my dick, "Who owns this cock?"

"Sir, you do and the body and soul of this slave, too, Sir."

He knew better than I, once he placed his hand on me there was no way to stop Pete from rising up to see him. Yes, so what if I call my cock Pete, there are other men who have stranger names for their cocks if they would own up to it. Pete had ruled my mind and body longer than my Master had; now, even he is submissive to our owner. Pete silently shrieked when Sir held up before my eyes the inside of the codpiece that he was going to place over him. The codpiece was filled with copper wired pinpricks. I damn near purred until he snapped it over my friend Pete.

Hunter snapped the codpiece into place, trapping Pete under a thousand tiny pinheads. I imagined hearing Pete screaming his defiance as the metal pins bit into his softening flesh. There was a struggle at first as my cock softened from initial shock of the new experience, then began enjoying the sensation and rose to the occasion, driving the pins deeper. I was winching in pain instead of Pete and all Master Hunter did was watch my face and laugh. "We have time, eat something off the tray that mike brought up to us. But don't get too full, you are part of the entertainment for the evening." His laughter made me worry but I followed orders.

Master walked over to his humidor and chose two cigars. One he pocketed the other he cut and lighted. I was nibbling on apple and cheese slices when he came to me. "Tonight, you may cum. Hold off until you cannot take it any longer. Now finish up those two bites and let's get you finalized for your part of the evening entertainment." He walked to the bed and returned, holding out a rubber gas mask by the way it looked. He paused, set down his cigar and held it out to show me. "This is something you have not experienced before."

My hands were positioned at the front of the mask. Together the rubber hood and mask were pulled over my head. Once in place, there were two huge eye plates before my eyes and a long rubber accordion tube hanging down from my nose area. He lifted the tube, "Inhale deep, can you breathe ok? Nod your head." I nodded affirmatively. He put his cigar into the end of the tube. "Breathe in normally." The eye plates and my lungs filled with this tobacco smoke. It felt like him exhaling into my lungs, something I loved for him to do. With the smoke clearing, he held up two eye plates of a much darker color. "These will go on just before you're positioned for tonight's party. Now let's go down to our guests."

I opened the door to the bedroom and followed him down the steps. There at the foot was J.D., who followed us into the den. Hunter moved forward to meet his guests and I was led off by J.D. I was taken into the small dining room, which was to serve for tonight's dinner party. Master Hunter loved showing off his slaves when he had a chance and tonight was no different. Perhaps it was his pride or his need for artistic expression, but tonight's performance was going to include me. A small platform was set up in the center of the dining room, where the lights seemed to shine up from underneath the platform and there was a hoist hanging from the ceiling.

J.D. led me up two steps. Gentle pressure on my shoulder indicated that I should kneel. Once down, he bound my hands at my back. Ok, I thought...this would be a breeze because so far nothing is at all painful. So what if electrodes were built into my cod-piece and each pinprick was a contact point? I saw nothing that would give me trouble until J.D. pointed to the six small tables set around the room encircling the platform. Each table held a small box from which wires ran down into the floor.

Stepping away to grab the hoist cable, J.D. lowered the hook from the ceiling. That damn hook was attached to my wrist restraints and I was lifted up, forcing my head downward to look at the floor. The pain was just beginning to build in my shoulders when he added straps around my tights and unzipped the zipper at my rear. Another slave was added to the platform, his cock was inserted into my ass and we were bound. His ankles to mine, his legs to mine and his arms were bound opposite mine, thus we were linked together.

Stepping down, J.D. went to each box and flipped a switch. Either I or the other slave squealed and squirmed to his delight. He left the switches, walked back to the platform, put the darkened eye plates over my visor, patted my ass and stepped down. Before he left the dining room, he adjusted and turned up the lights on the two slaves locked in a love embrace. The cock in my ass was squirming down my inner walls. It actually felt good, even if we were both being used to entertain our owners.

The guests arrived. Each in their own time pushed one or more of the buttons on their boxes and watched with delight as two rubber mannequins shrieked, squirmed and humped away. Instead of hanging with this horde of horny bastards, I chose my only way out and fled to my memories.

****

Hunter and I were sitting out back on the wooden porch one sunny day. Actually, He was sitting while I was being used as his boot stool his boots rested heavily but almost tenderly on my backside. He was chuckling out loud as he read what I used to refer to as a real leather man's magazine one that he had confiscated from J.D.'s room. J.D. had paid for such a disrespectful act of self-indulgence earlier that day and was off counting grains of rice with his Master as punishment.

Hunter was reading the advertisements within the personal ads column out loud. One particular caught his attention, it begged to be rewarded with a severe case of humiliation therapy, proclaimed Hunter. The ad read, "If you are a real Top who wears real boots, meet me in New Orleans for the Mardi Gras. Let the World's Best Boot Black service your boots. Contact me either here or online WBBootB@aol.com."

Sir was heehawing at the ad that he had just read; his boot rose from my ass and stomped back down getting my attention, "Damn, slave, this sounds like something you would have written. I think this 'Mister Wonderful' needs a lesson in humility, Hunter style." His boots rose off my back, one slammed into my ass hard enough for me to look back towards him to see what he wanted. "Get off your knees you lazy good-for-nothing slave! Go find Handler Dan and ask him to join me for dinner tonight. Ask mike for a chip so you can pass into the Handler's quarters. Run, slave, I'm already missing my boot rest."

My feet sprouted wings as I ran into the kitchen and found mike, hastily explained and bounced back and forth from one foot to the other until he placed a colored chip onto my collar. With that silly little colored chip, I could gain access to the secure zone, the Handler's living quarters. As if fire was following my heels, I ran the mile down into the caverns seeking out Handler Dan. I could not find him at his quarters and had to search out the daily work orders. I found him supervising a team of mules in the new cavern. He told me to tell our Master that he would join him after the changing of the guards; which would be in about a half an hour. With a pat on my ass I was sent back to Hunter with his reply.

I found Sir on the back porch having a boiler maker; he saw me running into the house and bellowed for me. "Next time I send your slow ass down, I am going to turpentine it so you can find some speed, slave. You took too fucking long to get down there and back. Did you blow every Handler down there? What took you so long?" With a slicing of his hand he cut off any attempts I might have had at a reply. He looked up at me and frowned. I was standing while he sat - a major mistake on my part. We have a standing rule; slaves keep their heads lower than their owner at all times. "Drop where you stand fuck up, on your back and crawl under my boots!"

Doing as I was ordered, my legs spread and his boot slammed into my cock and balls. He ground down, leaned over his leg and asked, "Did you find Handler Dan and is he coming to dinner, fuck up?"

My fists were tightly clenched and pounding the wooden planking below my body as his boot ground into my unprotected cock and balls. Through clenched teeth I spoke, hoping he heard me clearly. "Sir! He will be along when the shift changes, Sir!"

He let up the pressure he had been maintaining on my cock and balls but held his boot in place. "Hump the sole of my boot, but remember, slut, you are strictly forbidden to cum. Get busy, slave!" I was tuned out as I set about my task, humping and grinding my cock on the rough under-sole. I was extremely thankful that he was not wearing a Vibram soled boot. Past experiences have taught me just how brutal an assignment of fucking the sole of his boots can be, with a Vibram sole rubbing my cock raw. The sole of these boots were not just flat soles; they did have a small ridge that allowed the boot to hold into its stirrup.

Dan arrived, having stopped by his quarters for a quick shower and new uniform. He entered so quietly that I was nearly startled out of my wits. Laughter that sounded as if someone was uncomfortable at what they were witnessing was heard coming from the front porch of the main house. Dan stepped around the corner into view, "Master Hunter, Sir, how can I be of service to you my Lord."

"Ah, Dan finally you have graced us with your presence. Thank you for joining me for dinner. Come sit over here so we can talk." Sir pointed to a nearby chair then looked down at me. "Get Dan a boiler marker, slave. Make his Southern Comfort and a glass of beer and bring me another. Make mine Jack."

Once I was out of their way, Dan dropped to his knees beside our Sir, Master pulled his face up to his and they exchanged a big wet kiss. Dan stayed there until I returned with the drinks, then he ordered me to bring him a pillow. He remained on the floor at Sir's side while I knelt on the opposite, holding a tray with snacks and one of his cigars. Master noticed the cigar, looked over to me and patted my face. "You are learning to anticipate my needs, slave. That's good, real good."

I smiled inwardly and focused on holding the tray so both men could access the goodies mike had sent to them as a way of teasing their appetites before dinner. Lightheartedly, Hunter was talking to Dan about the ad he had read in the leather men's magazine. "Dan, I want you to answer this advertisement. I need to be in New Orleans on business and you'll be accompanying me."

"Thank you for the offer, Sir, but I cannot leave the command at this time," replied Dan. But he was not prepared for Hunter's response.

"Bullshit, Dan! I did not ask you! I said you'll attend me in New Orleans.

Commander Schmidt agrees with me that you need time off the base, as do I. Besides, everything is being taken care of by Castle and you are being offered a choice you cannot refuse. Do you understand me? If you need to tell the other Handlers something, tell them you won a trip to New Orleans. Hell, I checked your records; you have not been off the hill for over seven months, not even taking your standard 24 hours off every week. Being a workaholic is one thing, but you're heading towards burnout and you are just too damn good at your job to have that happen."

Dan's head fell to his chest while Hunter was talking. He looked up slowly and turned to Hunter. "Ok, Sir, as you wish. I will attend you during your trip to New Orleans, Sir."

"Now, Dan, before we go I need a big favor from you. I want to teach this guy a lesson while we're down there. I think its time we burst a bubble or two. Are you'lling to make a boy earn his self appointed rank and title?"

Dan's smile covered his face ear to ear, "Sir, I am looking forward to it. Besides, if he is that good, we just might need him here to replace 9-745. I thought it was supposed to be the worlds best." His laughter got my attention and his compliment made me smile.

"One thing, Dan. This is the first time I have left the hill without taking my slave...so you just might have to fill the bill if this boy does not work out. Are you up for that aspect of the game?"

Dan studied his boots then chuckled, then tossed back his shot followed by a long swallow of beer. He looked over at me then turned towards Master. "How long do I have to seduce this man, Sir?"

"I will give you one month," and Sir laughed heartily, "but only boot pictures, no nudes and your final picture will be you on my hog in your thigh high boots and a jock, nothing else!"

"Errrr, Sir, I just don't know about that. It seems I am putting up all the effort and I am not getting anything out of this but a trip to boring New Orleans during Mardi Gras. I am not that much of a drinker or care much for large crowds. And I like country music, not the blues."

Mike stepped out from the kitchen to announce dinner was being served. Master and Dan rose and I followed after I picked up there empties. The table was set for J.D., Master and Dan while mike and I served the men. Master Hunter explained his plans to J.D., who immediately suggested that Dan stay at home and he go in his place since Dan does not have any idea what a slave has to do to care for our Master. Their teasing banter made the dinner go faster and, after dessert, the men went into the den to continue the conversation.

Mike and I joined them after we had finished with the kitchen, bringing coffee and freshly baked cookies. The men-folk were having way too much fun at this ruse than was necessary. Mike assisted with Master's permission in creating a new profile for Dan, fitting his new role. I joined Master and J.D. who were pouring over blueprints for modifications to one of the waterfalls found in the new cavern.

Hunter looked up from his blueprints, "Dan, I will sweeten the deal since you were bitching a moment ago about the fact that you are doing all the hard work. I will have something made for you by my leather guild if you'll take that as a suitable bribe?"

Dan's look of surprise was cute, and then he stammered, "Sir, that's not necessary, really. When did you want me to go for the measurements?" We all laughed at his eagerness. Our leather guild's creations are highly prized as our artists are very special and extremely dedicated to their leather designs."

"Sucker!" Hunter poked at me kneeling beside him before cocking his head in Dan's direction. "I know how to seduce men too! They open at 6AM. Get there tomorrow morning before you go on shift and expect to be there an hour. Oh, and take your Dehner's and your thigh-high boots. I have something special in mind for you, boy!" His laughter had a sadistic ring to it, I knew that laughter well, and it meant he had something else up his sleeve for Dan.

Dan called us to silence, "Ok men, here is the sucker ad: 'So you think you are the world's best boot black? I think you're a liar. Or worse yet, a tennis shoe wearing geek who thinks he knows how to tend to a real Man's boots. I am 6'6", 210 lbs, 9" cock, work out 5 X per week, have dark hair, dark eyes and a dark soul. I will be riding in for the week of Mardi Gras on my Harley. My boots are thigh high black Wesco's and they have broken more wannabees than there are beads in New Orleans! Let's see if you are man enough to worship a man while he sits astride his Harley in all his glory. I hope you are not just giving empty lip service and are real, because I am. Email me now, boot slut! Powr1BootSS@aol.com.'"

Everyday both of them checked for an email. It took the World's best boot black over a week to respond to the first email. He was caught hook, line and sinker. Dan began sending him a few hot pictures of him in boots to tweak his interest and those emails almost made the boy swim with desire. It was only a few days before departure time when they received the *crème da la crème* email. I was in the office when Dan hurried in to read it to Hunter.

"Dear Sir, will you meet me on Fat Tuesday at the Café Dumonde at noon. I am eager to discuss more fully your plans for me serving your boots. By the way, you need not wear the thigh high Wesco's to the Café no doubt they are heavy boots and you might feel more comfortable wearing sneakers while we walk through the quarter. I am yours to do with me what you want. Until then, hugs and kisses, Jamie K."

Hunter began heckling Dan almost before he finished the letter. "So you are going to be wearing those sneakers, right Dan?"

"The hell I will, Sir! I don't even own a pair!"

Master turned serious, looked down at his laptop then looked back up at Dan. "Maybe this trip is a waste of our time, Dan? What if this boy is a total wash-out? Are you really ready to be my surrogate slave should he fail to please? What will you do to keep me happy, eh, Dan?" Hunter was starring into Dan's eyes solidly and Dan got wiggle-butt just sitting there under his glaze.

I knew what he was willing to do for Master. I knew and kept my mouth shut. Then the realization hit me about the trip. It was nothing but a ruse to get Dan off the mountain and into Master's clutches. This way he could find out for himself if the rumors were true about Dan's activities with the other male Handlers. Would Sir castrate Dan while they were in New Orleans for breaking the contract? I wanted to tell Dan to be careful on this trip, but knew he would not listen to this slave. Since my return from the pit, Dan seemed changed - or more awkward - around me.

J.D and I were left with a copy of Master's itinerary. They were to be hosted there by one of the New Orleans Shields; a Mistress Barbara and her mates who owned a fishing shack outside of N.O. that looked like a castle turret. The shack came with its own private dungeon and slaves to care for their needs, but the slaves had been declined.

The day before their departure, Master supervised my packing of his bags and added two suit boxes that had just arrived from the leather guild unopened. Boots, leathers, the standard gear for most leather men; as well as personal whips and toys. Another slave was doing the same thing for Dan in his quarters as mike had been sent down to help make certain Dan did not leave out anything. This being Dan's first trip off the mountain representing Buena Vista, certain formal gear was needed with all the accessories that would denote his rank. Once packed, mules loaded the luggage onto a delivery van along with a personal crate that was destined to arrive in New Orleans before our Master. This way all their gear would be unpacked and waiting their arrival as befits the Deus of Castle Enterprises.

Once the luggage was away, Master and I went to his office that I would pack his briefcase and he may speak with J.D. in private. I was busy packing his necessary items and downloading files onto his laptop when J.D. entered. They were discussing general items that needed to be taken care of while he was away. Master called me to the front of the desk looked over at J.D., suggesting to him that I should begin a new level of training to be his bodyguard. They discussed that for a while and the matter was closed. I would start the basic training right after he departed and I would continue it when he returned. I would be allowed to study three times a week when he returned and then I would be trained by the crack security team called the Black Watch. Clothes would be issued to me for the time I was with them. While he was away, I was to sleep in our suite along with J.D and mike. This was the first time he had left me since I had become his shadow and he was trying to anticipate all my needs. Details big and small were one of his specialties, that above all other perks won him more favor than you could imagine.

Once all the basics were complete, the end of that day was upon us. He took me upstairs to our suite and made love to me the balance of the night, giving me welts as well as a pleasant glow to remember him while he was away. After I awoke him by drinking his tiger piss and giving him his morning blowjob we crawled out of bed and he waved off the shower and shave, choosing instead to have me dress him. By his orders I placed him in ripped-crotch, worn, faded jeans, his favorite needle nose Justin cowboy boots, a ratty flannel shirt after which we ran down for breakfast. Once the morning duties were complete, he shooed me up the steps into our suite. One of the other house slaves had brought our lunch up to the suite. He fed me with his fingers and made certain that I ate as he ate. Lunch completed, the tray was placed on the dumbwaiter, lowered to the kitchen and Master called me to him. Together we lay on the bed cuddling and necking as he explained why he wanted me trained to be his bodyguard and some of what it entailed. He told me to call him every evening to report to him. This way we could be in constant contact even with the distance; he was trying his level best to put my fears at ease. I knew something bad was going to happen to him if I wasn't there to assist and care for all his needs. I just could not get the thought out of my head that Dan would not be capable of caring for my owner's needs as well as I.

He crawled to the edge of the bed, fished for something underneath and pulled up a box. This he opened and pulled out a severe hood with lots of straps; it honestly looked like something from a torture film. He pulled it over my head, lacing and buckling it nice and tight before he added the extra straps. I loved it.

With his hand pulling me forward, I was escorted to the St Andrew's cross in one corner of the room and bound firmly. My arms and legs were spread. My balls were gathered and bound deep into their sack before being drawn down and attached to the floor of the cross. He bound my balls this way because I tended to crawl up the cross when he laid a whip to my back. He leaned his weight against my back and licked from my shoulder up to each hand. His tongue ran down my spine, flipped around my butt cheeks before dropping towards the 'V' of my butt where he paused, teasing me to arch my back and tug on my nuts.

His hands teased my chest and then played expertly with my nipples. Rolling them to a sharp point before adding one of his tit clamps to them, then rolling the clamps between his finger and thumb to make me writhe in pain. I felt his heated breath on the back of my neck, followed by a gentle kiss. Then he bit me. The sharp contrast made me jump and moan into my hood as my butt ground back into his hips. He laughed; he was having fun teasing me, warming me to for what was to come.

Slaps rained upon my shoulders, down my back, over my butt cheeks and down onto my thighs. Then up again and down. A doeskin flogger replaced his hand before his tongue followed. Another bite - he ground his teeth into my flesh, I moaned laouder this time. The light flogger gave way to a medium flogger. By its feel it was the heavy mop. It slammed into me, knocking air out of my lungs. He was using both hands on the flogger like a bat, each blow forced another section of my skin to warm to his touch. His rough beard ran over my back, making me squirm and moan in delight. Another whip - one that had a sharp sting to it - awoke my ass and thighs to his gloved caresses and I found myself arcing my butt out to greet the flogger as it descended. The whips stopped, his breath returned to the nape of my neck. A loving kiss, followed by a deep bite, and he bit his way down the rib cage. I yelped in pain and pleasure of this moment as he grabbed a mouthful of slave butt between his teeth and dug them in hard.

He laid his weight back upon my body, rubbed his gloved hands up my arms. As they descended he attached clothespins one at a time. They ran from my elbow down to my ribcage and on to the tops of my thighs. One set established, he applied the other. Then he leaned in, adding his weight to mine pulling on my bound wrists helping me realize just how helpless I was to resist. A twist to my nipples made me wiggle my butt into his naked hardening cock that sawed between my open butt cheeks.

A fist slammed into my shoulders, followed by another, then his fingernails dug into the skin as he tried to rip it off to see what lay beneath. He flipped each of the clothespins on one side while he strolled down the whole strand with the other. I could no longer be silent and gave him the scream he sought.

He went back to work, as he wanted more of my screams. A paddle burned my ass raw, his teeth found their mark and one string of clothespins were ripped off rapid fire. I became a wolf howling at the full moon. My screams had to be heard in the kitchen. Still he played his fiddle, going for the deeper, richer sounds of anguish. Claws gripped my skin and tried to rip it off my bones. Fanged teeth chewed at any loose flesh, grinding into it, threatening to tear giant chunks off. Another clothespin zipper was ripped off and my voice reached a new level. The only response was his deep laughter in my ear and a quiet voice that ordered me to sing more.

Tit clamps got rolled and rapidly removed, then rolled again until circulation was forced back into the twice bitten nubs of flesh. One arm was released and repositioned above my head, then the other joined it. My ankles were released and, with a pull, I was flipped around facing him. He lifted my legs up and pinned them over my head before he took a belt to my exposed ass. Working it with layers and layers of pain until, just when I felt as if I could not take it any longer, his cock filled me. Pinned on his raging hard on, I lost all control and surrendered to his needs. He fucked my ass brutally, leaning his head in to bite my chest making me work to accept his hunger.

My hands were released and he pulled my legs around him. Using his strength he carried me to the bed, pinning my legs over my head. He slammed his hips into mine hard as he went crazy pile driving his hard cock into my manhole. Each time I thought I wanted it harder he must have heard me, because he complied until I felt as if my butt was raw and bleeding from the impact of his hips slamming.

He was like a madman, because he fucked me until I thought I could not take anymore and yet kept going. I wanted to scream for him to stop and still he continued reaming my guts out with his cock. My asshole got sore from his constant action. The lube seemed to dry up and still he was plunging his cock. Then, with a mighty bellow like a wild beast, he came and collapsed over me. He lay there for what seemed like an hour, catching his breath. His cock hadn't even softened.

I heard the laces and felt the buckles being released and helped him remove the hood. I pulled his face towards mine, he permitted me to kiss him and he kissed back. He began to slowly fuck my sorely ravaged butt as we kissed. I sobbed in his ear out of sheer pleasure more than the pain. His tempo picked up a pace and within a few heartbeats he shot his second load up my ass. His cock began its slow withdrawal from my battered and bruised ass lips. He fell asleep in my arms and would have remained there had one of the household slaves not knocked and entered to inform him of an emergency phone call.

When he returned, the mood had been dispelled and he was all business. Before he dressed he did take a moment to look at his handiwork and show it to me. I was somewhat shocked to see my back covered in freshly coloring bruises. I'd been accused of being a glassy eyed tripped out slave, and this time I had to agree with them. The balance of the afternoon was spent in his office taking care of the emergency.

****

My ass was still sore from Master's loving attention earlier. Thankfully the cock now in my ass was not as big as his, and I could relax at least one part of my body while we awaited the guests and our part in the party. The first jolt of energy made my cock scream, as it seemed every tiny pinprick in my jock cast out electricity that sent Pete screaming and trying to hide. The response the guests saw was my body arching and my butt grinding into the cock slave at my rear. A jolt hit him by the way he sprang forward, throwing his rod into me. I can only hope our dance and duet added to their digestion and pleasure derived from the party, because we were being put through the wringer for their benefit. Visually we had to have been enjoyable. Two well-muscled rubber clad slaves locked together by bondage and sexual frenzy, driven by their control on electrical stimulation devices set upon our bodies.

I heard the slave at my rear when they disengaged his arms and cock from my ass. He had cum while I hadn't; the chance was there but for some reason I refused to submit to their game. It was my only way of having some control over my body. I chose that I would cum when I served Master, never with others.

J.D. kindly rubbed the circulation back into my arms, then led me into the den where Master was talking animatedly to the guests. J.D. signed that I should kneel near his chair. For a time he ignored me, making a point with his cigar waving in the air. Then he noticed me and began removing my headgear. Once the hood was off, he pulled me protectively between his legs, closed his boots around me as if to say to all in the room, *this is mine and I am happy with it*. A bowl had been placed near him filled with tidbits from dinner, those he fed to me while he listened and spoke at great length about the future of our slave trade among the general population of America. I honestly did not hear his speech, being more interested at that time was I on what he was feeding me. I was lost in the simplicity of cleaning off my Master's fingers and all the pleasure we both seemed to derive. Being caught up in licking his hands, I'd failed to hear a question directed at me by one of the guests. Master snapped his fingers which got my attention. "Slave, you have been asked a question, respond."

Turning towards the guests I responded politely. "Forgive this stupid slave. What was the question again, please?"

It was the Mistress who was speaking. She seemed as if she had one too many cocktails and she had a very pronounced lisp to her speech pattern. "Slave, help me win a debate. Who works harder on Buena Vista, is it Cappy who is extremely absent tonight or Master Hunter?"

I looked up to my Master seeking an answer, hoping he would give me a clue. Instead I got a light tap to my leg, "Go ahead, 9-745, speak freely," he prompted.

"Begging your pardon Mistress," I began, "but it would depend upon what my Master has previously indicated as to who works the hardest. His answer is correct, Madame."

The guests hooted and hollered over my reply, thinking it to be the funniest thing they had ever heard by the way they reacted. Someone even suggested that I was so well trained that I could not speak for myself. Another demanded to see both of Master's hands, suggesting that his hand was in my ass making my lips move like a puppet. I could have answered, but knew the answer would be incorrect and thus found it easier to side with my Master. After all, his will is my will.

The Mistress pressed me for the answer once the laughing stopped. "Madame if you are seeking what this slave thinks, this slave would have to say in all honesty," I paused for effect and they all seemed to lean towards me waiting for the answer, "it would have to be the slaves of Buena Vista that work the hardest."

Again my response hit their funny bone. However, it was the truth! Madame thought that suggestion was ridiculously funny. She rose to her feet with the help of one of her slaves, bade everyone a good night and retired for the evening. Others took that as a hint and did likewise. We, on the other hand, sat by the fire. Just the two of us lounging together watching the flames, quietly drawing in the warmth and pleasure of being together. Hunter and I were both in our own thoughts, locked in silence and just enjoying the moment. It's nice to sit between your owner's legs, head resting on his leg, one of his boots in my lap. I ideally traversed his boot with my fingers and his hand lightly rested on my shoulder.

After the trip to New Orleans, there was a major change in our household. Dan was moved from his quarters, down in the subterranean depths of the slave-training compound, into the main house. Slave mike and I were sent down with Dan to pack his household belongings. It must have taken too long because our Master arrived in a huff and set about showing all of us what to pack. Dan's boots and uniforms were taken to Master's suite. Dan's bowling trophies were tossed in a box, along with a few select items Sir found that were of interest, those items were taken to Master's blacksmithing studio by J.D. What was left was given by Dan to his friends, his reasoning was that he was moving up in the world. Master was not pleased by what Dan was saying to his friends. I could read his low bubbling anger in his actions. Whatever was left was sent into town with the next able body going on shore leave.

Our Master called a family meeting. All of us, Cappy, J.D., mike, Dan and I were on hand. We had a nice dinner and afterwards the roundtable discussion began. Hunter basically announced that he had taken another slave, Dan. Then they went on to explain what happened in New Orleans. "Finally it was Tuesday and Dan made his way to the Cafe Dumonde while I engaged in a stockholders' meeting. Ok Dan. you finish the story." Master turned the storytelling over to Dan.

Dan's Story.

I arrived late intentionally and found my quarry easily. Both of us having exchanged photos I knew what my quarry looked like, and he did, too. I entered the café, grabbed a longneck and leaned against the wall watching the crowd's reaction to my presence. Hoping that the bootblack would make the first move. I spied him across the room surrounded by a group of adoring clones. Most of them were eyeing me as if I was the cock of the hour.

I decided to get this show on the road and walked in his direction. He was so fucking nervous when his friends parted and let me through to where he stood. Real smart-mouthed little shit, he was. He looked down at his watch and told me I was late. I told him to consider himself lucky that I was here at all. So I took a long swig off my bottle eyeing him as I lowered the bottle, "You agreed to my terms boy. Let's get the fuck out of here!" I turned and walked away from him, only pausing long enough drop the empty into the trash and to look over my shoulder to order him to follow. When he did, I damn near shit!

He was a handsome guy actually. Not my type, but a bet is a bet. The boy was thin, had street tattoos all over his arms, shaved head with hungry looking eyes, piercings in his ears, and - if I saw it right - in his tongue. I led him out to a rental car. That seemed to put him off base right away. He gathered up his courage and asked where my Harley was. I made up a lie, telling him the carb needed an overhaul. He seemed to understand. Honestly, I did not really care if he did or didn't - something about this boy just made me want to stomp the shit out of him.

I opened the trunk of the car and ordered him to get in. He looked like he was about to back out until I caught his shirt in my hand, pulled him closer, back handed his jaw and shouted, "Get the fuck in, boot slave!" He squirmed so handsomely I said to him, "You stupid fuck, you said over and over I could do anything I wanted. This is where it starts." He looked like he was going to cry. Instead of another physical backhand I gave him a verbal. "If you are so fucking hot for boots, slave, why haven't you dropped to your knees to kiss them yet?"

The stupid shit began to stammer and back off. "You want me to do that here? In public where my friends can see me? They will never let me forget it if I did, Sir. Please Sir; can we wait until we get to the motel? Please Sir?" Fucking whiner! I kind of went off. Told him that was his third fucking mistake to think and told him either he got into the trunk like a good boy or he could run back to his sissy pals. I was slowly closing the trunk in total disgust when he hopped in and I slammed the trunk hard.

It was a warm day and had taken me about 35 to 45 minutes to get from the fishing shack due to all the traffic to the café. It took me over an hour with him in the trunk before I got back to the fishing camp. I parked the car before going into the fishing camp to find Master Hunter. Once I had dinner completed for the both of us. Master ate dinner while I ran out to drag a sweaty slave inside. We were to be identical twins for the evening. Sir had the guild make us immaculate white leather breeches that we wore with our Dehner's; police shirts; utility belts and we were stunning when he had taken me out to party with the herd of others.

I went for the boy while Master checked the appointments in the dungeon. He relocated an old fashion boot-blacking stand under a spotlight and hid from view.

I opened the trunk and found a sweat-drenched and angry boy looking up at me with terror in his eyes. He begged me to take him back to the Café and the little shit even whined as he begged. I pulled him out of the trunk while telling him he'd had his chance back at the café now his ass was mine to do as I wished. "You did say I could do anything I wanted this shouldn't be a problem. This is what I want slave!" I grabbed him by his shirt and drug him towards the shack. He started screaming, struggling and kicking out at me, tearing his shirt in hopes of fleeing. I kicked out at him, catching him in the groin. That dropped him to the ground, taking the wind from his sails. While down there I cuffed his hands behind his back. Using his tattered jeans as a handle, I lifted him and flung him towards the shack door. He hit it hard and fell stunned.

I knelt down placing one knee in the middle of his chest and grabbed the back of his head forcing him to look at me. "Look at me, boot fuck! Look! Pure black leather boots that have your name on them and I plan to put that tongue in overdrive. Can't get any better than this, boy." That's when I noticed he was hard as a rock and loving what I was doing to him. He absolutely loved my treatment of him and he was even trying to hump my booted leg that was holding him down. What a pig, he wanted it rough! I started purring in anticipation of what this night might hold.

I stood up, placed one boot in the center of his chest. "Do not disappoint me boot slave, or you'll leave here so fucking sore your breathing will hurt!" Lifting him to his feet, I sealed his eyes behind a sheepskin blindfold. Grabbing his waistband and opening the door, I pulled him into the dungeon and literally tossed him into the room.

Master was seated on the bootblack stand, dressed in his white breeches, Dehner's, a blue police shirt complete with the utility belt, gauntlet gloves and one of his big cigars. My entrance into the shack with bootblack being flung to the floor put a big smile on his face. All he did was sit there and watch me like a fucking hawk for any mistakes. It felt as if I was in the spotlight and everything I did was being judged which made me as uncomfortable as hell.

The boy, Jamie, was struggling to get to his feet, my boot swung, catching him in the ass. The impact tossed him like a ball over the concrete floor. Making a leap, I forced my big boots between his legs, aiming my boot at his sweat-wet crotch. When it connected, he exploded with a huge *woof*! Damn if he didn't close his legs around my boot, trapping it, forcing me to slam his cock and balls repeatedly until he released my boot and begged for more. The next half hour was a melee of boots hitting flesh and clothes ripping until I got the shit down to nothing but his BVD's. And those I ripped off him after I made certain my boot sole was well imprinted into his ass cheeks.

I let him lay there winded as I stomped off as if I was pissing mad, tossing shit and screaming at him as I left. In reality, I ran to change clothes so I could be the identical twin of Master Hunter. While I was changing Master was having his way with the boy. He wanted to be the good cop. What a farce. I did a number on that poor unsuspecting bootblack and Sir had to be nice to him. It's against my nature it hurt. While I was changing into glad rags Sir went to the boy. Scraped his hide off the floor, gave water mixed with piss to drink from a bottle and put him into a special leather hood with no eyes, only an open mouth. He got feisty when Sir started putting it over his head, but his boot down his boy-cock helped him come to terms.

Since I was taking longer than Sir expected, he took advantage of the lull to place the new meat into more comfortable wrist and leg restraints. Hell, he even had time to add a bar stretcher just so he wouldn't try to run. Then he bound his cock and balls tight with some old bootlaces and pulled his nuts down to the leg stretchers. That made him groan so good that I finally returned, looking hot as hell in breeches, boots. Sir backed away, taking the seat in the old fashion boot stand. We wanted to fuck with this lad.

I returned taking the side opposite Master on the boy and Master backed away as quietly as an elephant. Sir had to have a coughing fit to cover my steps. What a klutz! "Disrespect of your Master. That's going to cost you slave!" Hunter laughed. I made the boy put out his hands and feel the boots so he could get a reference. The change in wardrobe seemed to confuse him. I took that moment to add a leather collar and leash. With a tug, the boy climbed to his feet and struggled to follow my lead. We walked a short distance and I handed the leash over to Master, who was sitting all pretty-like in the bootstand, waiting for this moment.

I drew him towards my boots until he bumped into them on the foot rests, his hands went out to find them and he waited. I ordered him to kiss the soles of my boots and the boy jumped back like he had seen a ghost or a rattlesnake. I ordered him not to fucking worry about it. "Kiss the soles of my boots or I will rip the hide off your back. Do it now!" All it took was one swipe of Dan's deerskin flogger to get him back to the proper position. That boy knew how to clean the soles of my boots almost as good as 9-745 but he fucked up when he ignored the welting and skipped to the uppers.

I helped him retrace his steps by guiding his face around the welt inch by inch until he got the hang of it and could do it for himself. The boy tried to do a shoddy job on licking and sucking Sir's leather boots, but a couple of smacks with the flogger helped with his motivation. During a piss break, Sir swung down and let me take point, seeing as it was coming to the next phase of his re-education on boot blacking; polish application. Sir just did not trust this grunt to do a good job. Thankfully, he listened to my inner voices.

Master helped me with the boy seeing as he was on the floor and I was up in the chair. With Sir's guidance, the boy did a fairly good job on my boots, but I would too with a huge pair of size 15's slamming into my butt for any screw up. The boy knew he was in way over his head and sinking rapidly into a quagmire. I held the boy while Master rebound his nuts properly for the next phase of his challenge, boot polish application blindfolded. Master was seated in one of those big chairs they use in a church, all wood and no comfort. He was waiting as patient as he could to have his boots polished a crop slapping lightly on his boot like a cat's tail when playing with a mouse.

I pulled the boy between my legs and started talking to him. "Boot fuck, you are about to be tried. Seeing as you are the World's best fucking bootblack, we think you can polish our boots blindfolded and not get black paste polish on our white leather breeches." The boy swallowed so hard I could actually hear him and the color from his body seemed to drain down into his ankles. Our laughter only made him flinch, as if he had been hit. This made us laugh even more sadistically. God, we were enjoying ourselves at the boy's expense. The boy tried to weasel out by saying *Sir, I forgot my boot polishing kit*. We laughed again and gave him all he would need. I handed over a big tin of Kiwi Parade polish and his torn tee shirt, then I explained his handicap. He had to apply the paste to our boots using his bound nuts to rub the paste on to the leather. Hell, I had seen 9-745 do it plenty of times on Master's boots. This boy being the World's best, he should be able to do it blindfolded. But the boy started crying like a little baby and I gave into him. I even allowed him to use his fingers to apply the wax as long as it got rubbed in real good.

The boy did a kick ass job on Masters boots and didn't once get any black polish on his breeches. He was almost too good. I started wondering if the hood had eyeholes. Then it happened. The boy was starting to buff Sir's boots and failed to realize his rag had gotten soiled. That was all it took for Master to go ballistic.

Sir stood and the heavy wooden throne fell to the floor in a loud crash behind him; I went to reach for the boy to protect him and got caught by Sir's heavy boot then he started screaming. He screamed not at the boy but as me! "What type of worthless boot black did you bring me, slave? This can't be the World's best boot black that you promised me, is it, fucker! Look what he has done to my pants, boy, look!"

Both the boy and I freaked. I'd never had his anger aimed at me this way. Always he treated me with respect, but this was something else, it went deeper, it was as if he was channeling anger from other mishaps into this building rage and aiming it all at me. His face grew beet red as he shouted, making me feel like a worm. What was this anger all about? Did he know what I had been doing in the caverns on my days off? Did he know I had gone against our contract by sucking off other Handlers? How could he know? I had been so secretive after I had been almost caught that one time.

Hunter grabbed the boy and jerked him out of the way. He turned looking at me and ordered me to strip out of that costume. I don't deserve to wear it. It was the tone he used with me that really made me worry. He returned to the boy, removing his hood, making him fast to a set of pipes running up the wall and giving the boy a big bottle of colored water to drink. He turned back saw me standing in the middle of the dungeon with a face full of shock, wondering what the fuck was going to happen now. Knowing full well this was not part of the script and wondering where it was going to take me.

Hunter crossed the short distance, flipped open a butterfly knife and literally cut off my shirt. That got me motivated enough to strip down and stand before him naked, scared silly, head bowed and looking at my feet. "Since your boot black is a total fuck up, you're going to show him how it's properly done so his time here is not a total waste of my time. Drop to your knees, slave, and get that tongue onto my boots. Or so help me God, I will castrate you here!" At first I was stunned; then my cock got hard. He picked up my utility belt as he walked around me, doubled it and swung it at my ass. I jumped, looked into his eyes and realized just how dead serious he was that moment.

He had to have heard my knee bones cracking against the concrete because I dropped like dead weight to the floor and fell forward. Another blow to my ass made me move forward until my head was between his boots. One came down on my back. Without so much as an order, I put my head onto his boot and began kissing it as if my life depended on it. He was in one of his rare rages! Once in, there is no stopping him until he is finished destroying whatever is in his way. I was trembling out of fear what might happen in the next few minutes.

The blows to my ass were nothing. I knew what I could handle; I'd taken worse beatings from other Handlers downside. The boot on my backside moved and came down on my head. He ground my face into his boot. Even I heard him shout through the pain. 'You fucking broke the contract, you stupid shit! Now there is no going back, you are mine, nothing but a worthless piece of human flesh under my boot!' His boot shifted under my chin and lifted me to my knees. A gloved hand closed tight around my jaw and he turned my head. Commanding "See that bag? Bring it here, stupid. Bring it to me!' He pointed to a wheeled bag that was medium sized and stuffed by the protruding sides.

I ran and fetched it. Dropped back on my knees and held it out to him. "You only think of yourself. Not any more cocksucker, not any more! Hold the bag up high!" It felt like it had to have been at least fifty pounds. Slowly he unlocked the bag, unzipped it and flipped the flap right over my head, not giving me a chance to see what it contained. My arms started shaking as he was rummaging in the bag and his voice made me push it up until my arms where fully extended. Finally he found what he was looking for, pocketed some items and ordered me to set the bag down. Master held before my eyes a length of heavy logger's chain. Then he began, "Are you certain you can no longer be a Handler, Dan?"

I shook my head then replied, "Sir, I am lost without you, Sir." My cock got hard when he locked it around my neck with an equally huge padlock.

"Get up on your feet you no good slave and grab your ankles!" His finger lubed my ass just enough so one of his special butt plugs could be forced up my asshole. Straps running between my legs and around my waist locked it. My ass adjusted to the pressure as the plug walked deeper. In his excitement to make me his slave, we had almost forgotten the boy that I had brought to him. Hunter grabbed my chain collar and literally hauled me over to the bound boy. His hand shot out and caught the boy's upraised cheek then slammed into mine. "Now that I have two worthless boot slaves' attention, I am going to give you both a chance to please me; that is, if you can."

The boy was released from his bondage but not his collar. Hunter walked towards the boot stand and climbed into place. He grabbed the boy's collar, took his head into one hand and smashed the boy's nose into his boot. "This is a shitty fucking job. Redo it or I will hang your balls from my rear view mirror." Hunter grabbed my head and smashed my face into the other boot. "Your boot black fucked up. Remove the dried paste and redo that boot. Both had better be perfect or I will take your nuts, too! Both of you - get to work!"

He leaned back, fired up one of his old stogies and watched us work. I buffed the old paste to a high shine. Sir was not pleased and I felt a crop sting my back, then heard the boy yelp in pain. I dropped to my knees, lifted his boot gently from the footrest and applied my face to the under sole. The boy followed suit. He watched and copied whatever I did, and when I screwed up we both got punished. It went for what seemed like hours until his boots got a bright mirror finish. 'On your hands and knees slaves, put your heads on your hands and raise those asses,' Master barked as he climbed down from the bootstand.

We could hear him walking around, then I felt him as his boot slammed hard into my upraised ass. I must have risen up like I was going to strike him, because a paddle slammed into my butt hard; hard enough that I saw stars in my and my head went reeling. The boy broke his silence too as Sir bellowed, "This shine sucks, boys. Hell, my grandmother can do better shines!"

Master straddled the boy's upraised ass, pinning him in place with his legs and boots. One paddle strike followed another and another until the boy was shrieking and begging to him to stop. I tried to hold my place. Either I looked in his direction incorrectly or did something that displeased him because he laid that paddle onto my ass until I was howling as loudly as the boy. Master's anger seemed to grow in proportion to his size, like an atom bomb, his anger mushroomed and spread out. He lifted the boy from the floor, screaming at him. "You got paste wax on my white leathers, you little fuck!" He pushed the boy to the floor and Sir's boot held him in place. He ordered the boy to count.

Christ almighty, Hunter was furious! He wasn't joking; even if the black wax on his leather pants was part of the plan from the get go, his anger wasn't! Hunter was flogging the shit out of the boy's backside and the boy was doing his damnedest to maintain the count. When it reached fifty, Master shouted down, "Shut the fuck up or I will give you something to really cry about!" Hunter turned to me then, "Get your ass off that floor, faggot!" He didn't wait for me to get up, but latched onto my collar and pulled me to my feet. "You said that boy was the best boot black in all New Orleans," then he winked at me, "you know what I do to liars, don't you slave?"

I took my cue from him and dropped onto my knees and begged him to forgive me. Instead I saw a flicker of a thought pass from one eye to the other and almost knew something was afoot before he replied. "I am going to teach you two liars a lesson you both won't soon forget!" He went to the small suitcase and pulled out a slave harness, tossing it in my direction. "Put that on that liar over there and make it tight!"

The boy put up a struggle, wanting no part of being in a slave harness until I backhanded him once and whispered to him, "Don't say one fucking word, boy, or you'll get us both in more trouble than either of us can handle. Just do as he says!" Jamie stopped struggling and even helped get into the harness when he looked into my eyes and saw my fake terror. Of course it could have been the blood on my lip. Hunter helped me into my first harness. It was not the usual slave fare on Buena Vista. I knew as soon as I got home a much heavier and far more functional model would replace this light harness, maybe even a mule's harness. Seeing as I am as hard-headed as one of those animals.

Faded well-worn denim landed before both of us, with Sir demanding to put them on. We squeezed into these skintight Daisy Duke shorts. They were so short my balls hung out of the leg, and they were so worn that if we so much as farted we would have blown the ass out of the seat. White boating shoes dropped, almost hitting me in the face. "Put them on. These, too," when a pair of dirty white muscle tank tops was tossed near us. Mine hung almost down over my Daisy Dukes. He ordered us to our feet once the shirts were in place. His knife made quick work of the rotten cotton, exposing my harnessed ribs. He ripped the lower half of my shirt off, tossing it to the floor in disgust. The boy got equal time, then Master backed away, studied us, walked to his bag and returned with his shit-eating smile covering his face. Flourishing a big black magic marker, Hunter approached us. On the boy's shirt covered chest he wrote, *Worlds Worst Boot Black* before he walked over to me and wrote *Man Cunt Slave*. He stepped back to admire his handiwork, shook his head and pulled a choke chain collar from his pocket before the boy. "I am going to only ask you once before you are to answer," he starred down at Jamie, "do you want my collar and to be my slave?"

Jamie studied the floor before looking up and smiled, "Sir, more than anything in the world I would love your collar. But, I am already owned by another, Sir."

Hunter only laughed and patted the boy on the back. "You're too good to leave unattached for long. Help me, Jamie," said Master to the boy, "hold his arms for me."

Jamie proved to be stronger than he looked. Hunter bound my elbows at my back and secured my wrists. Jamie tugged my shorts down below my knees while Master bound my nuts in doeskin, then wrapped a bootlace around my cock. A leash was attached to my collar and Sir led us towards the exit. "Let's go meet your daddy, boy. It's high time my slave and I got acquainted with the New Orleans Shield mates."

Master opened the car trunk and ordered me into it. I felt betrayed by the turn of events, wasn't my surrender to him enough? Jamie lifted my legs and dumped me into the same trunk he climbed out of earlier. Before Master slammed the lid he told me he was ashamed of me. His message given, the door slammed and I was locked into darkness. They climbed into the front, turned on music probably to cover their conversation and we drove off towards what I hoped was New Orleans.

Lying there in the dark hot trunk listening to the whine of the tires on the pavement was a trip I did not want to have repeated soon. Master must have taken a perverse pleasure out of finding every railroad track, every pothole and every curve in New Orleans. Our original plan was to meet up with Shield mates at a bar on Bourbon Street, but as things had gone so far, even that could have been changed. The trunk light blinded me, but it was really good to see Master looking down. He helped pull me from the trunk of the car and steady me before he grabbed my leash and forced me to follow. We were nowhere near Bourbon Street by the looks and smells of the area. We were parked on grass, big tree limbs with Spanish moss hung over us. Motorcycles, vans and old beat up pick-up trucks seemed to be everywhere in rows. Rock and roll music that switched to Conway Twitty's crooning voice was heard coming from a ramshackle looking shed of a building. Old Christmas lights twinkled off and on around the roof of the place, making it look like a redneck idea of paradise. Men clutching women were partaking of pot and god knows what outside of the bar, a few stopped whatever they were doing to stare at our little parade then went back to getting it on.

Always the one to make a grand entrance, Hunter released my leash, grabbed me by the seat of my pants and tossed me over the threshold where I stumbled, skidded midair and fell hard on the floor. The room stopped dead in their tracks. Hunter entered, dragging a boy on a leash. You could've heard a pin drop by their reaction, eyes seemed to peel back to get a load of Master in his pants, boots and police issue leading a male on a collar with another on the floor struggling to climb back up to its knees.

Having gotten their attention he announced to the room, "I hear tell this is the baddest assed biker bar in the bijou! Got two worthless slaves that are here to earn their wings in boot blacking and I got two kegs on tap for any takers." Hunter walked over to the bartender, who handed him two huge steins; he held them up, "Two beers, and one yard of beer per hand for anyone who needs their boots cleaned by these worthless slaves. Any takers?"

This place was the pits. It stank worse than any of the old D.C. baths. The bar floor was covered by god only knows what. I could see broken beer bottles, peanut shells, cigar and cigarette butts, not to mention the unseen shit that lay below those layers of crud. A huge black nasty looking boot was pressed under my nose and I heard over the loud music a voice bellowing, "Hell yes! I'll take that deal!"

Hunter passed to the man the two big steins of beer while I was relocated, as was the boy in another corner of the bar. The greasy slob of a biker that Hunter had given the beers was eyeing both of us over the rim of one mug. Master released my arms but attached our leashes to rings set in the floor. "Which one you want working on your boots?"

The toothless wonder with the greasy long hair said, "Ah want dat one!" I got the lucky choice and, with a vicious slash from Master's whip, I was dropped back on the floor at the worst pair of grunged of boots in the world. They looked as if he lived in them, shit in them and I heard him saying his boots ain't never been cleaned. I was hesitant to put my face to them. Hunter got me in the proper mood with the aid of a few well-placed blows to my thighs and ass. "Pull over a chair and set down brother, the fun is about to begin," Hunter said.

I'd seen enough of Master Hunter's handiwork today to even consider crossing. I must have worked the better part of an hour on those shit-crusted boots before I could even get the crud loose. However, I counted myself real lucky because I could catch a glimpse of the boy with a line of boots waiting and his tongue mouthing a evil bitch's boots with disgust clearly written all over his body. I didn't dare look up; I knew my line was probably just as bad. Everyone wanted free beer at whatever costs.

Whenever one of us finished a pair of boots, Hunter would ask the owner if they were satisfied by our tongue action, the shine, anything to draw attention down to us kneeling and sucking leather on the floor in this slimy bar. If Hunter did not like the job that we did, he made certain we improved our style by laying my belt on our hides. My thighs and ass blistered after about four pairs of boots. The boy had to have been hurting bad, as he had done twice as many. I lost count of the boots I licked clean while kneeling on the floor of that god awful smelling bar before Hunter called a halt. He bought another keg and gave the balance of the remaining keg to those waiting in line. I hurt in places even I did not know could hurt and my mouth tasted like shit. We were permitted to gargle one beer between us before he lifted our leashes and we departed that hellhole.

When we got back to the car, he pushed us both onto the hood, face forward; making us both reach as far across the hood as was possible, then spread our legs. He growled, "Don't even dare to assume that I'm finished with you fuck ups yet!" Fuck! He was still pissed with the boy and me. He was so fucking pissed that he ripped off what little clothes we had on and took the belt back to our thighs and asses. It was bad enough to have that being done in the bar parking lot, but when the biker chicks and bikers encouraged him in his efforts that was all I could take. I moved to block one of his blows and got nailed for my trouble. Both of us rode in the trunk on the way back home, neither of us spoke the whole way. We were just too exhausted. Neither of us noticed that the car had stopped and that we were home until we were blinded by two flashlight beams aimed into our eyes.

Two well muscled policemen pulled us out of the trunk. Hunter was nowhere to be seen. When I asked about his whereabouts, a fist was slammed into my gut and I was told to shut the fuck up if I knew what was good for me. Both of us got cuffed right there on the city street. They did nothing to cover our nakedness from the onlookers. Then we were tossed in the back of the squad car. The cop called into base telling them they have found the troublemakers and were bringing them into there, 1020.

Lights and sirens blaring, we passed through the traffic at breakneck speed to where I hoped the police station would be. I was more concerned about the whereabouts of Hunter than I was about my nakedness or the way the boy and I both looked. I wasn't paying attention to where we were going. When I did notice, it was too late. We were not anywhere near a police station but down in the warehouse district. I started screaming and asking where they were taking us. They stopped the car, keyed open my side, pulled me out and shoved a penis gag into my mouth. This was not standard police issue; that I did know.

The older of the two grabbed my ass cheeks gave them a good squeeze then patted them. "I'll take this one, you can have the boy. We can teach them both a lesson they'll remember about being polite around authority." The bastard laughed as he pushed me back into the car and they drove on. We made a turn off the main road, slowed and pulled up before two huge metal doors. He honked his horn twice, then twice again before the door opened and we drove into a darkened warehouse.

I was pulled out of the back of the vehicle by the older cop. When I turned my head to see if the boy was ok having heard him cry out I got my face slapped. He barked a command, "Eyes forward and on your feet, meat!"

We walked a short distance to where a chain hung. I was attached to the chain, the gag removed, after which my arms were hoisted up over my head until I was just barely able to stand on my toes to stop the swinging of my body. I was scared to death, crying out, "What have you done with Master Hunter?" But the cop had disappeared back into the darkness of the warehouse. The only light, it seemed, was on me and I was hanging from a hook like a side of beef.

The warehouse felt huge. I heard the sound of leather hitting flesh in the distance, then a scream what I took to be the boy crying out. I was studying the floor just past the light. I noticed something shining there, and then it moved. I called out to whomever it was to show them. Master stepped forward. He looked up towards me hanging there and whispered, "What are you?"

I panted trying to grab enough air to fill my lungs, "Your slave, Sir."

He replied, "I am going to be harder on you than I have been on 9-745. What are you?"

"Sir, your slave, Sir!" I screamed in response.

He looked down at his boots then up at me again, "So it is witnessed. So shall it be. Take it down."

The lights in the warehouse were turned on as I was lowered to the ground. Everywhere around me were men and women, some of them from the bar tonight and others I hadn't seen before. Around us was a huge dungeon, the Stations of the Cross scattered all over the warehouse floor.

I permitted myself to continue downwards once my feet touched the ground until my knees kissed the earth, and fought the chains until my forehead was to the ground. Bowing humbly to my owner, my life and my reason for living, the Shield mates cheered. The New Orleans Shield mates were present to witness my acceptance of my new station in life. No longer a Handler. Now and forever a slave to my only Master, Hunter, as I have dreamed for over a year.

Dan stopped and the room feel quiet. It was Hunter, standing and motioning that we exit the boardroom that broke the stillness. En masse we adjourned to the blacksmithing studio. Once Cappy heard about the new addition, he seemed to get disgusted and left the room. J.D. followed soon after. Slave mike and I listened to their story as if it was the best soap opera we'd ever heard then we gathered Dan between us and escorted him out the back. Little did he know what was planned for him over the next few hours. Master followed the three of us to the studio.

Crossing the threshold, just about everyone grabbed a hold of some part of Dan and helped him onto the pillory. I got the pleasure of cutting his uniform from his body and giving him the last haircut he would need for a long time. By his cursing, he was not pleased by the changes. But this was the only way for us to help him realize he was no longer a Handler, only a slave.

The night progressed much as I remembered mine. Dan, who from here on out would be known as 9-777, received his collar and leg shackle that would mark him for a Buena Vista slave until time stopped or he was sold. He, like I, was disillusioned somewhat by the rapid changes once he had returned home to the mountain. Still, 9-777 looked stunning in his wet mule harness hanging by his wrists glaring as all of us withdrew into the side room.

Cappy and Hunter were discussing how they could disguise 9-777's face from being seen by his friends within the Handlers. They chose to keep his head locked into a leather hood until the leather guild could create a leather helmet that would conceal his face. Hunter thought it might be wise to add a brand to the slave, thus changing it from freeman to slave and giving the Handlers something other than the hooded head to be curious about. J.D. was sent into the forge room to set up the numbers and drop the brand into the flames. Hunter, mike and I took hold of 9-777, pulled his arms behind his back and bound them tightly. Additional ropes were added to lock him securely between two wooden support beams; it was imperative that he not wiggle from side to side when the brand was set.

Dan, 9-777, was not at all happy with what was planned. Master paid little heed to Dan's raving. After all, Dan had fucked up Hunter's well-laid plans in hopes of coming to serve Master quicker. A slave that thinks of its needs first is twice damned. The brand was placed to 9-777's flesh just above the right nipple, marking him for life as the slave he will now become. Dan could not hold back the scream that tore from his lips and echoed down the valley. He passed out once the brand was lifted.

When he awoke, his hands moved to his head there he found what his head already knew, it was encased in a heavy leather hood. Hooded he may have been, but he was with his family. Master Hunter was asleep on the bed and I was on the floor, waiting until my brother revived. Once he did, it was my job to awaken our Master. That had been his standing order when he had carefully rubbed ointments into his new slave's chest. Using my mouth on his cock brought Master awake quicker than calling his name. He looked down at me sleepily, "What's the problem, boy?"

"Sir, he's awake, Sir."

"Bring him to me and get in the bed yourself."

I lifted 9-777 and helped him as carefully as I could without touching his burned pectoral muscle, and got him into bed beside our Master. Hunter scooted over, taking an outside edge and pulling Dan between the two of us. Quickly as his fingers could spin, Master removed the hood and tossed it across the room. "Why do you boys always have to make it harder on me than it should be?" Hunter rose, pulled 9-777's arm under his back and had me do the same. Master grabbed a hold of my collar, dragging my face in 9-777's direction. Master leaned forward, kissed Dan deeply, raised his head and kissed my lips just as tenderly.

"Tomorrow 9-745, you and I will take this new slave 9-777 into the caverns below so it will be hooded. For that matter, 9-777 will not be seen out of this room without that hood locked over his face. Do you both understand?"

"Sir, yes, Sir!"

"Once the helmet is created Dan, your face will be locked away and you'll be taken to the fields. There you'll learn respect for your Master, since you could not respect yourself as a Handler. Consider this your punishment for disrespecting me by servicing seven Handlers while you were under my contract. They, too, are being reprimanded. All have been reduced in rank and, like you, they knew the rules. So your name is mud and most of them are thankful you are gone."

It was a good feeling to be lying beside my Master and knowing that Dan was between us. We were wearing our only permitted phi's in his bed. I was wearing hand irons while Dan was shackled, both hand and foot, to the bed. Master loves to hear us rattling in our sleep. Once Sir had gotten 9-777 bound as he wanted, Master resumed his place of preference between the two of us.

Drifting off, he pulled me closer and whispered into my ear, "Open your legs, boy." One of his knees pushed between mine and he snuggled closer. He loved using us like body pillows, only we are a lot warmer and a hell of a lot friendlier when he wanted something more than a hand job. Nothing finer in my book than to have a big old grizzly bear of a man wrapping me in his arms - one of his legs between mine and him breathing in my ear. It's better than home cooking and twice as cozy.

The alarm startled us awake. As he lay there brushing away the sleepiness from his eyes, I released Dan from his night bondage and went to start Sir's bath while Dan cared for Master's needs. Normal morning routine; a nice long blowjob and drinking Master's piss. Dan tidied the room while I bathed and shaved our Master, then it was back to Dan for dressing while I tidied the bathroom. Master went downstairs while we shaved and showered. We were to join him in a few minutes after taking time to place 9-777 in his hood and leg irons before joining Sir in the kitchen for breakfast.

Cappy joined Master at the table. The creature that looked like Cappy was not in his normally perky morning mood. This man pretending to be Master's friend was a snotty nosed evil twin with a grudge. Cappy sneezed brutally. Master told him to say it not spray it and laughed. However, the evil twin was not amused and told Hunter to fuck off. Then he laid into Master, "Leave me the fuck alone! I feel like shit and do not want any Goddammed mother hens watching over me. Check the mike's backside, he tried last night!"

Hunter looked over to mike, "Turn around mike, let us see!" Master whistled in appreciation while Cappy grunted his disapproval and shoveled in another spoonful of his crème of wheat. "Just trying to help you when I sent them to you with chicken soup, you used to like it. You sound as if you could use some fun in the sun. How about a nice all-expenses paid two-week vacation? You have a few weeks coming to you."

Cappy growled, "Tell me Hunter. Where in the fuck am I going to get the time to do that? We have a slave auction coming up this spring. Someone has to do the work. All you seem to do is gallivant around and add slaves to your household. On the other hand, I work for my living!" Hunter's eyebrows knitted together across his forehead when Cappy muttered the last comment. "Boys front and center!"

We converged upon our Master. "We have six weeks to do some planning on what we will be packing for a two week vacation. It will be over 90 degrees where we are heading during the days and can be cool at night. We will, after the slave auction is completed, be going on a vacation that will be covered by Castle Enterprises." Cappy, having finished his breakfast paused and looked at Hunter. "I will not leave Buena Vista unattended."

Hunter ignored the anger under Cappy's outburst, stood up, leaned forward on his hands while looking down at Cappy. "You'll go on this vacation one way or another. Play your little games with others Cappy, but don't even pretend to play them with me. I will make you pay dearly." Hunter ordered mike to feed both Dan and me, then send us into the office.

Cappy abruptly stood. The chair at his back fell loudly in the quiet room and as he departed the room on Hunter's heels said, "I do not need this shit from Mr. High and Mighty!" A door slammed shut. We could hear two voices bellowing over each other and then silence. I had finished eating my breakfast and stood before the door of Hunter's office. There wasn't so much as a sound coming from beyond the door. Scratching lightly on the door, I was ordered in. There on the floor behind Hunter's desk was Cappy kneeling, his hands locked to his ankles and Master talking to him quietly in hushed tones.

Hunter noticed my entrance, lifted an envelope and held it out in my direction. "Take this to Commander Schmidt and take the new slave with you on a leash. Wait for her answer and make certain you do not give that letter to any one other than the Commander. Do not let anyone else see that letter. Do you understand me 9-745?"

"Sir, yes, Sir!"

Our feet sprouted wings and we ran like a deer in the forest just for the joy of the run. We ran past slave gangs as they were being led up to work in the spring fields, down around Handlers still sucking down coffee and around a corner where I slammed right into Doc just outside of the Commanders office. Doc climbed to his feet and began verbally assaulting me as he pulled himself together. I apologized and tried to get all his papers off the floor and back into his file folders. While I was being berated for being a total lack-witted screw up of a slave, the door opened out stepped Commander Schmidt to see what all the commotion was.

Doc wanted my head on a platter by the way he was screaming and jumping around. The Commander thought different of that, but assured him that I would be taught to look around corners before I left her office. 9-777 and I were admitted to her office, once the door closed, she held out her hand. "Hunter's letter."

She read it then reread it in silence while pacing the room. She stopped in front of 9-777 who held a stance of superiority. She looked at me then back at 9-777.

"This one is new to me, what's its name, 9-745?"

"Sir, its 9-777, Sir. Master just added it to the household and plans to send it to be worked like a mule, Sir."

"Bow your head in the presence of a superior, slave 9-777." Dan did not move fast enough to suit her. She had been standing almost opposite him when she ordered him to lower his head and change his stance, which looked like a parade rest for the Handlers. Her boot slammed into his stomach so fast it made my head swim and Dan crashed backwards into the wall.

She lifted him by his collar long enough to look into his eyes. Studying them hard, she smiled. "9-777, that hood is only going to save your hide a short time. Once those you used to reach Master Hunter realize who is within that hood, you are going to suffer. Seven good men lost their well-earned ranks, a considerable amount of their retirement fund and pay due to your indiscretions. The brand is a good idea but your eyes will tell on you faster than your body. Keep them lowered at all times slave!"

She turned to her desk scribbled a note on a piece of paper put that into an envelope then looked up at me. She handled the letter to me, and then stopped me. "Wait, slave, if I know Doc he is out there listening and waiting. Grab your ankles!"

Twenty swats over my upraised ass gave me more than enough reason to fly back to Master's office in record time. I handed him the letter. In turn, he handed me a list of chores that would've been best accomplished in a week, all to be done today. Before I departed to fulfill my chores list, I humbly begged to speak freely to Sir about what Commander Schmidt had said to 9-777. He accepted her comments easily and took note to see if there was a way to cover his eyes.

Departing his office I ran into mike, who was freaking out about Hunters ordered dinner by the lake. Calming him down, we set about planning dinner and suggested that he beg Hunter permission to go to the Handler's kitchen for special assistance. Mike posted a note for all house slaves. Dinner was to be served by the lake, fire pits had to be set out, for the evenings were still cold. Cushions had to be taken for the asses of our guests, a table made of wood and concrete had been built down there long ago. A St Andrew's cross would be needed and six of the slaves for the auction would be serving this evening. Hunter took any and all opportunities to display our fleshy wares to our guests.

I had a huge armload of soiled linens in route to the laundry room when I saw Master escorting six guests into the lower domain. I knew the tour would be a major eye-opener, especially for one guest who thought the above operation was the sum of our estate's secrets.

Mike was in a tizzy, ordering food hampers to be brought from the below kitchens, preparing his side of the main course and getting things packed for the party by the lake. I had been sent ahead to lay out the fire pits, mound the wood and light the torch that burned brightly in the lake when guests were present. While there, I helped supervise three mules - one of which was 9-777 - as they set the awning over the table, set up the St Andrew's cross that had been ordered and generally police the area of anything that would be considered unnecessary for this evening's perfection.

Once completed to my level of satisfaction, the mules and I ran over to the logging area and they were put back to heavier work while 9-777 and I ran the mile home. Arriving, I found Hunter and his guests in the den. I moved briskly into the kitchen, dried off and sent 9-777 to the den with a huge tray bearing a coffee service. I followed afterwards with light snacks until dinner. Hunter had me serve, he took his coffee, sat down in his chair, lifted his boots and 9-777 crawled under into what should have been my place. The simplicity of that act did not go unnoticed by the guests, but then Hunter was pointing out the joys of owning property such as 9-777. I stood at my Sir's left side in the position of an attendant slave. (Meaning: hands at my back, head lowered with my eyes constantly looking to see who needed refills or anything.) It was my part of the soft sell, a way of detailing to these new wannabee owners the pleasure of having a slave. A slave, after all, is better than any butler, valet or maid, as we're trained to use our natural need to serve.

Chapter 6

Patience is not passive: on the contrary it is active; it is concentrated strength.
Bulwer

Having completed my chores for the party and inside the house, I went to do some of mike's, such as slopping the pigs, feeding the chickens and collecting their eggs. Heading back to the house I saw Cappy's pick-up hastily turn on the gravel road in a hurry to depart the mountain. I thought it kind of odd, as he'd just returned from a 24-hour leave. He'd been into the city to get medications for his cold, so I thought nothing else of it. I told mike when I brought in the eggs and went outside to do the chore we all endured - chopping wood for our fireplaces. It was a chore even our Master enjoyed doing splitting wood for winter. This was the best way to heat our cabin.

Mike had gone way overboard packing the hampers for the damn picnic as he tried to anticipate everything anyone would consider wanting. It looked like he had drafted every existing hamper on the compound and they were stuffed to overflowing. J.D. and I packed the mules, enlisting 9-777's back for the job as well as ten others. Slave mike must have told J.D. by the way he was behaving, he seemed more nervous than I had ever seen him. He even dropped one of the hampers, breaking a considerable amount of wine bottles in the process. I was asked to find Master to voice their concerns and I went off to find him. He and his guests were in the recreational hall going over lineage of some of the slaves. I entered the room quietly and prayed silently that he would see me. He summoned me to his side.

"Sir, begging your pardon, Sir. J.D. requests a moment of your time. There has been a minor emergency that he needs your assistance, Sir."

He excused himself from his guests and I held the door into the pantry through which he would quickly access the kitchen. There he found both boys and J.D. winded.

"Sir," said slave mike, "Our Master has left the premises. 9-745 saw him nearly run over some chickens in his hurry to get off the mountain, about two hours ago."

"Is that right, 9-745?" Hunter asked with concern in his voice.

"Sir, yes, Sir. He was driving like a madman, gravel shooting out from his tires like he was pissed at the world, Sir."

J.D. spoke up, "Sir, I have checked our cabin. The place is torn to pieces like he was in a hurry - or looking for something. He took his duffle bag, his leathers and left no note. That's not normal for him, Sir!"

Hunter looked over at the boys, "I can't depend on him any more. Wait until I get my hands on him!" Hunter walked over to the phone, dialed security. "Has Cappy come your way? Time? He did what? Did anyone get hurt? OK, I will send someone down; take him to the infirmary pronto!"

Hunter hung up and then dialed three numbers fast. "I need two men on the front gate and take a new pole down when you go. Get a small team of Handlers to repair it. We have had a breach. No, it has been contained but one of ours got hurt. Yes, now!" He put the phone back down. "That stupid little jackass ran through the gate. Louis said they tried to halt him but he just sped up and ran right through the wooden pole. A piece of the pole cold cocked Bill and he's bleeding pretty badly from the cut."

I could see Master's anger beginning to boil as he snarled, "Damn his hide. This time Cappy has taken one step too far over my line. Once I find his ass, this time he will be punished." Hunter was talking more to himself than the twins, who did not take this news well. I coughed trying to get his attention, it worked, and he looked first at me then saw the twins. "Ok, boys, back to work. Focus on the meal tonight and our guests. I will put out an all points bulletin to find him. 9-745, ask the guests to join me in my office I got some calls to make then you return here to help mike and J.D.." As Hunter departed the room, I overheard him sigh, "I am really tired of his dying queen theatrics."

With guests in tow, I escorted them into his office. He was talking to our police force down in New Market. "Carl, put out an APB. Cappy has flown the coop and I want his ass, pronto. No! Do not hurt him, just detain him. One of my men got nailed by his antics at the gate and is in the hospital. Thanks. Call me when he's caught."

The guests were settled in his office and I was about to go back to the kitchen when he stopped me. "9-745, I need a coke with lots of ice and ask the guests what they want." Orders taken, I ran to get him what he needed and returned to hear yet another conversation. He had called the local Shield mates in our surrounding area and asked them to be on alert for Cappy's arrival. Not to detain him but just return the call if he showed up.

"9-745. Tell the twins. The matter has been handled. Cappy will be found tonight and I will have a long heart to heart with him. Go help the twins and if you see 9-777 send it in here. Dismissed." One thing that has to be said for the twins, they knew their Masters; both Cappy and Hunter. These slaves were professionals and must have been used to Cappy's disappearances. Once I assured them by telling them what Hunter had done, they put their emotions on the back burner and set to pulling off this party by the lake.

Master and his guest of honor rode down to the lake in a rickshaw pulled by none other than this slave. Ever since I'd been in the stable I found this act of service to be one of the most gratifying for both Master and slave. However, the honored guest's boy/slave was totally insane when he found out he - like the other slaves - had to run beside the cart. The rickshaw was only for the elite.

The matter was squelched when Master grabbed a hold of his collar, added a leash with padlock and attached it to the side of cart. Master climbed in and commanded that I giddy up. I moved off, leading a small fleet of rickshaws down the path and half-dragging the still mouthing bitchboy at our side. In my mind I heard the Public Broadcasting Station announcer speaking, *Look at the temperament of the black widow spider, how she controls her victim. The creature does not even know the blood is being drained from it until it's too late.*

Cappy's unexpected departure had left its mark on my Master. He was unnaturally edgy tonight. When the boy started showing his ass, Master stopped the rickshaw, stepped down and grabbed the boy with not so much as a 'by your leave' from the boy's owner. Whatever Hunter said made the boy pale and shut up long enough to have a pleasant ride down to the lake. Torches lined the way and the handsome awning over the table along with the nearby fires set a wonderfully barbaric scene.

It was a fun evening even without Cappy's presence. Commander Schmidt, along with a few of her hand picked Handlers, attended tonight's dinner. In the past, Dan would have been with them; tonight he tended the fire pits and stayed away, not wishing to call attention if at all possible. None of the Handlers were so foolish as to refuse an invite to one of slave mike's dinners. Tonight was no different, as mike and the kitchens had gone out of their way to impress the guests. Mike had created a dinner that would have impressed or shamed most houses; bass bisque, smoked pheasants, a ton of fresh vegetables, home made breads, slave churned butter, wines and a most fitting dessert his specialty fresh raspberry tarts.

The dinner was almost ruined by the loudmouthed bitch when he did not find a table place set for him. He flat out refused to kneel and be fed by his owner, thinking he deserved better. Master made a sign to me. I turned and grabbed two mules, together we grabbed the mouthy bitch and placed it onto the St Andrews cross. 9-777 strapped it in place and added a gag. The balance of the evening was uneventful save for a few gagged moans from the thing on the cross.

During dessert and coffee fresh from our fire pit, Hunter asked for some music. I picked up on his cue and positioned two mules on either side of the bound boy. The mules were instructed to pinch the little shit along his body, not to leave any place without marks until it squealed and sang. The chamber music was very enjoyable - most so for the Top that claimed to own the piece of shit that was providing us with his lovely voice.

Dinner was about finished when Hunter excused himself and asked Schmidt to join him by the fire pit. He requested her to act the hostess while he was away; there was a matter he had to take care of immediately. She did not even question him, knowing too well the recent events of the day. Commander Schmidt returned to the table just before Hunter called to 9-777 to follow him. They went together, leaving me to tend to chores, the dinner and the guests.

Hunter hates electronic intrusion at any private function and will be the first to destroy a cell phone to his dinner table or event. He believes there's a time for work and a time for play, but never at the dinner table. Often I have seen Hunter act upon a feeling with positive results. If anyone stays around here for long, they eventually get used to the idea that anything you do wrong or have a problem with, Hunter will know even before you mention it to him. It gets real spooky some days when he is online with his talents.

Hunter stopped before slave mike and gave orders that he and J.D. were to sleep in his suite tonight. While I watched my Master and the new slave walk up the road with 9-777 holding a torch to light his passage, Commander Schmidt was speaking. "Honored guests, Master Hunter has some family business to attend to and has asked that I offer to you some of our private stock for your entertainment tonight. One of our entrances is only a short walk from here, when you are ready, we can walk off some of this meal and this will give you an even broader perspective of our compound.

"Oh, Mr. Brooks, Master Hunter has suggested a mule that may be to your liking. One less argumentative than that creature you brought with you. Please do not worry a moment about him; he will be taken care of this evening as befits his rank. Rest assured he will be kept securely until you claim him tomorrow." Almost affectionately she put her arms through two guests' arms and led them into the dark beyond our torches. That was when it dawned on me these were potential buyers. That was why they got the royal treatment and the tours. If they had been real friends of Hunter's or

Cappy's, we would have eaten in the cabin instead of here on the lake.

We ate tidbits of leftover food while policing the area. Slave mike was good at keeping a tidy kitchen and, whenever a course had been finished, packed the soiled plates then had them returned to the main house. There at the main house they would be cleaned by other slaves and replaced in their cabinets within the pantry. With only had one dessert course to actually clean up afterwards, we would be home before the guests even found their way onto a playground. We quickly extinguished the fires and made our way back to the cabin so we could enjoy the leftovers before the cleaning crew got to them.

We'd just had a good meal, gotten the soiled linens into one of the dryers when we heard the front door creaking open. It was too soon for one of the guests to arrive home or so I thought and went to check it out. Poking my head around the kitchen door I found Master Hunter entering the door without 9-777. He looked bone weary and sad by the looks of his eyes. He saw me, signaled that I should come to him and whispered, "Where are the twins?"

I replied, "Sir in the kitchen, Sir."

"And the guests, where are they, slave?"

"Sir, still within the underground Sir."

"Excellent! Go get the boys and have them join me in the den. Bring me a cigar, a beer and a double of bourbon. I can sure use it tonight." He laughed when he was looking at me, "Was the mousse good?"

Sheepishly I looked up from beneath my eyebrows to make certain he was smiling. "Sir, yes, it was good Sir!"

"Go get the boys and wipe your face before you return."

We joined him in the den. Mike, the ever watchful mother hen, brought him a sandwich. "Please Sir, eat. I watched you picking at your plate all night pretending to eat. We are all worried, but you must keep up your strength so we can be strong. Please, Sir, eat."

Hunter scuffed the boy's head lovingly and took the sandwich. He took a huge bite; started chewing as if ravished then paused took a sip of his beer, "If you want something go get it. No booze, but something to eat. If I didn't eat, neither did you."

The offer was just too rare. We ran to the kitchen like it was a party, and returned with a big bowl of fruit and glasses of orange juice. Hunter had finished his sandwich and was sipping on his bourbon by the time we were all seated around his feet. "The Virginia State boys picked up Cappy and turned him over to our gang of thugs. I found him in New Market in the police holding cell and had a long heart to heart with him there. He was not a happy camper! I got it from him with both barrels and I let him vent all his frustrations unchecked.

"First of all. J.D. and mike, to put you at ease; Cappy is still with us but is going on a leave of absence immediately. After what he said and what I said we both need a cooling off period. He has not taken a vacation for as long as I have known him, so the next three weeks is something that he's earned. He will be back with us in time for the great vacation to the South Pacific.

"Twins, you have a choice. You may stay at your cabin while he is away. I would prefer for this weekend that you stay here in our cabin. Afterwards we can play it by ear. My home is your home; this you both should know well by now. J.D., you have been Cappy's shadow slave for too long. It is time for you to be elevated. You'll fill his boots while he is away. Cappy actually said that you can run this place better than him and have been because he'd been shirking his duties due to his frustrations.

"One thing J.D., the old lady that is with us this weekend. I highly recommend that you get into her good graces. She operates one the oldest and best medical schools in the States near her Shield. I can guarantee that if you can fill Cappy's boots with the farm that I will personally see to it you attend that school when you are ready. Mike, you'll attend school, too. One more thing, Carl and Pappy picked up two more runaways. They are undergoing reorientation and will be placed with Doc for rubber transformation; there may be two new rubber creatures underfoot here for a while. Be attentive to them and keep them busy, do not let them stop working until I call a halt. Now that everything has been said and done. Leave a light on for our houseguests and will one of you please help me to bed. That bourbon has done the trick, I am feeling much better!"

I couldn't say whether it was the additional company in the bed or the bourbon that he had drunk last night, or the fact that he snored like a freight train all night. But Hunter woke up in a randy-ass mood. The sheet was tented when I rolled over on my back. Within my mind's eye I could look down upon our bed and the view was something from out of our past. Three collared slaves encircling their owner, all like kittens snuggling together to get warmth from each other. Pillowing his feet was my responsibility, with mike to the left side and J.D. the right. We were awake, waiting, exchanging looks one from the other. Waiting until we saw the signs of him awaking, and then the debauchery began. It was full frontal assault on our owner and Master.

Rolling over, mike and J.D. lapped their way towards his nipples, each laughing as they tried to keep his powerful arms pinned to the bed. Sir lifted his feet and opened his legs, inviting me to work my tongue between his toes and up. His moans became very audible, which signaled to all that we had to renew our efforts. I drove my tongue under his balls he elevated his ass so I could get what I sought. J.D. was working on mike's butthole as I did a headfirst dive between Hunter's butt cheeks until I found gold with my tongue. Now we had our Master at our mercy.

Each of the twins had served Master Hunter as his slave when this slave was elsewhere. All of us knew how to please this man, and today all of us wanted to drive him fucking nuts with our combined actions. It was rare that the three of us got together in his bed, so we decided last night to jump his bones one way or another.

I rose up for air and found mike crawling across Master's chest, lifting up his ass in preparations for mounting that precuming monster we all loved to have rammed into us. We must admit we we're spoiled, we love his cock. But mike really loved his cock. When mike got Hunter's cockhead aligned, the boy just dropped like a dead weight until Hunter's balls were sucked into that boy's hole.

J.D. and I crawled up to hold Master's arms to the bed as he was reaching for mike. This was, after all, our rape scene. We pinned him to the bed and began nibbling on his neck, chest, nipples - whatever flesh we could find to put under our mouths until he began crying out at us. "You little bastards!" He laughed, "Oh God, mike, what you can do with that ass. Damn you all!"

Slave mike had a sadistic side to him by the way his was treating Hunter's cock with his ass. Mike would rise almost off the thing then inch down slowly, then inch up, pumping his cock with his ass muscles clenched tight. The boy was gifted with how he could make that ass work. Mike leaned forward as if to kiss Hunter on the lips, then arched his back, slamming down on that cock of Hunter's with such gusto the bed rocked from mike's assault. At one point, mike twisted around on Hunter's cock while spiraling upwards then slammed back down, making Master roar like a wounded lion, screaming, "Evil slaves!" Then he burst out laughing and closed his arms around me, pulling me to him forcing a kiss before his hand closed around my balls.

J.D. had moved off Master's arm in preparation for Hunter's attempt to take control away from us. Master's legs grabbed purchase in the cotton sheets was just lifting off the bed when J.D. buried his tongue eyebrow deep into Hunter's ass and darted in for the kill. Master tried holding mike up but succumbed to the tongue and mike signaled an arm waving victory.

Mike decided to bring it home and quickened his pace. At first mike had only been toying with Hunter's cock as if it was just a peppermint stick he might have been sucking in and out of his mouth. Mike turned serious and began pounding his ass into Master's hips fucking, for all it was worth while we kept Hunter's hands occupied.

Our Master's voice began at a low rumble, picked up volume like an earthquake drawing nearer until it reached the sound of a speeding locomotive. We stopped all action and even held our breath. That sent him into a fit of cursing as he tried to toss J.D. and I off his arms to get at mike. Mike tilted back his head and laughed. "You are my captive, now, Sir!" The he resumed his journey more slowly than before, making Master beg like a wounded animal. Having heard this we all cackled like witches around a bubbling pot.

Not getting his way, Master's hands turned vicious as he worked them under my legs until the found what he sought. With a lunge, he grabbed my nuts, closed his hand around them and squeezed. My response was a sick yelp and a call for help.

J.D. started chewing hard on Master's nipples while I fell forward onto his chest and grabbed a mouthful in passing. Another nipple snared and being ground into raw meat by two hungry horny slaves, Hunter had to release me to get at J.D. and I withdrew to the nether regions for a renewed attack on his rich cleft. Like a worm working itself between heaving mounds of flesh, this slave crawled between his legs and took both his balls into my mouth. adding my teeth to J.D.'s attack on his nipple. Together we had him begging, "Stop! Don't, stop, stop!" Master bellowed, "If I get my hands locked around your nuts J.D., I'm going to…aargh."

Mike stopped again, allowing us a chance to grind our teeth and make him suck air in pleasure. We definitely knew our man, he was so close to cumming, if we weren't careful he would blow his load and we wouldn't have our small victory. Master had pushed himself up on his elbows during the lull. "Oh, you evil little bastards, which of you came up with this idea? When I am out of this I will make all of you pay for this and if I have my way, and I do, we will do it again. My way!" He fell back when mike leaned his weight into him and burst out laughing while kissing mike. Three sex-crazed slaves attacked their Master, demanding he blow his load into mike's open manhole.

He ordered J.D. and I to his nipples. "Chew them like you mean it, you fucks!" he said through panting lips. He moaned in pleasure as we expertly were expertly driving him towards climax. "Harder, mike, harder," he bellowed, and mike's slap-slap turned blazing fast and more forceful. The bed shook under his ass slamming into Hunter's hips, forcing his cock deep into mike's butt. Hunter screamed, "Oh, God, I'm coming!" at the top of his lungs, which sounded like a bear growling as his cock gave up its juice. Mike rose up and slammed his butt down once, then twice and collapsed over onto Hunter's heaving chest.

We pigs were down on Hunter's cock, slurping up the ass juices before his cock even pulled free from mike's butt. We heard Master grunt. That gave us our cue, he was pissing his load into mike's ass. As mike slowly rose, Master's cock fluids flowed from his well-ridden rear and down Hunter's cock to be sucked by the awaiting tongues at the base of his obelisk. Nectar from our god, sacraments bestowed upon the humble. It was a feast that put J.D. and I over the edge, we exchanged kisses and our tongues could not get enough of Hunter's cock nectar. We ate our Master's cock then dived into mike's open asshole, seeking more of our God's juices. He let us nurse his cock until he came again.

We laid by his side resting from our efforts when he began to speak. "After considerable thought, I have made up my mind. You two twins bunk here while Cappy is off playing like the horny goat we all know he can be. Jesus mike, I could eat a horse after all that you three put me through. Go fix us some pancakes, sausage, gravy and whatever else you can find in the kitchen. I believe we all deserve a good meal after all that exercise. Besides, today is going to be a tail buster!"

Mike climbed to the edge of the bed, grinned his big toothy grin, and put his hand on our Master's chest. "Sir, it has already been a tail buster. You may go back to sleep. The day is done." He quickly sidestepped Hunter's reach for him and laughed. "Breakfast for an army in about 30 minutes, yes, Sir!"

Then mike turned to us, and began issuing orders, something totally out of his nature, "J.D., you bath him, 9-745, lay out his day-wear, skin tight leather and lace up boots. While they are bathing, strip this bed and let it dry. We have been pigs!"

While they bathed, I ripped apart the bed, laid out the new linens for later application and pulled out suitable clothes, his knee-high lineman's boots and red sox. Finished, I knelt to await his return and to dress him. I could have been upset to have shared my bed with two other slaves, but thought nothing of it. We were his to command and use as he saw fit. If he was happy I was happy.

He entered the room and stopped before me. Using my head to balance, I pulled him into his leather pants, applied his red socks and helped him into his lineman's boots before rolling the tops of the socks over the upper shaft like he prefers. I stood, helping him into a leather t-shirt that he wanted, and laced the sides. Adding a belt to his pants, I slipped his cock and balls into the leather pouch he called his jewel bag before slipping that into his pants and dressing him down his left leg. I dropped and kissed his cock, then dropped lower to kiss his boots. He was now ready for whatever the world would bring him.

Just as he was to depart the room, J.D. and I were ordered to clean and shave before we joined him in the kitchen. We had twenty minutes to get ready and I was to shave J.D. As the elder, J.D. went first with the shower. I patted him dry, then gave him a quick shave with a dry razor. He returned the favor for me. We actually beat Hunter's time and arrived in 17 minutes, only to find him not in the kitchen but in his office.

Exiting his suite, we damn near ran over a groggy guest, Mistress Jan. I was sent ahead to return with a carafe of coffee and a mug while J.D. saw to her needs. She joined us for an informal breakfast at Hunter's request. We all had to stifle a giggle when, as she was sipping her coffee, she asked if we had bears up here. Master wondered why and she told him that she had been awakened by the sound of a bear roaring. He put her fears to rest saying that we rarely had bears here this time of year, as they were still in hibernation. That seemed to soothe her ruffled feathers.

J.D. was trying to help mike and me in the kitchen, but was getting underfoot and being an absolute nuisance until Hunter called him over to the table. "J.D., sit and join us. Quit hovering around the slaves. They know what to do and how to fix our breakfast. Take Cappy's seat!" Hunter turned to Mistress Jan by way of explaining why J.D. was breaking protocol. "J.D. is taking over Cappy's duties while he is off the mountain on an errand for me. Besides, the boy is due elevation and I was thinking. Columbia has a good medical school; we may be sending him down there for the balance of his training if he proves he can handle responsibility."

Mistress Jan blew a gasket (and her coffee) halfway to the other side of the table at mention of the Columbia Shield and its medical school. She became venomous when she spoke, calling it a Voodoo practicing school for witchcraft, not medicine. However, her school was the best in the nation, one that even non-slaves attended and fought to purchase a seat in its halls.

Breakfast was served, thankfully. Between mouthfuls of syrup soggy pancakes, Hunter suggested that they speak privately in his office after breakfast. She agreed. "Besides," he said, "I want damn good trading terms on that man, he's one of my finest."

She laughed, and then sighed deeply. "You are such a controlling bastard Hunter. Is that why I love you, that we're like two peas in the same pod?"

He sopped up a big bite of pancake, making the fork do a complete circle as he chased the last drops of syrup before he spoke. "Controlling bastard, am I? What does that make you, my dear?" He filled his mouth with the last bite and chewed with relish as she chewed on his words.

She laughed lightly, "Ah, Hunter, my love. You simply do not have the right equipment to please little ole me?"

He opened his mouth as if to play 'see food' and stuck his tongue out at her. "I got a tongue don't I, girl?" He was doing his best to bait her and we tried our damnedest to keep silent. Mike and I ate our pancakes in the kitchen while poor J.D. had to eat his on the front line, with those two bantering like two young roosters trying to outcrow the other.

"Yes, Hunter. But dear heart, you would want to use it on your terms and not mine. One of us would have to bottom, and I know I'm not going to do that after all I've gone through to claw my way to the top. Nor will I permit you to bottom. Although it has been a passing fancy of late to see you riding me with that big old cow tongue of yours, it would be fun to see the great white Hunter trapped in his own net."

I had just taken that time to fill everyone's coffee cup when Hunter, looking over his mug at me, mumbled, "Oh, but I am trapped."

She looked in my direction and saw me blush. Her laughter was warm and pleasing to hear when she looked at him. "Trapped, huh? How nice to hear that coming from you. It's about time, my friend." Hunter slid back his chair, I ran to help her with hers. "It is a charming one, that's for certain. Tell me about how you made it into your glove. Now that I have seen it, I want one too. It's absolutely delicious." They departed the room none too soon for my tastes, as they were talking about me.

Hunter paused at the door. "J.D., send one of the others into my office when the other guests are awake and have had breakfast. Put a heavy collar and arm binder on 9-745. I will need him about 11:00." Master put one foot over the threshold and stopped abruptly. "Sorry J.D.. Give me a few days to get used to your new rank. Use 9-745 as you see fit, bring it as I have asked when its near 11:00. Thanks J.D. Oh, by the way. Mike, that was one hell of a stack of pancakes you fed me. Next time I get to feed you."

We laughed as he stepped beyond the door, taking Mistress Jan into his office where they could discuss J.D.'s education and what we of Buena Vista might have to exchange with her Shield for his education rights. J.D. sent me about the house policing and tidying up after our guests. When they poked their heads out of their quarters, a coffee carafe with fresh brew was awaiting their pleasure just over the threshold of their suites. I maintained a low profile, working quietly in other rooms without making undue noise. Dusting bookshelves, moping floors, waxing the furniture, generally cleaning up the house trying to get a day up on the next week's chores.

J.D. found me in the recreational room. He'd found what I had done my damnedest to bury, deep into the closet; Hunter's favorite toy and not mine. Arm binders! The bastard was going overboard to make an impression on our Lord. He had found the shoulder coat with two individual sleeves. Each sleeve got laced up tightly before being laced together across my back. Straps over my chest locked the sleeves in place and, with the addition of another strap from my hands to my nuts, there was no way I could escape without help from outside hands. As much as Hunter loved this toy, I hated it. But he would always find it when he wanted something to show off to guests.

Damn if J.D. did not find the most brutal of collars as well. What had I done to him that he was treating me this way? He locked the old Victorian style collar around my neck. It was designed to force my head in a humbling position, always watching my feet or Sir's crotch. Which wasn't all that bad, since I had a great view. As if this wasn't enough, he'd found Hunter's private stock. J.D. added the face straps to my head, buckling them tight before adding Sir's mouth-watering codpiece to the straps. Even he laughed like Hunter at my expression as my eyes glazed at my owner's scent.

Trusssed up like the Christmas goose, J.D. knocked on the door to Hunter's office at 11:00 sharp. He entered first, waited until the talking stopped and turned when Hunter commended him. "Good work, J.D. - I wondered where he'd hidden my favorite toys. Thanks for finding them." Sir rose from behind the desk, walking towards us at the door. "You and Mistress Jan need to talk without my influence."

Hunter and I left the office together. We dropped down the steps into the cavern. Once there, he dropped the leash and let me follow him as I'd been trained. He led me to Schmidt's office, where he spoke to her about the new recruits and if the transformation was complete. Then he spoke to her about Dan, 9-777. "Katherine, only you and I know about his aptitude test. We both knew this could happen. The psychological test showed that he was borderline, but leaned more towards being a bottom than a top. It was worth a try. We did our best by him, Katherine." There was a long silence between them. "Now he is where he belongs; with his Master where he always wanted to be.

"How are the men that got reprimanded? Any problems since the hearing?"

"I feel sorry that they got caught up in this, as it was actually my mistake that he was placed here instead of where he needed to be. I think I can help them recover some of their money, but I may have to put them on special detail." Hunter searched her face for a few minutes, "I want these two new recruits worked overtime, pushed until they drop. This is the only way I can get into their heads and make them realize just how fucked they are. This one taught me to remove the kid gloves. Love must not be a factor when you're training a slave!

"Think about this Katherine. If you think it will work, arm them with stun batons and have four of them escort the new slaves into my presence when Doc is finished with them. It's high time they meet their owner!" The door at Hunter's back was banged heavily, then burst open as a black shiny body stumbled over the threshold and fell with a rattle of chains to the floor. It was a Vulcanized rubber thing with Doc standing on the threshold, grinning like a lovesick cow.

Hunter closed the distance between the black thing on the floor and dropped to one knee to study it. "Good work Doc. Is this the suit or is this one it is borrowing until its suit is ready for occupation?"

Doc's laughter erupted and I cringed, remembering his talents applied to my raw torn skin. "Just thought I would drop by and let you see one of them. The suit is borrowed. It will be about another week before all the pieces cure out for both of them. You did say you wanted them both in heavy rubber suits, yes?"

"Hell yeah, Doc! I want it so their own mothers wouldn't know them. Lock their cock and balls behind a watertight flap, catheterize their cocks too. I want total control over everything. Nothing gets in or out unless I say so. Can you do that for me, Doc?"

It was as if Hunter had just given Doc someone's death warrant by the smile that occupied that evil fuck's face. He seemed to have a grudge against these two new recruits. Doc spoke quietly, in a whispered snake-like voice. "Thought you would see it my way, Hunter. They both need to be punished severely. No one does that to you and lives to talk about it, no one!" Doc made the sign of a knife being drawn over his throat and laughed. "We just finished making their body casts. I plan on putting them into a suit like none other, even mine. A suit molded just for them and using their own body to make the casting fit. I can guarantee both of them will remember this lesson. Once a slave. always a slave. Besides, bondage and pain will change their minds. Just like it did that one behind you."

"One more thing Doc. Put copper connections into their codpieces. I just might need to start a fire somewhere. I want to fry their nuts as I see fit. After all, their nuts, like their whole bodies. minds and souls, are mine to use as I see fit." Hunter kicked at the rubber thing on the floor, his boot made it grunt. Instead of crawling away, the body rolled closer, almost imploring Sir to kick him again. Hunter turned away in disgust. He grabbed up my leash and stepped towards the door, but paused to ask, "Doc, when will they be ready? I need them for an experiment as soon as possible."

Doc paused and counted his fingers before replying. "I will have them at your door on Sunday next week. Is that soon enough my Lord?"

"You are a good man, Doc. That will give me plenty of time. See you later. Doc and Katherine, give me a call." Hunter looked in my direction. "Heel slave!" We walked down the corridor in the opposite direction we had come. Down a long corridor lined with small shields of the crafts guild beyond each door.

We stepped into a small office and were greeted by a leather craftsmen working on a pair of chaps at a table. "Good day, Master Hunter. How can our craftsmen be of service to you today?"

Master pulled out a folded paper handed it to him. As he unfolded it, he whistled in anticipation, "Sir, I take it you want total encasement. Laces on sleeves, torso and legs?"

Hunter cut in, "No, I have that already. I want him sewn into the suit. Do you think you can do that for me? Let him have an opening zipper at his crotch if you must, so I can have access to his cock, balls and ass. Oh, and fit it with Dehners, I want this one marked as my property well. See to it the Dehner's have an additional strap at the ankle so I can add a padlock, and another one around the top. Once this piece of meat is wrapped up, he will not be permitted out for a month or more. Can it be done, Ralph?"

"Most assuredly, Sir." The man laughed and pointed in my direction, "It seems to like the idea. Look at its cock, Sir!"

Hunter turned. "That's next on my agenda for today. Thanks for pointing it out Ralph."

"Sir?" What is your timeline for this project, Sir?" Asked Ralph, the portly old bearded bear of a man.

"You have about six weeks to have it completed. I will send it down tomorrow for the measurements, thanks." We left the guild area and moved into more familiar turf. Hunter and I traversed the length of about 4 football fields before he found all the answers he needed. Then he went to check on the foul-mouthed spoiled boy from last night. A Handler was called over to open the cell; the boy was lying in a bed of straw in the corner. When he saw Hunter he made as if to crawl away.

Master turned to the Handler, "Get it to its feet!" The boy was lifted by its neck to stand before Hunter, who eyed him carefully - like a man checking a horse for its worth. Having made up his mind, he turned to the Handler. "Ok, here is what I want you to do to that whiney-ass bitch. You'll need an apple or an orange and tube socks for this punishment. Hand and Glove: The Pit of his glam wardrobe, dirty him up a little, rough him up some, bind him spread eagle and beat his backside with the fruit until you have mush. Only his backside and not over the kidneys. Once that is done, find a clean cell or have him clean a cell, doesn't matter. Put its worthless hide on a t-bar kneeling, lock it down tight and give it no more than an inch for movement."

Hunter pulled the Handler aside outside in the corridor. "I will be trading one of our oldest mules for this piece of shit. I want that boy to be as foul-mouthed as it can when its owner comes to see it today. Understand me, no visible bruises; the fruit will give him deep tissue bruising that will show up next week. It's what I learned to do to get a confession before they went to the judge. Help the boy be all that he can be. I want him abusively evil to his Master. You have until the dinner bell for this to happen; afterwards I will be bringing his owner here. Do you damnedest, Handler!"

I was shocked! I had never overheard Master conspiring against another in this way. As we walked off, leaving the boy and Handler to get acquainted, I wanted to ask him so many questions. He must have known my inner turmoil as he began speaking his mind. "If I am right, and I usually am, that boy is part of a gene pool that I want utilized for our benefit. He looks like a distant cousin of that old whore dog William. If he is who I think he is, he will be worth a fucking fortune once trained like you! Imagine selling him to a foreign government for a few million! Hot Damn, what an embarrassment!"

We exited by moving a shelf that was in the pantry and entered the kitchen. Mike smiled at us and asked if he could take it off my hands while Master was poking around in kitchen. "Lunch looks good! Got any samples?"

Mike laughed. "For you, Sir, anything."

Hunter's eyebrows seemed to knit together, then he looked puzzled. "Why so much food mike we only have a handful of guests?"

"Sir, you may have forgotten. This is the third Sunday of the month. Handlers will be joining us for lunch so we can discuss the upcoming changes you requested, Sir. This time my kitchen and the one below have made enough food to feed those with bottomless pits for stomachs. I won't allow those people to go hungry. Besides they whine badly when they think someone has something the other one doesn't." Mike laughed, shaking his head. "Worse than children when it comes to eating."

Hunter laughed. "Then I had better wait for lunch. A banana - that will tide me over. We may have sold that old mule 5-493 to the new houseguest last night. Cross your fingers and toes, he may trade in his loud-mouthed bitchboy for that old mule. He will bring us a tidy profit once we determine his gene pool." Master grabbed a hold of my leash, and then turned to mike, "Where are the guests?"

"Well fed and in the smoking room. J.D. and Mistress Jan are on a long walk around the grounds. Sir, do you think J.D. will be accepted to her school?"

"Mike, if I have any say in the matter, he and you'll be attending school in another year. I want my boys to be the best that they can be. Besides, you two richly deserve all the benefits that Castle Enterprises can shower down upon you." Hunter had crossed the distance between he and mike, taken the lad's head in his hand and pulled him closer when he spoke.

There it was, proven again. Hunter's paradox in action. One side brutal, cold and calculating, the other side warm, loving and tender. I love this man so much, because I fear him just as much as I love him. Lost in my own thoughts, I failed to hear him call and got jerked forward to follow his departing back. We made our way to one of the side porches where we found the men smoking and talking over coffee.

"Morning, gentlemen. Well, not so gentle, having just come from the slave pens and seeing your handiwork. I don't know if I can just loan out slaves to you all again; such butchery, such brutality! I applaud you! Bravo!" Hunter was joking with the men as he leaned back on one of the roughhewn logs that acted as a banister around the porch; I stood at his side, quietly studying the men.

"Well now Mr. Brooks, I hear tell that you found something more to your liking last night? Is that true, then, that you liked that mule you were using last night, huh? That 5-493 is a good one, for certain." Hunter turned me so my arms where nearer to his hands and began adjusting the straps across my back, loosening them slowly, letting my arms relax but not removing the binder. He paused to look over his shoulder at Mr. Brooks. "Ever thought of trading in your boy for a more improved and better model? No? Well, think about it. You deserve happiness and I bet that boy is a drain on everything. Your money, your sanity and your sex drive. Who tops, you or him?" Hunter paused for dramatic effect, then continued. "Nothing meant by that statement. Mr. Brooks." Hunter held his hands out, palms up, as if to hold back Mr. Brook's anger. Then he laughed. "Love sucks, doesn't it? Well, here we fix that. Here our slaves fear us first and love us second.

"Down, 9-745." My knees cracked as they hit the wooden floor and I watched as Hunter moved off returning to the house and returned a moment later with a cigar in his hand. He was preparing for what we called stupid pet tricks. I was going to serve as his ashtray that for Mr. Brooks would be an eye opener and hopefully a revelation into the many uses of owning good slave meat.

Sir leaned back, stretching out his long frame then squatted resting his back on the wooden planking on the banister. He was in his element, talking to these men as he played idly with his slave. Tweaking its nipples, rubbing his hand down its belly and feeding it his ashes, then waiting with his hand upheld for my kiss. I loved any and all time I had with him and hated being away from him more than a moment. His trip to New Orleans had been hell for me if our phone conversations had anything to say about it. Never in my life was I so grateful for a telephone and the twins as when he was gone that week.

Butch, who was a short-bearded gentleman from Alexandria, was talking about the fun they had last night in the pigpen with their chosen slaves. I only heard a portion of their conversation because Hunter was filling all my wants and needs; nothing else seemed to exist beyond him unless he called my attention to it. Butch was crowing, "Damn, Hunter. I may have to trade in my slave for that one last night. He was handsome and could he take a beating. The damn creature actually purred when I started cutting him with the single tail!"

Hunter cocked his head, "Now Butch, are you certain you want to trade in your model for a young stallion?"

The shock on that slave's face was precious. The slave was an older gent, perhaps in his fifties. He had been kneeling quietly near his Master, holding an ashtray between his teeth when he heard his Sir make that comment. The slave opened his mouth and the ashtray dropped, spilling its contents and making the slave very alert to any sudden movements from his Master. His Master opened his legs, pulling the slave in-between the two outstretched legs. "You know Hunter, that isn't a bad idea. How much do you think I could get for this good-for-nothing lump of tainted meat? I have made it love tobacco just so it could be referred to as smoked meat." He chuckled, opened his fly and pointed at it with his finger.

The slave went about pulling out his short stubby cock and balls, looked up at his Master who nodded and gobbled all into his mouth. "Still Hunter, I found this one to my liking three years ago here. I like his devotion and eagerness." The slave was making a ruckus as he slurped, huffed and puffed while he was sucking off his Master's cock.

Mr. Brooks watched Butch's slave, then looked over to me as I was nuzzling my Master's hand in hopes that he would scratch my itching head. Then Brooks cleared his throat looked up to Hunter. "What does a mule go for in these parts?"

Hunter looked over to Brooks while he scratched my head roughly. "It all depends on their training. Our mules are, as you have seen them, well-defined muscular males and females. They are designed for hard labor. Here they are used for plowing the fields, logging, clearing the land, pulling out stumps and dragging heavy loads, but they can be of used in other ways. Most of our mules are bought for their docile nature and their heavily muscled bodies. Most are sold to city dwellers that want bodyguards, or want to see them on the weight-lifting circuit. But there are other uses for them. Ever wanted to be carried from one room to the other once you are home from work? You can with a mule. Ever wanted to literally beat the shit out of someone? With a mule you can, hell, they'll beg you for it and even ask it to be harder! Besides, with the new technology developed by Castle Enterprises we can program your mule for almost any given task. It is just that simple."

Hunter let him think while he busied himself with more adjustments on my arms as my hands had begun to shade towards blue. He finally gave up and released my arms, removed my neck brace and sent me with it to our suite with orders to return. I did not find them on the porch but in his office when I came back. Hunter was moving in on the kill, about to make a sale to Mr. Brooks. Hunter directed me to get them drinks. Sir ordered me under his desk, thus out of the way to target any of Mr. Brook's concerns.

They talked about the trade-in, where he had found the boy, what knowledge he had of the boy's background, family etc. All of which was entered with fast key-strokes into Hunter's laptop. The phone rang and Hunter answered. "Yes, Lt. Phillips. Please do some quick labs on the boy in cell block four, I'll need fingerprints and a retina scan as well. I need information stat; he may be a trade-in on mule 5-493. Thanks!"

I was called out and put before a keyboard and monitor. Master directed me to call up the data on 5-493 and translate our encryptions to Mr. Brooks. "Sir," I read out loud, "5-493 has been with us for 3 years, all the while within the mule camp. It is trained in rudimentary cooking skills. That means he can cook basic foods, but nothing fancy. It shows here he has talent in that field and with future training will be able to provide you with excellent dinner and party fare. He was brought to us by his brother and sold outright. At the time of his entrance he was 247 lbs and had a large gut. Here, Sir, is a picture of him before the training." A double click summoned the picture and we all made disgusting remarks at seeing him naked. "Here is his most recent image, Sir." Another double click pulled his well-defined heavily veined body up on the scene opposite the grossly over-weight image. The transformation was incredible. In the before picture the slave hung his head in shame, the newer image had him holding his head still lowered - but with pride.

I went back to reading the file on 5-493. "It now weights 182 with less than 3 grams of body fat. It loves heavy workouts and took the runner-up title for power lift-ing here on the base. It is a donor, meaning it is a sperm donor and has a 99.9 rating within the gene pool. His sperm creates babies. Health status is excellent overall but he must maintain a very high fiber diet due to an accident that has since healed and he has a slight limp when it is tired. Its psychological profile says it equates food and pain as love. There you have it, Sir."

Turning back to Master, I found him pouring over figures as they scrolled over his monitor. He was muttering to himself. "Did you find anything else in the pig pens that suited your tastes, Jim?"

Mr. Brooks looked puzzled by even being asked that question. "Why are you asking me that, Hunter?"

"My mistake. It seems there is another buyer a man in Tennessee who has placed a bid on 5-493. He is trying to raise the money for that mule." Mr. Brooks was sputtering when Hunter held up hand for silence while keeping his eye on the monitor. "If you want 5-493, there is a chance. The farmer has listed two mules that he wanted and he needs only one for what he has in mind. Don't get your drawers in a knot, Jim. Let me tell you the pros and con of owning a mule for your slave. This way, at least you have been apprised of its qualifications before you take it home and become dis-satisfied."

Hunter snapped his fingers; I turned off the monitor and dropped to my rightful place at his boots. One was lifted and placed on my bent back the other went under my tongue. "This animal, 5-493, is a work mule. Jim, do you work out in the gym? You'll need to become a member with this creature. He has to work out daily on heavy weights to maintain his muscle mass. Make him carry you from room to room when you're home, sit on his back when it does push ups, things like that. Be creative. As a sperm donor, his cum is precious to our firm. Do you enjoy sucking cock? What you do not consume yourself needs to be preserved, placed in one of these cups and frozen. We can pay you about $800 per pint for this one's sperm. If you add yours to his cup, you'll taint the batch and you'll be fined $1500 as others have tried to do in the past.

You'll need heavy irons and shackles on him to keep him feeling as if he is loved. The more you whip and dehumanize him, the more he will love you; it is only a thing for your pleasure. Get over the fact that it might look like a human. Believe me, it isn't any more a human than that pen is a butterfly. 5-493 thrives on hard love, it makes it tick, and makes its cock hard. If you do not own a heavy-duty steel cage, buy one. It's necessary for this creature. Anything else he will escape from if he can. We have them if you have need of one. Place this one in its cage when you go to work, it will be overjoyed when you return to beat him and force him to make you dinner before taking his ass to the gym. Never, ever, leave this one alone in your house unguarded or without being firmly locked in its chains. It is a binge eater and if he escapes he will literally eat his way through your house. No sweets - not even pet snacks - they have too much sugar. It gets fed either our slave food or very small portions of white meat and a fucking ton of freshly cooked or raw veggies. Any questions?"

"Will a dog cage work for him?"

"No way. This is a beast who will chew his way through those tiny bars using his teeth." Hunter went in for the kill. "Tell me, what about 5-493 did you like?"

"Every damn thing! The one thing that sold me on him was the way he dropped to his knees and begged me to beat the shit out of him. Then when I was finished, he begged to suck my cock. Not that boy, he was constantly making fun of my cock becuase his was larger. But that slave chewed on it and gobbled it down as if my cock was the only thing that could satisfy him! I loved it! When I shot my load and he'd drunk it, he rolled over onto his back, spread his legs and begged me to kick his nuts if I liked how he had served. I was totally amazed when I was stomping the living hell out of his cock and balls, it shot its load after begging me permission. Damn, it was fucking wonderful! I want that slave, damn it!"

Mr. Brooks continued even faster. "You know, I just might be going through my mid-life crisis but damn, I like it! I've never taken a risk to be me! Always cautious, forever safe; I wear two condoms just to fuck the boy. Does that give you an idea? I want that slave to be my racecar! How much is it?"

Hunter cleared his throat; "Remember, it's a sperm donor with a 99.9% rating, a trained mule, docile, a valuable worker, certified fully submissive and we can add two programs to him at no extra cost to you. Our asking price for 5-493 is $62,000 dollars."

Mr. Brooks whistled at the named price then spoke to Butch at his back. "Does that sound fair to you, Butch?"

"Wait one minute, Jim, remember you have a trade in. Let me see what Lt. Phillips has to say about it." Hunter picked up the phone and called Lt. Phillips. He made a dramatic face spoke in quiet tones before hanging up. "Seems the computer is down for a few minutes, lets move on to more important matters." He began typing on his keypad and the monitor filled with numbers and notations on our new client Mr. Brooks. Hunter took a sip from his coffee cup then proceeded. "According to your financial records, you can afford about three mules at that price."

Mr. Brooks looked over his shoulder at Butch, who just shrugged his shoulders and nodded his head no; as if to say he hadn't given Master the information. Hunter continued reading the files. "Oh, well that explains it. You are the bank president for Prestige Banking Corporation. No wife, no kids. Ah, you have a Swiss bank account, how interesting."

Brooks yelped and jumped out of his chair. "What? How did you get that information?"

"Get a grip man! We have the most complete information system on this planet. We have some of the youngest, brightest minds hacking out information as we need and they get paid handsomely for their services. Yes Jim, a Swiss bank account and a private account in Columbia. Maybe we can set you up with one of our banks in that country. Someone that will not skim a tidy edge off your hard earned bucks. Besides, it's in our best interest that you succeed in life. Castle Enterprises believes in taking care of its own investors."

Master leaned forward as if to take Mr. Brooks into his confidence. "Slaves are like highly negotiable bonds. Work them as long as they make you a profit then sell them and get yourself another. Hell, Jim, once you have bought a slave you have joined one of the most satisfying and elite clubs in the world. Castle believes in taking care of its people and sharing our profits. So it will behoove you to join one of the Shields if you buy, because they are all slave owners and they can help you with those little problems that might some times arise. Plus, Castle has small hospitals within some of the major cities should your animal get damaged and have need of repair. Always a wise move to insure the line. Excellent to note, your last blood test certifies you as a slave owner. You do not carry any diseases that we keep out of our communal gene pool. This is all good to see," Hunter said with a smile.

I was summoned from below the desk and ordere to go see who let in the cattle. I returned to notify Master that the Handlers were beginning to arrive for lunch. He turned to Mr. Brooks. "Think about what I have said while my team joins us for lunch. I will make certain that you, Mr. Brooks, sit next to the men who trained your mule. They can answer any other questions you might have. After lunch we can go see the mule and confirm the sale if you are still so inclined. Come gentlemen, my team is arriving."

Opening the door, we entered a human sea of men and women in black, blue, brown and sun-bright yellow uniforms making their way towards the buffet line. They parted for us as Hunter led us up the rank and file before he paused to introduce Mr. Brooks to two Handlers. They were told to answer any question concerning 5-493, since Mr. Brooks was considering purchasing the animal. Once they were put aside, Hunter made his way towards the huge fireplace where he could stand and watch his team at the buffet line.

It was fun to watch him work his way down the line. Checking to see if everyone got what he or she wanted, talking to one about something important before moving over to speak to another. No other Founder took such good care of his people as did my Master. We had fewer employees leaving our ranks and a whole list of people wanting to join, so we could have the pick of the litter. Perhaps that is why Dan's episode hurt Hunter the most and Cappy had only added to his burden. Still today, none of that was present. He was in his element with his team and loved being there seeing to their happiness as they did his.

He had the ability to remember a face and a name, rarely getting caught offguard by someone who may have added a mustache or beard. They loved the way he moved among them, talking about things they enjoyed outside of our base. He was proud of his team and rightly so; they responded to his nurturing and discipline. Few people in the outside world cared enough to get involved with an employee and make them part of an intricate team. He took individuals and meshed them into a unit, just like he had done for us slaves in the household. The Hand and Glove was an apt analogy for all his Buena Vista teams.

Every six months he would have such a gathering as today, but today was special. He had some major life changes that had to be told to everyone up front so there wouldn't be any hurt feelings or misunderstood orders. He believed that all of us on Buena Vista were a huge extended family and, like a family, we had our arguments but nothing that could not be settled. All personnel were welcome to his table and he even went out of the bounds to extend his hand to the craftsman guilds. Once (or if it's good, twice) a year, there were huge picnics in their honor. His attention to detail showed in every smiling face as they dined today and yet, there was Cappy's seat empty until Hunter fixed a plate for J.D. plunked him down with an ordered to eat.

I was ordered to fix two plates for him and another for mike. All of his family was seated save me. I knelt at his side to dine from his fingers. That was my preference to being seated at the table and eating with a fork or - worse yet - from a bowl. J.D. fed mike and Hunter fed me this way all, with his extended family dining around him in the dining room and den while extra slaves from the caverns made certain all were being fed properly. Such was our family.

Chapter 7

A man is a worker. If he is not that he is nothing.
Joseph Conrad

Hunter pushed himself up to his feet, walked to the center of the tables and cleared his throat. "Ladies and Gentlemen, and I use that term loosely," he paused for their laughter, "please note that there is a new marshal in town; meaning while Cappy is away on business, J.D. is taking up the slack. If I have my way, and I usually do around here, J.D. will soon be elevated. It's been his ideas that have helped our top-side production double to support our downside. Please treat him as if he was Cappy. Only better. Thank you all for coming today and thank mike and his staff for all their hard labors."

The people began applauding, catcalling and whistling to show their appreciation to mike and his staff and Master laughed heartily. "Mike's food is the web and I am the spider. As I need to talk to all of you in the easiest manner possible. Oh, stop groaning; you are being well fed aren't you?" He turned serious. "Folks, you have no doubt heard the rumors, have seen the Black Watch Security people crawling the under-caverns and have seen many a stranger running around with measuring tapes. Well, part of the rumors are true. Buena Vista is about to get a major facelift. The greatest part of the retrofit will affect each of you here. Why is this happening now; simply because in the last year, we pulled off the most successful slave auction ever and the most profitable. When you go back to your duties today, check your dividend accounts. Each of you has received a sizeable chunk of the profits." They began banging their fists on the table as a sign of their appreciation and he had to hold up his hands to get them to calm down. "Eat some more cake, have another round at the buffet, just sit quiet because there is a lot more my family needs to hear today.

"Buena Vista is the oldest constantly occupied Manor house with in the Castle Enterprises Corporation. Due to that fact, Castle Enterprises has decided that we need a major facelift and retro fitting that befits our rank and status. Wait one moment hear me out before you start applauding…what this means for us is simply larger living quarters, more slave storage, training grounds and new equipment throughout the caverns. We are to have the most advanced security system known complete with retina, hand and implant security checks installed. We will have a slave monitoring system as one of you suggested; each slave will be implanted with a microchip. Plus there will be increased living and workspace for the guilds, an underground spa and better gym equipment. We will be harnessing the newly found underground river for added electricity within our growing underground city. That's the upside of the matter, but the downside is that we may have to endure dormitory living below ground or tent city above while they are doing blasting and laser mining.

"A lot of the work started in out of the way areas last January, all of which is complete. Now they want our living and work areas. It means that your personal spaces will need to be crated and locked in storage. But this also gives you an incredible opportunity to go as a complete team on a vacation the likes of which I rather doubt will happen again

"Almost all of us are on the fringes of burnout. We will more than likely be toast after the spring sale this April but we will get through it. Why? Because we are tough. We have something to look forward to. We have been rewarded by Castle Enterprises with an all expense paid vacation!"

The room exploded in sound and the fluttering of white napkins being flung into the air as everyone gave an audible reply to his statement. He let them enjoy the moment then held up his hands laughing and calling them to order.

"Folks, calm down, folks! The vacation is an all inclusive trip to the South Pacific. We go as a group and play as a group. Can you handle that? It's only for two weeks and afterwards you'll have one week to use as you see fit before you report back home. Then comes the challenge of getting us back up and running before the October Manor Run. The construction foremen believe they can get the major construction work done in the living quarters while we are off the mountain."

Hunter was walking back towards our table when he stopped. "One more thing I should add. Cappy is away hiding about to $20,000 worth of prizes on islands in the South Pacific. There are detailed maps, clues and charts for those of you who want to play the game. We gamers will be housed on one of three-masted ships. He then spoke with mike, asking him on one of the three ships that have been chartered for our cruise. For those of you who would prefer a quieter getaway, we have charted a five-star hotel for your needs, but that puts you out of the game for the duration of the vacation. Blueprints will be in your mess tomorrow as well as a slave who will sign each of you up and give you each your clues. They are all the same, but you must utilize all the star maps, water currents and your brains to find the buried treasure."

He turned, signaled me to get another plate of food, turned back, and held his hand up. "One more thing. There will be at least one Pirate party while we are onboard those ships, get an appropriate costume. Fraternization within our ranks will go unpunished amongst my whoring Handlers while on the high seas, but bring it back here and brother, you'll face my wrath. Get it out of your system, marry, or become partners so when you are home, we are a closer knit family than before! Hey mike, where is my dessert!"

With that bellowed command he sat down and enjoyed the balance of his meal in the relative quiet of being in a college dinning hall. The whole room was buzzing with excitement. Butch and Mr. Brooks came to sit near him as Sir finished up his lunch. "Have you made up your mind after talking with 5-493's Handler's, Jim?"

Mr. Brooks hung his head, and then looked up, "I really want it, bad! I have tried a dog, even a cat but I'm still alone. I want this manimal like nothing I have ever wanted in my life. When you are finished with your lunch let's go back and talk money."

Master was mopping up the last residue of gravy on his plate with a roll, he sat back, looked at me and plopped the chewy morsel into my mouth. "Jim, I can think of no better dessert. Let's go talk."

Sir rose, crossed the room to where J.D. was sitting and spoke quickly to him. Sir spoke with mike and asked him if I was needed, then signaled that I should take the guests into his office. They followed me well and I offered them cigars and a drink should either need fortification. Cigars were accepted and I prepared them as Sir had taught me with one exception; they were lighted by their own lips while I held their fire. I waited, having placed a cigar in his ashtray should he wish it, standing in an out of the way corner with bowed my head to watch the room.

Master entered abruptly, laughing at something someone had said. "Good to see it has taken care of your needs. Drinks anyone? No? Then down to the business at hand." Sir sat behind his desk lifted the laptop screen and began typing in his clearance code. "Lt. Phillips must have his computer up and working. Let's see, that piece of work that you brought with you is a class A piece of work. When did you two meet? Two years ago, huh, well prior to that he had two arrests. One for selling crack and another for prostitution. Wow, his M.O. is that he finds older, wealthy clients and milks them to support his habits. Does he live with you? No? Check your valuables when you get home, I guarantee something is missing. Wait one moment …let me check something."

Master began rapidly hammering on the keyboard then whistled, "Seriously, look in your house. He has recently made a deposit to his bank account, one you probably set up for him, and the deposit was $5,000. Did you give that to him? You have a well-known coin collection if I remember correctly; I can almost guess where that piece of shit got his spending money. Would you want one of our security team to come to your house? No charge, call it a friendly gesture. They are the best of the best. If they can get the clues they just might be able to help relocate your missing objects. I will send them a note now and someone will meet you at your door tonight when you arrive home.

"Ok, down to business. We can take that boy off your hands but he will not be trained here. He will be shipped over to another house for training. That way should you think of trying to get a few more kicks in later you know he is off our grounds. Now, Jim, tell me what you own in the way of proper gear for maintaining this mule you are about to purchase. I need to know if you have any heavy whips, a private play space, a steel animal cage, a private gym, do you happen to have any leg irons, handcuffs any of the so called tools of our trade as slave owners?"

"I did once but come to think about it. I haven't seen that steamer trunk in a long time," Mr. Brooks got a distressed look on his face. "I wonder?"

"A few more questions, if you please, about your trade-in." Sir bagan firing off questions, checking off the answers as they were giving. "Does he have his own apartment, yes, does he have a car, you bought it, ok. Do you know the address; excellent…let me get that entered properly. Do you want the car for your personal use. Do you happen to have a set of the keys to the car. Do you have insurance on the vehicle, as I had hoped you did all you could for him. It is a shame he ran away. OK, let's get to work hammering out these prices, shall we?" Master was set up for the kill.

"$62,000 for the mule slave 5-493 and I can give you about $10,000 for that piece of work you brought here."

Butch spoke up, "Hunter, can't you sweeten the deal any?"

"Only if you are willing to waiver your finder's fee, are you ok? Then I can offer you $12,000 for that untrained creature. But remember Mr. Brooks, you'll be receiving from your insurance company full payment for that car and return of your valuables if my team can track them down. Also, as an owner of a sperm mule with a 99.9% status you'll be earning $800 to $1000 per pint for its frozen sperm. Most mules can produce that twice a month and yours can produce more than that if you milk him twice daily as we have. One of the Handlers will show you how to milk him. Really, it's easy. He really is a cash cow and a true pig, hell of a manimal!"

Sir finished his calculations. "With your trade in that will be $50,000 for the mule. Did you want to take it with you today or did you want to make changes to your home prior to his arrival? Master was about to add more to this mans sale than he could even imagine. Let's go down and see the mule. I had him brought back in from the fields earlier just in case you wanted to see him before you returned home. I don't know about you gentlemen, but I really love some afternoon sex before a nice long nap; especially on a Sunday. Better than any boring football game in my books. Come on, let's go be owners of men and get nasty."

Hunter continued talking to Jim Brooks to give him a sense of security and control over this beast as they headed down and about the extras that can be added. He described a team that will come in a retrofit any existing room, giving it its own air exchange, soundproofing the walls, ceilings, floors, building in a cage, large furniture all usually within a week. If he wanted his animal shipped to him, he would arrive crated like a statue from some art house, be uncrated with all the materials hauled off. The animal could be suited for the delivery in rubber or leather gear, just in case you would want to take the beast out. As a new owner, he was at liberty to attend local training classes, attend functions and meet other owners with their pets. All said, we turned and entered the mule zone. Bars of color over the door told all that could read our code just what type animals were stored and trained within the bowels of this cavern.

We were stopped by a Handler and escorted into the pigpen; bound there to a heavy upright buried into the ground was the Charles Atlas of mules. This animal was nothing less than a slab of pure muscle. It was growling and snapping at those around it until it saw us enter the arena. Once it saw Master Hunter and its new owner, it dropped to its knees placing its face to the floor.

Master asked the Handler for the keys. Walking past a whip rack, he chose his weapon and moved to stand before the cowering animal. "Get on your feet, you worthless lump of flesh," Sir growled at the creature. "Move so much as an inch and I'll rip you into shreds!" The animal held his breath as Hunter keyed the locks holding his arms to the whipping post. He barked, "Down, beast!" and it fell forward on its hands and knees. Master stood there for a moment, then kicked it in the ribs. "Lower, mag-got!" 5-493 stretched out its arms and legs until its body lowered and Master climbed upon the animal's back. The animal held its position until commanded. "Up, slowly." That animal showed its control over its body as it slowly rose from its position and lifted its hands from the floor all while Master stayed firmly planted on its back.

Master jumped off, walked a short way and began to sit while knowing full well there wasn't a chair in sight. The animal rushed to get under him before he landed on the ground. Hunter patted the slave's butt, ran his hand between those two slabs of muscle and then stood, turned swinging the whip high overhead and down to cut a deep red welt on the animal's hide. 5-493 made no sound. Master repeated the blow, then kicked the animal with all the force his booted legs could muster. The animal rolled with the kick and came up smiling. Hunter shouted, "You are a fucking puny mule slave. Give me 50 push ups now!" Master walked over to Jim handed him the whip. "Go play with it. I got my own to play with." Sir gave me a wink and I followed.

My Master put me through my paces, encouraging Jim to put the beast 5-493 through his. This way the pig pen was filled with the sounds of leather hitting flesh that ended in a joint fusion and the bearish roar of yet another climax claimed from my Master. We withdrew to a private sector where we could cuddle and watch the new owner as it laid claim to its prize and subjugated it thoroughly. Finished and completely satisfied, Master Jim joined us in the quiet room. Hunter cocked his head, "Well, how did you enjoy kicking its tires and checking its engine? Think you want it, Jim?"

Jim laughed, nodding his head. "Hell, Hunter, you know I do."

"One last thing you have to do is tell that piece of shit that you have traded him in for a better model. That's the easy part then we go sign some papers. Jim, if you don't tell him, he will try to escape and get damaged in the process. Besides, it's only fair that you tell him. This way he knows there's no going back to you, that you are finished with him. Let's get this over with and be done with that job," as Master stood up, walked over to an intercom box, depressed the button and spoke into the box. "Bring chains for 5-493 and we will need an escort to the slag zone." Two Handlers entered the arena, 5-493 stood there calmly as they secured its arms and legs in heavy logging chains then ordered it to follow them into the private room. Hunter stood before 5-493, "pick him up and carry him comfortably mule."

Chains rattling with each step, the mule walked to where Master Jim was sitting, scooped him into his arms like a baby and lifted him into his arms. I'd been around this big beast for years when working out with the mules on several occasions. Before he always held a totally blank expression but when he picked up Master Jim, he had a smile.

We cut across corridors this way and that until I was lost and entered one of the darker zones. At no time during the long journey did either Master Jim or the brute that carried him have anything to say; the simple act was saying enough for all. Hunter, however, kept up chatter about how riding a mule always gives him a hard-on as well as answering questions from the Handlers about the South Pacific vacation. I kept silent. I remembered these past corridors too well.

Our little caravan stopped before a rank smelling cell. One of the Handlers shown his flashlight into the cell where, kneeling and bound to a T bar embedded in the stone, was Master Jim's boy. He was in pain, glassy eyed and was gagged. Hunter had the Handlers rap on the cell door. The boy looked up slowly, then realized who stood on the opposite side of the bars and began shrieking through his gag.

Hunter spoke up. "Boy, your ex-lover has something to say to you. Listen carefully to what he has to say and remember." Master backed off and gave a flourish with his hand as if to say, the floor is all yours.

Master Jim said, "5-493 put me down on my feet." The beast obeyed him but stood at his back as if waiting other orders. Perhaps the animal knew this was a turning point in its life. Who knew with these brutes? Often they are a mystery within themselves. Master Jim put his hand on the cell door, found something disgusting and rubbed his hands on his pants quickly. Jim turned to look at his mule, "Down slave, head to the floor."

The beast followed his order to the letter and Master Jim placed his boot on the animal's head. "See this slave, Bobby? It is your replacement. He will not bitch at me or steal from me like you have. This animal will go home with me as my property and you'll be staying here to be trained. Maybe one day you, too, will be like this slave. At the very least, you'll be more obedient." Jim turned to the nearest Handler. "Open the cell door will you?" He looked up to Hunter who to ordered the door opened.

Master Jim entered the cell, opened his fly, hauled out his cock and let the stream of piss wash over his ex-boy. "This is somehow a very fitting end to our association." He zipped up and closed the cell door, walked to his new slave who had moved, kicked him hard and looked down at it. "I do not remember ordering you to move. beast! Now put me back in your arms and carry me back to the pigpen. Fucking worthless hunk of meat, move on."

As they walked off, Hunter gave a command to the Handlers. "Take that one to processing make certain they draw blood on it as it may be contaminated and only suitable for a work detail outside of our firm. We have just sold 5-493." Masters Jim and Hunter withdrew into the office where they hammered out the final details, while I was sent back to work helping mike and the other staff as they finalized the clean up of the lunch. Just about the time my duties had drawn to an end the two men exited the office shaking hands. Masters' parting comment to Jim was that the animal would be delivered in about a month then they broke each going in their own direction. Hunter towards the kitchen and Jim back down into the caverns to check out his new purchase yet again.

My Master sat down exhausted at the kitchen table, ordered a cup of coffee and sipped it quietly when I knelt before him, "Sir, begging your pardon, you look exhausted. Let this one give you a massage."

He looked up smiled, "We've sold 5-493, thank God! Come. Oh, mike."

Mike turned, laughing. "Sir, it's already completed, sandwiches and a small bottle of wine are prepared for the guests' return trip. Congratulations on the sale, Sir."

We returned to his office. He ordered a cigar, a brandy and sat down in his wing-backed chair, he pointed me to his desk, "Take notes first, then you can make the calls to the teams while I rest here. We need to call the Black Watch security team and have one of their detectives report to Master Brook's house this evening around 9PM. Next, we need to call the outfitters. They need to make an appointment to get into Jim's home for the retrofit of his spare bedroom. He wants it soundproofed, an air exchange system and sound system, a slave bondage bed and a heavy duty cage, plus a hoisting system if possible. We need to call the leather guild; 5-493 gets a complete set of leathers and a rubber travel garment and a sensory deprivation hood. They need to send up an agent to measure Jim's arm so he can have three custom whips made for him, he wants a set of leathers and knee-high linemen boots. God, what else...delivery will be in standard crate and we need to notify the hospital in D.C. as well as the area Shield that a new owner will need the welcome wagon. Read it back to me."

I complied while he released a huge yawn. "Call the leather guild now; ask Randal if he will send up a boy to get measurements from Mr. Brooks and tell them he may be located in the mule pigpen with his new slave. Also tell them he needs new leathers, boots and three whips. They'll know more when I fax out the information."

"Sir, don't forget the sensory hood that they need to build for 5-493, Sir."

"Yeah, right. Ok make that call now and I am going upstairs for a quick nap. I worked hard this morning. We just turned at tidy profit of well over $100,000 for 5-493 and all its appointments. Join me once you are done." Hunter kicked out our guests and the new owner of 5-493. They went back to D.C. by limo, carrying a well-stocked hamper filled with goodies from mike's kitchen. One of mike's hampers was not something easily denied. Mistress Jan had helped J.D. come to the terms of his barter to her house while he underwent medical schooling. Mr. Jim Brooks had come with an asshole of a slave and was leaving with one of the finest mules within our stock pens. Delivery would be in about a month once his house was prepared for the animal and suitable changes had been made to his living quarters for its use.

No sooner than the door closed and the limo departed when Hunter declared it play time. He wanted J.D., mike, and this slave to race him down to Cappy's cottage. His reasoning was that he'd never been invited in and now that Cappy was oddly vacant we might find clues to his whereabouts. Having had a good massage and nap, Hunter was in a playful mood. He turned, grabbed mike within his arms and tussled the boy's handsome blonde hair. "You'll race me to the cottage, and you too J.D." He looked at me, "I may have to chase you with a switch, and last time we ran anywhere you lagged behind, watching my ass! Anything on the stove that will burn, mike? Ok, first creature to the door gets my cock!"

J.D. tripped Hunter in his eagerness to get out of the house while mike and I ran like the wind, laughing as one pulled ahead of the others. J.D. caught up to us and did his damnedest to push ahead. At our rear was Hunter, running as fast as he could to catch up. Slave mike reached the door first, this one second, then J.D. and Hunter. All of us paused to catch our breath before entering the small cottage.

Three of these cottages existed on the topside. One for Cappy, one for the Deus Mistress Beatrice and one for that twisted fuck Doc. They were all laid out the same; a nice long full-length front porch with an overhang and rocking chairs. Entering, we stepped into the den which opened onto a breakfast room, and kitchen. Outside of the kitchen was a small back porch with steps down to the ground. From the den, taking a small hallway you would find the bathroom and a huge Master's suite.

Hunter was looking over the house and whistled, "Who keeps this house so clean?"

"Our Master, Sir", they piped in unison and laughed.

"Jesus! It looks like he dusted before he left, which could explain his rush to get out of here." Hunter was walking through the cottage with a seriously perplexed look on his face. "This reminds me of something. Fuck! The way this house is set up, the placement of the rooms it reminds me of our..." Hunter coughed, hoping that he'd covered up his mistaken words, "...a house in 'Nam. I wonder..." His voice trailed off for a moment before he resumed. "Boys, as I see it we need to look around and find clues. J.D., tell me what is missing from his closet and his toy chest. Mike, see if you can find any correspondence. I know Cappy hates computers so I doubt if he is doing it the modern way. And you, 9-745, read these letters with mike see if anything odd pops out that'll tell us where he has gone."

J.D. returned to announce to Hunter that Cappy had taken his chaps, boots, bar vest, motorcycle jacket, gloves, whips and his private toys. Again Hunter's eyebrow looked like a wooly caterpillar on his forehead, "Well, just maybe he is gone to get him some strange."

"Sir," Slave mike was holding out a picture, "here's packet of letters from a boy called Jason who lives in Richmond, VA."

"Damn, mike that boy could be your triplet. Are there more of you boys around than you know about? No? Ok, Richmond Virginia is Rob Roy's turf. I'll give him a call to see if he can give his old army buddy a favor. Maybe he can find Cappy and check on him to see if he's all right. We're all worried about him," Hunter said. Then he turned to the boys, "Go to the closets and bring me your rubber or leather gear. I need to see what you two have."

J.D. his head bowed said quietly, "Sir, we don't have any extra gear. Only a few odd clothes should it get cold. but nothing else, Sir." By the way J.D. was acting he was embarrassed to have to say this to Hunter.

Hunter blew up, "What? Give me that goddam phone, mike!" Hunter punched in some numbers, spoke to someone on the other end of the line. "This is Hunter, code 3347-12250, tell me just how much money is Captain Hicks' account? Oh, you cannot give out that information? Give me your name please; thank you Anne Givens, now pass me to a supervisor." Hunter waited, drumming his fingers across the tabletop while the boys ran to pack their meager belongings and returned.

Hunter started in on the supervisor. "This is Bruce Hunter, code 3347-12250. Do you know who I am? Check your file. Good, you know. Give me the amount in Captain Hicks' account. That much? Excellent. Thank you. Oh, when was his last draw on the account? Indeed, thanks. Please tell Anne Givens she did only what I would expect from her." He hung up the phone and turned to us. "Come on boys, you're staying at the main house. Take one of the guest bedrooms for now to dump your gear, but you're sleeping in my quarters. Let's go back home. I got some work to complete before we call it a day."

We walked quietly back to the house and as we entered, he started issuing orders. "Twins, gear upstairs, you 9-745, to the kitchen and pull out that sandwich platter. Start laying out items you know we all will eat, and I will join you in a few minutes." We ran to do his bidding and I watched him stalk off as if the weight of the world was on his shoulders. What was bothering him so?

I laid out everything I thought any of us would want to eat. Sandwiches, fruit, leftover pie, chips, a handful of sodas, milk and was about to make him a pot of coffee before mike entered. "Too much, way too much. Let's make this a simple meal!" Mike put back half the items I'd set out then directed me to bring in the really heavy paper plates. Together we took all the items into the den where we found J.D. adding wood to the fireplace. He, like Hunter, seemed to be occupied by something other than just life.

Master announced to the room, "Rob Roy is on the case. He is a great snoop dog and if Cappy is there, he will find him and the boy Jason. Boys, fix me a plate. And each of you gets one. 9-745, go get a sketchpad and pencils from my office. We have to put our heads together and think of a uniform that will be suitable for our slaves when they are in public. They need to be seen as limo drivers, van drivers going between sites with an owner, so something that marks our property without being too loud and screaming. Your collars and harnesses will be a part of you until the time comes, but I want something that gives you slaves a punch up on the gene pool. Eat and let's talk this out, all of you have excellent ideas and I value your insights." We all blushed at that statement and he pretended not to notice how it affected us.

"J.D., you'll report after breakfast to the leather guild. You'll be measured for clothing that befits your new rank. Do this, because this is an order. Mike, you are to report about the same time to the general merchandise unit for jeans for both of you, shirts, and you will stop by the leather guild and be measured, too. I am tired of watching you two suffer cause of that old queen's need to horde."

Three slaves and their owner sat pouring over and discarding ideas about a uniform while they ate then our Master joined us on the floor using my butt to pillow his frame. This way we discussed and debated the possibility of a house livery; something that all of us could wear easily and still look sharp in public. Our selection was leather tunics which would cover our torso and - depending on weather - bondage shorts or bondage pants with boots.

What we didn't eat was returned to the kitchen, the plates were burned and we turned out the lights. We withdrew to our suite, where we undressed our lord and gently put him to bed. He pretended to be sleepy because as soon as he was in bed he asked the twins, "When you put Cappy to bed, what did he have you do for him?"

J.D. winked at mike and motioned his hand at me to stay in place, sitting on the edge of the bed. "Well, if it would please the Sir. Recline in your bed and leave the driving to us." Hunter laid back on one of his arms as the boys wiggled down to his toes. "Our Master rarely bathed, Sir. That is, in real water. He much preferred our method of bathing."

They proceeded to lick, suck and chew each of his toes, then his arch, heel and began a slow tongue bath up his ankles and legs, missing his crotch and along his ribs, into his armpits, around his neck, over his face to grab kisses in route back down his chest. Both nipples got sucked, licked and chewed, then they went down to his belly and J.D. signaled that I should crawl in amidst them. J.D. squirmed under Hunter's legs, lifting his lower body and drove his tongue between Master's ass lips, mike went to work chewing leisurely on Master's nutsack and I was permitted to gobble down his cock. I dropped on that as if it was the last meat in town! The three of us milked him of yet another load and crawled back into his arms when done.

Both mike and I were not having any success at sleeping. We both were tired; it was just that we both of us were without bondage. Thankfully, mike was the one that begged him for restraints. "J.D.," Hunter bellowed, "take mike down to the floor, put his cock in my pig's mouth and fuck that pig's ass raw! Make it good, because it's been a long time since I've had the pleasure of enjoying a good old fashioned porno movie played out in front of me."

The twins were overjoyed with this gift and they dragged me down on the floor. Mike got his cock hard and shoved it into my mouth while J.D. bound his brother to my arms, then found a belt and laid into my ass. Daring me to bite mike's cock all while he beat my butt white hot, then he dropped behind me and shoved his cock into my butt. Damn, did those two boys know how to set a mind reeling! For awhile, I thought I was being ridden like a bicycle…one in and one out. Then they must've reached their level of endurance because they both started fucking my holes hard. Both blew their loads in unison and I had one hell of a time swallowing all mike was depositing down my throat. The boy must have not been milked in a long time by the way it felt.

Hunter was applauding our efforts, ordering J.D. to clean me up in the bathroom and mike into bed. Exiting the bathroom, we two stopped dead in our tracks. There was mike bound to the headboard, his arms bound at his back, his legs spread eagle and attached to the sides of the mattress and Hunter lying back in the 'V' of the boy's legs smiling. "Come on you pigs, let's get some sleep. Mike, keep that thing out of my ear," Hunter laughed and told J.D. to turn out the lights.

We awoke early and went into the bathroom - leaving mike where he was bound. Returning, Hunter ordered us to pull out a sleep-sack, mike was released and allowed to piss or shit. He was placed into the sleep sack, laced up tightly, buckled securely and we departed to make a mess in his kitchen, giving mike ample time to recoup his lost sleep. Once breakfast was completed, J.D. was set about his tasks and reminded of his need for a fitting.

Hunter turned to me while he was scratching his balls absentmindedly. "Come here." I ran to where he stood, his arms pinned me to his chest. One hand grabbed my chin, lifting it. "Love you, meat." He clamped his lips on to mine, holding me there for the longest time before pushing me away with an order. "Dress me in leather today; I will be taking my Harley for a much needed ride. Dress me accordingly." A slap on my butt put me in motion.

I thought of putting him in his green leather police uniform from Germany, but chose something I liked better. I hoped I would be the one removing them later. I put him into skintight leather pants and his thigh-high lace-up linemen boots, a leather shirt, gloves, leather doo-rag and his heavy motorcycle jacket. He put me into a double cobra hood, lacing it tight, kissing my lips, and then zipping the hood front closed. My hands were bound to my nuts and we took the private elevator. After few steps we turned and I was bodily lifted by other hands and laid out on a slab. There I was bound tightly in place, my hands freed and rebound. A body settled on to my chest and the hood was unzipped. Hunter stood above me looking down. "Everything I do to you is to control you to another level and to prove to you that I love you, slave."

A hand grabbed my cock and I squealed from the shock, I'd forgotten about the piercing he had placed in my cock when we were last in Miami. Something brutally cold slipped into my cock like a sound filling the piss slit. Hands rolled the sound around, then I felt a twinge as something was passed through my cock against metal. The hand dropped my cock and try as I might I couldn't lift it off the table.

Hunter climbed off; they unbound my body and helped me to my feet. I must have been in shock because between my legs was my cock weighed down by one of the most evil looking chrome spiked balls I could've ever imagined. My cock hung down between my legs as if it was locked in place. No manner of urging, except with my hand, could get it to rise. Hunter must have liked the look on my face because he laughed and pulled me into his chest. "It's new yet, you'll get use to it. This way I know you are secure when I am away. Now get on your knees, slave."

Damn if they didn't insert a chrome plug into my ass. Hunter showed me one while men were working the plug in my hole. It looked like a normal plug except at the base there was a lock like on a doorknob. Putting the key in and turning it, the plug opened up, irising wide, thus making it impossible to remove and making this slave like a virgin, locked within its Master's chastity devices. "Neither of these devices will stop you from working or doing your chores, I have seen to that. You and two others are wearing these devices; they mark you as mine better than any brand. I want you to go upstairs, release mike and drag his sorry ass down here for measurements. When done, you both have house chores. I want them all completed before I return tonight. Hold dinner until I arrive. Now, go!" He swatted my ass and I ran off feeling alive and more aware of my Master than I had since the boys had moved in with us.

I had the run of the house and I was by myself. I could have let my old self out of its tomb but dared not screw this up; I knew deep in my heart this was one of his tests. Instead, I did as was ordered, ran upstairs woke mike, got him out of the sleep sack and fed him a power bar as we walked back downstairs for his measurements. While there, I was shocked to find out that I was also destined for more measurements. We left there and went to the General Store where there were two huge bundles waiting J.D. and mike. We took both topside so they could explore the new wardrobe at Sir's leisure.

He must've gone while I was still down in the caverns. I missed feeling him in the house; it seemed to be quieter than normal. So mike put on music and he joined me with the house chores, together we got more accomplished than I could've in one day. Dinner was baking slowly in the oven, fresh vegetables were scrubbed and ready for a pot, and dessert was done and cooling when J.D. arrived. He notified us that our Master would be home by eight and to have dinner ready. Until then, we were to finish the chores. J.D. retired to Hunter's office to complete some schematics on a crop rotation he and Hunter had been working on for the spring planting.

We heard his Harley coming up the mountain and I ran to greet him. I had been lonely all day, mike must have noticed because neither he nor J.D. ran to the shed where Hunter stored his bike. I must have sounded like a love-sick cow, because once he stopped his bike I ran into the shed and dropped to my knees, kissing his boots as my way of welcoming him home. He must have missed me as well, as he pulled me up, had me straddle his legs and he pulled me to him. "What's this, little shit? Did you miss me today?"

I was kissing his chest and pressing myself into his jacket to get closer to him. He scooted back on his bike and I found my ass wiggling into his 'V' as my legs closed around him. He leaned forward, propelling my back across the gas tank. He pinned my hands, then leaned his head on my chest. He was tired and his trip was almost a waste of time. Still, the outing did him good. Having the wind in your face and the power of a heavy hog between your legs has a way of driving almost all bullshit out of your mind for my Master.

He released my hands to hold me, his head turned and he kissed my naked torso then moved over to bite down on one of my nipples. My yelp shattered that loving moment of him holding his slave. He pushed himself up and ordered me off the bike, stepping off before pulling it up on its kickstand. "How was your day, slave? Did you get everything on my list accomplished today?" He asked me this with a wiry smile curling across his lips but was shocked when I said yes…with mike's help.

We were walking back to the house, my arm wrapping around his waist and his around mine. Neither of us spoke while we walked, just enjoying the silence of the woods and the beauty of the night sky as two lovers. He paused and sighed, "Tomorrow just might prove to be very interesting day for us." With that bombshell, we crossed the threshold and I took his jacket.

Dinner was served to our Master and J.D. while mike and I dined in the kitchen. Afterwards, those two retired to the office to make plans for the upcoming slave auction and I was left alone. Once mike was finished with my services, I took his jacket upstairs, pulled out some of his boots and proceeded to give them the spit shine he loved. The men entered the room, saw me and laughed their asses off as I looked up with my face covered with black boot polish. Hunter screamed in mock terror, "Kill it! Kill it! It's a boot vampire!" He ran to where I stood to put his dirty boots in my face and taunted, "You missed a spot." I made a grab for his boot and he danced away laughing.

J.D. stepped up pointed at his disgraceful boots. "Do you think you can do anything with these, 9-745?" I growled in his direction and asked him to leave them with me for a few days. "What, you want me to go around barefooted until they are done?"

Master chimed in, "J.D., mike go get the bundles and bring them in here for me to see. You did open them, right?"

"Oh, no, Sir! I wanted J.D. to be here when we did." Their boots ran hollowly down the hallway and resounded as they ran back. The twins were laughing when they dropped the 2-foot tall paper bound stacks of clothes. They looked at Sir and he nodded, as if to say go-ahead and tear into them.

I witnessed something that day that I will remember the balance of my life; two grown men crying out of sheer joy and gratitude. They opened the parcels, pulled out a couple pair of button-fly jeans for J.D., one pair for mike, heavy shirts, short sleeved shirts and tee shirts for both men, socks, a new pair of combat boots for each and, for mike, a handsome white chef's coat, white pants and a tall chef's hat. Tears began streaming down their cheeks, "Sir. It's just too much."

They both did their best to climb into his lap and thank him. He held them easily until they quieted. "More will come your way now that we have your sizes. Its high time you two look the ranks that you both have within my household. J.D., go turn on the hot tub, let it heat up. Mike, set out towels for four, set up two massage tables and 9-745, undress me. This week we need to rest up as much as we possibly can. The next three weeks are going to be ball-busters!"

We all were in the tub soaking when he shared the bad news. He had ridden over to Rob Roy's camp, spoken with him and the boy Jason. No one had seen or heard from Cappy. He told them that he thought he knew where he was, and that by Sunday he would know for certain. All three of us slept in some form of bondage that night and he took his revenge or pleasure of us in the morning, as was his right as Master.

The spring slave auction was just around the corner. Within nine days we had to get the house primed for incoming guests. The same mules that normally worked out in the fields were put to work erecting tent cabins out in the fields nearest the stables so electric and running water could be pumped to the bathing tents. Slave mike was underground early on Tuesday, arranging a menu for the upcoming event with the other Master Chef on the compound and was gone most of the day. I was sent with a handful of light duty slaves to dig the roasting pit, transferring fire rings to designated zones and to haul racks of dry wood to those individual sites. Hunter went downside to check on Doc, who, according to the phone conversation I overheard, was having a bloody tantrum.

Everyone was exhausted when they sat down to dinner. Hunter voiced his concerns about Doc failing to keep on his prescribed medications. J.D. requested permission from Master for him and mike to sleep in one of the guest rooms. His reasoning was although they loved the sex, no one was getting quality sleep. Hunter accepted his reasoning, but added that they could sleep there after a good night's rumble. His laughter told us who the real pig was in the family.

The four of us enjoyed the silence of the house and the crackling of the fire. Two men sitting side by side in comfortable arm chairs with two slaves leaning under their boots. True friends comfortable with whom they are and whom they are with only share silence like that. Two loving couples went up to bed, bade each other good night and went to our suites. Once in the bedroom, Sir unlocked my cock and butt thus giving him what we both needed.

When breakfast was complete the following morning and we'd all gone about our assigned tasks, all of us - including Hunter - had overslept due to my failing to waken on time. My poor ass got a blistering. Still, it must have been needed by all of us; else wise it would not have happened that all four of us slept almost three hours more than our norm. Hunter had gone to work off a budding anger in the gym, J.D. was off doing whatever he does, mike was ordering food supplies for next weeks delivery and I was alone again, off to carry out those endless tasks that we slaves have to do.

I was upstairs vacuuming the hallway when I heard a commotion in the downstairs entrance hall. J.D. ran in screaming, "Security team at the main gate just called, we have guests arriving by the busload! Get Hunter here, stat!"

I ran to the nearest phone calling the caverns below and told the main checkpoint below to find Hunter and get him topside, "Guests are arriving in buses!"

Damn that man, he must have known all along. He walked in just pretty as you please with a big toothy grin on his face, heard the news and began barking orders, "Mike! Get the flagon of mead, J.D. fetch the Welcoming Cup and you, get your leash." Hunter was the axis point from which three figures spun off to find and return. "You know the drill. J.D. you hold the cup, mike the flagon and you, on your knees at my boots. One, two, three…get the door slave."

We stepped out onto the front porch where we could hear the busses as they chugged up the graveled road. It sounded like an invasion was coming up the hill. The first vehicle pushed itself over the knoll as we stepped off the porch. Two black Hummers followed two black Trailways buses that were followed by one ¾ ton canvas covered truck; all pulled within five feet of our front steps. The Black Watch security team had arrived early!

A tall, well muscled cinnamon skinned Indian stepped from the first Hummer just as Hunter stepped down to the ground. The Indian walked around the vehicle as if his boots held unlimited power. Each boot had a glossy mirror shine from which two well-proportioned legs in a black uniform extended. He stopped before the vehicle, drew himself up straight and sharply snapped to attention, then saluted crisply. "Captain Steve Golden Squirrel and the Black Watch Security team, reporting for duty as ordered, Sir!"

My Master returned the salute just as sharply, "Welcome home, Captain." Hunter turned took the cup from J.D. who poured honey mead into the Welcoming Cup. "Welcome, Captain to you and all your Black Watch command to our manor home, Buena Vista." Hunter put the cup to his lips took a long swallow then passed the cup to the Captain who extended it high over head before pouring a few drops to the ground. Then he put the cup to his lips and tossed the balance of the cup down his throat. Traditional values for non-traditional people, they're still a necessary part of our life.

The rules of tradition met, Hunter opened his arms wide and stepped forward. Captain Squirrel did the same and they both patted each other heavily on their backs. Captain Squirrel shook his head, "Damn, Master Hunter, too few houses celebrate the old traditions like Buena Vista. It is good to be home!"

"Hell Steve, you know me. I like those traditional values; a man is the King of his own Castle, a slave in every home, even spare the rod and spoil the slave. It's all tradition." Master scanned the crew and the vehicles. "Did you bring the whole division? Who is left guarding the White House?"

Steve laughed, "They have their own guards and we have ours. Yeah, I kind of brought the whole shooting match. I know you could use some extra hands for the auction with all that's happened, and I know some of my people could use some quality down time, light duty. Hope you don't mind, Hunter?"

"Not at all. The more the merrier, I say."

Steve stepped back. "Let me introduce you to my field command, then you can review the troops, Sir."

Hunter turned back to mike. "Take the cup and wine back inside. Call Schmidt and inform her that a full division of Black Watch is here. She and her command had better be here in a nanosecond if not sooner. Go!" Mike ran to do Sir's bidding and hopefully Hunter could drag his feet long enough for our command to be on hand for the review of the troops.

Both Hummers emptied of men and women, all making their way towards our position on the steps. Hunter held out his hand as I did my part, putting their names to their faces. When next he would meet them with me at his side he would be informed of their names and ranks and not look foolish before his peers. This was one of the more endearing jobs we personal slaves get to contribute to our owners, memorization and recall.

The driver, Lt. Eric Wilson, was a handsome big blue-black man, well defined chest, bald head with a big gold earring in his right ear; hung like a horse and very nasty as a top. The passenger in the second vehicle was a wiry man, nice chest, with a warm smile that seemed to illuminate his whole face with teeth; his name was Second Lt. David Wu, demolition specialist. The fourth person had gone to the bus instead of in Hunter's direction. She looked like a spitfire. She walked with a bounce to her step that gave me the impression that she was just plain deadly, with shocking bright red hair. We were informed that she was Sgt Major Peggy Glover. Her whistle could be heard loud and clear.

A sea of men and women in their black jumpsuits and boots exploded from the buses. Each of the divisions held out their arms, getting placement before forming two distinct rows of commandos at parade rest. Sgt Major Peggy Glover stepped down her people with a practiced eye before making her way towards us as Commander Schmidt and her command exited the main house. They dropped down the few steps and another round of introductions was made.

Sgt Glover suggested the manor Lord and Schmidt join her with inspecting her troops. When Hunter and Katherine drew close they snapped to attention and our team walked amongst the finest security team within our Castle Corporation. Many countries copied our Black Watch, but only the England and Lao Manor's had anything that could match this group of devoted people. When they completed inspecting the troops Hunter turned to Schmidt. "Commander, please see to it that all their needs are met. Please notify both your teams that a barbecue will be held this Friday night at 1800 hours. Cocktails for officers an hour earlier." Hunter put his hand on Squirrel's arm, pausing him for a minute. "Get them settled and report to me for a briefing."

Master and I watched the teams unloading trunks of equipment. Schmidt sent in a few teams of mules with Handlers to help with the heavy lifting and, by the way the Black Watch team reacted to their presence, you would have thought they hadn't been privy to our training records. Our mules out lifted them four to one. Admiration of the mule teams rose as each heavy crate was lifted and carried to its destination. Our teams were like bulldozers working with men with shovels; our animals beat the security team easily. We would have stayed there most of the afternoon if a phone call hadn't broken our reprieve. Hunter went to his office and I to my house duties.

An odd incident did occur during the barbecue that set the teams on edge. Lt. Eric Wilson in the company of two other team members was fired upon by sniper in the woods while on a routine perimeter check. No one was hurt, but this indicated that someone has a grudge with either Lt. Wilson or one of the other men in his crew that evening.

After Friday night's attack on Lt. Wilson's team, security teams traveled armed and extra precautions were mapped out more completely for security checks. Whoever fired upon those men of the Black Watch left enough evidence behind to indicate the shooter was one of our own. Footprints led Captain Squirrel back to one of the old entrances to our caverns and down into an unused section that was occupied by that twisted fuck Doc.

Saturday seemed to take care of itself as Hunter met with the command of both Handlers and security for the greater part of the day. J.D. took me underground to assist with the next big show in hopes that my experience on the block would help the new stock find better owners. I helped the new stock create and perform, repeating their stances while displaying their strong bodies and handsome physiques. I was ignorant of the best way to show off my body when I went on the block, so I made them understand what was expected of them.

My Lord found me somewhat unfocused when I returned to the main house and made the afternoon something we both richly needed. I got the best of the deal. Being a bondage pig, my Lord was kind enough to place me in a sleep sack with a rigid back. Soft leather encased me from my shoulders to my feet; each arm slipped into a sleeve within the bag, and then laced up snuggly from my ankles to the nape of my neck. Once secure with the laces, heavy belts locked my ankles, calves, thighs and my arms to my sides, this slave was purring. With Sir kissing on me, I knew he was enjoying my confinement as well. When he was lacing me into the bag he saw to it that my cock and balls were left out of the leather folds. He laughed, saying someone had brought him something to play with. It was a larger application of something he'd made from two old hypodermic syringes for sucking the nipples from the chest; however, this was placed over a well-greased cock. The suction made my cock swell down into the clear tube and made me extra hot. With the addition of two nipple cylinders this slave was fired up and ready to play. My Lord had other plans and work to do, so with the addition of one of his hood and gag, he departed my side. He did return once to remove the cylinder from my cock, then disappeared to leave me traveling outside space and time until he returned.

I felt him as he climbed into bed, removed the gag and replace it with his balls. I sucked on them tenderly until he bored of that and placed his ass over my lips. While I ate his superbly tasty daddy-dank, he teased my extremely sensitive cock by rubbing the underside of its cock head with his thumb. The light sensation on my cock was replaced by a pleasure-pain when he began rolling the crown ridge between his finger and thumb. One hell of a way of making this slave increase its tongue action. He used my nipples to turn up the volume on my lapping tongue dance. Between his use of my cock head and the nipples, this slave's tongue was boring a hole to China. He gave up using my cock head, gathered my balls and began slapping them to offer more encouragement to find a way of burying my head into his asshole.

Believe me, if I could I would've been shoulder deep eating that man's asshole. All was going well until that damn phone rang. He cursed as he moved to answer, then replaced my gag, slapped my head gently and departed. As much as we both hated interruptions, when he returned there would be no stopping him from getting what he wanted. Later that day he gave me two loads, and that evening we had a private orgy with the twins. That is to say, he had a private orgy with the twins while I was locked into a canvas postal bag hanging from the ceiling. They sounded as if they had fun and, well, I had mine. There was always enough to share when it came to satisfying that man. Little did I know how that was about to change as two new mouths were about to be added to our pig trough.

Sunday, Hunter was called below to receive two packages from Doc and I had to accompany him into the depths of that man's depravity. Having had one too many associations with that depraved little fuck - if he was really a doctor - this slave did not wish to be in his presence without the protection of my Lord. Even then, this one could be put into Doc's hands without so much as a blink of an eye if my Lord felt it would better my understanding.

Doc greeted Hunter as cheerfully as a cat who had been caught playing unmercifully with a mouse. That man's insidious behavior made me feel queasy. Just being near him! Plus, I secretly hated the little bastard for what he had tried to do to me after my correction and the pit.

"Always good to see you, my Lord. It is a lovely day today, isn't it?" Just the way he said it made Hunter tighten his grip around my neck. He was indicating that I should pay close attention for later recall at Master's request. His fingers tapped out a code into my neck observe and be aware. "Sir," continued the doctor in a coy conceding voice. "If my work pleases you Lord, may I ask a favor of you?"

"Why of course, Doc," then Hunter thought the better of his reply. "That depends on what the request might be, Doc."

Doc giggled his not quiet normal laugh, "Sir, I want to go hunting on the grounds," Doc said the last in a rush of words. "I saw a handsome buck the other day. Stunning animal looked to have a huge rack and I just felt this need to possess it. Could I possibly go deer hunting?" Doc laughed at his sick joke.

"Doc," Hunter composed his thoughts carefully, "I thought you were against needless slaughter of wild life. Why the change?"

The doctor took Hunter's left hand. "I just don't know. I just felt I needed to have it. It would get me out of the caverns; you are always after me to get into the sunlight more. This would help, yes it would, to make me feel better. You know about myself," his head started bobbing up and down. "Yes, this would help me a lot. Fresh air, sunlight and hunting are good for the body. Please say yes; please think about it, please! I got a place all picked out for it in my cottage, where it can hang. So lovely, those beasts." Doc danced and skipped around as we walked down the corridor like a man having just been given a totally new lease on life. Wildly excited, happy and even smiling one of his least liked smiles, one of those smiles that always said to me, this slave was going to hurt bad. My body shivered just watching the sick bastard, he was hiding something. It showed in his eyes and how he pretended to hide his hands at his back. What few hairs I had on my body did their damnedest to lift as that sick fuck danced around us in a wide circle as we made our way down into his twisted domain. As we dropped deeper into the cavernous depths of the corridor, it was interesting that more and more rubbered things crept out to see who was traversing the corridor with Doc. We'd moved beyond the corridor, having entered Doc's private domain. The walls changed from chipped rock face to white sterile walls and we entered his hospital. I always found it odd how Hunter would have such a creature as Doc around, but they have history as does Cappy. I wondered what it would feel like to have your own personal time bomb ticking around you and no way of knowing when it would explode.

Hunter was talking again. "Did you have any problems finding the answers I needed from either of them?"

"They confessed to everything and anything. I asked them politely, I really did. But when you have a man by his nuts they usually confess to anything. How much can you believe from times like these?" Doc's eyes seemed to stare off in space as his voice seemed to wind down. Doc was like a wind up toy. Once its key was heavily wound and released it talked, danced, giggled excitedly but as time drew out its ability to hold on to a subject seemed to peter out, fade, then stop. It took Hunter's questioning to rewind the creature and set it on another tangent of wild hand gestures vivid adjectives and mournful nouns.

Doc was talking to himself then looked up and announced, "One is a whore and the other is a traitor. He betrayed you, my Lord! Both of them betrayed the sacred trust!" Doc's hands turned into claws before transforming slowly into white knuckled fists, and he spoke through clenched teeth. "They hurt for you, but I got the last laugh."

He backed away and opened two twin doors of a retired operating room. Doc led Hunter across the room to a huge chair set up on a raised dais. With a bow and flourish of hands, Doc asked him to be seated and he pointed where he wanted me, down on my knees resting beside my Lord. It was a very barbaric scene that I held in my head, something from one of those Conan comics I must have read as a child.

Doc started, "If confession is good for the soul, that whore is fresh as a newly sprouted daisy. Once it started talking there was no stopping it; but then, I did just happen to be sawing on it at the time, names I got, places, too. All for you." He snickered into his hand at his private joke then began singing, "A tisket, a tasket, now it has a black and blue basket. I cut him here. I sawed him there. And now I got what sticks to his underwear."

Hunter leaned forward in his chair and demanded of Doc, "What do you mean, Doc? Sticks to his underwear? Tell me, Doc! Don't play games, Sir is not in the mood for games today! Doc!"

Doc was no longer listening to Hunter but was off in his own tight little world. The man was literally standing on one foot as he spun around. He stopped, turned to Hunter who was speaking in a loud voice. "What on earth do you do with all those foreskins you take from every man that comes to you, Doc?"

Doc's face seemed to be perplexed, he became real quiet and then switched into a southern drawl with applied hand gestures. "Well, I's stretches deem and I's stretches deem again. Some's I makes into pillaws for my head, some's into curtains around my bed and some's I puts in da vats. Deem little ones I just makes into chewing gum, good stuff too, never really wears out. Amazing stuff, dat's what's I says."

I damn near puked on the floor at Hunter's feet when he spoke of his chewing gum. Every time I had been with him he had been chewing hard on some gum and every place I may have seen him in the corridors he was almost always chewing!

He turned on his heels and ran out of the room as he departed he hooted over his shoulder, "On with the show!" A naked slave who, by his physique, was an incredible power-lifter with slabs of muscles opened the twin doors. It was another one of Doc's creations. A thick black rubber hood with one oblong eye in the center covered this muscled slave. Huge pleated tubes exited either side of its nostrils, giving the hood a nightmarish image of some multi-horned demon. Where its mouth should have been was another tube that ran to a funnel on top of its head; this giant was nothing more than a urinal. The hood was locked around the slave's neck by a band of silver metal and a padlock. It was an odd effect that slave and its hood had on me. For once since I was most thankful for the wand Sir placed into my cock and its added weight. There was no reason to show my approval of one of Doc's creations knowing my Lord that Doc might be allowed to place me in one.

Two of Doc's goons in rubber pants, boots and long gloves entered, each holding a chain running to a fully encased, hooded and tubed thing in black rubber. The first in was 9-777, Dan, and the second I assumed would be Cappy. But my guess had to be wrong. The second creature seemed taller, had broader shoulders and even the way he walked was off. So if that wasn't Cappy, then who?

9-777's encasement was handsome yet oddly brutal. Black skintight rubber coated his legs, arms, hands and neck as if painted in place showing off every muscle the creature had under the casing. Its ribs and waist were trapped in what resembled a heavy accordion pleated corset that curved around its butt, slipped down into its crotch area and rose up to its shoulders. Buckles on either shoulder had to release the back panels. A bar of silver metal ran from one nipple to the other. Doc stepped forward to show off his creation. Flaps opened to reveal what looked like an adornment to the body suit, but was actually a piercing. The metal ran through one nipple out over the chest and into the other. Doc sounded like a fucking car salesman, coldly detached as he detailed his craft. Giving the codpiece a jerk, the unit snapped off. Inside was a black cock bound in silver metal, its balls locked into heavy ball weight. Proudly he announced *the flap does not leak* and displayed a small tube under the nuts where the water drains into two butt panels that could be drained without removing the flap. Bands of rubber-covered metal encased each wrist and ankle, allowing for multiple bondage positions. The creature was bent at its waist, showing a flap that snapped over the asscrack. When removed, I saw the same knob and key unit that was housed in this slave. Extra padding was built into the knees and elbow area. Even its boots were rubber, designed so the shackle link was exposed for use even while the creature was booted.

The creature rotated slowly, before the goon dropped it to its knees using a baton at the back of its legs. Doc stepped up to show its facial covering. He produced a key that unlocked the metal band from around its neck. Two large tubes ran from its nostrils, giving it plenty of air for hard labor. Its mouth was plugged with a large penis gag; it too has a hole through which piss or liquid nutrients may pass. Its eyes were covered with Mylar bubbles, giving it an alien look and the balance of its head was covered in protruding nubs. Doc, having released the mask, pulled it off the creature's head to reveal another mask under it. Straps ran over a well scraped hairless head, holding an anatomical face plate, giving it a non descript blankness around its eyes, leaving its mouth and chin area open. Those were Dan's lips and eyes burning out of that blackness. The gas mask was repositioned and pulled into place, the collar lifted and locked. Doc pushed a protruding tube back into the mask, forcing 9-777 to accept the penis gag back into its mouth.

Hunter seemed as stunned by Doc's rubber creativity as I was of one of Doc's creations; this transformation of Dan into slave 9-777. If I hadn't seen his eyes I wouldn't have known for certain who was in the suit. I hoped no one else would catch wind of who's in that suit. Least of all the Handler's that 9-777 betrayed.

9-777 was placed on its knees before the throne. Doc gave it a passing kick and it fell over, crawled to Hunter who elevated one boot and the creature crawled under. Good, I thought. 9-777 knew its place.

Doc called the second creature forward; its head was bowed and it must not have seen Doc's gesturing hand. His hand dropped to a box, one that was not unlike the one Hunter had used when I was on his big boat. Doc turned the knob and depressed the button. The reaction was instant as the creature gave a muffled scream, dropping to its knees while trying to reach its groin with its chained hands. His finger lifted and the air went out of the creature's lungs. It seemed to deflate before us.

Hunter rose to his feet before Doc could press the button again, stepping over 9-777 across the short distance and swung at it with his boot. It was like kicking a bag of flour on the ground; the boot went in but did not move the bag. The creature did, however, raise its head when Master stepped over it and walked back to the throne in disgust. As Master moved away, the creature put out its hand as if to grasp the boot and crawled forward, following Hunter painfully back to his throne. Hunter had one boot up on the dais when he turned abruptly, stooped down, grabbed the thing's hooded head and shouted, "Are you happy now, fuck up?"

He slammed his body back into the chair and drove his boot back into position on 9-777's back. His mood darkened considerably the longer he sat there and he was enjoying grinding his boot into 9-777's rubber hide. If I did not get him out of here fast, I thought he would be in a mood none of us could handle safely.

The goon moved forward and grabbed the smaller creature, who was crawling towards Hunter. Doc began the singsong chant of a salesman. "Both suits are alike in many ways, both have back flaps should you wish to beat them, copper contacts within their codpieces and drainage, ass plugs and cock locks. Both hoods have interchangeable parts so they can have filtered or limited air down to the size of a pencil lead. Personally I found this one loves the smallest setting on its air supply." Doc snarled, "It's taken too much for granted for too many years. It has gotten soft, but no more. Doc has seen to that. Even with this one's boots off it cannot feel the floor beneath its feet. I encased its feet in heavy rubber, no more slip ups for this one, none needed." He laughed, hugging himself.

Doc released the lock at the second one's neck, dropped the collar to its shoulders and backed away. "This one, if you noticed, has clearly humanoid features on the exterior of the mask. Its breathing tubes were lowered because I noticed it breathes mostly through its mouth. I found crushed bones here," he pointed to a place just above the nose on his face. "A little air enters its nose but most of it is sucked through its mouth." He paused, then giggled, "It will be able to suck in limited air when your cock, my Lord, is stuffed down its throat. Very limited air."

He pulled off the outer rubber hood of the creature's head to reveal a face I hadn't seen before. Doc ordered the goon to open the unknown slave's mouth and inserted a surgical clamp, grabbing the tongue and drew it out. "It came to me with too many piercings in all the wrong places, eyebrows, nose, lips and tongue. I split its tongue added two spherical piercings in hopes that it would give you more pleasure, my Lord. Plus, I opened a hole in the cartilage of its nose so it will hold a large bull ring, most suitable due to its bullheaded nature."

The goon pulled the hood back into place, Doc pulled out the bullring and inserted it through the rubber into the creature's nostril and out again. He took the ring in hand, nodding to the goon. "If you'll notice, it obeys better when someone has its ring in hand. Use it, my Lord, to bind it to a cross or the floor. If it rips out it will take its nose off. Then it will look like the pig it is!"

Master stood, up applauding Doc's craftsmanship. "Bravo, Doc! What incredibly talented hands you have and how creatively twisted is your mind, you are a genius. How can I repay you for your time and effort?"

Doc bowed before his audience before jumping at Sir's offer. "Let me go hunting in the woods tonight. I want that stag bad, Sir."

Master thought for a moment. "I will let you go, but we must do this right. Let me get you a deer tag and license from the local Game Warden. Once I have that, then you can go. Will you promise me that you'll not go hunting until I have the license and deer tag? Promise me, Doc?"

Doc studied the floor, then looked up to search Hunter's eyes to see if he was telling the truth or a lie. "You'll let me go? Oh Sir! Yes I will wait until I have the tag and license. Can I have them by tomorrow? Please?"

"It will take two days; promise me that you'll wait until Wednesday. The papers must be processed so you can go hunting on our land. By Wednesday all will be ready and you can go on your big game hunt. OK?"

"Oh, Sir! Yes, Sir! Wednesday I get to go hunting! Yeah!" Doc began to skip around the room, then he looked over at the second slave, suddenly stopped, walked over to it and started cursing a blue streak.

"What's wrong Doc?"

"There is a tear in its fucking suit." Doc kicked the beast.

"Can you repair it or replace the panel, Doc?"

"Yes, but I wanted you to take them home with you tonight," he whined.

"Can you replace the panel and bring it up with you for dinner tonight; will that give you enough time, Doc?"

"Oh, yes." His head was nodding in excitement, "Yes, that will work and I can see those lovely boys again. Those sweet twins, so lovely they are together, lovely twins."

Doc seemed to be starring off in space. His head snapped up and he took Hunter by his arm, leading him towards the door. "Go now, and take that other one with you. I will be along for dinner with the other nasty beast in a few hours."

Hunter was dismissed just that quickly by Doc and Master looked at me signaled *grab the leash* and I joined him on our way back up the corridor with 9-777. As we walked Hunter directed questions at me, "Doc is normally weird. But wasn't he a touch out there more than normal, boy?"

"Sir, it's like he's no longer in touch with reality. That is, if he ever did have a reality, Sir." As he asked, I shared my observations. I followed Sir's lead holding the leash to 9-777 and did not notice when we deviated from our path. He stopped at the nearest phone, a booth at an apex of two corridors. He made a call and spoke animatedly to whoever was on the opposite end of the line. Hanging up, he returned and we continued down the new corridor. Entering the hospital wing, we found the nursing station where he spoke to a collared nurse in full uniform. "Can you tell me if Doctor Wentworth is available?"

She studied a clipboard, then moved to a microphone. "Code 1, Dr Wentworth, Code 1."

The phone rang; she picked it up, spoke a few seconds and directed us to the third door down the hall. We entered without knocking and found the doctor on the opposite side of a desk. She rose, extended her hand and asked him to sit. She was a rotund woman, big breasts, big hands, big smile and big cigar.

"I bet I know why you are here." She started directly onto the subject.

"How long has Doc been without his medications?" Hunter asked her.

She flipped over a day calendar turning the pages. "I took him off them about five to six months ago, why?"

"When did you last see him, Dr. Wentworth?" Hunter asked her with ice in his voice.

She flipped back the pages then flipped them forward, "About two months.

Why?"

"Tell me, Dr. Wentworth, did you read his file before you took him off his medications?"

She coughed, "Honestly no. I assumed his problems were post traumatic stress syndrome - he was a highly ranked Vietnam veteran, wasn't he?"

"You did not read his file, yet you assumed to know what was wrong with him." Hunter leaned towards her, "Then I will inform the police department that it's your fault when he kills again!" He jumped out of his seat and started leaving the office. She shouted at him loudly, "What do you mean, again! He was a Vietnam vet, for Christ's sake. What does the file have that I need to know about?"

Hunter turned abruptly and made a cutting motion with his hand. "Read the file! He not only killed for the United States, he killed for pleasure. Read the fucking file and pack your bags! Since you took him off his medications, you'll now become his personal physician. You'll be flying with him to D.C. where he will be housed in a private asylum. You'll help him recover!" He slammed the door as we departed and exclaimed as we hurried down the hallway, "God, I hate doctors! For just these stupid reasons, so fucking high and mighty! They honestly do more harm than good!"

We stopped at the nurse's station and he asked her to call the Chief of Staff. Once the call was connected, she asked him if he would like to take the call in a more private setting. He denied privacy, "Elizabeth, we have a situation here. Your highly honored brainchild Dr. Wentworth failed to read the profiles before taking Doc off his medications. Yes, that's just what I said! Until your Doctor proves herself capable, I want her reassigned to Doc as his private nurse until he improves. I do not care how you do it, Elizabeth. It's that or she no longer works in our sector, and I mean world-wide! She can wipe her ass with her degrees for all I care!"

Hunter kept right on talking and did not notice that Dr. Wentworth had left her office and was standing right next to him. Her face had gone from a blush red to a pale white as he talked. Master turned, saw her there and resumed talking to the Chief of Staff. "Yes, Elizabeth, someone has been taking pot shots at the Black Watch security team, one man in particular who could pass for the man in Vietnam that Doc butchered. They could be twins. The same man that Doc tortured and skinned to death! We could not find the man's privates or skin when we finally found Doc. It took me seven years to get him back to some form of normal and this stupid cow of yours has destroyed my friend's life due to her own arrogance! If Doc or Lt. Wilson is killed in the next few hours I am personally seeing to it that your Doctor goes to jail for the crime. I will get him to D.C. and our asylum. Talk to your stupid brain child." He abruptly passed the phone to Dr. Wentworth whose mouth had dropped open in shock after what she had just heard coming from Hunter. "Talk to the Chief of Staff, you now have a new assignment!"

Hunter turned in his rage to get away from the hospital. We took a side trip and stepped out near the blacksmith shop. He said nothing and no one spoke to him. Just the way he walked said *leave me the fuck alone*. He leaned into the breeze cutting it apart like a knife through paper. He was determined to reach Lt. Wilson before either of his friends got killed. I let him walk ahead as he stormed into the Black Watch camp and began bellowing for Lt Wilson.

We caught up with Lt. Wilson in the command tent and Master asked if the Black Watch was armed. "Just tell me; do you have a tranquilizer gun? Preferably a rifle that can make a long range shot?" Wilson seemed perplexed by Hunter's request.

Wilson spoke to an officer who checked an inventory list. "We have one, but we did not bring it with us on this trip. We did not think we would need it."

Hunter's legs seemed to give away beneath him and he fell into a chair, put his head on a hand. "Fucking damn!" He sat there starring into space, pulling down on his lower lip. "Do you have anyone that you could call and have the gun brought here by tonight around eight this evening, but no later than dawn tomorrow?"

Lt. Wilson directed the request to the communications private, "Ask command if it's possible. Hunter, can you give me some explanation what is the emergency and why you need this rifle?"

"Yes I can, but I just don't want to make it public information," Hunter put out one hand as if to stop something midair. "Where can we talk in private?"

Both Lt. Wilson and his communications private seemed puzzled by his request so I injected. "Sir's, would it be possible to talk in one of your Hummers? It's pretty private, Sir's?" Both men agreed and withdrew.

I knelt and had 9-777 do so in an out of the way location. The two men were gone about a half an hour before they returned, barking out orders. Lt. Wilson told the communications private to make the call and Hunter called J.D., who joined the party in the tent. He and Hunter had a pow-wow and he ran off to use the secure office phone. One way or another, the tranquilizer gun would be here by dinner.

The local game warden came to our aid loaning his gun, high-powered laser sights and loaded the half a dozen charges for deer. That would be more than enough to take down what game in the sights tonight. The game warden chose to stay so that Doc would feel more secure. Like Hunter, he too had served in Vietnam. His reasoning for staying was that it would seem odd if he came here and did not issue a hunting permit and a deer tag. The warden was BV family like so many in the surrounding county. He'd arrive at the cabin in time for dinner, but chose to remain with Lt. Wilson until that time. We three departed and returned to the cabin.

As Hunter entered the cabin, he ordered me into the kitchen for sandwiches and a pail of slave drool. Slave drool was the nickname given by the slaves for the liquid nutrients that were usually served via a bucket and a rubber cock. By sucking the cock the slave got fed. Entering the suite, I found that Hunter had removed 9-777's outer hood and under mask, 9-777 was kneeling its knees spread, hands at its back and with its head lowered. I stood rooted to the spot, watching and waiting for him to see me.

"How dare you fucker's think you know me well enough to second guess me?" His open palm slammed into the kneeling slave's jaw, jacking its face in the opposite direction. The slave returned its face to original position, eyes forward head bowed. "Why couldn't you wait instead of becoming a cock crazed whore?" His boot slipped back before being slammed up, pinning the slave's nuts between boot leather and the metal that encircled its nuts. The animal fell forward, retching and unmoving. Hunter stepped over the motionless form and, as he did, asked his final question. "Why must those I love the most always hurt me the dearest?" He stalked out to the back porch, threw himself into a chair and sat quietly with his head in his hands.

I let the door slam and prayed silently he hadn't seen me when he was speaking to 9-777. I stepped out on our private balcony set down a plate, adding a nice cold beer and then knelt between his legs. I rambled to him about nothing in particular, allowing him time to regain his weakened façade. He sighed a long deep shuddering sigh, put his hand on my head, let it slip down to my chin and turned it up so I could see him. He pulled me into his lap and I held him as his head dropped onto my chest. I held him, offering him my strength and giving it freely. I felt as if his soul was crying. For all his hardness and harshness, he is a very tender-hearted man. We sat there unaware of time, one man giving another comfort. He kissed my chest, raised his head and kissed my lips tenderly. Placing his forehead to mine, he thanked me and I slipped back down to my knees. Once again all was right with the world.

Together we shared the sandwiches and the beer. Neither spoke; we had passed beyond physical words as we communicated with touches, looks and light kisses. All this he sucked into his heart, drank into his soul, replenishing and repairing the damage done by other's carelessness and eagerness to be with him. Even 9-777 felt it and crawled out to join us. Tentatively its rubbered hand slipped forward to rest on Sir's boot. He jumped at first as if stung, but settled down and allowed that things hand to rest lightly where it lay.

Each of us has our pit. Hunter was entering his. 9-777 would be dwelling in a pit housed in rubber until its body adapts and can feel Master's lightest touch. A thing sealed in black rubber no longer permitted to feel, taste, see, hear or smell until Master forgave the man within the suit. They say a body cannot live completely covered in rubber, its true. However, should precautions be taken that one part of the body remains exposed to the elements, so the pores of the body may breathe, the body can endure almost anything. My concern was how long would it take for Master to heal?

Hunter rallied. "Prepare me a bath, tonight I must betray a friend; so that, I can help him." Sir followed me into the room and ordered 9-777 to him. "Do you know why you are in this get-up? To protect you from Handler's who would love to get their hands on you. Men you counted as your friends and fuck buddies, betrayed because none of you could follow the rules, so you got punished. You have been watched for almost a year, even before 9-745 came into your grasp. You betrayed yourself."

I was moving about the room setting out his evening clothes, polishing boots, tiding the balcony, listening zealously, and watching them together. 9-777 cleared its throat as if to speak, but Master's head started shaking negatively. "I do not want to hear any excuses from you; I am not in the mood to forgive right now. I want to hurt, crush and destroy those that have hurt me at this moment. For now, you must wait on me!

"Boy, bring me that gag you hate, the wide straps and one of my filthy jocks."

All items placed within easy reach and I was ordered into the bathroom to attend the bath. He joined me a few minutes later, allowing me to undress him and place him in the tub. While he lay there I massaged away the knotted muscles in his neck, shoulders and back. This time I was not pulled in beside him. He lay alone, allowing the warm water to flow around him as I knelt at his side in silence.

After he dressed, he departed the room and left me to complete my tasks. 9-777 was bound tightly by straps and laid in a steel barred cage. Its mouth was gagged and Master's jock tied tightly over its mouth and nose. Tears streamed down both of its eyes. It now knew the severity of Master's control, and like I once did, now it must learn to fear our Master.

Dinner was something from out of a Fellini film. Too much drinking, laughter, and gaiety as I ran the courses back and forth from kitchen to dining room. The guests were an odd assortment of people. Besides Doc, there was Dr. Wentworth who'd dropped in to apologize and was ordered to remain, Joe the game warden, J.D. and

Peggy Glover (the Sgt Major of the Black Watch). They spoke mostly of hunting.

Doc arrived with time to spare and danced a jig when he realized the game warden was present as Hunter had promised. When he was given the hunting license, the little man went off! Doc held it high in his hand and pronounced to the world that he has been given the right to kill for God and Country again, that he had been liberated, then laughed and was about to leave when Hunter told him he was here for dinner. Doc rambled something about having his fill of the sweetest meat again and smiled.

During dinner, Doc refused any wine saying he had to keep his wits about him if he was to bag his buck. Then he giggled with his hand cupped over his mouth. Normally Doc had a huge appetite, eating damn near anything in his path when he came to Hunter's table. Tonight he ate only vegetables, a salad with no dressing and muttered over and over about the sweetest meat. Then he would smile a huge toothy grin, smack his lips with an *mmmmm, good!* and rub his tummy.

Wentworth sat in stunned silence, having finally read the files on Doc. It was as if finally someone had turned on the light as she realized she was at fault. She knew exactly of what Doc spoke of when he giggled over his sweetest meat and smacked his lips, relishing the thought of a nice thick steak. Still, pretenses were kept up with the laughter somewhat forced. Doc did not notice - he was oblivious to what was about to happen to him once he left the party.

Dessert was served at the table, strawberry shortcake with, Hunter announced, the first berries of the spring. We looked to Doc to tell him since it was his favorite. Doc didn't even taste them as he rose to say his good nights and was about to leave. Hunter stopped him, asking what the rush was. Doc looked up, "It's the dark of the moon, my Lord, like the last time. It's still the best time to go hunting. I must grab my gun to go bag my buck. Wish me luck, my Lord!"

Hunter pulled the little man into his chest. "Good luck Doc. Happy hunting!" Master returned to the table and sat down heavily as we all waited in silence. Someone muttered something, but Hunter chopped the air demanding silence. Then we heard it; feet running up the hard soil over the wooden planks until a lone figure burst through the front door, exclaiming, "He is down!"

The room exploded as we all ran to where Doc laid crumpled on the ground, a rifle at his side not far from the blacksmith's shop. Hunter began bellowing orders as he dropped to the ground and pulled the little man into his lap. He found the dart and tossed it away. "Bring a vehicle; the hospital in D.C. is waiting." Someone ran after a Hummer his boot stomps going softer as the distance grew. Hunter looked up, "Wentworth, I hope you're packed. If not, tough shit!" She tried to tell him that she was not going with him.

He cut her off. "You'll either go with him tonight or you are retiring from the medical field for the balance of your life! One way or another. you are off my base and you'll return to your place of origin as a slave and repay every last cent Castle invested into your schooling! You are indentured until you have paid off your debts, slave!" Hearing the anger in his voice, seeing the set of his jaw and how he cradled Doc she had to have known not to press the subject, and she bowed to his wishes. Hunter asked the Sgt to escort her to the hospital. Help her pack and get her off Buena Vista. "She either goes with her patient or to jail. Either way, she's out of my hair!"

The transportation vehicle along with two of the Black Watch medical staff and Lt Wilson arrived. Carefully Doc was loaded onto a backboard, straps were added securing him for the trip and Lt. Wilson assigned two paramedics with their equipment to monitor Doc. Wentworth returned with her pink doctors bag and the vehicle departed. All of us watched the tail light slip over the darkened road going down the mountain.

Hunter's shoulders slumped as Lt. Wilson came up to him and put his arm around his shoulders. He spoke with Hunter quietly as they walked back to the cabin. He walked my Master into the cabin sat him down and placed a tall brandy in Hunter's hand. When Hunter didn't immediately drink, Lt. Wilson suggested politely that he take a sip. It was as if Hunter was in a dream as he stared off into space. One sip of brandy reactivated the blood flow in his veins and he came to slowly.

After a double helping of strawberry shortcakes, Lt. Wilson departed for the night. Hunter reclaimed the black thing that had been unable to move due to being chained to its place. We retired to our suite, one thing locked in a cage another in tow. Hunter permitted me to feed them both and even allowed me to remove 9-777's gag while it was fed. Hunter had withdrawn to the balcony while I fed the creatures. It was as if their presence just made tonight's events too raw for him. I stayed my distance and was given permission to release a portion of the second slave's gear so its body could breathe.

I slept on the floor until he pulled me back with him in the middle of the night, chaining my hands to the headboard and roughly fucking my ass. Afterwards he rolled over into a deep sleep and I lay there listening to him snore. He turned and began muttering in his sleep, "No more Mr. Nice Guy, no more." The balance of his words were destroyed by a loud snore.

In the morning he added chains to my feet, tossed the cover over me and added a gag with the order to sleep. It was damn early and the sky outside was still dark when he moved over to where the second slave lay bound. Master toed the creature awake, released the creatures butt toy, slipped his cock in and worked that man's hole as he punish-fucked the beast! Hunter rolled the little man's legs and body into a tight ball, standing above it and driving his cock down as if it was a dagger. From the automatic sensor lighting, it was like he was stabbing the creature with his cock. Not caring if it could handle his meat, but raping slave butt. Having had his first load, I knew he could control his second to come easily or make his cock endure until he wanted it to blow. He worked that slave's hole until he lost interest and crawled up its body seeking another hole to rape. I heard the all too familiar gagging that told me he had found his mark and was now fucking the depths of the creature's throat.

The first bands of light were tinting the sky while he took his pleasure with the rubber creature. Sir stopped throwing his hips, looked down and whispered, "Now are you happy?"

His cock plopped wetly from the creatures lips and I could have sworn I heard Cappy's voice reply, "Yes, my Sir, yes." Hunter rose, behind him the sky was coloring blue. He stood out as a black-silhouetted shadow with a cock bobbing midair as he walked towards the cage that held 9-777. The door was opened, he dragged 9-777 out and flung it across the room to where the other slave lay. Like a tiger, Sir threw himself on them, tearing out 9-777's plug and replacing it with his own. A dramatically brutal orgy ensued.

"Get over here, stinky." Hunter grabbed the second creatures rubber covered body and drug it into the fray. "Eat my ass, you little fuck! That's right, bury that tongue deeper, deeper!" Hunter had his cock impaling 9-777 as the slave he called stinky kept its head buried, giving him room to move like well practiced moves on both their parts.

One head buried cheek deep, the other's cock buried balls deep and the slave beneath them, spreading its ass cheeks to give him more depth. And I hurt badly. My swollen cock remained locked within my Master's chastity watching, wanting to be part of the scene as it played out on the floor below me.

Never had I watched him fuck by inches, he always had taken the full length of his cock in hip shattering blows. He gave himself over to the tongue buried deep and fucked the helpless slave slowly as it mewled in frustration. He pulled stinky off his ass long enough to withdraw his cock and put the smaller slave into the cleft of 9-777s cheeks with an order to eat it clean. Sir ripped the gag from 9-777s lips and allowed it to mouth his cock until he grabbed its head, tilted its chin up and impaled its face. He raped the slave's gagging throat, giving himself over to pleasure; he became a steam fed piston feeding his anger into his heaving loins. He came, voicing a pent-up rage that left him slumped over his heaving creatures, withdrawing his cock and ordering the second slave on it. When he'd had enough, his hand knocked the little slave off his cock and his foot kept it in place. "You'll be a fitting gift for a warrior."

The slave beneath his foot begged, "Please Sir, no."

Hunter slipped his weight and body over to the slave straddling its chest. "What did you say, slave? You brought me to this. You tried to run away from me! Once, when I let you go you returned and you said you'd never leave me. Then you begged me for this. Now you have it. I will always love you, but you would serve me better elsewhere." Master's head was nodding, "You belong to Buena Vista. Like others before you, you'll be placed where you'll serve me best."

When I was permitted to move from the bed, the smaller slave had his headgear back in place and was slumped over in rejection. The back panel had been removed on its rubber suit, showing shoulder blades to ass crack. There, painted in fine line tattoo was an image of the Virgin Mary. This was not Cappy, but some other slave who I would never know unless Sir told me.

Both 9-777 and I attended to my Master's needs while the smaller slave tidied the living quarters. Returning Hunter to his bedroom, I was ordered to empty the traps on the small slave's suit and then to do the same for 9-777. Completed, the three of us dressed him and escorted him downstairs for him to have his coffee.

The whole household was up. J.D. had just left for his duties and mike had taken the liberty of preparing two buckets for the new slaves. Master took his coffee to the table and sat in silence until mike asked what he would like for breakfast. He had been sipping in silence, starring off while allowing the coffee to help return his senses. "Before you feed them," he pointed at the rubbered slaves, "both of you piss in the buckets." Mike looked at Sir than over at me, but knew that tone of voice. He had better follow the order to the letter. I'd just pissed upstairs, so not much of my drippings would be in the buckets; mike gave a sizeable bladder load to each. "Now they may eat, put them before the bucket's."

Having had my share of sucking on those damn buckets I knew the humiliation that it could cause a body, still it taught a slave a valuable lesson. Sucking cock gives one nutrients, taught how to suck and drink the cum like goo down one's throat without gagging.

"Fix me a big omelet and take care of 9-745's needs, too. More coffee, 9-745." He looked over to the slaves sucking on the buckets, "Finish it boys, it may be your last for a long time."

They renewed their attack on the rubber cocks, working them for all the fluids their buckets contained. When the buckets were empty, they withdrew their heads while kneeling and belched. One of the bad things about the buckets; when you sucked you got a lot of air along with your meal. Hunter ate in silence, only pausing to demand more coffee and finally to make his demands of the day. "9-777 will be with you today, so get the house spotless for the incoming guests. If that's completed, hood its head and go below, use it to clean the guest quarters. Make one suite ready for immediate occupation and go to that whore Dr. Wentworth's office, box her shit and find her sleeping quarters. Pack it; that crap can be sent to her in D.C. when the next delivery goes out. Then call pest control let them delice her quarters and office. Come stinky, you are with me."

That was the last that I saw of him until dinner when he returned with Lt. Wilson and stinky.

Chapter 8

Let them hate, so long as they fear.
Lucius Accius

According to the story that this slave has been able to piece together from tid-bits of information gleaned from my Master and other conversations, I believed I knew Doc's history. Doc was once known as Doctor Teddy Rosenthal and was stationed from his internship on a ship going to the Vietnam conflict. He must have been a cute looking young man, because three Marines guards, one black and two white, bustled him into the brig. There they gang-raped him, using him every possible way and even sold his ass to others for a price. When he was finally discharged from the brig, he was a changed man. On the surface he was the same caring doctor his other friends had known. None were wiser as to what had happened to him in the brig that weekend. Under his façade, he was a smoldering rage bent on revenge.

Hunter and Doc had become close friends while in basic training. Later, they were separated for specialization and reunited when stationed together in Vietnam. At that time, Hunter and Cappy were sharing a bungalow off base and Doc became a regular overnight guest. The three men were out painting the town, blowing off the blues when they overheard from a bragging belligerent Marine how there was nothing finer in life that to split a white man's pussy. Doc disappeared soon after hearing the Marine talking about how he and his buddies stalked, trapped and captured this young thing and used it all weekend until the boy begged them for cock.

Hunter tried searching discreetly for Doc; he did track down the Marine's pla-toon and found out their Sarge was missing in action. Hunter checked the whorehous-es, flop house and opium dens, making indirect inquires concerning the whereabouts of the two missing men. He'd almost given up when something odd came across his desk; a report of recently stolen medical supplies. Going to the hospital supply unit, Hunter found that Doc had also requisitioned surgical supplies and had stolen the items while the officer was checking his papers.

Hunter had asked his closest buddies to help with the search; it took almost two weeks to find Doc. He was located in a Quanson hut near an abandoned supply dump. One of the trackers found him and summoned the collective; they waited and watched until Doc left for supplies. The temperature over there was in excess of 100 degrees in the shade, so they thought it odd to see Doc leaving the hut wearing a burgundy black long sleeve shirt and pants. Two men to followed him with a radio, just in case he should return sooner than expected.

Before they even entered the hut, Cappy and Hunter thought it was going to be really bad inside. Flies were blocking out one of the windows. The team made their way slowly into the hut. Those first in were first to leave, they ran out to vomit from what they witnessed. Black flies swarmed the rooms, swarming over mounds scattered around the hut. The odor in the hot hut was beyond disgusting and the heat burned it into their nostrils and clothes.

They found a curtain dividing the room into two sections. Just over the curtain, they could see the slumped head of the Marine that had disappeared. From their point of view, nothing seemed out of the ordinary with exception that the Marine was silent. The curtain gave them reason to worry; it was covered with reddish brown handprints and the color of dried and baked blood on a white sheet.

Nothing prepared them for what they would find once they pulled the curtain back. What they saw made them all vomit into their gasmasks as they ran from the hut. They found the Marine, the poor bastard, barely alive. He'd been skinned from his chin down to his ankles, all the skin had been expertly removed from his body, flayed in giant sheets. And the realization hit them. It was the clothing that Doc was wearing when he left. Only the man's head retained the true skin color. Everything else had been peeled off his body, his cock and balls were missing as well. A shot of morphine was administered to the suffering Marine. That quieted the man as they laid him gently on a cot until they could figure out the possible reasoning behind Doc's insanity. Two other disgusting finds were made that day, the heads of two white men packed in buckets.

The mystery ended with Doc's return, carrying a bag full of fresh greens and flowers. It was by the way Doc acted - as if nothing was wrong - and upon finding Hunter and his men inside his hut. Hunter noticed blood running down Doc's arm and asked him if he had been cut. Doc laughed, then sobered quickly and told Hunter the story about a trusting young doctor on a flagship and how three Marine animals had gang-raped the young man. But the voices had corrected that situation as he now had the power and nothing would hurt him again. Doc, who had been sitting while they talked jumped to his feet screaming, "I got his power!"

Doc tore at his chest, ripping the buttons off his shirt to reveal the skin of the black man draped over his body. Laid casually like a silk shirt over his shoulders and he was wearing the man's legs like pants. "I got the power,' he screamed, "I got his power! And he can never hurt me again!" Before anyone could stop him, Doc jumped to his feet and fled the hut. Two men followed but lost him in the market place crowd. When they did finally find Doc, it was days later, and the skin, cock and balls were gone.

Doc retired to a psych-ward, his captive was taken out into the field and left for one of our patrols could find him. It was spread that he was kidnapped, tortured and skinned by the fucking evil enemy. A few villages were burned with the occupants killed in honor of the other two dead Marines. When their heads turned up in yet anther village, they too were destroyed. The true incident was swept under the military carpet like so many others.

Hunter kept tabs on Doc while he was transferred from one VA Psych-ward after another, until the new administration thought it would be wise to put the old nuts out on the street. Hunter brought him to his Buena Vista where he could keep Doc under heavy medication, lock and key. Pills had kept Doc under control and nothing had given Hunter reason for concern until Lt. Eric Wilson had stepped onto Buena Vista soil. Then all hell broke loose.

Master had to switch gears immediately after Doc had been taken off grounds. The following day guests - sanctioned, prospective buyers - began to arrive. Master and his team had to become welcoming hosts, showing off the animals that would be on the block and otherwise showing the visitors why it was great to own a few slaves. 9-777, stinky and I did our damnedest to show our guests that we're the gears of the household.

The slave auction went unbelievably well for Buena Vista, netting us a tidy profit of $3 million plus and what our craftsman guilds earned in their own sales to new and previous owners. Shipping of our precious cargo began immediately and would be finalized before the end of the month. Hunter was so pleased by the sale that he gave everyone above ground a day off for rest once the guests left Buena Vista. There would be a huge feast to celebrate the success of the spring sale.

Life on Buena Vista had been running pell-mell towards the auction. Once over, with half the cargo in route to new owners and the balance waiting until their containment units could be constructed, Buena Vista paused to give a huge collective sigh of thank God that's over. Then we heaved a huge hurray for the next step, the after the auction blowout party followed by a few weeks of packing before we would all go on a huge collective vacation. Life was good!

Good for all except those who made the mistake of angering their owner. Such was the case of 9-777. I'd risen early and had taken the other two with me, leaving Sir to rest in bed. I was bringing him back some breakfast when I heard a commotion in the bedroom. When I entered, I saw 9-777 go down after Hunter had kneed him in his nuts. Master's face was bright red and when he turned to see who was at the door his eyes were bloodshot and evil. He told me to get the fuck out and leave him alone…he would take care of this situation without help.

Listening at the door, I heard a scuffle, a muffled groan and then I heard his screaming. "Stupid fucking slave, you do not think, you obey!" Silence, then I heard his whip hitting flesh and I fled back down the steps. I knew all too well the sound of a whip in anger. Silently, I prayed that he would be a merciful God and continued muttering my prayer as I went back to my housework.

A barked command over the intercom brought me back to the suite, where I found 9-777 facing the wall, arms attached to shackles midair, its back panel open and its back covered with angry bleeding welts. This was not Hunter's anger; this was a show of his pain. 9-777's face had also received his attention, or more likely his fists by the way one eye was swollen and lips busted and bleeding. I was told to cut it down and clean it up; it has to function tonight as the bartender. Hunter crossed the room swiftly as I lowered 9-777's feet to the floor. "If you so much as fuck up one drink," he said, shaking the slave's head. "One!" He turned to me and demanded, "Clean that fool of a slave up. I'm going to soak in the spa."

I hoped the hot water in the tub would drain away some of his anger. Thankfully for 9-777, stinky and me, it did help him relax. While I cleaned up 9-777, I tried to get out of it what had happened. It honestly did not know. Hunter just blew up on it. Which was totally out of character for my Master - unless the slave had stupidly had touched one of his more raw nerves of late.

Master returned more relaxed and knelt to aid with my cleaning of the slave's back, the slave made the mistake as if to draw away from Master's touch. Hunter grabbed it, flipped it by slamming his barefoot into its ribs and straddled its heaving chest. "Refresher course, 9-777. Never, ever refuse your owner anything. No matter how badly you hurt, no matter how ill you may be, never say no to me with body, mind or soul! Both of you into the bathroom, now!"

What goes around comes around. I remember a very similar lecture given to me by Handler Dan after he had beaten me senseless about never refusing him service. Once Sir's needs were met I was permitted to finish cleaning 9-777's back and install a heavy leather hood with a large open mouth. Once sealed around the thing's head, Hunter added chinstrap and a prick ball that rested just on the tongue of the slave. Any attempt to speak would give it pain, hell, just having it in your mouth was pain, swallowing was pain. I knew how brutal they can be for long term wearing; they make you salivate which makes you want to swallow. It's doubly damning.

Hunter had ordered his kilt, but when I turned to assist with his dressing I found him instead having chosen his skin tight black leather pants that showed off every muscle that man had, he looked stunning. His shirt was a handsome, deep emerald green and over his left shoulder he laid a black and green plaid wool sash that got pinned by a huge silver broach. He had chosen a soft boot that ran up and over his knees for the evening. Buckles locked them around his thighs cavalier style. I was ordered into a green pair of leather shorts with a black codpiece that he had made for me. Before we departed the room I was ordered to find an arm binder and put stinky into it.

We found stinky in the kitchen assisting mike. There was a brief scuffle when stinky realized the arm binder was for it. Master's boot and anger held the slave to the floor while I trussed it up like a goose with its wings pinned at its back. Its bull-ring was installed and Hunter added a leash handle hanging down before the slave's hooded face, a barbarically beautiful function. Stinky was forced to its knees near the den fireplace while Hunter took 9-777 to the bar and locked it firm, warning again of the consequences it if it screws up. The animal was visibly shaken by his statement andheld its silence.

Over 180 people joined in the celebration of the spring sale's success. The den was a swarm of people in different states of leather attire at its best. These people did not fashion themselves after bikers, but came from all walks of creativity. Some wearing only primitive loincloths, others from out of nightmares with billowing trench coats, some wearing nothing but boots, bra and jock. It was mind reeling statement of pure hedonism. Just stepping into the room would have made any leather lusting slave attempt to get a hard on, serving them drinks kept my mind focused and on its duties. Even when someone cupped this one's ass or grabbed at its cock in passing, gestures permitted by the Master of the house. They knew it just like I knew it, *once owned, off-limits*; the overtures flattered an aging slave nonetheless.

The slave kitchen staff had gone overboard to make these people feel secure - if security meant food. They laid out a spread that could be hard to have been equaled by other houses. A cow, pig and hens were roasting over open pits; fresh vegetables were laid out on huge flatbeds, hot breads, sweets cakes and a tanker of beer had been brought in to give the horde plenty to wash it down. Small buckets had been issued as they entered the arena. Each held about two pints of fluid and Sir made certain they had their fill. Most of them knew the following day was a workday, but they did not falter in their attempts to drink the tanker dry.

Master strolled through his partying horde with his hand on stinky's nose ring leash, a proud owner by the way he walked. I was on assignment to the kitchen until the food was laid out, then I would return to Sir with a tray of tasty bits for us to eat. When I did find him again he was without stinky. 9-777 stood at his side, proudly displaying his Sir's handiwork by turning to allow Handler's to see. Pride in a slave is a double-bladed sword; Hunter saw what it was doing and dropped it to its knees for view and within sight of his people. A slave brought him a chair, others were placed around him and a small court seemed to appear out of nowhere.

The sky above our head exploded with a wild array of colors and sparks. The crowd hushed their mingling voices, holding their collective breath in anticipation of more fireworks. Instead, Hunter's voice booming over a loudspeaker called them. He stood above me; 9-777 and I were kneeling at our appointed sides. The slave on the left was closest to his heart, my place, and other slaves on the right. His people moved towards him and crowded around, waiting patiently for him to begin. Their smiles radiated their trust in this, their Lord.

"Lords and Ladies of Buena Vista, welcome to tonight's celebration our spring sale. An amazing success, all due to each and every one of you. Give yourself a well deserved round of applause!" He began clapping and they followed suit, waiting until they quieted before he began again. "We have all profited from this sale, your bank accounts will show the transfer by tomorrow noon of your part of the profits." They went wild, catcalling and applauding this announcement. "We netted $3 million! This is the largest sale to date! In addition the leather guild brought in $525,000, the blacksmith made well over $1 million in future renovations and steel sales, the rubber guild brought in $457,000 and I, personally, want to thank you for your hours of hard work. Your pay and profits will reflect my appreciation." The crowd cheered when they realized they would be receiving profits from almost $5 million.

"Guildsmen, since your families are here with you, please see to it that they do not wander beyond the beer truck or beyond the canvassed wall, that is for the adults only. Now, Lords and Ladies of Buena Vista, while I have you here I need to make a public announcement. Starting tomorrow Buena Vista needs for you to begin packing all your unnecessary items. Crates are available within the dry storage units off from the kitchen, units 1 thru 7. You have one and a half weeks to get everything packed, because in two weeks we will be going on vacation. I hope you treasure hunters have done your work. The treasure is incredible, ranging from a brand new custom chopper made by our own Rob Roy, custom leathers made by our leather guild, custom thigh-high boots and - if my fading memory recalls - about 500 pieces of gold bullion."

His final words for the evening were, "There's a beer wagon over there and a soda wagon over there for those of you who have the dawn patrol. The day after tomorrow our work is cut out for us. But for now, let's party!"

His people moved like a tide, swarming around him, thanking him, patting him on the back before departing to continue with their aspect of the party. The crowd finally drew apart, allowing this slave to approach him bearing a tray heavily laden with all the necessary and unnecessary food groups. The slave at his feet was placed on its hands and knees as its battered back was transformed into a tabletop. Kneeling between his legs, my Lord allowed me to feed him between chats with his people. He was not put off by any of his people nor did he choose to live among only the higher ranks of his officers. All were welcome and he was genuinely concerned for all of them.

My Lord had drunk the best portion of two buckets when he decided he needed to piss. Normally, I would have drunk his piss right on the spot. But with children present within the partying horde, he took me behind the beer wagon. That was where I found stinky, laid into an old bathtub, its arms freed and body covered in a tub of piss. A hand-scrawled sign was posted on a fence post, *In or On, all piss for free!* Stinky seemed to be in heaven, coaxing men to play their hoses over his body or when he turned and presented his funnel going directly into its mouth. Happy like a fish in water was stinky at that moment. Hunter and I emptied our bladders and returned to where 9-777 waited.

Lt. Wilson joined us, trying to juggle a tray of food and eat from it. 9-777 was kicked in his direction by my Master and at first Wilson seemed leery to use the slave's back until I took his tray, toed the slave between the man's feet and rested the tray on the slave's backside. Numerous other slaves ran around feeding Handler's and guildsmen, still others were tending the roasting beasts and others were detailed to serve as sex slaves behind the curtained fence. It was to that area that we withdrew after a fashion. After the dungeon Master had claimed 9-777, it had been placed in service to care for the masses. According to my Master, it would break him of that need for excess.

Master had me on a short leash, with the slave taking the lead to cutting a path and alert others to his presence. We passed the piss troughs, the beer tanker and its lines, beyond to the canvas wall erected to keep our sexual freedom away from children's prying eyes. Besides any children with common sense would have been in the opposite direction to where there was a slave run merry-go-round and other simple devices for entertaining children.

Moving beyond the tented wall into a world of shadow and light we found many couples enjoying their own form of pleasure with slaves. No matter where I turned I could not find 9-777 until Hunter lead me to the front of a line. What I saw made me pull on my leash to flee. Hunter pulled me back, placed his elbows on my shoulders and pulled my head around forcing me to watch. "Yours was rape, this is nothing of the kind, and this it wanted like you did your rape. After this, it will never want it again. I know 9-777 better than you; this is just what it needs to get its head back in proper focus. After tonight it will be a better slave. Believe me boy, I know of what I speak."

Hunter captured a heavily muscled mule that was moving through the crowd without Handler or leash, placed it on its hands and knees as a chair. He pulled me down and forced me to watch the vulgar show that was unfolding around 9-777. They had him bound over a wooden barrel, his head and ass were elevated and his mouth open for all takers. Two lines of men had formed, some openly fisting their cocks in anticipation of blowing a load in their Lord's newest slave, 9-777.

This slave shivered as it watched, being held in Master's arms as first one man blew his load into an open mouth then another in its ass. This slave remembers just how hopeless it felt when it had been used so cruelly by police officers. Every time I tried looking away, Hunter forced my head around to watch what he called the transformation of his slave. It was an uncouth way to milk the fight from 9-777 and this slave knew it would work; it did on me for a time.

Hunter pulled me with the 'V' of his legs, placed my arms under this thighs to wrap them around his boots as he rolled my nipples. I watched the boorish sights of men using slaves however they wanted. Not only 9-777 was bound and open for service. Other slaves were trapped, being fucked or made to suck whoever approached. Refusing even the slightest cock was not permitted and a few received punishments while others waited their turn. If we were an outside society this action would have been life-threatening to all that partook of the forbidden fruit. However, on Buena Vista soil with people who were fanatical about getting tested regularly safe sex had been taken to new heights. Here it was the accepted norm.

Hunter leaned down to me while rolling my nipples, making me squirm as my cock struggled against his chastity. "I want them to fill his bowels with their cum. Fill his throat, too. When it stands again before me, the cum will dribble out of his mouth and ass lips. It needs to remember this night for the balance of its life as you do yours. Look at me, 9-745. Go fetch me two cigars and when you pass stinky drag it out of its tub and bring it here. It's time it earned its keep as well. You have 15 minutes before I depress the button at my belt and blow your nuts heavenwards. Dismissed!"

When I returned with stinky I found that 9-777 was suspended by its ankles with a catch basin was below its head, vomiting up what looked like massive volumes of cum. I wanted to run, but stinky held me in check, making me take him before our Master. Master made me focus not on what was going on behind me, but on taking care of prepping him a cigar and serving as his ashtray. Even there, straddling one of Sir's boots, this slave was forced to listen to 9-777 gagging and puking as the numerous loads of cum poured out its body and into the basin. Once 9-777 was lowered another slave measured the contents of the basin. There was always a contest amidst the slaves to see who could take the most.

One of the Handlers approached Master, speaking over me, asking if stinky was ready for its term of service. Hunter must have seem my revulsion, he pulled my face up to his by the collar and spoke clearly. "Stay here, don't fucking move one muscle. Or you'll be next!" He rose, dragging stinky behind him. The men at my back cheered as stinky was tossed over the barrel and they bound it in place.

I had just risen to run when Sir grabbed my arm, spinning me as I fell to the ground. "Where do you think you are going, 9-745?" I had no answer for him, instead I chose to look at the ground. "Get me a wooden lawn chair and be quick about, 9-745!"

Returning to him with the lawn chair I found 9-777 released from its suspension. Hunter indicated where he wanted the chair placed. I dropped to my knees to the ground beside him. He leaned, back stretching his booted feet across the ground, saying, "Watch 9-777." Master raised his hand, crooked his index finger towards 9-777 who was where they laid it. 9-777 crawled on his belly to where Hunter and I sat. Its tongue shot out of his rubbered face, a brilliant pink in contrast to the deep black rubber that contained its body, and tasted its Lord's boot sole. Sucking and licking on them as if it was his lifeline to sanity, the tongue previously coated with cum was now coated with blackish brown soil from the ground of Buena Vista.

Hunter felt me tense up as the men went to work on plugging stinky's holes with their cocks. He changed my focus with a light slap on my face. "Go to the den. Bring me a large brandy and you better install a couple of cigars in my humidor. I want you nearby me and not running around later."

I ran to his office found the needed items in his desk drawer, withdrew two of his Churchill's inserted them both into a condom each and installed them in his private humidor. I found his private stock of brandy and his large brandy snifter. Carefully, so as not to destroy the cigars in my ass, I ran to my Lord and halted mid-tracks as a jealous rage came from nowhere. 9-777 was walking its tongue up my Lord and Master's leg. If looks could have killed, that slave would have been dead on its knees. Instead it got something it was not expecting. Master put his boot sole squarely on the rubber thing and stomped back on the face, hard! The swiftness of the attack was a shock to 9-777 as it knocked back over to lie on the ground. 9-777 crawled to Hunter's boots, placed its bleeding lips to them and began tracing patterns into the soles. Watching Hunter and 9-777, this one realized these tactics seemed to please the slave and the Master. Hunter drew his boot back, making the crawling slave follow the boot sole. When the creature was near enough, Hunter grabbed hold of its collar to pull it between his closed legs, trapping it.

"Hands behind your back, slave!" The slave obeyed and bowed its head.

Hunter's open palm slammed into the slave's face as he bellowed, "Cock suck-ing whore!" The slave's head flashed to one side and returned, looking down at its Master's crotch and licking its lips. "Does it have anything to say for itself, slave?" Hunter laughed hard, "No? Then you are a cock sucking whore?"

9-777 cleared its throat and whispered, "Sir, this slave needs its Master's strength, Sir."

Master laughed, "You are going to get a lot more than that, 9-777. Pull my cock out of my pants, dog! Now suck it all the way down your throat like it's been taught. Hold it there. Do not move, just nurse it." Snapping his fingers this one dropped besides its Lord, opened its mouth and was fed the ashes from his cigar. He pulled me into his leg, rolled my nipples to expertly force all my attention on him. This was a game he loved to play with slaves, fill their mouths with his cock and make them keep it in place until their jaw grew tired. God help the slave that dare allow its jaw to close on his meat. It would have all its teeth pulled in a heartbeat, if not beaten down their own throats with his fist.

Others pulled up chairs and joined our ranks, watching the crowds of milling men and women as they practiced the oldest form of hedonism, pure unadulterated debauchery. Those that chose to gather around Hunter and his slaves were close friends of the family. Golden Squirrel had one of his slaves sitting quietly in Japanese bondage at his feet. Peggy Glover had a male slave literally peeling grapes and feed-ing them to her. Katherine had bound her female slave's breasts in rope, making her lick parts of her body as she pointed.

Time was called on stinky's duty. Like 9-777, it was suspended over a basin where the fluids caught were measured and posted on a growing line of other such disgusting tidbits of the slave contest. The winning slave would get nothing special out of the contest except the knowledge that it had served its owners well and maybe an extra ration of food in the morning.

When stinky was released it dropped and lay prone on the ground. Hunter called its name a few times. Either stinky was out cold or he was refusing to come to Master. Instead of getting upset as he would have if 9-777 would have pulled this shit, Hunter chose to ignore the slave on the ground and chose to wait for it to regain consciousness on its own. Hunter looked over to Lt. Eric Wilson. "Tell me Eric, have you ever owned or trained a stubborn slave?"

Lt. Wilson laughed a deep bass chuckle. "Never found one that was enough of a pain pig to handle what I like to dish out."

"So you are a mean motherfucker, are you Eric?" Hunter pointed to stinky, who was pushing itself up on its hands. "Maybe you're just the right man for that crea-ture over there."

"Sir, I really do not consider myself to be a mean motherfucker. But I do tend to get brutal when I get a hard on."

"Eric, I need a favor from you." Hunter stared directly into the eyes of the Lieutenant. "I seem to have one too many slaves underfoot right now. I would be honored if you would take stinky under your boot over the next two weeks and teach it what pain is all about. However, there's a catch that goes with that creature. It must never be allowed in public without its headgear firmly locked in place. No one but you and I must know who that rubber suit contains until its appointed time. Are you game, Eric?"

"Thank you, Sir, for your kind offer," stated Eric to Hunter, "but I have more than enough to do getting my teams established, demolition started and the various other teams familiarized with the crisscrossing tunnels. I keep getting lost and so do most of my people. Honestly, I don't have the time to train it in two weeks."

"Eric, I don't want you to train it. I can do that once I have whipped 9-777 into shape. I want it to suffer for the next two weeks, that's all. Make it suffer. Teach it about your kind of pain. I want him so sore when you return it to me that farting hurts. You can do anything to it with exception of snuffing it, maiming it or breaking any bones as it still must perform for me when returned. Stinky is a captured runaway. Besides, it knows the underground caverns like it knows the back of its hand. It was well trusted once before it betrayed its owners. Tell me Eric, how many runaway slaves have you had the displeasure of tracking down since you have been with the security team?"

"Only ten, Sir."

"Did you like that search and seizure routine? Did any of those slaves ever get a punch in on you before you took them down?" Sir paused through the lieutenant's silence. "I see by your reaction that they did. Ever wanted to pay them back? Now's your chance with that piece of shit over there. Take it home tonight, let it feel your displeasure, use it any way you want. Fuck it until it's blue in the face, make it beg in Swahili for all I care. But use it hard and work it harder. Do me the favor of keeping it over the weekend. If it doesn't prove valuable to you - even as a dog on a leash leading you around the underground tunnels - return it. We have quarters for you and your officers underground already primed for your relocation. The housing was used by Founders, so they may be a little larger than you're use to. Seeing as they are going to those that will be caring for my estate while I am gone, I trust your team will approve. Your team might as well have some benefits while my team is off the mountain. It's the best we can offer; private suites for each of you, easy access to the main gym and spa. The area is sound-proofed, as some of the Founders thought it too close to the slave compounds. Your team will be taken to them tomorrow, so be ready to move underside. I will take no excuses; just consider it hazard pay for all the other shitty details you and your teams have had to endure in the past. Come by the cabin tomorrow around noonish," Hunter laughed giving him a pat on the arm. "Oh and here's stinky's leash. Attach it to his nose ring, it minds better that way. Thanks Eric, I think you'll like this one a lot, it's 100% pig."

The moon was well past its zenith when the party began to wind down and couples began to depart towards their quarters within the caverns below. The last I saw of stinky was when Eric attached his leash to the nose ring, ordered it to follow and led it off with its hands cuffed behind its back.

Master bade all those around him good night, picked up 9-777's leash and put his hand to lifting me to my feet. The three of us returned to the cabin where we found slave mike with company other than his brother. Hunter sighed with relief to hear mike begging for more cock. That boy has a bottomless pit for its hole when cock is at hand. Master tossed a tired 9-777 out into the room, where it crumpled like a Raggedy Andy doll. Hunter walked to where it lay and ordered it to rise. The creature lay there, starring at the ceiling high overhead.

Master turned to me, "Get me a brandy and warm it, prep me a cigar and bring me a cap full of brandy." Dropping to one knee, Master scooped 9-777's head into one hand and lifted its face towards him. He poured the small shot of brandy into the slave's mouth. It coughed abruptly then sat up. Master walked it over to the standing Tao cross, spread its arms and bound them in a position that the slave could watch us from across the room. My Lord dropped into the chair, took the proffered cigar and a long swig of brandy. "Nice boy, warmed just like I love it."

He tried prying off his boots, but gave up and put me to work. He hadn't used me all night sexually before the Handlers or guests, instead chosing to use 9-777. He'd forced me to watch things this slave would have preferred not seeing again even if it was on someone else. Still, this slave was a touch jealous that Master chose to use me in more menial ways than he would if 9-777 or stinky was not around. Yes, I realized after I had time to analyze my thinking, I was jealous of them.

Hunter must have known that I was jealous of how he chose to use me tonight. He pulled my head towards him, exhaling blue tobacco smoke in my direction and cupping my head in his hand. He was relaxing as the brandy, cigar and my presence helped him to unwind from the evening. His hand rubbed my face and his finger crossed my forehead down my cheeks. "9-745, I love you. The others are just slaves, but you own my heart. Remember that."

This slave melted into his hand and kissed his open palm as tenderly as his hand had caressed my face. My love for him was detailed in my devotion to his needs. Our quiet time was always good and would have been better if 9-777 hadn't broken the calm with one of his noisy moans. Hunter saw me seething with anger as I looked at 9-777. "Do me a favor slave. Fetch me a suitable belt to beat this piece of shit into silence."

Like an impala, I sprung to my feet and raced into the closet, found that one belt with hundreds of holes. We all hated the one that one I brought back and extended it out to him. Master did not take the belt from my hands, but instead he looked down to me. "Take that belt and give him the brunt of your fury. Give him the warm-up he deserves, then I will have a go at him. Show him just how much he angered you tonight, then show him how much you love him - using only that belt. He needs the pain to show it how much we care and love him. Give it to him, slave. Show him that you really do love him, but do not slack your pace or slow your hand. Remember, he needs this to understand our need for him to improve!"

Slowly I approached 9-777 with the belt draped around my neck. Hunter told me to loosen the panels from around his ass and thighs. Boy you are to work only the front of his body I will refresh his back. Show him how jealous you were of him tonight. Show him how much you care!"

I stood before 9-777 thinking of things he had done to me while I was with him. I needed more than just my own jealousy to fuel my fire if I was to hurt this slave. My first swing was a light slap that made Master boo me from the sidelines. The second swing brought tears to 9-777's eyes as I recalled how he had taken my love and betrayed me for the sake of a few extra bucks in his envelope at the end of my shift. My anger got the best of me and I lay into that thing's flesh with every ounce of anger I could to burn into its hide. I did not know until I couldn't swing anymore that I had been crying while I beat him. Tears streamed down my cheeks and dripped off my chin with each blow that I burned into his thighs. When I stopped, I dropped to my knees and kissed his raw welts. It was the only way my mind could rationalize and tell him that I would always love him.

Hunter did not beat him after I was finished, but released it from its bondage and ordered it to crawl towards our bed. Master touched the slave's face until the slave rubbed his face on his owner's hand. I saw Hunter smile as he bound his slave to the foot of the bed and added a spreader bar between its ankles before returning from the bathroom with a piss soaked jock to install in the slave's mouth. Then my Lord walked to my side of the bed. "Undress me." He climbed in over me, pulling me to him as he turned out the lights and bade 9-777 goodnight. Master was healing.

My Lord woke early, put on his running shoes and shorts, added blankets to both of his slaves and departed. When he returned, he had two randy slaves ready to care for his needs. Master was right, last night's heavy use of 9-777 helped it come into its own and focus on the needs of its owner.

Once this slave was released from its bedroom bondage, it was permitted to release 9-777 and was directed to remove its encasement. Two slaves bathed their owner using only our tongues. We took breakfast in the spa where our Master was soaking and fed him. 9-777 gave him a deep massage and ate out his ass while this one laid out his clothes and prepared his shaving gear. All morning was spent taking care of our Lord's needs. In return, he gave us both what we needed - his cock and his pain. Each of us suffered equally under his blows and humping hips. That day, two separate slaves became a team focused on serving their Lord and Master. My petty jealousy had been taken away when I used the belt to express my anger on a creature lower than myself.

When we departed, 9-777 was hooded, gagged and locked into heavy bondage shorts. I was permitted to wear my finest slave harness and nothing else but combat boots. 9-777 was to be with Sir today, I was sent to find Lt. Wilson and lead his team to their new quarters. I'd show them around the area that was set-aside for them while we we're away. This way, I spent the balance of the day helping Lt. Wilson and his people get acquainted with the tunnels and helping them learn to read the slave marks written on every conjunction within the caverns. Every slave within our compound was bilingual. We all spoke English first, the second language was our slave chit. Broken symbols etched into the stones gave Handlers and slaves alike their own symbolized language.

Entering Master's office after these duties, I found him sitting back in his large black leather chair, one leg crossing the other, his boot resting on a slave who was in turtle position. (The turtle slave was on its hands and knees, elbows touching knees firmly, head tucked between hands and hands at right angles in toward the head. Done thusly, the slave in turtle position is tucked into a tight rectangle box shape and a firm foundation for boot rest or a table.) I entered his office, knelt beside his desk and waited until he acknowledged my presence. He looked up, smiled, and said "Report, slave." He laid aside his writing and turned to face me. I reported all that I had accomplished in his name while with Lt. Wilson and his team. His eyes twinkled in the light and he smiled. "Good boy. How did they like there new quarters?"

"Sir, may I speak freely, Sir?"

"Yes, slave, speak freely your findings."

"Sir, this is, and I quote, 'better than the Carlton-Ritz, awesome, absolutely fucking incredible. So this is how the Founder's lived.' Sir, its odd downside, Sir."

"Explain that statement, 9-745, what did you observe. Should I be concerned, boy?"

"Sir, nothing for you to be concerned about. It's just odd to see so many Handlers smiling and laughing in the corridors. They were actually helping each other carry crates into storage. Everyone, including Handlers and craftsmen, is smiling. It seems last night's party was just want everyone needed, Sir."

My Lord brightened. "The party and the additional profits that found their way into their bank accounts this morning. Good to know, slave. Go ask mike when dinner will be ready. I'm starving."

The party seemed to change the mood for all of us on Buena Vista. Everyone had a smile in their step as they went about the task of securing the estate, battening down the hatches in preparations for a group leave of absence. During dinner. Hunter told us that the mule 5-493 had made it successfully to its Master in Alexandria and, from what Mr. Brooks was saying, he couldn't be happier. J.D. reported that 1/3 of the storage was filled with personal belongings of the Handlers and that we may have to open up other storage elsewhere. Hunter suggested opening up some of the inter-rogation rooms due for retrofit later in the project. Or to use the dining hall, and just to double strap the crates so no one is given reason to snoop while we were away. Both J.D. and mike asked if anything had been heard from their Master Cappy. Hunter informed them that they would see him soon, he awaited them in the South Pacific. The boys seemed greatly relieved with exception to J.D., who seemed distraught that he has done things here on Buena Vista since Cappy's disappearance that his Master would not have foreseen possible. Hunter told him that he acted in faith and Buena Vista in mind and had his seal of approval.

After dinner, Sir received a phone call from out of state. I was with him when he took it and was shocked at what I learned. We discovered the trade-in that Mr. Jim Brooks left was a very distant bastard Kennedy relation. The slave had been trans-ferred to Castle Holdings where plastic surgery would enhance its facial characteristics to make it look more like the father than some of his own. Its brain wipe had been suc-cessful and it was now undergoing a complete history reboot with implanted memories. The creature was tainted, something was found within its gene pool that would not permit it to be used to full capacity. Therefore, it would be sold to a third world country where cleanliness is not always a virtue. The beast would still be a valuable asset no matter where it was placed. How our people governed its placement was beyond me.

That was the last night of quiet time, as our house became the hubbub of Handlers. For a time, it looked like every security person on the estate wanted to per-sonally meet Lord and Master Hunter. It was interesting to see them hanging on his every word, like he was a grandfather or a demi-god! At the main house everyone was packing their belongings and getting ready for the final push into paradise. Our first shipments of goods were leaving tomorrow by plane and would be waiting for us when we arrived. I was ordered to have 9-777 fully geared and ready when Sir came for it that evening. It should have anticipated this action, but it had been kept so busy pack-ing and hauling shit that it more than likely just blanked it out of its head. We walked down the corridor to shipping. It climbed up on the waiting slab, laid back and let me secure it in place. But when the door opened and the shippers arrived, he freaked. It finally dawned on 9-777 that it was being shipped to an unknown destination.

I didn't know if it had been sold. I was in just as much shock as 9-777 when the slave shippers stepped into the room and began preparing 9-777 for shipment. They stripped 9-777 of all its rubber, placed an oxygen clip into its nose and turned on two tanks. Whatever was in that breathing tube took the fight right out of 9-777. It became quiet almost instantly once it had a couple of lungful of that enhanced air. His skin had turned a brilliant white since it no longer got sunlight. The body had taken on more muscle while it had been with us. Constant activity, forced workouts with Hunter and controlled food intake had taken some pounds off this creature and given it a more defined slave body. If it had been handsome as a Handler, it was in its peak as a slave.

The shipper's were careful with the property; one of them always had their hand on it, keeping it aware that they were there, calming it as others worked. Braces of foam were placed between its legs once its holes had been clearly flushed. Its arms were wrapped in a thin absorbent material. The same material was wrapped down its torso, buttocks and on down over its legs. Then came the condom of rubber, a thin membrane that stretched over its feet and rolled over its body to its chest. It was like watching mummification with the high priests of ancient Egypt working on the dead. It could have been if we stepped back a few centuries to that period, as the shippers were bald headed and very dedicated to their positions in life. They held a 99.8% delivery rate for all their slaves arriving alive without harm or damage.

The eyes of 9-777 never left my Master's or mine. My Lord was seated in a high director's chair at my back and I stood before him, both of us quietly watching the proceedings. After the rubber membrane was rolled into place, the packers slipped his feet into neoprene rubber boots and rolled a larger sheet of neoprene up his legs to just above his hips. Handlers had discussed ways that slaves could escape these shippers and their methods always work. Once the pendulum is set in motion, it cannot be halted save by my Lord's hand. Today he did no such thing.

Two strong packers released 9-777's hands and helped it sit up while three put its arms into what looked like a neoprene waist coat that got zipped down the middle of its chest. Thickly padded gloves were slipped onto its fingers and hands; these had long gauntlet sleeves that were zipped down its arm. If it escaped the confines of its crate it would find it impossible to release itself from the wrappings, those heavily padded gloves make the fingers impossible to move.

It was time for 9-777's head to be covered. Hunter slipped off his chair and told the shippers to leave him. Hunter stepped up to 9-777's head, snapped his fingers and indicated with his hand that I should approach on the other side. We both stood there looking down at him and he looking up imploring us with his eyes to stop.

Master broke the news. "9-777, you have been sold. Private auction, someone saw you flitting around in the background in your full rubber suit and they made an offer I could not refuse." He let the words sink in before he continued. "You are going to an owner that will love and treasure you. Be happy about that 9-777, you'll be his second slave. He plans to have you branded, marked as his private stock and you'll become his pain pig."

"Sir, please, no! Please, Sir, please!"

"What's done is done, slave, the money has already changed hands. In two days you'll be with your new owner. You'll come to love him like you do me." Hunter leaned forward and forced him to accept his kiss. "Say your farewells now, 9-745!" Sir's voice betrayed him, I realized the sale of 9-777 was not in his books.

I kissed 9-777, hugged him and offered him inside tips on letting go once the shippers returned. I licked off the tears that were streaming down his face until Master snapped his fingers again, calling me to him. The shipper's returned to complete their job. Nose plugs, gag glued into his mouth, and earplugs with programming tapes. Hydraulics lifted the contained slave up, its crate was pulled into place and it was lowered into the foamed box. Sir watched, standing near 9-777's head as expanding gels were installed around the slave, locking it into the crate. The last sight that 9-777 saw was my Lord mouthing *I love you*, then the box closed and the music began. A narcotic spray would soon take him down into his new routine and he would awaken with his new Owner's face looking down on him. That first face is the one upon which the slave fixates. After that it is owned by only one, that face, whoever it may be. So many changes occur between being shipped and received that it was important for the owner to make the first impression.

A part of me was happy that 9-777 would be serving his true lord and yet I cried silently as we made our exit in silence up the lift to topside. Hunter placed his arm around my shoulders and whispered, "He is not lost, he was sold to me."

I stopped midstep, turning to look up at my owner. "Sir, but why the crating and you telling him he was sold, Sir?"

"You know why, 9-745. I need it fixated on me. The programming that it is undergoing now will be accepted to a depth even our other programs cannot reach. It feels betrayed right now, like you did. Now it will accept and absorb all that those very special CD's hold for its future." I could not stop myself and began crying out of joy that my brother in slavery, 9-777, would be at my side from here on.

Hunter slapped my butt, "All our bags packed boy? We fly out tonight with our crate in tow. They'd better be ready or your ass is mine!"

"Sir, respectfully, my ass is yours any time you want it, Sir!" We stepped out of the elevator into the pantry, catching mike and J.D. comparing notes in their own twin gibberish. By the tone of their voices, whatever they were discussing they were excited by.

All the major luggage would be departing with us; those left behind would be bringing only duffle bags. Order of the trip was that Hunter, stinky and I would travel with the first wave of cargo, followed tomorrow at dawn by the Handlers and their slave property. It would look like a sea of black uniforms in combat boots hitting the airport at dawn. They were to be escorted by a small portion of the Black Watch security team so that all would be on the Castle Enterprise jumbo jet and off before the airport got chance to realize who had invaded their private turf.

A knock came to the door. Lt. Eric Wilson entered the office leading a very sore stinky by the nose ring. The slave crawled in on its hands and knees like a human dog. Lt. Wilson took the indicated chair while I shut the door. "Master Hunter, thank you so very much for the loan of this slave. I cannot tell you how much fun it has been having it under my care. As per your request, Sir, it is bruised from its neck down to the soles of its feet." He laughed sadistically, "That's why it is crawling instead of walking up right. It made the mistake of pissing me off last night, so I caned its feet. Nothing's broken, but it will hobble or crawl before it walks for a few days. Helps a slave realize its place in my world."

Lt. Wilson leaned forward, pulling the slave's leash towards him. He nodded his head while looking at the slave. "I just might have to take a slave, Sir, and I find this one to my liking." He unsnapped the leash from the dog stinky's nose ring, pointing to my maste. "Go to your owner, slave." Stinky licked Lt. Wilson's hand as he withdrew the leash, slowly turning to first look in the direction of his owner then back at Wilson. Finally, Eric had to kick at it to get the manimal moving in the correct direction to Hunter.

Hunter studied the creature as if he was trying to make up his mind. The manimal crawled around the desk; Hunter leaned forward and stroked its back. By the reaction of the manimal, Hunter might as well used a hot poker instead of his hand, the manimal flinched and would've drawn away if Hunter hadn't grabbed and caught its nose ring. "Good work, Eric. By the looks of it, it's been giving you a run for your money. Did it?"

Lt. Wilson laughed, "Once it realized who was in charge, it gave me no problems. Actually I taught it that pain is pleasure, pleasure is pain, mirror against mirror reflections of the same. When I can afford it, I would like to own a creature just like that one, Sir."

"Eric, I have been doing some reading and thinking for the past few weeks. Is it true you grew up on a family farm, studied horticulture and animal husbandry in college? How the hell did you come to be associated with the Black Watch?"

His head dropped then Lt. Wilson looked up with a huge smile, "Sir, how did you come by that information, if I might ask?"

"You should know by now. I learn everything I can about people I am considering adding to my permanent staff. Tell me, Eric, how much do you make a year with the Black Watch? Would you like a chance to prove the theory I read of yours about manimal husbandry? Join me for dinner, and we will discuss the possibilities of your new assignment. 9-745, go get J.D.; I have an errand for him to do."

Returning with J.D. we stepped into a deep conversation about the possibilities of cloning slaves and DNA splicing, J.D. entered on my heels, "Sir, how may I be of assistance, Sir!"

"You'll need to find a cart as stinky cannot walk. Please take it down to processing. Here are my private CD's for its crate; it will be leaving in a few hours as will I. Drop it off and return quickly, I need to cover some interesting aspects of tomorrow's journey for you and the merry horde."

I was sent to the kitchen to assist mike while Hunter and Eric carried on their conversations. Mike did not need me, so I ran upstairs to confirm that we had gotten everything packed and began bringing down his luggage for the trip to the south Pacific. We dined simply that night in the kitchen dining room away from the others, who were milling around and hanging out at Hunter's cabin until they had to go elsewhere. Eric and Hunter carried on their conversation until J.D. arrived. That's when Hunter dropped a bombshell. "J.D., do you think you could work with Eric if I can help him realize his future is best with us here on Buena Vista?"

J.D. seemed perplexed. "Sir, why do we need that much security? Or does Lt. Wilson have other qualifications that will benefit the estate?" J.D. was ordered to make a copy of Lt. Wilson's profile to take with him on the cruise so that he and Hunter could have a nice heart to heart about the hiring of Eric.

Lt. Wilson seemed to get a little huffy while the two of them spoke, and called a halt by slapping the top of the table. "Major Hunter, I am not one of your slaves that you can talk around in this fashion. I have not said that I will leave the Black Watch team, nor have I given you any indication that I am seeking employment anywhere else, Sir!"

"Forgive me Eric, you are absolutely correct. With Cappy gone and knowing that J.D. will be attending medical school in a year, I need to find someone who is capable of handling the farm. I like your caliber and would be honored if you would consider it while we are away, nothing more," Master replied. "I can almost guarantee you a lab if you'll think of it seriously. We need brilliant thinkers like you! Besides, anyone that can make stinky behave like you were able to can't be all bad, now can you?"

Master looked down at his watch, "9-745 are you finished eating? When you take the bags out front, check to see if our precious cargo is on the truck. I will finish up here and be along. Eric, please consider my offer. It's a once in a lifetime deal.

Think about your future. Take care of my estate we will be back in two weeks." They hugged then Hunter turned to J.D. "Come with me." A ¾ ton truck was waiting outside, I climbed in while slaves laoded my Lord's luggage and the "precious cargo." 9-777 was stenciled on the outside of one crate and the other said dog, which was somehow fitting for stinky. Checking my inventory list of luggage, we were ready for when the Master finished whatever he was doing. The ¾ ton truck drove off, leaving me to stand by the limousine. Still no Hunter, so I went in to find him.

Handlers thinking they could pry more information about the treasure hunt had caught him. Politely as one could manage, I walked between them, plucked at his arm and suggested we leave. He caught my hand and made a quick announcement to the group. "It would seem my slave says it's time that we hit the road. See you folks in the South Pacific in two days. Safe journey and please do not make J.D. lose any more hairs than he already has! You won't like it when he is mad."

They escorted us to the car and stood there as we drove off. We were off the mountain following the taillights of our cargo truck when he looked at me with a twinkle in his eye. "Is that all you are wearing on the plane, slave?"

I froze. I hadn't thought of anything but getting him ready and I had run out of the house in nothing but a slave harness and boots. He laughed at my dismay until tears ran down his face and then laughed some more. When he quieted, he pulled a duffle bag out of a storage compartment and tossed it to me. "I bet you're glad your Master takes good care of you, slave."

We had two hours to kill before we got to D.C. and we killed those two hours well. He put up the window that divided our space from the front of the car, had me grab on to the handholds on either side and plowed my ass as we whipped around the curves of our mountain range. Satiated for the moment, I knelt between his legs teasing his cock with my tongue, hoping I could nurse another load from him before we hit the lights of the city. He let me have my way.

Once at the airport, we were taken directly to the tarmac. Hunter oversaw the loading of our private stock into the cabins that we would be occupying for the flight. We were taking the private jet placed at his disposal by Castle. The executive chairs were lowered into the floor and the crates were secured on top. Cargo nets and straps held their crated bodies in place even as they were held by the bondage within the crates. Having them nearby seemed right, gaving Hunter and I both a sense of security that our men would be with us for the long haul.

Chapter 9

By suffering comes wisdom.
Agamemnon

We arrived early by a day at our final destination and the kick off point for our Pirate Cruise, Pago Pago in the Polynesian islands. Since we had arrived ahead of schedule, we were housed in a private home of one of our stockholders. Our slave doctor had come ahead with twenty support staff, some of which were on hand to assist with the uncrating of our beasts.

No matter how exhausted we were, Hunter demanded that they be uncrated even as the doctor assured him they would be safe for yet another day in their crates. Hunter did not want to risk it. He found a crowbar and started the process, ripping and tearing at the planking that encased our slaves until the doctor pulled him aside and allowed the other slaves present to release the hidden latches.

The slave's made quick work of their job, removing the screw latches, popping apart the sides and freeing 9-777 and stinky of their gel packs. The shippers back on Buena Vista had sealed both slaves' eyes with tape, making certain only their true owner would fill their vision upon reawakening. We stood back, allowing those trained in the process give our private stock rebirth. Hunter turned to a slave, demanding a tank of oxygen. The slave looked to the doctor, who nodded his approval and the slave returned with a tank on wheels. Hoses were connected and tested; the most crucial part of the uncrating is when they disconnect the breathing tubes. Watching them work silently, I allowed myself to think about rebirth. How few have the pleasure to really first hand aquire that knowledge. The sheer joy of seeing your owner's face for the first time as your body and mind are freed from captivity. There is no way to express in words the delight that simple act gives to a focused body and mind.

Christians were Born Againers; Metaphysicians experienced rebirth; both of those only experience it in a spiritual sense. People coming out of coma experience something of what we slaves endure when placed within a crate and are shipped to an unknown site. A physical rebirth, very akin to what we slaves have happen. Locked into a womb by those that trained us to serve, bound by whatever means that suits their nature. Placed on a bed of gel that molds to our bodies, allowing us to float in a sea of tranquility. Our air filtered....

The doctor working over 9-777's crate barked, "Oxygen!"

Quickly, quietly they attached the hoses and the air began cycling into 9-777's lungs. The body under the doctor's care jerked as the muscles in its body contracted then settled back down. The doctor studied the monitors that displayed heartbeat and brain activity before turning to Master. "Sir, they are coming around and are ready to be viewed. We will step out of the room so their impression may be more complete, Sir."

All the packing materials and extra packaging was taken from the room as the doctor and the two slaves departed. Hunter grabbed me by my shoulders, forcing me to look into his tired face. "What you are about to witness cannot be revealed to anyone or anything, do you understand, 9-745?"

I gave him the reassurance he needed with a curt, "Of course, Sir. Whatever

I am about to witness is not to be told to anyone. It remains our secret, Sir."

Hunter turned not to 9-777, but to stinky and began removing the headgear until a very familiar face began to take shape under his prying fingers. I stood in shock. This, the slave stinky, the one that I had fucked on command, had watched J.D. paddle because it got out of hand, had seen it blow J.D. afterwards and had been given into Lt. Eric Wilson's care for tenderization...This was Cappy! Captain Jonathan Hicks, Master Hunter's soul mate, best friend, and now slave...Christ! The lies, fucking lies and deception put across to the twins! I just couldn't wrap my mind around what was being revealed to me as Hunter carefully released Cappy's gagged lips then slowly peeled off the tape holding its eyes shut.

The slave's eyes fluttered as it looked up into Master's face, seeing him as if for the very first time. The beginning of a tiny smile crawled from one side of its mouth to the other, giving bloom to a rich, full-toothed smile. Hunter held one hand lightly on Cappy's freshly shaven head, the other under his chin. Master's head lowered and he raped the slave's mouth with his lips and tongue. "Welcome home, slave. Damn, I've missed your sorry ass, boy." He laughed, "The twins are going to kill us once they find out." Cappy's eyes never left Hunter's face and tears began trickling down. Perhaps it was the eyes' way of cleaning itself, I thought, or Cappy's happiness leaking through. Nothing mattered as I watched the two unite, this time properly as Master and slave. No more hiding the reality of their love and devotion to each other. Few can handle an hour-long relationship, fewer can say that they have had a relationship that has crossed decades.

I went to find the doctor and the other two slaves. They took Cappy into another room to finalize its release and give it the necessary bodywork it would need to come up to working level. I found Hunter working his hand under the rubber and neo-prene suit until he found 9-777's right nipple. I stood watching as he rolled this slave's nipple, making it intimately aware that its Master was present. A motorcycle helmet was over the slave's head. It had been modified and contained the programming system we used to implant deep knowledge into our trainees. Shield lifted, the head released from the containment of the helmet, Hunter lowered it easily and passed the helmet in my direction. The posture collar was released giving him access to the hood that covered its head. A soft leather hood was unlaced by the ear, this too he worked off this new slave's head, the gag was pried from its lips and the slave closed its mouth, sucking on his finger as he tried to dislodge any remaining glue that might have been left by the gag.

Sir took his time to play his finger around the slave's lips, teasing them to life as he was teasing its body and mind into focusing zealously upon seeing its Owner. The eyecups were dislodged and any residue of glue was picked off before he reached for the tape that would permit 9-777 to see its owner. With an abrupt pull of his hand, the tape was torn off the slave's eyelids and face. The sudden pain made its eyes open quickly and flutter until they gave it a clear view. When slave 9-777 saw the face of its one true owner, tears began to stream down its cheeks and there was that joy in its eyes. Hunter cupped the slave's head and the slave moved his in his Lord's hand one touching the other, whispering a simple yet ever so meaningful, "Welcome home, slave 9-777." Their lips met and Master's lips lingered sucking on the slave's lower lip. His hand indicated that I should fetch the doctor. Hunter had already peeled the shivering slave out of the first layer of rubber and was about to cut the membrane. The Doctor drew back gently Hunter as other slaves entered and finalized the process. Once out of the containment bondage, the slaves were carried outside and lowered into a very warm pool. Other slaves were with Cappy, helping it to regain movement, this they did as well with 9-777.

Master and I sat on the sidelines watching until he could take it no longer and ordered me to undress him. I was ordered to join him in the pool. Together we cemented our bond with the new slaves of Master Hunter. It was an odd sensation to be granted permission to fuck a man I once feared. Both of these slaves had used me in their own fashion, all to justify my Lord's plan, this I knew now. Afterwards, all of us curled up and slept in our host's guest bungalow near the beach and were awakened by a gong heralding the setting of the sun. Torch runners ran down the seashore lighting torches, adding excitement to our first night of many as they drew closer to our bungalow.

We were like puppies lounging on the floor of the bungalow, huge pillows buffering our bodies from the hard wooden floor as we rested from the long journey we had made to get to this point. Each of the men around me were in some form my equal and brothers. We belonged to a society unlike any known in this world, our own private niche in the world. Sir and those of like mind had made this all come to be.

A naked female slave coughed to catch our attention, taking us totally by surprise. "Forgive this one's intrusion my Lord," she was directly looking at Hunter as if he should have known her. "Food is being brought to you here so that your rest may be more complete, Sir. My Lord and your host requests an indulgence of your time tomorrow." She bowed, backed away and two other females carried in huge platters of food. One looked like it was roast pig and hot and steaming vegetables, the other contained fresh tropical fruits. Once set before us, the slaves withdrew and disappeared.

Hunter ordered us on to our knees, hands at our backs, heads bowed. He ate in silence for a few minutes, using his finger to put the greasy pork into his mouth, relishing the food and making us watch. He held his fingers in my direction, "Lick them clean." I did as ordered. He propped himself up on big pillows, attempted to snap his fingers and couldn't from the grease. He flashed a delighted smile and ordered, "Feed your Lord and Master, slaves."

He reclined back into the pillows and allowed us the pleasure of feeding him. He fed us as much as we fed him. The dinner transformed slowly from just good eating to *really* good eating when the dinner turned from dining to pleasure. An all out orgy occurred with our Master being the central figure. Fresh guava was fed to him by 9-777, the juices dripping up his chest had to be licked off tenderly. Spicy roast pork, rich with hot peppers, tickled both his taste buds and mine when he took a bite and forced it into my mouth. Four pigs under the stars had the best damn dinner they could have ever imagined that ended with a dessert that all of us needed to cement our new life.

We bathed in the warm ocean after our free-for-all and returned to the bungalow finding our mess had been whisked away. There, in place of the chunks of meat, half eaten guava, and pineapple wedges was Sir's passion of passions; liqueur made from passion fruit. When mixed with champagne, the two chill him out and make him sleep like a baby. He rarely allowed us alcohol, but tonight he permitted us each a taste of his favorite drink. It was an incredible taste of strawberries and melon that with a touch of sweet. He drank more than was necessary, to the point that we had to carry him to bed. He wasn't totally blasted - he still made sense and his words were not slurred when he looked up at us. "Finally, I got my heart's dream around me. All of you in my bed. Maybe your weight can stop it from spinning."

More fruit and skewered shrimp were waiting for us when we crawled out of the bungalow and ran to the sea. There we played like boys on a lark instead of one Master and three slaves. When we returned we found a note attached to a small suit-case of gauzy flimsy clothes in pastel shades and a bottle of homemade lotion. The note read "Apply the lotion on the men with the white skin, pour in into their skins or they will burn badly in our sun. The rest of you use it as well. Forgive the clothes; they are all we have that might fit your slaves with the lily-white skin. It will allow them to catch the good rays of the sun without burning. All of you please join me at the main house. When ready, sound the gong and a car will be sent for you."

Hunter did not need much of the lotion, but he made certain the balance of his team got it liberally rubbed in everywhere. He did not want any of this property dam-aged by the sun's rays and he laughed his big evil laugh when Cappy and 9-777 put on the flimsy clothes. They looked like rough whores from a harem, and my poor Master was laughing so hard he practically pissed on himself. None of them were amused, especially when I was laughing at them and he caught me humiliating my own broth-ers. I was then forced into proper gear for the sun. By his command, I sounded the gong and turned to dress our Lord. His leathers were nowhere to be found. Our Lord got away with wearing nothing but a loincloth of the flimsy material and we got the last laugh. No matter how we tried to cover our smirking faces, he caught us at it. "Wipe those smirks off your faces, slaves. Don't make me stop the car and cut a switch or three!"

No car arrived, but a slave-carried divan did. Eight beautifully matched brown skinned, black haired women ran across the sands, carrying on their shoulders a shad-ed pillowed draped cot. They stopped just before the bungalow and Master stepped up on the platform. He ordered us to follow as the women lifted him and trotted off. The women didn't slow until they reached a huge colonial house where we were escorted into the cool interior of the home of Doctor Phillip, our host.

About the time our eyes adjusted to the dark interior of the house, we spied our Master's missing clothing laid out on a settee in the foyer. Dr. Phillip appeared extending his hands out to Hunter and greeting him cheerfully. "Did you have a nice ride in my car, my friend? Sleeping arrangements were suitable, my girls have told me." Dr. Phillip was Germanic by the way he looked, pure blood, blonde hair and blue eyes added to a handsome bearish body. He looked like a friendly pear with legs, and very detail oriented by the looks of his female slaves. It was suggested that we be sent out back where we would be cared for, as he wished to speak to Master in private.

We exited to an outdoor kitchen filled with women in various states of undress. All of them burst out laughing, seeing us wearing their clothes. They sat us down and brought us cool drinks and began flirting with us. They had to know we were slaves, we wore the same collars as theirs. We were eventually led to our appointed seats where fruit was brought to us. Every time we one of us rose to assist with a task that we men would have normally performed we were led back and something was brought to us in hopes of keeping us out of their hair. We were out there for what seemed like hours until our Master appeared.

God, was he a sight for sore eyes. A man, and what a man, standing there on the porch wearing his knee high boots, thin leather pants and no shirt while holding a whip in his hands. It was like something out of *Gone With The Wind*. The women were swooning at his approach and we men were kneeling and drooling. After all, this was our Master. The divan was offered for our return, but Hunter wanted to walk. Our host offered a guide instead. A child led us along a path to the bungalow and we took to the sea as the sun was setting. We ran back to the bungalow laughing while Hunter was grabbing ass and slapping it. Busting through the curtains we discovered two female slaves laying out huge dinner trays of hot and iced foods. One knelt, asking permission to speak with our Lord.

All ears turned in their direction as she began to talk, "Sir Hunter, our Master has explained to us what it is you have given. We are very thankful for this gift." She leaned forward and kissed Hunter's bare, sandy feet, then rose and ran out.

I had the honor of holding his cup while the other two were feeding our Master. I had been studying the rim of the cup and had missed his mumbled comments about wine twice. He grabbed my leg. "Ok, 9-745, what's on your mind?"

"Sir, you were nearly naked, what did you give them, Sir? Forgive me, I am being a nosy slave."

He blushed bright red, laughed nervously, then smiled. "I left them a load of my sperm. Dr. Phillip wants babies! He went on to purchase samples from each of you; the three of you impressed all the women. In a few days they will receive a package of frozen sperm from each of you. Soon we faggots will be fathers!" We all got drunk on just the thought.

Three male slaves carried his luggage onto the three-masted schooner, one of four that had been rented for this trip. Once we were taken to his quarters, we began to unpack his belongings. They had been kind enough to give him the captain's quarters, the largest of the suites aboard the ship. Having found out how much this trip was costing him, not Castle Enterprises, we felt they should have given him more of a red carpet treatment than they did.

Our exhausted family arrived and found slaves on the wharf assigning rooms. All went quietly to their appointed locations found their luggage had arrived early, had been unpacked and stored. Almost all crashed into their waiting beds, those few who did not got to watch our ships cast off. The ship's motor tacked as we set out of the bay, then the sails were unfurled and we caught the wind. It was enormously romantic for this slave as I was kneeling besides my Sir while he watched our sails billow in the wind and we flew across the waters.

Each ship had a dinning area where food was easily accessible for all those that had chosen to sleep before eating. It was a quiet night on board, few moved about with exception to the sailors on the craft and our Lord. He was finally enjoying himself and most of all, he was relaxing. Sir was lying back into 9-777's lap while Cappy massaged his feet with his tongue. Sir had me resting my head up near his lap. We were on a darkened side of the ship keeping to ourselves when we heard boots approaching. They stopped abruptly. "Sir! What are you doing, Sir? God, have we missed you Sir!"

Cappy looked up with Master's foot still in his mouth and turned his head to Hunter. "Sir, shall I handle this or did you want to do the honors, Sir?"

"Well, stinky, he is - as is mike - your slave. Maybe we both had better handle this."

J.D.'s eyes seemed to grow to the size of plates then he collapsed like a marionette that had just had its strings cut, "stinky? STINKY!" J.D. shouted, "Oh, God, what have I done to you Sir?" He looked to Hunter, "Sir?" By the tone of his voice he was demanding an explanation. "Oh, Sir."

Slave mike appeared. He surveyed Hunter lying back into 9-777's lap, then noticed Cappy down at Master's feet with one wet foot inside tongue shot of his face.

Mike looked at me, then down at J.D.. "Finally, Sir's, you two can stop playing those god damned stupid tricks. As if you were fooling any one." Mike dropped to his knees and hugged Cappy then crawled up and hugged Hunter. "My Sirs, it is about time you both came out of the closet. Of all people, you should know you can't hide your true nature from people that you love. Right J.D.?"

He turned to J.D. who was still in shock by the way he kept shaking his head back and forth. He kept trying to negate the idea that his Master had been our Master's slave all along. Mike crawled over to J.D. and wrapped his arms around him. "Brother, don't tell me you really didn't know? Didn't you see it in their eyes, J.D.? It was written in bold strokes our Master has a Master." Mike was trying to comfort his brother.

Cappy spoke up. "Sometimes a daddy needs a Daddy that's all, J.D.. Nothing has changed!"

J.D. blew a gasket. "The hell! I am running Buena Vista now because you ran off, dammit!"

"Nothing you hadn't been doing for months. All those ideas that I laid to ground were yours, your ideas were what brought Buena Vista's crops to life, not mine. I was hurting badly. I really needed my Sir to beat the living shit out of me and I had to see if you were ready. Being stinky was the only way I could get what I needed and had earned. In Vietnam I was Master Hunter's owner, now the roles are reversed and here I am, happy to be serving all my men. Please be happy for me. Please." Cappy had put out his hand to caress J.D.'s arm, the touch of which sent a shock of electricity through J.D.'s body.

"You want me to be happy for the two of you," J.D. said in a most taunting voice. "Why the deception? Tell me? Why?"

Hunter was speaking. "It was the only way that Cappy could see you as I do. No longer a boy, but a man capable of handling his job, capable of handling medical school. We both had to know and that was the best way to prove it to both of us. Besides J.D., mike, as I see it, the deception proved to give me an insight into the two of you that I would not have normally seen. Both of you are cool when under fire." Hunter continued, "It's a win-win situation, twins. J.D. will attend medical academy next winter session and mike, you'll be attending culinary school about the same time. But both of you have to train your replacements or neither of you go."

"J.D., mikey, are the two of you ok with what has happened? No doubt J.D. you're hurt by what has happened." Hunter was questioning J.D. trying to get something out of the twin but it was like pulling teeth to get him to open up.

Looking up at his brother he asked, "How long have you known they were playing these games?"

Mike grinned. "Lets just say for a long time, brother; but then your head has always been in a book or on other matters on the farm. I was inside where I could watch them daily; watch them play their silly games."

"I am really having a hard time getting my mind to accept this, mike," J.D. said as his brother comforted him with a hug. He looked down at Cappy, who was back chewing on Sir's toes. "What do I call him? Cappy, Sir or Stinky?"

Hunter dislodged Cappy's mouth with a kick. "None of them. His real name is Jonathan, from here on he is slave jonathan or double zero. He and I have been together before the numbering system was even born."

Mike was the one to finally raise the question. "Sir, how did you get the name Stinky?"

Hunter laughed, "It's a joke from basic training. We would lie in bed during basic and Jonathan's farts were worse than any tear gas. Our division dubbed him Stinky and the name stuck."

Everyone laughed, including J.D.. His mood was lightened considerably. Mike was sent into the galley to see what he could rustle up while jonathan and 9-777 went to find suitable drinks for all of us. We had a proper family meeting that lasted until the early dawn hours. It was good for all of us. We laughed at mike as he told tales on Hunter and our brother jonathan, how they tried so damn hard to hide their big secret and failed completely with all except J.D.

Our ships dropped anchor not far from the first site of the treasure hunt. They ran gangplanks between the ships; One fore, one aft, to link the four ships into one. While we watched, native divers dove below to retrieve our dinner. Each galley on each ship was to prepare one main course, roasted pig, stuffed flounder, crab, lobster, sea urchins, shrimp and other delicacies of the ocean.

The good Doctor Phillip had sent along mass quantities of his homemade jungle juice that allowed a body to tan rapidly and not burn. Both 9-777 and slave jonathan gave proof to the value of his product. They had gone from pristine pearly white flesh to a nice healthy glow of reddish bronze within the short time they had been exposed to the sun. Others would need the services of the lotion Doctor Phillip created.

Hunter's merry band of slaves lounged on the deck for the greatest part of the day until he yawned and demanded a nice nap before dinner. As one, we retired to his cabin where he was massaged and put to bed. Those that needed additional rest slept with him, those that did not prepared his evening wardrobe. Sir woke ravenous and set 9-777 to the galley for food. It returned with a pitcher of chilled laced fruit juice and fresh fruit. By our Sir's leave, we all dined on the fresh fruit. While he sipped his drink he was thinking devious thoughts. He made up his mind and began barking orders.

"Lay out the chrome eggs, ball stretchers, trailer hitch butt plug and shackles, the bag of chain and padlocks." Then he sent us in to shower, with orders to shave each other and return. We knelt before him in our new pecking order, I at the front, 9-777 mid point and jonathan at the rear. It was slave jonathan that got the first installation, receiving the trailer hitch butt plug and a chain from his shackle to 9-777's.

The slave 9-777 was fitted with a heavy chrome ball stretcher to which a ball crusher was attatched. Its ass got plugged with Sir's condom wrapped cigars and it got shackles from its wrists to its balls and balls to its ankles. 9-777 paled when it was informed that it would pay tonight for its indiscretions while it had been a Handler on Buena Vista soil. It tried to beg its way out of whatever Master had planned and was suitably gagged. I got the chrome eggs inserted into my ass, my cock and balls bound neatly and was ordered into heavy bondage shorts sans the codpiece for the evening.

I had the honor of dressing my Lord in wine colored skin tight pants, Dan's thigh high Wesco boots and a silky bellowing blouse, gloves, and a single tail whip was hung from his left side not so much for effect as for use later. He had me pack an interesting selection of beating tools in a duffle bag; paddles mostly but a few quirts were tossed in for affect.

Sir was enjoying the tongues of both jonathan and 9-777 working their way up his boots when the door burst open and J.D. stormed in. Waving his costume before tossing it on the floor at Master's feet, he snarled, "I refuse to wear this damn outfit Sir! I will not debase myself before all of Buena Vista!"

Hunter turned cold like a nor'easter. "Oh, yes, you will, little slave! You'll be wearing that and jumping through hoops if so I command!"

"But, Sir?" J.D. seemed to halt mid-thought. "Sir?"

Then Hunter's mood lightened. "Besides, I had it made just for you and in your color, purple!" Hunter was nodding his head as if to say *yes you are going to do this*.

With his chest sunken, J.D. sighed. "As you wish Sir."

Slave mike ran into the room wearing a harem outfit that left nothing to the imagination. It had far less cloth in it than the outfits the boys had to wear when visiting Dr. Phillip's plantation. Hunter whistled at mike's costume. "Damn it boy, by that outfit I take it you are out to get laid."

Slave mike blushed the hottest pink any of us had ever seen, then he changed the subject. "Why isn't J.D. dressed? The hordes are demanding your presence, my Lord. Please come soon or they will come fetch you, so I was told by Lady Katherine and her merry men, Sir."

"OK, mike. Get your brother dressed in his costume for the evening. If he rebels, call me on the phone. I will send help. Do not let him bully you on this one. It's that outfit J.D., or your education." Hunter laughed, grabbed my ass, gave a jerk on the chain and we exited the suite.

Hitting any room just like this deck with Hunter at ones side is like entering a gasp. Everyone pauses mid-sentence or mid-bite. They look over at you, sizing you up and then return to their conversation. That was just what happened until Hunter gave a mighty tug on the chain attached to 9-777 and two additional slaves popped into view. Silence reigned supreme, followed by an audible massive intake of air and release as they realized who it was. *It's Dan and oh (gasp!) my god, Cappy in chains, what the fuck?*

Hunter took that brief shock to merge with the crowd of onlookers, moving through them while dragging the chained animals at his rear. He knew where he was going as he stood a head or more above all of us and could see the targeted people. There was a clump gathered around Commander Schmidt, in deep conversation with a Handler. We approached at cruising speed and were upon them before anyone spied our approach. We stood quietly on the outside of the knot until someone realized who was at their backs. By their reaction, you would have thought the Moses had sprung up from out of the deck. They parted like the waters before giving us access to the center and Commander Schmidt.

"My God, Katherine you do clean up nicely. Stunning outfit, what little there is of it," he leaned over and gave her a peck on the cheek.

She eyed him carefully, "Can't say I haven't seen that old outfit of yours before, Sir. But at least you do have the presence of mind to bring some interesting accessories. Care to explain yourself or why you brought them with you?" She was pointing to 9-777 when she said it.

"Oh, I just thought everyone here needed to see what happens to someone who betrays the sacred trust between Handlers. Dan is no more, this is 9-777, it is my new slave and the other one you know. It's jonathan, my oldest slave who you may have known as Cappy. I thought it time for all of you to see what I have been hiding in my closet these too many years. We can talk about it more once we eat."

We heard audible gasps from people behind us then heard Katherine reply, "Oh, My God!" Hunter and I turned to look; J.D. in all his splendor was standing above everyone on the poop deck. The outfit was incredible, but on J.D. it was awesome. He was wearing a purple brocade knee length coat, a ruffled shirt of white satin, skin tight knee-length satin pants in lavender, white hose, buckle shoes, a tri-cornered hat with feathers, a silky handkerchief in one hand and a tall walking stick in the other. But what totally made the outfit on him was the white pancake makeup, rouged cheeks, a big black mole on his chin and big black curly hair that rolled down well past his shoulders. Everyone stopped mid whatever to stare up at our fop.

Like a drag queen in command of her audience, he ranked the group standing before him until he found our Master. He lifted his hat and bowed to him, then spread his arms wide and bowed to everyone. "Me Lords and Ladies. I a humble servant come before you to humble itself by orders of My Lord Hunter. As you know, my Lords and Ladies, each of you has won this trip by right of service above and beyond those of any other house within this world of ours. You are the Crème de la Crème; the crème of the crop, the best Handlers known and this is Castle's way of showing their appreciation with this trip and the booty hidden on that distant shore!"

Pandemonium broke out as they began cheering and otherwise going nuts. J.D. started waving his arms until they quieted. "As you know, Our Lord is among you. We have - and this is a surprise even to him - just received word that Lady Beatrice, our reigning Deus, has appointed our Lord Hunter as her chief executive. He is in line to be the next, Deus of Castle Enterprises, Unlimited!"

Someone in the crowd shouted, "Three cheers for our Lord! Hip hip Hooray!" Everyone started patting each other on their backs and those closest to Hunter did the same to him. "Speech, speech," the crowd implored of Hunter.

He made his way through the throng of people, climbed the steps up to the poop deck and held up his arms for silence. "My fellow hedonists, lend me your ears," he laughed loudly. "Listen up crew. As of now, the rules that apply to Buena Vista no longer apply! We are off the soil. This means you can suck, fuck, be fucked or beat by whomever you choose as long as they consent to your advances. Anyone get out of hand and you'll answer to my fury. Now if you would please turn and shut up, the sun's setting. I turn the floor back over to J.D."

Everyone watched the sun sinking into the ocean, a most awesome sight for those of us who were landlubbers. We turned as one towards J.D. who was calling out to us, "Lords and Ladies fair, there are pillows a plenty around all the decks. Put your backs or butts on them, appetizers are going to be served by our slaves. The decks are connected, so make certain you are back on your ship before the twelfth bell. They will be separated and your belongings will be on one ship with you on another. Let the debauchery begin!"

Hunter grabbed slave jonathan's head and kissed its lips firmly. "Take 9-777 and make it carry the heaviest platter out to serve our crew. If he falters, lay into it with this whip. Don't allow them to think it's the slacker once known as Dan. Help them to understand what has happened with you and that one."

They had to have noticed because I sure did when Hunter grabbed his friend/slave/lover of decades and planted a big wet kiss on the man's upturned face. The late Captain Jonathan Hick's face turned red after the kiss that only balanced in color by the welted handprint Sir laid across his ass. Sir turned back to where I stood. "Go make me a place next to Katherine and her lot. I will be along in a moment."

The slave jonathan was still standing beside Master when I overheard Sir speak, "We have no more reason to hide our affection from these people or the twins.

Go, slave and do your duty." He went off to find J.D. They talked a few minutes before Hunter returned to where I stood awaiting him and his pleasure. He dropped onto a pillow, leaned back and patted the floor looking up at me. "Kneel here, slave."

People in various forms of pirate costumes wandered by, greeting him as their Deus. The night was shaping up nicely. First course was brought out by none other than our two slaves jonathan and 9-777. The Handlers, especially those that were punished by having a reduction in rank and pay, seemed to go out of their way to want to terrorize 9-777.

Three of the Handlers that suffered from the punishment approached Hunter while he was eating. He stopped them, "Gentlemen, 9-777, the man you knew as Dan has been punished far more severely than any of you. Not only did he loose his pension, his pay and get permanently reduced in rank to that of a Buena Vista slave, it was sold at a private auction. If any of you who can prove to me that you did not have sex with him willingly on Buena Vista time, then I will rescind the punishment. But remember the rules of the Handler's Rule Book. Chapter 1, Conduct of Handlers Section II, paragraph 4, reads, 'Handler's are strictly forbidden to have sex with other Handler's on company time, on company property.' There are no exceptions to the rule. Failure to comply and each person will face a council of their peers for punishment. Possible punishments include: reduction of salary, reduction of rank, repeated offenses, reduction of freedom-enslavement.

"Gentlemen, I would take advantage of the lack of rules placed upon you over the next two weeks. You may screw, fuck, suck, beat, cum in, cum on, eat as you desire with anyone you desire who is a Handler or crew. But you may not touch my slaves. Dan and my property and are branded accordingly. Look at 9-777. Study it and see if you are willing to risk all for a chance at it. It owns nothing; not even its cock, ass or air. I own it all."

Lady Katherine leaned over to the three Handlers. "This is the last discussion we will have on this subject. It is officially closed. Now run along like the nice boys I know you to be. Git, before I sick my bitch slave on you." Katherine laughed; a trilling sound and her bitch slave started snarling at the men.

It was a beautiful star-filled night for the first party. We lost track of jonathan and 9-777, as they were busy serving food to all on board. On the other hand, we roamed from one ship to the others until we had eaten from everyone's table and seen all the Handler's having a good time. Alcohol in all forms was partaken heavily by the way the people were acting. Of course, it could have been the freedom of the open sea that made them all relax and just let go. Couples paired up rapidly. All ships were equipped with some dungeon furniture, if not they made due with the ropes, pulleys and banisters. There was a whole lot of sex going on throughout the night and we did our share as well.

Everything about that first evening on ship was grand. I fed Hunter tidbits of food from my fingertips and licked the residue off my own fingers. He had laid back into the pillows taking pleasure in this new world. I was amazed when we took a poll at Buena Vista and found that about 2/3's of the staff here tonight had never traveled outside of the United States. Here, they were 3/4's way around the world from their homes, enjoying life in a tropical setting.

Everything was going great until a band of Handlers passed by where Master and I were on the pillows, two or three of them winked at Master. I knew then that they were up to no good; someone and I prayed it wasn't 9-777 or jonathan was headed towards hot water. We heard a scream from ship number two as they pounced on their intended victim. It was J.D. they had in their arms. We heard them count to three and a mighty splash as J.D. hit the water between the ships. A lifesaver was tossed; J.D. clung to it as he was raised out of the sea looking like a wet peacock in all his pirate plumage.

As the Handlers were hoisting him up and out of the water the crowd around them started chanting, "Lift him, lift him, lift him!" The term had two meanings in our world. The first meant that they wanted him lifted to his new position as foreman of Buena Vista and the other explanation meant they wanted to toss him back into the ocean but from a higher position. I prayed it was the first; they wanted to see J.D. elevated to his proper position in life as Buena Vista's foreman, the same job Cappy once held. As one ship started the chanting it was picked until all of the boats were imploring, "Lift him, lift him!"

Hunter had followed the Handlers at a distance and was there when J.D. put his first foot back on the ship. Hunter grabbed the twin and pushed everyone away from him. "Which of you fuckers tossed this man into the ocean," he snarled "Speak up now!" Those closest to Master had stopped chanting when he took J.D. under his arm, but only for a moment. The chant was renewed with greater intensity until Hunter held up his hands. J.D. had lost his wig to the water. His pancake white make up was running down his face, as was the red rouge. The poor boy looked like a soggy mess as he stood their dripping water and white make up onto the deck.

Master looked down to J.D. "Your peers want you lifted. How say you?"

J.D. looked up to Hunter. "Aye, Sir!"

Our ship seemed to take on more people who wanted to be part of this event and we would have probably capsized if the crew hadn't cut the gangplanks on all the ships. They circled around our ship making certain all could witness the transformation. Hunter had walked away from J.D., he turned back and shouted to the crowd gathered around them. "Make him ready for elevation, people!"

The cry of a banshee was heard when everyone dove towards J.D., ripping and tearing at his costume in a rush to get it off him. The torn rags were tossed overboard and J.D. was physically passed hand to hand overhead until he was dropped before Master Hunter. J.D. stood there in nothing but his slave harness.

People were cheering and yelling until Hunter held up his hand. "No longer will your body be contained by a slave harness." He extended his hand like a surgeon and a knife was slapped into his open palm. He took the blade to J.D.'s slave harness near where it connected to his slave collar and sawed through the leather. Commander Schmidt stepped forward and sawed away another section. The slave jonathan stepped forward and removed the balance of the harness while bearing a huge shit-eating grin.

Hunter and Lady Katherine Schmidt said in unison, "Walk with your head held high." Then Hunter continued, "The leg shackle will be removed when you depart us for medical training and the collar can only be removed if you buy your freedom after you've completed your doctor specialization." Master signaled that I should bring him his pewter goblet. "Everyone raise your cup to our new foreman of Buena Vista, our own J.D." he proclaimed with his goblet aloft. "May he govern our crops and our people as well as his predecessor!"

The smile that covered Master's face said another stone to his foundation was well laid. The Handlers had done something similar to Schmidt when she took office as the Commander. *Give a little/get a lot* Master always liked to say. J.D.'s acceptance by the Handlers was paramount to his game plan. That man was always plotting out a course only he and a few others could follow. His ships almost always gave us a great return, so it must work.

J.D. was pulled into Hunter's arms and Sir spoke in a theatrical whisper. "Take slave jonathan downstairs to my cabin. In the closet next to the bathroom is something far more befitting your new rank...and it's not purple. Change and return to me here. Now go." Hunter dropped back to the pillows and was nibbling on my nipples when J.D. strolled back into view. The applause said they approved his new wardrobe. He was stunning. Beaming with pride, he stood before Hunter in a chromed jock strap, knee-high lace up boots and a bar vest. Hunter asked him how he liked it. The boy was stunned, having never earned leathers before.

"J.D., this party is in your honor. Go make a pig of yourself." Hunter rose up on one knee as the boy kissed, sharing a private moment. "J.D., I expect to see at least one slave or Handler in your bed tomorrow and it better not be your brother. He is on his own private mission for me."

J.D. looked at Sir quizzically. "Mission? My brother, Sir?"

Hunter laughed, "Yes he is to find a Handler that can keep his ass toasty warm and plugged the balance of the trip. If we're lucky, we can get a break from that nympho ass of his. Good night, Foreman!" The gangplanks were reinstalled on all ships and the partying began in earnest. They now had more than just their freedom from Buena Vista to celebrate; they had J.D.'s promotion.

We joined the celebration following on J.D.'s heels to be with the others who were enjoying the ability to pass from one ship to the next. We had misplaced two good slaves in the melee and were out to find them. Climbing on the third ship, we found jonathan strung up by its wrists. A Handler was working on its backside with a huge quirt like flogger. Each time it struck, the slave screamed, "Thank you Sir! Can I have another, Sir?" Hunter left it in capable hands and we moved over to the fourth ship, seeking our runaway 9-777. To its dismay we caught it on its knees sucking off one of the same Handlers that had approached Sir earlier in the evening. Neither the Handler nor 9-777 noticed Hunter's presence until he spoke. "I don't remember anyone asking permission to use my slave tonight, do you 9-745?"

"Sir, no, Sir!"

"9-777 spit that out, now!" It did as ordered, hung its head with shame. "Handler Rodney, isn't it?" Hunter spoke in his iciest tone.

"Sir, yes, Sir," replied the Handler. His face flushed from excitement of the situation. Or from having gotten caught up in partaking one of the forbidden fruits on this tug.

"Rodney, I don't remember you asking 9-777's owner if you could use his slave?" Hunter looked at me, "Go find me a whip!" I tried to point out that he was wearing one, but he grabbed me by my collar. "Are you deaf? Do as you were told!"

I returned with a braided cat of nine tails, dropped to my knees and held it up for him. Rodney was still present, his cock was soft and he looked worried. Hunter backed off a few paces, took a few swings with the cat. Stepping closer, he laid the whip over 9-777's back repeatedly as the animal screamed in terror and pain. Rodney went ghost white watching Hunter's whip cut into the slave's back, bringing blood to the surface. When Hunter stopped, he tossed the whip aside and looked over to Rodney while wiping the sweat from his face. "Don't let me catch you with him again unless you have first approached me," he intoned gravely. "Understand me, Handler?"

"Sir, yes, Sir!"

"Dismissed, Handler!" Hunter looked down on 9-777. "Get your ass up, slave! Move your lazy cocksucking self towards our cabin. Now, slave!" Master's boot slammed into 9-777's ass with such force that the slave was almost kicked to its feet. It moved before us, turning its head from time to time to see if we were still on its tail.

We arrived at our cabin and I was sent for the first aid kit. When I returned, Hunter had 9-777 free from its chains and laying over the bed on its stomach, his cock in its mouth. He was shouting down as if by the loudness of his voice 9-777 would hear. "Every hole in your body is mine, slave! That cock, those nuts, and even the air you breathe is mine, all are only on loan to you until I wish to take them!" Master blew his load down slave 9-777's throat, then pulled the first aid kit from my hands. Together we cleaned its ripped and torn shoulder blades, added ointment and put it to bed on a floor pallet covered by a sheet while we slept in the bed above it.

Sir needed to make an impression on both of us: even in our sleep, what was his was his. 9-777 got restraints and a spreader bar on its ankles and this slave was securely hooded before having both hands and feet bound for bed. We'd been asleep for a few hours when a cock-crow heralded the new day. Sir groggily rolled his body over to seek the familiar turf of the depths of my hole. While he was nailing my ass-hole, his hands wormed under my chest to find my nipples and they got pulled, rolled and pinched until I entered the agony of ecstasy. His cock sent chills up my spine; his hands put fire into my chest and somewhere in my mind the two met as Hunter and I came together. We both shot our loads as one. I locked within his leather bonds and he locked within his slave's ass.

After his cock had withdrawn. He released me from the hood, putting one arm around me protectively. "By now 9-745, you should know that I love you very much." I kissed his heavy musk scented chest and licked the sweat off his nipple as I snuggled in closer basking in the afterglow of great sex. If I could have I would have tongued him all over but his arm wrapped around me protectively as if to keep anything from harming me again. Hunter was silently thinking, then he spoke. "Slave, I need to know if you love me?"

I cleared my voice, "Sir, may I speak freely, Sir? May this slave be brutally honest, Sir?"

He pulled me off his chest, turned his head to look down on me as if say *What are you going to say to me slave*? The room was illuminated by only a small night-light burning in the head. That gave me just enough light to see him and he me. This light afforded me a chance to watch his face as he studied mine, seeking an answer before it issued from my lips. "Well yes, be truthful, boy."

Using my head, I pushed back just a little giving us a hair's space between us. "Then to answer your question, Sir, do you remember back when you humiliated me outside that bar that cold winter's night by padlocking my balls in the parking lot? You scared the shit out of me, but I knew you were my destiny. When I was in my leather stud stage, only you loved me. God knows I hated myself enough, but you loved me. Then I saw me through your eyes, and I hated you for showing that to me. Later I loathed you when I was in the pit and yet that was where I found the seed you had planted within me. No man in my life has ever completely changed my world as you have. For the longest time I could not fathom the depths of your love. In the depths of that dark pit, the seed you planted took root and grew towards the light, feeding off of my ego, disenchantment with the world as I saw it. Holding on to the only one true thing anyone had ever given to me that did not fade, love. Yes, Sir, I do love you, but realize, Sir. You made me love you. I didn't want to do it, I really didn't want to do it. I can't think of a day that you have not occupied my mind. If that's love, Sir, than I am head over heels in love with you, Sir."

His strong arms closed around me, crushing me to his chest as his lips sucked the life out of mine. He clung to me, nuzzling my head with his chin while tenderly kissing the top of my head. "I want to formally make you my Number One and my glove. Before you agree, realize to formally become my property will mean you'll receive the personal brand that sets you aside from all other slaves."

I tried to answer, but he placed one finger over my lips. "Ssh, boy, let me finish. Two other slaves will join your rank, each will be branded. You'll be always be my Number One, the other two will be ranked by other means. I need them for other reasons. Nothing will change between us. You'll remain my slave as we are now, even into eternity. When we die, your and my ashes will be mixed and be as one. Yes, I love you slave. But that will not stop me from beating your hide, roping it, loaning it out as I feel is necessary. My people say, 'Love has no beginning or end. Love is always going beyond the great beyond, it knows no boundaries nor dimensions it is what it is.' So, 9-745, will you accept my brand and become my Number One slave for the balance of your life?"

"Sir, I am yours to command, Sir"

"True you are, but I need an answer from you boy. Your answer, not mine. You know what I want, it's just that simple. Ever since I saw you that first time, I knew that you would be mine to rebuild, recreate. Until I created my greatest Masterpiece. Answer me in your words, not mine."

Thank God the nightlight was low or he could have seen my face more clearly. He must have felt my tears as they flowed down my cheek to land on his chest. "Sir, ever since the pit, you have been my God. I worship you my Lord, gladly will I accept your brand to my flesh." I buried my face into his chest, letting his warm musky scent fill my lungs. I did love this man more than probably he would ever know. The brand would be an outward notice to all who saw it that I belonged to my Lord and Master as his number one slave. He never did anything without foresight and well laid plans. The branding reflected his foreknowledge of being promoted to Deus. Soon all would be playing his game of chess, where all the old rules need no longer apply.

Having the answer he sought, he pulled me closer and fell asleep even as my mind kicked into high gear. Who were the other two he had chosen to receive his brand? My thought was one would have to be his oldest and most devoted slave jonathan hicks, simply because he said he would not permit it to run away ever again and he would make certain everyone knew who it has been for years. The second slave that would be branded I could only hope would be the same creature that was feigning sleep on the floor at the foot of our bed, 9-777. But 9-777 had already been branded with its number.

Many men and women of the Founders wore brands to denote their rank. My Lord had a long intricate brand that changed whenever he had to go to Castle for business. It had to take many turns under the iron to have completed its woven pattern. That brand flowed up from his left wrist almost to the bend of the elbow. Where would he place my brand? Would it be on my right forearm, my buttocks, my triceps or hundred other locations so all would see and know what I was to him? Would it be a clearly defined brand or something in our private symbolist jargon? How would he do it? When would he do it? My body was fidgeting while my mind raced with thoughts about the branding. I damn near jumped out of my skin when he spoke in my ear.

"What the fuck is your problem, slave? Go to sleep."

"Sir, forgive me for wakening you. My mind is running a hundred yard dash and I just cannot get it to stop."

"What's bothering you boy?"

"Forgive me Sir. Will my brand be as serious as the one on your forearm, Sir? Who else will be given your brand Sir? This slave is being nosey and should be punished, but my mind just will not stop, Sir."

He let out a long sigh, "No, your brand will not be as serious as is mine. After all, I am one of the elders of our clan and an original Founder! The other slaves are none of your concern. Now go to sleep."

"Please, Sir. Talk with me a few more minutes. I need answers to some questions. Please, Sir."

Sir rolled away from me. Reached under the bed and began rummaging within a suitcase under the bed. He found what he wanted and rolled back into position at my side. He sat up on one elbow looking down at me with a huge shit-eating grin plastered all across his face. One hand lightly tapped the cheek of my face. "Open that mouth slave." When I did, he wedged a penis gag between my teeth and buckled it tightly behind my head. Kissing my forehead, "Now, go to sleep. We'll talk in the morning."

He rolled the opposite direction away from me, pulled up the light blanket over both our bodies and returned to his snoring. My mind continued circling like a vulture in the air. Finding no answers, my mind turned off and I dreamt of his cock being slid between my teeth and his cum filling me. The first rays of the sun peeked through the porthole over the bed.

While I lay at his side, he rolled back over in his sleep tossed one leg over my two bound ones and used me like a body pillow. I nearly joined the ceiling tiles over our bed when his tongue snaked out of his mouth and found my ear. He nibbled and sucked on the lobe before he bit my neck and began worming his tongue down my body. It stopped to nuzzle my armpit or to chew and suck a nipple. One hand descended towards my hardening trapped cock. Fingers closed around my balls. They closed tightly and squeezed until I moaned beyond my gag. His fingers dropped my nuts and went between the 'V' of my legs, finding my hidden rose. He finger fucked my hole while he chewed my nipples and all parts in between.

I was turned onto my belly; the ropes around my ankles and thighs were not released nor were my hands. He eased his cock into my ass, held it in place as he fingered my throbbing cock. If he would have removed the penis gag, he would have heard me beg to fuck the shit out of that hole. Instead, he heard the wanted muffled moans he wanted. Pressing his weight down, his cock slipped deeper into me. His weight on my body trapped me, held me captive and his hips began the slow measured pace of a runner doing stretching exercises before a marathon.

Today there was no pressing business to be attended, so he dedicated all his time and motion into filling my hole with as much pleasure as we both could endure. Once he built up steam, his cock took me to new heights as his fingers played me like an organ, turning one knob, biting down on another while his hips moved with their own beat. Like a cart, Sir drove me up a long hill of sensations until we stood on the tiptop, then we slipped over the edge together. I blew my load onto my chest and his, his splattered deep inside my heart. His I ate without tasting, mine he fed back to me by way of his hand. Slaves do not waste their cum; if not sold to the sperm bank it's recycled time and time again.

We raided the galley and were chased by an oriental cook, and we took our stolen fruit, mugs of coffee and breads to the upper deck. We watched the sunrise and the poor groaning souls still on deck from last night's party. The three other ships were sailing beside us, sails full, and we were gliding on the wind as men shouted from one ship to the other. We shared the quiet morning nestled in the pillows while the ships cut through the teal waters, dolphins racing at our side. God, it was almost as beautiful as the man sitting next to me licking fruit pulp from his hands like a child. We lay there that morning, enjoying our own company. His head was in my lap when a thought struck him. "I hope you realize from here on out you'll have to keep some secrets. Much of what I do or you witness cannot be spoken of with others. It stays between you and I. Understand, Number One?"

He turned his head, closed his eyes and went back to listening to the gull's overhead. Periods of silence between friends and lovers can be more meaningful than constant chatter; those silences mean you trust one another, a rare commodity in these days. The ocean had its affect on me. It lulled me into a calm and I was unaware of his hand being extended until he tapped me on the shoulder. "We need to check on 9-777, and to find out where in the hell jonathan is. Go by the galley and bring us more coffee - and whatever else you can steal," he laughed. "I am going below. Join me, and if you see jonathan bring it with you."

Returning with a tray of goodies stolen from the galley, I found my Master seated with 9-777's head buried in his lap. Sir was applying more ointment to his tattered back while speaking to it quietly, calming it. "9-777, you'll stay with Number One, I should have foreseen jonathan would slip back into his old ways and should have anticipated the Handlers influence on you. Slip up again and this torn back will be the least of your worries."

"Sir, I spoke to the Captain of the Watch, jonathan has reported in, it's on Spitfire the third boat of our fleet. It will rejoin you as soon as possible, Sir."

"Oh, it will, will it? Damn right it will, and it will find itself in a heap of hot water when it returns! Number One, go back to the Captain of the Watch and ask him to radio all ships. Please ask him to direct a message to J.D., mike and jonathan that they are to report to me when the ships drop anchor. We're holding a family meeting while everyone else is on shore; our first treasure hunt begins today."

I returned to find 9-777 tied into a tight little knot of human flesh, gagged into silence and ignored. Hunter was studying his laptop, humming as he clicked over the keys. I was ordered to shave by an absent minded Sir, who was absorbed in whatever he was doing. Having fed him coffee, sweet meats and a puffed pastry, I finally knelt at the side of his chair and waited for him to find me when he wanted.

I'd been there for about an hour when the first knock came to our door. Mike entered with a huge sheepish grin and bags under his eyes. Master looked up, did not say anything but returned to his work. Another slave joined my kneeling in silence. The slave jonathan joined us a few minutes later, yet another one found its place on the floor. J.D. followed on the heels of jonathan. Master greeted J.D. with an open handshake and hug. "Come, the rest of you stay where you are, we will be back in a few minutes."

We who serve heard a loud cheering from those gathered on the decks. "First treasure, 200 pieces of gold bullion, the first one to find it," boomed from loud speakers. "Return to the shore and wave the flag. Our airhorn will blow three times, that tells everyone that the treasure has been claimed and you are to make your way back to the shore. We need a count of those going ashore, stop by the slave over there and get a number. We will not depart this island and move on towards the next big treasure until all bodies are counted."

Hunter got on the microphone. "Does everyone have their maps, charts and sound footwear?" The crowd roared in excitement.

J.D. spoke next, "First one to find the treasure need only depress the trigger with their thumb, this will record here on our computer who won. Then I suggest you start digging, because this one is buried and if you don't return with the gold, you are shit out of luck! This way, no one can clobber you and steal your find. We'll have it on record who was the actual winner, plus we have video cameras hidden all over the island. We get live feedback so we can watch you whores running around like chicken dogs."

Hunter bellowed, "Captains of the Watch, are the boats launched? Diving and snorkeling gear can be acquired at the aft of the boats. Happy Hunting! On the count of three, get the fuck off my ships! 1...2..." We could hear feet running across the deck, the splash of bodies hitting the water and the cheers of people paddling inflatable canoes as they moved towards the island.

The men joined us a few minutes later. Hunter poured himself a cup of coffee, offered one to J.D., and brought the two cups to the table indicating to J.D. that he should sit. Both men sipped their coffee in silence. It was time for the family meeting to begin. The slave we now knew as jonathan cleared his throat. "Let's go back to the beginning, shall we, Sir?"

About the Author

I was born where "good ole boy" applied to both men and women. Where "honey and darling," were applied to all women, and they did not think it to be a sexist statement. Where being politically correct was something city folks did because they failed to respect, honor and take pride in all those with whom one associated. Where a man's word and handshake are more binding than any piece of paper. Where honor, pride and respect were a state of mind - the *hum* in *hum*anity.

Experience, they say, is the key to being a great artist. If that's the case, well, I am a frigging Picasso or one hell of a writer because I've done my share of hell-raisin' and placating while here on this good ole Earth of ours. One thing I have learned to be an outstanding truth - and something that we tend to forget - is: "Everything is connected to everything." Poison our Earth mother and we ourselves are poisoned. Heal her and we are healed.

I graduated high school in '69, then went to Morehead University for a start on my degrees. I've been a retail merchant, badge carrier, training and educations officer within a branch of the Old F.E.M.A. I'm a healer and medicine man within the Hiawatha Shawnee Hidden Society out of Kentucky. I came to Florida to cross-reference Woodland tribal magic with that of Tropical tribal magic and found an expanded universe that's absolutely awesome. I moved to Miami, Florida in the early 1990's to undertake the fire vision and survived. People either love or fear me; it's just that simple. Then Miami to Ft Lauderdale (aka Ft. Leatherdale) due to the amount of leathermen and women who have moved into our beautiful city. Once in Ft. Lauderdale I immersed myself within the leather community became a public figure. I became a leather tailor and later ran a leather business with Amy O'. In '99 I was the president of Leather University, an educational faculty teaching safe, sane and consensual S&M, B&D arts and sciences.

In 2000, I was involved in a major car accident that broke more parts than I thought possible. The accident awoke a sleeping childhood disease, polio, bringing it back as post-polio syndrome. I was told I would live the balance of my life in a wheelchair but a Sensei taught me water karate and I regained my limbs. In 2003, I found the love letters that my slave had returned to me while he was on a road tour. The love letters became the premise for the story *Hand and Glove*.

www.ingramcontent.com/pod-product-compliance
Lightning Source LLC
Chambersburg PA
CBHW051651260626
47170CB00004B/1444